P

'Beaumont strikes
the dark heart of
in Ukraine. *A Spy At War* is the best sort of espionage novel,
shimmering with authentic tradecraft, geopolitical intrigue and
a gritty exploration of betrayal and revenge'
  David McCloskey, former CIA analyst and author of
The Seventh Floor

'Charles Beaumont is that rare combination in spy fiction:
a genuine former intelligence officer who is also a first-class
writer'
  Charles Cumming, author of *Kennedy 35*

'With his second novel, Beaumont has cemented himself as
an author who both fearlessly tackles hard subjects and spins
masterful tales. *A Spy at War* is daring and unflinching, a must-
read for anyone seeking to understand the insidious nature of
influence politics and soft power that defines modern warfare
and espionage. Fast-paced, compelling and riveting, this is a
story that will leave you haunted and moved'
  I.S. Berry, author of *The Peacock and the Sparrow*

'This second espionage thriller from former MI6 operative
Charles Beaumont underlines his quality'
  Daily Mail

'An unadorned take on the brutal realities of the Ukrainian
war, told with literary flair and an insider's insights into the
corrupt political forces at work behind the trenches. Smart, well
written, darkly humorous'
  Paul Vidich, author of *Beirut Station*

'Angry, propulsive and very, very timely. It also feels like Beaumont's home turf – and is all the better for it. If *A Spy Alone* was his cry of rage as a citizen, *A Spy at War* is his cry of rage as a spook. It's the ex-SIS officer's professional world of untested sources, Whitehall chess and long waits in foreign cities, capped with a great portrayal of the life-on-the-edge strangeness of a country at war for its survival. Topping *A Spy Alone* was a tough ask. Beaumont has managed it'

Dominick Donald, author of *Breathe*

'Many works of fiction will be inspired by the war in Ukraine, the seminal European war of the 21st century. Charles Beaumont literally blasts out ahead of the field with an effort that is both cinematic and compassionate in depicting the frontlines of this terrible conflict, and merits its own Netflix series. A worthy sequel to his debut masterpiece'

Dr Fiona Hill, CMG, former US National Intelligence Officer for Russia

'*A Spy At War* is a classic of the spy fiction genre. Beaumont's portrayal of the contrast between a dysfunctional, working-from-home Whitehall and the horrors of the Ukraine war is particularly powerful. The new ambiguities in once clearcut international relations are there too, as well as the perplexing diversity of modern security threats we face... Its denouement is both shocking and unexpected. A real tour de force'

Christopher Steele, author of *Unredacted: Russia, Trump, and the Fight for Democracy*

'Beaumont has done it again: a gripping spy thriller, this time set in war-torn Ukraine, which is so true to life you feel you are there. It's also about Britain, now, and how so many in the Establishment have sold their souls for Russian gold'

John Sweeney, author of *Killer in the Kremlin*

Praise for *A Spy Alone*

'A debut thriller of high fluency, this is first class'
The Times

'A highly accomplished novel from a new writer of great promise'
Financial Times

'Five stars. One of the best books I've read in a very, very long time'
James O'Brien, LBC

'Beaumont is at the forefront of the espionage genre, capturing the changing nature of intelligence: soft influence and business deals are overtaking stolen secrets; long-term insinuation is replacing Cold-War tradecraft. A brilliant read'
I. S. Berry, author of *The Peacock and the Sparrow*

'Everything a John le Carré fan could ever wish for... This author actually has something to say. That's a surprisingly rare thing nowadays. As a result, Beaumont... has turned out an urgent, troubling book.... What this novel shows is how powerful a book can be when the writer looks the country straight in the face and writes about what they see. Le Carré used to be very good at doing that... Now Charles Beaumont has done it, too'
Private Eye

'Beaumont was a bona fide British intelligence officer and it shows. This is a marvellously confident debut, sharply observed and exceptionally well-written'
Charles Cumming, author of *Box 88*

'Authentic and compelling'
Tom Fletcher, author of *The Ambassador*

'*A Spy Alone* is as intricate as it is absorbing, as fantastically entertaining as it is disturbingly plausible, and is delivered with the confidence of a writer who knows how to handle the highest stakes'
Tim Glister, author of *Red Corona*

'*A Spy Alone* is a cracking debut novel by a former MI6 spy. If you read it, the Kremlin won't like it'
John Sweeney, author of *Killer in the Kremlin*

'A clever, thrilling spy story that brings the feel of Eric Ambler's shadowy political intrigues right into today's world'
Jeremy Duns, author of *Free Agent*

'A well-written and atmospheric tale of espionage. It hits hard at some of the real issues facing Britain and the world today'
Dan Kaszeta, author of *Toxic: A History of Nerve Agents*

'Charles Beaumont's debut novel has such a ring of authenticity about it that it reads like an inside job. But there's much more to *A Spy Alone* than being well-informed and highly credible: the plot is clever and tight, the story is gripping and the characters are all well drawn. A highly recommended espionage thriller'
Alex Gerlis, author of *Every Spy a Traitor*

'Propulsive, authentic and eye-opening, *A Spy Alone* is clearly written by someone with first-hand experience of the secret world'
James Wolff, author of *How to Betray Your Country*

A Spy at War

Charles Beaumont worked undercover as an MI6 operative in war zones, on diplomatic missions and in international business. His work spanned two decades and four continents.

Also by Charles Beaumont

The Oxford Spy Ring

A Spy Alone
A Spy at War

CHARLES
BEAUMONT

A SPY
AT WAR

CANELO

First published in the United Kingdom in 2025 by

Canelo, an imprint of
Canelo Digital Publishing Limited,
20 Vauxhall Bridge Road,
London SW1V 2SA
United Kingdom

A Penguin Random House Company

The authorised representative in the EEA is Dorling Kindersley Verlag GmbH.
Arnulfstr. 124, 80636 Munich, Germany

A CIP catalogue record for this book is available from the British Library.

Print ISBN 978 1 80436 480 2
Ebook ISBN 978 1 80436 481 9

Cover design by Tom Sanderson

Cover images © Arcangel; Shutterstock

Printed and bound in Great Britain by Clays Ltd, Elcograf S.p.A.

Look for more great books at
www.canelo.co
www.dk.com

To my family, with love and thanks.

'It is not the critic who counts; not the man who points out how the strong man stumbles, or where the doer of deeds could have done them better. The credit belongs to the man who is actually in the arena, whose face is marred by dust and sweat and blood; who strives valiantly; who errs, who comes short again and again, because there is no effort without error and shortcoming; but who does actually strive to do the deeds; who knows great enthusiasms, the great devotions; who spends himself in a worthy cause; who at the best knows in the end the triumph of high achievement, and who at the worst, if he fails, at least fails while daring greatly, so that his place shall never be with those cold and timid souls who neither know victory nor defeat.'

Theodore Roosevelt, speaking on 23 April 1910

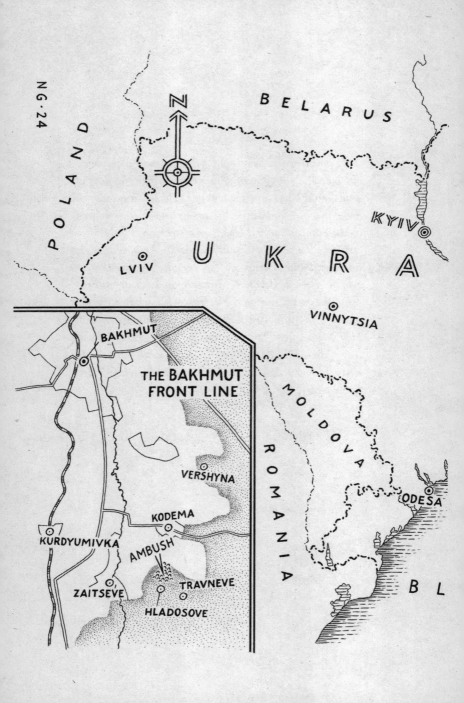

THE **FRONT LINE** IN **RUSSIA'S WAR** ON **UKRAINE** – AUGUST 2022

Russian-occupied Ukraine

SUMY

KHARKIV

L I N E

Dnieper

KRAMATORSK

LUHANSK

BAKHMUT

Area of detail

DNIPRO

DONETSK

ZAPORIZHIA

R U S S I A

MARIUPOL

KHERSON

C R I M E A

0 km 175

0 miles 100

A C K

S E A

Prologue

Kyiv

23 February 2022

Since Stoly knew he was likely to die later that day, he woke early.

He had lots of things to do and no time to waste. But a lurking anxiety was getting in the way of his thoughts, impossible to shift. A feeling that he was standing on the thinnest of floors over a dark, bottomless chasm.

The previous evening, as he walked home, he had paused by the flower clock in the Maidan. Just a normal winter evening, the buildings glowing in the yellow floodlights, the drone of rush-hour traffic, occasional tooting horns. There were a few other pedestrians, but it was mostly empty. It was hard to imagine it as it had been eight years earlier: the crowds, a sea of humanity washing into every space; the acridity in the air from the fires, Molotov cocktails and gunshot; the cries of those who had been hit, and the soft murmuring of those who comforted them in their final moments, the roars of anger and defiance, the determination not to be intimidated, even by the snipers on the buildings above. Above all, the energy and determination of a great mass of people all with a common goal. *The Revolution of Dignity*, they called it, because they had realised they could end their humiliation by Moscow and its oligarchs.

As he relived those moments, Stoly shivered, more with emotion than cold. It was chilly, but not freezing the way it was supposed to be in Kyiv in February. Unseasonal, as it had been in 2014. He paused, staring at the towering independence monument, and felt a brief jolt of adrenaline as he recalled that moment when they knew they had won.

Vidstávka! – Resign! – the crowd had bellowed, with such force that he had *felt* the sound, as much as he heard it. And, hours later, Yanukovych had gone. Not so much resigned as run away.

But this wasn't a fairy tale, and not everyone got to live happily ever after. The Russians hadn't signed up to dignity. Instead, they had taken Crimea and invaded the Donbas. And then things had started to get difficult for Stoly.

He had always hoped that one day he might be able to explain his actions: an elderly mother living under Russian occupation in Donetsk; a private life that was… *complicated*. Money troubles. Everyone had to make choices, and Stoly had simply chosen the guys who tended to win. But now he had that sinking feeling of someone who knows they won't ever get to tell their side of a very complicated story.

Stoly dressed quickly and quietly, doing his best to behave as if it was just another day. Whilst in the bathroom, with the door locked, he put the tap on in the sink. As the water splashed, he used a small coin to open an access hatch to the boxed-in cistern. He reached into the void behind the porcelain and pulled out a small unlabelled envelope. He stuffed this into his trouser pocket and replaced the panel, noisily brushing his teeth and making gargling noises.

In the kitchen he said little to Iuliia, but they weren't really talking to each other any more, so that was normal. His hand was shaking as he poured his coffee, and he wondered if Iuliia had seen. She probably just thought he'd had too much the previous night, which was true. He gulped the scalding liquid too quickly and then stepped into the hallway. As he reached for the latch on the front door, he paused. He was about to give his usual grunt of 'Have a lovely day,' but the inadequacy of it struck him. This might be his last day. He should say more. But what?

As he pondered this, he heard Iuliia's footsteps in the corridor. Hand still on the latch, he craned his neck round. She was looking at him blankly.

'Forget something?'

He didn't want to forget. He wanted to remember. The good times: Iuliia laughing on a Crimean beach; their wedding day; the times they had made love; her eyes, with the little flecks of amber in them. Try to hold on to those memories.

'No... Have a lovely day.'

As soon as he was clear of the apartment block, he pulled out his phone. Opening the Telegram app, he sent a message to Sergey confirming their meeting later. He then sent another message, this one to an unfamiliar number, pausing as he tried to figure out the right wording. How do you tell someone you have never met that you have information that could prevent a war, without coming across as a crank?

Stoly strode swiftly towards his office at the Cabinet of Ministers. It was one thing to have just a few hours to try to stop a war. It was quite another to do that while pretending to have a normal day at the office, just another civil servant managing the ebb and flow of government business.

Everything seemed distressingly normal. The gate guard was as dopey as ever. In the office there was a buzz because of the special Cabinet meeting in a few hours' time to discuss the crisis with Russia. Secretaries were lining up empty briefing folders on a large table, ready for the ministers' papers to be inserted. The sound of fast typing and whirring printers. The mild tension of an important deadline.

But it didn't feel like a country preparing to be invaded.

Stoly couldn't do anything but wait. He had the advantage of a reputation for quietness – the grey man in the corner, known for his diligent attention to detail. Not the sort of person to spend his day shooting off messages on his phone. But if someone had been keeping watch on this particular day, they might have noticed him nervously checking Telegram every few minutes.

He was finding it almost impossible to concentrate.

With just seven minutes to run before the paperwork deadline for Cabinet, Stoly still hadn't finished editing the steering brief. Olexiy, his severe but fair-minded boss, marched over, clearly angry.

'What's going on, Stoly? You forget there was a Cabinet meeting today?'

Stoly was sure he sounded like a man about to succumb to a panic attack. 'Sorry. I just had to double-check a couple of things,' he stammered, scrolling through the document.

'You've got two minutes.'

The paper was ridiculously inadequate: plans for diplomatic engagements; appeals to the United Nations and the German Chancellor. What would be the use of that against an invading army? Stoly looked around the room at his colleagues: Andriy, busily chatting to Nataliia about plans for the weekend – no doubt hoping he could persuade her to join them; Olena updating some spreadsheet; Lyudmyla offering to bring everyone tea; Olexiy, pacing up and down and casting resentful looks in his direction.

Stoly wanted to stand up and shout, *'The Russian tanks are about to roll in. We have to do something!'*

But instead, he corrected some grammar, tidied up the punctuation and released the document for printing.

Then Stoly's phone vibrated.

His heart skipped a beat as, snatching it up, he saw a new Telegram message. The office was emptying now. The briefing folders were on their way, and the Cabinet meeting was about to start. People were either taking the chance to grab an early lunch or attending as note-takers. Stoly opened the message.

Almanac 1200.

He had been expecting a clear answer. Maybe 'Thank you for contacting me. Meet me in the Maidan at lunchtime.' A specific instruction, at least. *What the fuck is Almanac?* He started to type the word into Google and then stopped himself.

Was this some kind of codeword? Would he be leaving a trail? Sergey had told him to be very cautious of anything he did on his work computer.

He looked around the room to confirm he was alone. Andriy's computer had been left unlocked. Typical, sloppy Andriy.

He sidled over and tried to act the part of having a good reason to look for something on a colleague's desk. As he did so, he opened a new incognito browser window and typed in the word 'Almanac', needing a couple of tries as his hands were now shaking. Google obliged with 76 million results, none of which were of any use. Stoly cursed silently, took a deep breath, and tried to think.

It's for a meeting. It must be a codeword for a place.

He tried again, typing 'Almanac Kyiv'. And there it was: a pretentiously named organic cafe that happened to be a few hundred metres from the headquarters of the SBU, Ukraine's security service.

There will be a meeting. Perhaps it's not too late.

'Looking for something?'

The voice was Andriy's; he was at the doorway, staring quizzically. From his position, Andriy could not see Stoly's hands. Stoly could feel the colour rising on his cheeks, his right hand frozen on the mouse of Andriy's computer. He tried to close the browser window without looking at the screen.

'Well?' Andriy was starting to sound suspicious now.

Stoly realised he hadn't said anything. 'It's a bit embarrassing… I came over to your desk for the stapler. And then…' He realised he was barely coherent, but his mind kept blanking out. So much stress and he couldn't think clearly.

'Then what?' Andriy was clearly angry.

'Then… Well, you know that I am supposed to remind team members about IT security – software updates? The security people are pissed off that we haven't done the latest ones. They've given me a list and you're at the top of it. I realise I should have just told you, but I thought it might help if I set the updates going.' Even as Stoly said this, he was ashamed of himself. *Couldn't I have thought of anything better?*

'Really?' Andriy sounded as though he almost believed it. Stoly *was* the sort of person you'd ask to take care of something this boring. He leant into the faint hope.

'Yeah. IT gave me a really rough time about it yesterday. I totally should have asked you, but... I suppose I was worried you'd be dismissive about it.' Stoly had decided to take the path of self-humiliation. Today wasn't the day for worrying about his reputation. 'I know I should have discussed it with you, sorry. I was just trying to help you,' he concluded, desperately.

Andriy shook his head, but there was a ghost of a smile around the edge of his mouth. Andriy was the man who organised parties, was always the ringleader of a lunch out of the office, or an after-work drink. Stoly was the guy he avoided inviting.

'Stoly, I get it. I'll do the updates. But not right now, okay?'

And Stoly realised that he was going to get away with it. He felt pathetically grateful, but couldn't show it.

'Well, make sure it happens today,' he said in his best mock-severe voice, as he headed out of the room.

By the time he reached the street, Stoly had just twenty minutes to get to the meeting, which Google had told him was a twenty-five-minute walk. He wondered about hailing a cab but there weren't any, so he began a sort of high-speed shuffle, down the hill to the Maidan and back up the other side. Despite the February weather, he began to feel sweaty and overdressed in his padded winter coat as he slogged up the steep incline of Sofiivska Street. He tried to hail a trolleybus between stops, but of course it ignored him. At the broad boulevard of Volodymyrska Street, he glanced up at the golden spire of St Sophia's Cathedral, gleaming in the weak winter sunshine. He permitted himself a little glow of inner triumph: he was going to get there just two minutes late.

Two minutes is okay, when you're stopping a war.

Just before the SBU building he needed to cross the wide, six-lane street to get to the cafe. The traffic was moving quickly, but he spotted a gap he could make at a jog. As he reached the centre-line he paused, cars whooshing in front and behind him.

And then there was a car pulling out of its lane into the centre of the road. Stoly felt a sense of disbelief as it came straight for him. Time slowed down. Enough for Stoly to get a clear view: it was an old Volkswagen. One of the ones they use for taxis.

He'd known it might end today, and now he knew how. Had Sergey's people seen his message to the SBU? Or was it the SBU tidying up loose ends before the change of regime? Did they already know what he'd been up to? Either way, it didn't matter any more.

And then a screaming horn, Dopplering as it whizzed past. Stoly saw a gap and raced for the far pavement. He bent over, his chest heaving, until he caught his breath and stood up, looking round self-consciously. His little escapade appeared to have generated an audience; he spotted a couple of middle-aged men watching him as they chatted on the other side of the wide road, like a pair of spectators at a very niche sporting event.

Sergey had often told Stoly to think about his surroundings, to take note of possible followers. Stoly knew this stuff was important, but somehow it was never the right time to focus on it. But on this occasion, he was going to meet an officer of the security service of Ukraine to talk about a matter of national importance, and two blokes seemed to be assessing his ability to cross the road.

Just a couple of guys who heard the car horn and looked up. Anyone would do the same.

But he didn't believe that. Not really. Running on nervous energy, he cut down the side street and could soon see the awning of the cafe, proudly displaying its silly name:

_MANAC. His entrance was unsubtle: he opened the door and stood on the threshold, panting, the other customers frowning as he let in the cold air. It took him a couple of seconds to gather his senses and take in the surroundings – exposed brickwork, steel beams, trendy crowd. And then, in the corner, he saw a face that was recognisable, if not familiar. He walked over to the small table. Sitting on the padded bench seat against the wall was a grey-skinned man, tiredness visible on his unshaven face. He was staring at a large black coffee in a china cup before him. This being a hipster establishment, the cup had no handle. Without moving his head, the man turned his eyes upwards to look at Stoly. His face barely flickered with recognition, and for an awful moment Stoly thought he'd found the wrong person.

'We're having this meeting, right?' he stammered, feeling faintly ridiculous.

'It's "a matter of national importance", I understand,' the man replied, using Stoly's words from his earlier Telegram message, but sounding sceptical.

Stoly took this as enough of an invitation to sit down. He'd made it this far; the car had missed him. The two blokes weren't surveillants. Perhaps it was going to be okay.

'Petro? Everyone calls me Stoly. We met – briefly – at Kira's wedding... Not sure if you remember me?' He felt the need to establish their common ground, but Petro seemed entirely unmoved.

'I'm sure you are very busy, Stoly. Cabinet's meeting today, right?'

So he's checked up on me.

'Er, yes... But this isn't really about my work... Not directly...' Stoly had resolved to tell the SBU. But he hadn't figured out what he was going to say, and he wasn't sure where to start. And then there was the risk that half the SBU was working with the Russians anyway. *Not Petro, surely? He's proper Ukrainian, always there in his vyshyvanka at family events. Yes, he trained in Russia, but everyone did in those days. He's one of the good guys.*

And then Stoly remembered that he thought of himself as one of the good guys... But he was working for the Russians.

'Do you need a coffee?' Petro was probably trying to sound solicitous, but it came across as impatience.

Fuck it. I've got to tell someone.

'The Russians are going to invade. Tomorrow.' And then Stoly remembered to reply about the coffee. 'Maybe in a moment...' He paused again, searching for the right words. They wouldn't come.

Petro looked confused and decided to ignore the question of coffee. 'You've been watching CNN? Reading the BBC? This is all over the television and every news website: the Americans and their sidekicks in London are telling everyone that Russia is going to invade.' Petro took a long swig. 'If that's all you wanted to tell me, I should probably get back to the office.'

Stoly wanted to stand up and scream. But, instead, he took a deep breath and spoke as clearly and quickly as possible, leaning forwards so that his low tone could not be heard on neighbouring tables.

'The Russian invasion starts tomorrow. The plan is to topple the government in the next ten days. They're sending armies in from all directions, they'll be in Kyiv in hours. And not like in 2014 – fake separatists down in the Donbas – proper invasion, huge army, headed straight for Kyiv.'

Petro sighed. He looked as if he had been working twenty-hour days for the past few months. His eyes had puffy dark patches under them. 'Yes, but their army isn't big enough for a full invasion. They won't do it,' he said with the tone of someone who had said exactly the same thing a hundred times before. Stoly reckoned he had about ninety seconds before Petro ended the meeting.

'There's a coup plan,' he blurted out. 'The moment the army crosses the border, they take over the government. There are

ywhere. It's not the invasion bit that matters. It's the
They'll countermand orders, tell units to stand aside as
he Russians advance. Assassinate people.' As he was speaking,
Stoly hadn't noticed a stiffening in Petro's posture.

Petro pulled out a small notebook from his inside jacket
pocket and a tatty biro. The end of the pen had been chewed.
He raised his eyebrows, and looked at Stoly as if to say, 'You
have about eighty seconds.'

Stoly shifted his body to allow access to his trouser pocket.
'I don't have all the details, but I wrote as many names as I
have here,' he said, sliding the envelope across the table. Petro
put it under the palm of his hand, but seemed disinclined to
open it. 'There's people in SBU, in defence, in ministries, but
I don't know much about them. But I know what's happening
in our office, in the Cabinet. The Russians step in and there's
a government-in-waiting: the Cabinet Office will issue policy
papers for new ministers, appoint new directors to the agencies.
The existing Cabinet will be told to stay at home to avoid
bloodshed. Some of them will be arrested or knocked off, I
expect.'

'Who's in the new government?' Petro was still sounding
sceptical, but with an undertone of urgency.

'It's complicated. Everything's complicated. But there's two,
apparently: a group around Yanukovych getting ready in Minsk,
and another one down in the Donbas with Oleg Tsaryov.
And the money sitting behind them is coming from the gas
billionaires, Dudnik and his people. The Kremlin will choose
between them at the right moment.'

'Right. And you know all this how?' asked Petro, raising one
eyebrow.

Up until this point, Stoly had still wondered if he might,
somehow, not have to say. But he knew it was hopeless. 'I, er…
I co-operated with them,' he said, choosing the word carefully,
'but it's different now. I'm not prepared to have them take over
the country.'

I've crossed the Rubicon.

He felt relieved.

Petro said nothing. He looked intently at his coffee, to the point that Stoly wondered if there was something wrong with it. He then looked straight at Stoly, blinked twice and took a long gulp from his cup.

When he finally spoke there was a sharpness to his voice. 'You're not prepared to help them take over the country, but you are happy for them to destabilise it. Just making sure I've got that right?'

Stoly sighed. 'There's a lot I want to say. Explanations, and so on. But I kind of think we have to deal with this invasion first.' He indicated the envelope under Petro's palm. 'That has all the names I know about, agents in the administration, details of the finances, and so on.'

'SBU?' asked Petro, putting the envelope into his pocket.

'Only one in SBU: Oleg Kulinich.'

Petro was trained not to overreact to surprising information, but Stoly was convinced this name elicited a double blink. 'Okay,' he said, still in a monotone, 'at this point I think I'm going to need to bring you in for questioning... Nothing too intense, you understand,' he added smiling. Stoly tried to look calm about 'nothing too intense' but felt intensely nervous. 'But given what you've told me...' He sounded almost apologetic.

'Okay, but there's two issues. They expect me back in the office in...' Stoly paused to look at his watch, '...half an hour. And, more important: I have a meeting with my Russian handler later. Nineteen hundred tonight. If I don't show, they'll know I'm talking to you guys.'

After his potentially demonstrative blinking at the mention of 'Kulinich', Petro appeared to have recovered his calm. 'You mustn't do anything out of the ordinary, either with your office or that meeting. Where's it happening?'

'Holosiivskyi. I walk along the road by the lake and he catches up with me. Two blokes getting their steps in after work.'

'So this is a regular debrief?' Now that Stoly had told the bald truth, Petro no longer had to feign bored scepticism.

'No. Sergey called it urgently and I confirmed this morning.'

'Sergey who?'

'I dunno. I don't know anything much about him. He's obviously Russian. Belgorod accent.'

'But you meet him regularly?'

'For the past year, yes.'

'And he called an urgent meeting? What about?'

'I don't know exactly, but it must be about tomorrow. Last-minute plans or something… You see, at the start, it was just about information. I gave them political information from the Cabinet. I know I am not supposed to do that, but honestly I don't think they got anything that isn't in *Gazeta*, or any other paper. But then things started to get weird. Around autumn last year.'

'Weird how?'

'They started to want me to take *active measures*. Could I – subtly, of course – encourage disagreements between two of the President's top advisers? Could I add a note of pessimism to the latest military assessments coming out of the Donbas? Could I make sure the estimate of numbers of Russian troops massing on the border was at the top end of the range?' Stoly paused. He had never spoken about this to anyone before, and he wasn't sure if it made any sense, or even if it was true. He had compartmentalised his relations with Sergey into a bit of his brain that wasn't part of the real world. It was his way of managing the guilt: perhaps wasn't even real. Except, of course, it was.

Petro wasn't saying anything, so Stoly ploughed on. 'And then they started telling me things: information about governments-in-waiting, orders for new ministers, all that stuff. I've been told I have to be ready tonight for the orders to go out from the Cabinet. Tomorrow. That's when I realised it's the moment. And I needed to tell you people.'

'It took you until now? Until you believed the invasion was only hours away?' Petro had not raised his voice, but there was now perceptible menace in the tone.

Stoly felt his voice quavering, which made him annoyed with himself. 'Let's just say that for the past few years I have been working to prevent my mother falling out of the window of her apartment in Voronezh… You know how these people work…' Petro stared at him, eyes narrowed. Stoly's sense of impending doom was coming back. This might be his last day. Maybe this was the only chance he'd get to explain himself. 'At first, I just thought, "These are the games the Russians play." Active measures, parallel governments. That's just their usual stuff, and real life seems to carry on anyway. It seemed so unlikely they'd go this far.'

Petro's response was short and to the point. '*Blyat!*' – Shit! He slapped the table in frustration. A studious type at a nearby table looked up from his laptop.

'I need to get back to the Cabinet,' said Stoly, squirming in his seat, knowing Petro could arrest him right away. 'Or I need a reason why I'm not there.'

'If you try to do a runner we'll find you and expose you. That won't help your mother very much. You will message me once you're back at the office, and you will call me when you leave for the meeting later. In the meantime, I will be checking this,' he said, gesturing with the envelope. 'And at some point in the very near future we are going to go over *everything*. Now, go.'

Stoly stood up, wondering what he should say. He couldn't think of anything.

'Sorry I never got you that coffee,' Petro added with evident disdain.

Stoly shuffled out of the cafe, realising that, once again on this nightmare day, he was going to be late, this time on returning from his lunch break. Olexiy would tut and make snide little remarks.

He had hoped to feel relieved, but now only felt worse than before, if such a thing was possible.

-

Within seconds of Stoly's departure, Petro had drained his cup, left a couple of crumpled notes on the table, and stood up to leave. As he did so, he pulled out his phone and began scrolling through his contacts. He ambled to the door, waiting a couple of seconds as he watched Stoly through the glass, shambling around the corner and out of sight. He then made his own way out onto the pavement, phone held to his ear as he waited for the call to connect.

'Oleks?' Petro sounded bright, almost energetic. 'I think I've just found something interesting. We might need to make some new arrangements.' He continued his call as he walked briskly back to his office in SBU headquarters.

-

Stoly spent the rest of the day editing documents that were supposed to be assessed by a meeting of the Cabinet subcommittee on transportation the following day. It was ridiculous: there were papers on bus routes, train schedules, and whether or not to raise the duty on diesel fuel because of air pollution. Nothing about the war that would have started by then, which would ensure the meeting never took place. He wasn't completely sure what he had expected after his meeting with Petro, but he had hoped for some reassurance, even if he knew he didn't deserve any. When he saw Petro's number come up on a Telegram call later in the afternoon, he felt strangely relieved.

'Transportation subcommittee?' Stoly found it vaguely disconcerting that Petro seemed to know exactly what was happening in his office. 'I don't imagine that will be taking place,' he said, flatly.

'We need to do something!' said Stoly in a desperate whisper, nervously looking around the open-plan office to see whether anyone was paying attention to his call. 'This thing kicks off in a few hours. I thought you would stop them!'

'We are taking appropriate measures,' replied Petro in pure securocratese.

Appropriate measures? What the fuck is that supposed to mean? Stoly dug his thumbnail into his index finger, fighting the urge to scream. He had thought he'd tell Petro and then the wheels would start turning. The system would do its thing. And Stoly would know, whatever happened to him, he'd done his bit when it mattered. But it didn't seem to be working.

'What measures?'

Petro ignored the question. 'Ahead of your meeting tonight you will need to meet me. Just for two minutes. Easiest if we do it before you get on the Metro. Meet me outside Mr Grill on Khreschatyk. Eighteen-fifteen?'

'Okay.' Stoly knew he had no choice.

'You've got a busy social life all of a sudden.' Andriy had come over to his desk. 'Never seen you take so many calls. Anything we should know about?' He gave a theatrical wink as he said this, grinning at his undeniable comedic talent. Stoly started to stammer something about organising a little surprise for Iuliia, whilst thinking about the fact that he had not organised a little surprise for Iuliia in years, and wondering if he would ever see her again. 'Anyway,' Andriy continued, 'I did those updates, no problem. And then I thought I'd better call IT to let them know – get me out of the naughty corner – and they didn't seem to know anything about it. Bit weird, that, isn't it?' He was still grinning, but there was a slight menace to his tone.

'Look, Andriy, I just pass on the messages. Not going to apologise if they've messed up somehow.' Stoly was surprised at his own brazenness. It seemed to work: Andriy shrugged and headed back to his desk.

The sun had already set when Stoly stepped out of the Cabinet of Ministers building, a vast, hulking monolith of Soviet architecture, its curved facade towering over the cobbled street below. He tried not to think about what lay ahead: an emergency meeting with his FSB handler... some kind of SBU intervention... He knew there was no turning back now. His sense of panic from earlier had subsided to resignation.

The streets were busy with civil servants heading home. They all seemed to be walking faster than him. He wondered if there was some special way you were supposed to check if you were under surveillance. Bit late to find that out now. He decided he would stop, pull out his phone, pretend to take a call and look around for followers. There seemed to be hundreds of them. Given that it was the end of the working day near a Metro station, he self-consciously concluded this was pointless.

As he turned into Khreschatyk Street he saw the red neon sign for Mr Grill, an incongruous hamburger joint, gleaming in the dusky night. He wondered where Petro would be, but focused on walking calmly and slowly down the wide middle stretch of pavement between little strips of grass and benches. In the February weather the benches were deserted but for one figure, hunched in a long overcoat. As Stoly approached the figure stood, perhaps too quickly, and he realised it was Petro, barely recognisable with his face wrapped behind a thick scarf.

'Sit down.'

Stoly felt the cold of the wooden bench against his thighs. Petro was sitting side-saddle, facing Stoly. He seemed to be fiddling with his clothes.

'We're going to change coats. We're about the same size. You'll get yours back later, but I'd check your pockets anyway.'

Stoly found his voice. 'Why?'

'You'll be carrying a wire. We need to hear what's going on. It's totally hidden,' he said, stroking the lapel as if he were a tailor appraising a fine bolt of cloth. 'Even if you look for it you won't find it. No risk to you, but it helps us.'

'I don't suppose I have any choice about this.'

'Not really.'

Petro sounded apologetic, which Stoly thought was nice. They shuffled around on the bench, Stoly stuffing things into his trouser pockets before switching coats as quickly as possible in the chilly air. It was odd the way the hundreds of passers-by seemed to ignore them making this peculiar exchange. It was a heavy overcoat, but warm.

'Okay, Stoly.' Petro's voice had acquired a work-mode formality. 'Two things: first – don't worry. You're having a meeting with Sergey, like all the other ones. No reason to do anything strange. Just behave as you would on any other occasion. Second...' He paused, searching for the words. 'You did the right thing today. I can't make any promises, but you have done this for the Motherland and that's been noted. *Slava Ukraini!'*

Stoly noticed that Petro wouldn't make eye contact with him. He felt a lump in his throat as he replied, '*Heroiam slava!'*

Pulling the unfamiliar coat around his chest to keep out the chill, he headed for the Metro.

Kyiv's Metro, with its wide thoroughfares and broad platforms, was rarely crowded. But it was busy during this rush hour. Stoly had to squeeze to get onto the first train heading for Holosiivskyi. For the second time that day he had to fight an urge to shout, '*The war is about to begin!*' at the top of his voice at the unwitting passengers whose only battle was to find a free seat.

The carriage thinned out as he got closer to Holosiivska station and Stoly started to wonder about the people that were left. There was a guy in a cap, pronounced gut, sitting at the end of the carriage, staring straight ahead. Didn't seem to be taking any interest in Stoly. But was he one of the spectators from when he was nearly run over earlier? He was the Ukrainian everyman: late fifties, overweight, scruffy overalls, probably a factory worker heading home after a tiring shift. You could see his type in every Metro carriage and bus; on every street, if you wanted to. Stoly shook his head involuntarily, as if he could make the thought go away.

Paranoia isn't helping.

At Holosiivska he realised he had to commit, stop worrying. He made a point of being first out of the carriage, heading swiftly for the exit, not looking round.

And so he didn't spot Everyman following him.

The air was noticeably cooler out of the city centre, a light breeze blowing across the wide road junction in front of the park. Stoly crossed carefully, setting out along the quiet track that ran alongside the lake to his left, the water inky dark. To his right, a wooded hill loomed over him, its trees' bare branches fusing seamlessly with the night sky. He knew that, within a couple of minutes, Sergey would loom up behind him, his footsteps always disconcertingly silent. He told himself he wasn't going to look round and give Sergey a reason to suspect anything. He was approaching the second old willow, its branches weeping into the lake. Sergey had always reached him by this point. He wondered if he was walking too fast and slowed, almost to a standstill.

And then he felt his phone buzzing in his trouser pocket. He pulled it out and took the call from a number he didn't recognise.

–

Only a few hundred metres away, unknown to Stoly, Petro and his younger colleague Yevhen were sitting in a battered Toyota sedan, parked against the pavement in a side road. They were both wearing an earpiece, the wires snaking back to a small black box sitting on the dashboard. The engine was off and the car in near-darkness, just a few flickering green LEDs on the front of the box glowing spectrally onto their faces.

Petro turned to Yevhen. 'Phone call.'

Yevhen nodded. Instinctively they both put their hands up to the earpiece, concentrating.

'Hello, my friend.' They heard a voice speaking Russian, very quiet, as it was coming through Stoly's handset.

'Lefortov?' asked Yevhen.

Petro nodded. Stoly had said he only knew his handler's first name. But Petro had been sure it would turn out to be Sergey Lefortov. It was a voice he had heard many times before, but always remotely, through intercepted calls and hidden microphones.

'Hello.' This was Stoly, coming through loud and clear.

'Different plan today. Take the steps up ahead, into the woods. I'll meet you up there on the little hill.'

The call came to an abrupt end. And then all they could hear was heavier breathing, as Stoly appeared to have picked up his pace. Yevhen was fiddling with his phone, using a tracker app to confirm Stoly's location. But it didn't seem to be working properly, and he cursed quietly as he repeatedly tapped the refresh icon. Stoly's breathing was now laboured as he climbed the steps into the dark woods.

'It's not working,' said Yevhen. 'Tracker's not updating properly. Should I get a visual?'

'No panic,' replied Petro. 'Perhaps walk in that direction, just in case.'

Yevhen gave a middle-aged grunt as he climbed out of the car, his body disappearing into the darkness.

The only sound now was the audio of Stoly making heavy weather of the climb. He had obviously reached the top of the steps, as Petro could hear him panting heavily. Then a slow crunch of shoes on gravel as he continued on the path.

'*Stoly?*' It was a new voice, with a pronounced Caucasus accent. Chechen, Petro reckoned, but it could have been Karachay.

A gasp, and then Stoly's voice: 'Shit! Who're you? I can hardly see you.' He sounded terrified. 'Where's Sergey?'

'Sergey couldn't make it. I'm Chovka.'

Petro knew instantly. He wondered if he had known the moment Sergey had guided Stoly up the steps. He jabbed at a switch on the little black box. 'Yevhen,' he called in an urgent tone, 'run. Get there, *now*!'

Petro's mind was racing: should he follow Yevhen? But then he wouldn't have the audio feed... Before he could make a decision, he heard Stoly again.

'No, I'm not doing this!' It was a cry of defiance, and then Petro could hear heavy footsteps. Stoly seemed to have left the path, as there were the cracks of breaking twigs underfoot and then the sound of a stumble in the dark.

'No!' Stoly was gasping for air, like a drowning swimmer.

And then, two sharp clicks.

Chapter 1

Kyiv

July 2022

A spy alone is the loneliest person in the world. Simone Sartori, who had left England a few weeks earlier only a few metres ahead of a police arrest team, was definitively alone. His cover story – that he was a Canadian-Italian journalist writing for a South African news website – was so thin that he dared not expose it to even the faintest scrutiny by actually behaving like a journalist and talking to anyone. The days when you could show up in a foreign country with a fake name and a plausible ID card were long gone. True, he'd kept himself off Facebook and the other sites, but nobody in the 2020s owns their face or their data any more. A decent OSINT researcher with a good photo of him would take about two hours to prove that Simone Sartori had never written anything for SA News Zone. Another thirty minutes and they'd find that he bore a remarkable likeness to Simon Sharman, a British former civil servant and suspected intelligence officer, who had gone missing in the UK after a series of highly suspicious events involving Rory Gough, a hedge-fund manager who held an advisory role at 10 Downing Street.

If you're in the business, war zones are like a professional networking event: you get to check in on the people in your industry, catch up on gossip, tell a few tall tales, and try to stay sane and alive. From what Simon had seen on the train in, all the usual suspects had come to Ukraine: the bodyguards, thick necks and shaved heads, tattoos on their bulging arms, monosyllabic; diplomats and media crews, more social, chatting with a nervous jollity that was meant to signal nonchalance; aid workers, serious, filling in endless spreadsheets on their laptops because Ukraine was going to be rebuilt one logframe at a time. And then there were those like Simon, travelling alone and avoiding getting into conversations. They would be the spooks, all pretending to be something else.

In the station at Przemyśl on the Polish border, Simon had kept his cap pulled low and paid extra for a single cabin on the sleeper train. As he walked up the platform he overheard a young diplomat talking at deliberate high volume to his colleague – 'Haven't seen you since the last flight out of Kabul.' – hoping he would be overheard by the coolly beautiful producer from Al Jazeera who was helping her colleagues lug their camera kit onto the carriage.

In wartime Ukraine, there were plenty of people who might remember Sharman from previous adventures. Once in Kyiv, it didn't take him long to figure out that he could head down to the Havana Café and encounter half a dozen acquaintances: the people who pop up whenever there's a war on, particularly one of those good wars where you know which side you're on and you can get a proper drink after work. 'Such a relief to be out of the Middle East,' he'd overheard a loud-mouthed Fox News producer say to his sound man, who appeared to share this opinion. Many of the hangers-on at the Havana could probably give Simon the head start he sorely needed, and would be happy to see him. But it wasn't a risk he was willing to run. For now, he would remain in the shadows.

And for that reason he was steering clear of the international joints, instead spending lonely hours in places frequented only by Ukrainians or, these days, by almost nobody at all. Like the cream cakes it served, the Café Kobzar was a perfect slice of central Europe: high ceilings, large gilt-framed mirrors hanging on walls painted a rich yellow, a chequered tile floor. Behind a marble-topped dark wood counter, a waiter in a black apron pulled the levers on a huge chrome coffee machine, the occasional searing hiss of pressurised steam assaulting the ears. But he didn't have to use his machine very often as the cafe rarely had much custom, the piped muzak easily audible.

It was getting closer to curfew time in Kyiv and Simon was wondering if he would have 'one for the road', which meant a fourth whisky. He'd tried to make them last a little longer, with a dash of water, and ice cubes that he crunched in his mouth. But he was running out of time, and another night alone in his Airbnb meant another night wondering what the hell he was doing in Ukraine, travelling on a fake Italian passport and an even faker Polish press card.

Simon had his complete plan laid out on a double page of the notebook that lay in front of him on the shiny table. The problem was, that double page was blank, save for a name. Which said all you needed to know about his plan.

Chovka Buchayev

'He's in Ukraine now.' So had said Vasya Morozov, a former GRU officer whom Simon had once recruited as a source of British intelligence. Vasya had long since cut his ties to the British government, preferring to pursue business opportunities with Britain's bankers and lawyers. But, perhaps for old time's sake, he had given Simon this one piece of intelligence about Chovka.

Turned out, Ukraine was a pretty big place and Simon didn't feel as if he was getting anywhere, sitting in an empty cafe, measuring out what was left of his life in coffee spoons. For the third night running, he was the sole punter as curfew approached. He kept a lonely vigil at a corner table, the choice of which would have gained him the approval of his trainers at the spy school in Cardross, allowing a full view of both the cafe and out through the windows to the street that led to it. And it was thanks to these well-entrenched skills that Simon saw a second customer heading towards the cafe.

Although he was a trained intelligence operative, it didn't make particular demands on Simon's professional skills to figure out that he was looking at an American volunteer soldier, making a slow, tired progress down the street towards the Kobzar. Just as you could spot an American tourist a mile off, from the specially designed hiking clothes they wear – even when the only hiking they're doing is round a museum – Simon knew an American combat veteran by the fact that he was wearing desert camo and carrying a sand-coloured backpack. Of course, they were now fighting a war in the fields and forests of northern Europe, but like every other American of fighting age, this one would have spent his military career in the deserts of Iraq and Afghanistan, and had come to Ukraine equipped from that war.

The man was peering into the cafe, squinting to see if it was still open. Artem, the barman, was coaxing him in. Simon felt a surge of opportunity: *just one guy, no real risk talking to him*. The newcomer was now standing in front of the bar and Simon could see an eagle, a globe and an anchor embossed on the left breast of his fleece, which was covered in dust and oily stains. He took the plunge, walking across to the bar to where the new arrival was waiting for Artem to stop his relentless polishing of the espresso machine.

'*Semper fi.*' This was a gamble, but Simon felt he was on the right lines.

'Huh?'

This didn't seem to be going very well.

He looked exhausted, the tiredness etched into a weather-worn face. He didn't exactly look old: Simon guessed mid to late forties. But he looked as though he'd lived what obituarists would call a 'full life'.

'*Semper fi.* You're a Marine, aren't you?'

'Yessir. You serve?' A quizzical look accompanied this question.

Simon had a choice to make. He had never been in the military, but he knew enough about their world that he could probably carry off being a soldier of some kind to an American Marine. But he was supposed to be an Italian-Canadian journalist, and the army he knew best was British. So he tried another angle.

'No, not me, I'm afraid. Journalist,' he added, pointing at himself unnecessarily, given that the rest of the room was empty but for Artem, whose profession as barman was not in doubt. 'But I spent time in Fallujah. I know what you guys were up against there.' Simon was doing as he'd always been taught when living a cover story: *keep it as close to reality as possible.* Nearly twenty years earlier, as a British intelligence officer in an obscure entity known as the Pole, he had spent some time deployed to a Forward Operating Base in Fallujah, western Iraq, where the US Marine Corps had fought a desperate battle to regain control from Islamist militants. The Marines had lost more people in a few days in that one small town than they had in the entire invasion of Iraq a year earlier. The city was left in ruins.

'Fallujah? Damn, that was a hot mess.'

'Well, you guys bore the brunt. I was there a couple of weeks later. Interviewed Jocko Toolan.' Simon hoped that using the familiar name of a well-regarded Marine commander would increase his credentials.

'General Toolan... Well, he was Colonel Toolan then.' The man fell silent, reliving those intense days.

'And you're a volunteer now? Here? On the front?'

'Yes, sir. International Legion.'

'Thank you for your service.' Simon said this with a slight stiffness in his spine, a formality to his tone. This wasn't a man in a bar; it was a target under cultivation. The man held out a hand, dirty, with crescents of grime under his fingernails. His eyes had that level gaze of someone who has seen more than they wanted to. He didn't seem like a talker, but he wanted someone to talk to.

'Thanks, man.'

'Drink? Artem here will take care of you.' Simon fixed Artem with a meaningful glance which he hoped said, *Now is not the time to start talking about the curfew.*

'I'm Simon.'

'Mike.'

They sat at Simon's corner table, Mike leaning forwards, hunched over his beer bottle. He'd been on the Donetsk front, fighting intense battles against Russian tanks. He'd lost several comrades: Americans, Swedes, Georgians. It sounded chaotic. And heroic.

'I spent half my service life wondering if there'd ever be a war with Russia. And when it came, I'm in the fuckin' Ukrainian army.'

'And the Russians? What're they like? As an enemy?' Simon had fought a secret war against Russia his entire life, but what they might do on a field of battle in a conventional war remained a mystery to him.

'You know, the thing I didn't expect is that they aren't one army. I was in Popasna. Just a road junction you'd barely call a town back home. But the fight there... It was like Stalingrad. There's nothing left...' Mike lapsed into silence.

'Because of how they fight?'

'Because of what war this is. In Fallujah it was bad, but we knew we just had to secure the place, bust out the AQ guys, you know? I mean, we're the Marine Corps, we make a mess. But nothing like what's happening down there, in the Donbas. The Russians just flatten everything. And when they take some ground and they find civilians...' His voice tailed away.

Simon felt the need to fill the awkward silence. 'I can only imagine... You said they aren't one army?'

It seemed to have worked: Mike's voice brightened. 'Oh, yeah. So I thought, you know, Russian army, few million men, Soviet doctrines, one way of doing war, all that. But what you see in reality... it's very different.'

'Different how?' Just get them talking. This was the key in the early stages.

'They have so many different groups fighting, different commanders, uniforms, equipment. There's this group called LPR, that's Luhansk People's Republic – some kinda bull-shit country they've got going down there. Those guys are running around with rifles straight from a military museum. But that's just the start of it,' he added, warming to his theme. Simon nodded eagerly. 'Okay, so there's this one time we're in the market in Popasna. I say "market"; there's nothing left of the place. It's just rubble, but that's what they call that area. Like I said, kinda how you imagine Stalingrad, just corners of buildings still standing. Nothing has a roof any more. It's all cinder block, and anything above six feet has been pulverised by Russian artillery. So you dig a fucking trench. Your shovel is your best friend. I'm fourth generation Marine, but I don't reckon anyone in my family has dug so many trenches since World War One.'

There was an intensity in Mike's face as he started to relive the experience. Simon only had to make occasional eye contact to keep the flow. 'So, one night I'm on a guard rotation with Patrik, my Swedish buddy. I mean, guard duty doesn't mean a whole lot 'cos most of the time it's just Russian shelling. How do you guard against that? But sometimes they do these crazy-ass attacks…'

Another pause as Mike drained his Obolon beer, the events weighing heavily. Simon asked Artem to bring a couple more. The fresh bottle seemed to revive him a little. *Mike has something he wants to tell me, some piece of illuminating information – it's not just an anecdote. There's intelligence.*

'Like I'm saying, this time we're having a few quiet hours. Dead of night, street lights failed weeks earlier, so it's proper dark. We're keeping an eye; Patrik and me, we've got night-vision 'cos we brought our own. Most guys have to rely on the Javelin CLU, but that works fine.'

Simon nodded. He didn't know it was called a 'CLU', but he'd heard that soldiers were using the sighting unit from the Javelin missile launcher, with its powerful night-vision capability. And he didn't want to break Mike's narrative.

'Patrik's like: "You hear something? I heard something." And I'm staring out of the trench we've dug and I ain't heard anything. But that might be because I'm not one hundred per cent sure I'd been awake. You ever do an overnight shift on guard duty?'

Simon had not — certainly not when he was being a Canadian-Italian war correspondent. And he wanted Mike to stick to the story, so he merely shook his head.

'So this is what it's like: you get into this space — you're not awake, you're not asleep. It's something in between. You hear things well enough, but you might not *see* everything. Anyways, Patrik is whispering to me, "I heard something," and he's pointing down-range. I pull down my NVGs and sonofabitch, there it is. Probably couple hundred yards out.' He started to mimic his alert, peering eyes, looking through his night-vision goggles, his head darting towards the faintest movement, like an overgrown meerkat. 'There's one of their trenches we thought they'd abandoned. And at first I'm only looking at little dark dots, but it's clear enough I'm seeing the tops of their heads, moving in that goddam trench. So I signal to Patrik, he's going to grab a couple of the other guys, I'm lining them up along my rifle sights. But I'm not gonna shoot yet. I've just got some shitty AK, it's pretty random past two hundred yards. But we've got Arkady manning the *Dushka*.' Simon knew this one. The ancient Soviet .50 cal heavy machine gun that had been bolted onto the back of pickup trucks by insurgents the world over. And used to devastating effect. 'I mean, with that thing we can hose 'em down once they're in the open. And *they* must know that, except, what do they do? They just pop up, like they wanna get shot, no covering fire, no recon as far as I can see.'

'What – they just ran at you?'

'Pretty much. It's like, *bang*! They've fired some shitty RPG in our direction, misses off to the right, and then I can see maybe ten, fifteen of them coming our way, shooting their AKs, *pap-pap*. They don't know what they're doing. Everything's going up over my left shoulder. You know that thing with AKs? If you don't know what you're doing, the barrel always drifts up, shooter's right. So I start to pick them off, and then Arkady fires up the *Dushka* and it's just ground beef after that. Real mess...' Mike fell silent again, holding his beer bottle out in front of him, looking at it quizzically as if it were an unexpected object.

Simon was also remembering his own, far more limited experiences of warfare: the hideous pink brightness of eviscerated humanity. 'So you got all of them? Mowed 'em down?' Simon's tone was somewhere between bravado and ghoulish fascination.

'Damn near. 'Bout half of them shot to pieces, other lot crawling around on the ground, screaming...' Mike shook his head, grimacing. 'Couple of the last ones to come over got pretty close to our trench. One so close I had to lean back to get a shot at him as he's coming towards me.' He was pushing against the back of his chair, his hands mimicking the trajectory of his Kalashnikov pointing upwards at his doomed adversary. 'He's not dead, just on the ground, moaning. Gonna bleed out. I woulda pulled him in, patched him up. I mean, warrior ethic and all that. But the Russians, man, their snipers will get you, even when you're keeping one of theirs alive...' Mike paused again. There was a point to this anecdote. A punchline, but they hadn't got to it.

'They're taking incredible losses, by the sound of things,' offered Simon, stating the obvious, anything to keep Mike talking.

He found his groove again. 'This is what I wanted to say: bit later, we get our artillery to drop some shit on that trench, clean it out a bit with the *Dushka* as well. Middle of the next day,

29

when we reckon it's pretty safe, we checked the bodies, what's left of them. First thing I notice, they mostly have a different build to the Russian soldiers. Skinny, more facial hair. And they're tanned, like Arab-looking. Straight away they remind me of the guys in Fallujah.'

Simon had a jolt of interest, an opening to be exploited. 'Were they from the Caucasus? Chechnya?'

'Not even,' said Mike, smiling as he waggled his beer bottle for emphasis. 'I go through some of the ID documents and, whaddaya know? They're real-life, genuine article, Allah-fearing Arabs. Some of them have Libyan ID, some Syrian. Can you believe it? Fuckin Ay-rabs fighting in that shit in the Donbas? I mean, it's kind of a joke: I go to Ukraine to kill some Russians, all my life I've been shooting at Camel Jockeys, and down there in the fucking Popasna market it's like I'm right back in Fallujah.'

'Arabs? In the Donbas?' Simon was sceptical. 'You really sure of it?'

'Sure as I see you in front of me. ID cards were genuine. No doubt… You wanna know how they got there?'

Mike had a familiar smile. Since they'd met for the first time minutes earlier, this might seem odd. But it was familiar to Simon from years of source handling: the moment your inter-locutor realises they have something worth telling, something of real value. Intelligence. Simon nodded, his eyes wide with anticipation.

'Wagner.' Mike paused for effect. 'Mercenary army. Russians didn't wanna put their regular boys into the fight, to have the mothers in Moscow see their sons coming home in body bags. So they fill the battlefield with the guys nobody cares about. That bullshit LPR army, Wagner mercenaries, Arabs they pick up in Syria and Libya, whoever they can get to show up. And I haven't even mentioned the Chechens.'

Later on, Simon wondered if he had been obvious. Had he blinked too many times? Had he twitched, straightened his back?

'Yeah, everyone talks about the Chechens,' said Simon, as coolly as he could manage. 'But are they really *doing* anything? I mean, Kadyrov is on Instagram all day but I reckon he's safely tucked away in Grozny.' He was referring to the brutal Chechen warlord. Ramzan Kadyrov, who liked to claim he was on the front line slaughtering Ukrainians but appeared to be more comfortable living it up in his gaudy palace, where clueless Western celebrities would show up at his parties and simper 'Happy Birthday, Mister President,' just as soon as their appearance fee had gone through.

'Yeah, Kadyrov's chickenshit. Don't think he's been within a hundred miles of the front line. But his guys… That's another story. There's not many of them, but you know where they are at from what they do. They're insane. So cruel. So, *so* cruel.' The word struck Simon. A Marine veteran of Fallujah had no illusions about warfare. The concept of cruelty seemed almost quaint.

'We lost some guys,' Mike continued. 'I don't mean KIA. I mean we actually lost them on a manoeuvre. We got separated and a couple guys in my unit were unaccounted for. I mean, we don't normally have enough radios to go around. We might be better equipped than the Russians, but that's about all. People have no idea how desperate we are for basic kit.' He seemed to be about to go down another rabbit hole. Simon was starting to remember that one of the many symptoms of post-traumatic stress disorder was an inability to concentrate.

'You lost some guys?' he said, a gentle attempt to steer the conversation back onto fertile ground. 'Did the Chechens take them prisoner? What happened to them?'

'Take them prisoner?' Mike sounded confused. He was feeling inside his jacket pocket for something, muttering to himself.

I've lost him, thought Simon. *Poor bastard can't think in straight lines.*

Mike was holding a smartphone he'd dragged out of the inner recesses of his combat smock. 'I wanna show you something,' he said. Simon was about to stop him, pull him back on to the subject at hand. But he had no leverage – just a tired soldier who wanted someone to talk to. *Fine, show me a photo of your daughter, whatever.*

Mike was fiddling with the photos app, his thumb swiping through images, muttering, 'No... not that one... Wait a minute... Ah!' His face lit up. He thrust the screen under Simon's nose.

In the picture there was a front garden of a small house, little more than a dacha. Once, perhaps only a few short months ago, it had been someone's little patch of heaven, where the flowers bloomed every spring and the birds would start their day chorusing the dawn. But now the garden was muddy, overgrown, the house shabby, pockmarked with bullet holes, the windows smashed. In the middle of the image was a pile of clothes – military uniform – on the ground. And then Simon realised it wasn't a pile of clothes: it was a person sitting on the ground, leaning against the metal railing in front of the garden. He had been confused because there was no head. Or, at least, the head was not connected to the body, but jammed on top of a wooden pole, just to one side. The metal railing had spikes running along the top, almost too grand for the humble dwelling it guarded. There were two odd objects either side of the body, impaled on the tops of the railing. Simon leant closer to the image, unable to identify these pinkish lumps. Then he got it: they were the soldier's severed hands.

'Oh, God!' He had been looking at the picture for no more than two seconds, but it was more than enough. He turned his head to one side, not wanting to see any more.

'Yeah,' agreed Mike, still holding the phone up. 'That's the Chechen way of war.'

Simon looked forwards again, his eyes drawn inexorably towards the hideous image. He couldn't take his eyes off the head. He hated the blankness of the face, the grey of the skin. Not for the first time, he found himself reflecting that there was something surreal about a head no longer connected to its body, offending the laws of nature. 'Mike, I've seen it. Put it away.'

Mike nodded, tucking the phone back into his jacket.

'That was Petro. Best watcher in the unit. He and Oleh went missing when we were doing a night sweep on one side of Popasna. They were just gone – maybe ten days. Then the front line shifted: we move forwards a few blocks and that's where we found him. We found his buddy Oleh around the corner.'

'They did the same to him?' As soon as he asked this, Simon wished he hadn't.

'No.' Mike looked as though this was a ridiculous notion. 'They just tied his hands behind his back and double-tapped him. Even the Chechens get tired of torturing people,' he added, as if it were the most obvious thing in the world.

'And you know it's Chechens did this? I mean, regular Russian army is capable of all kinds of stuff.'

'Sure we know it was Chechens. We captured a few... I mean, we don't do what they do, but we found out who they were.' He smiled with weak bravado.

'I'm following up a lead. For a story about the Chechens fighting in Ukraine.' As Simon said this, he realised he hadn't figured out his cover story in his *own* mind, let alone having it ready to explain to other people.

'What's the lead?'

'Well, I have a name – at least, it's a *nom de guerre* – of a Chechen who has been active in Ukraine, known for taking part in assassinations, torture, that sort of thing. Could easily have been the guy who did that stuff to Petro.'

'Yeah?' Mike had been slouched over his beer, but now he straightened up a little. 'You think that's possible? There's not that many of them. Even the so-called Chechen units are mostly made up of guys from all over Russia. What unit was this guy with?'

Simon felt slightly queasy. As if he was getting into more than he could really handle. 'I don't have the unit, I have his name. Chovka. Chovka Buchayev.'

Now Mike was looking right into Simon's eyes.

'To be honest, I don't know if the second name is real. But he definitely goes by Chovka. Means "jackdaw" in Chechen.'

A long silence, as Mike frowned, looked at Simon, and then shook his head. 'Chovka?'

'Yes.'

'So that's all you've got? That's it?'

'For the moment, yes.'

Simon knew a lot about Chovka's background. But in truth, he knew almost nothing about what he was doing now in Ukraine.

'That's a lead?' Mike sounded incredulous. 'A lead for a story? What's the story gonna say?'

'Well... It's a kind of deep dive. Into how these outsiders, Chechens – Arabs, from what you've just told me – how these outsiders have come into the war in Ukraine as part of Russia's motley crew. And how some of them have blood on their hands from other conflicts, other places.' Even as Simon said this, he felt it sounded incredibly weak.

'What places?'

'Well, Mike, the Russians like to use the Chechens for assassinations, sometimes across Europe... There's only so much I can say at the moment.'

'Huh.' Mike sounded nonplussed. 'That's really all you got?'

Simon nodded, feeling like an idiot, wishing he could say more. But he felt he might already have said too much. But inside his head, he could hear himself explaining, clearly, what was going on.

Chovka Buchayev killed my business partner Evie Howard. In Prague, about a month ago. I had to call her father. Will never forget that. Vasya Morozov, a former GRU officer with contacts all over Ukraine, told me Chovka's here now. So I've come to find him.

'That's all I've got for now, but I might be able to find his unit name.'

'Well, I don't know how fixed the units are anyways. I think it was the Akhmat Battalion we were up against, but like I said, a lotta them aren't even Chechen.'

'But would you know if they were there now?'

'I just came from the front. They're there. Akhmat Battalion. But the other way you find is by following the reports of massacres or torture. There was a story about them using some old hospital, bodies buried there, bad shit.'

'You know where that is?'

'They called it Pryvillya. Don't ask me where that is. But the Kadyrovtsy were there.'

In keeping with the crazed egomania of Chechnya's warlord, the Chechen soldiers were also known as Kadyrovtsy.

'That's their other name,' added Mike helpfully. 'Find a massacre and you'll find them. Or check Telegram. They post everything.'

This wasn't Simon's first war. But it was his first social media war, and he was finding the concept confusing at best.

Chapter 2

London

November 2017

'Social media is now a weapon of war.' It was one of those statements that people made to try to appear intelligent. *Thinking outside the box.*

'Social media is *not* "a weapon of war". It's a bunch of people wasting time on their phones.' Simon took a swig from his beer bottle and wondered whether the woman he was talking to was actually half his age, or just looked half his age. In spite of her youth, she was self-confident, not letting a slightly overrefreshed middle-aged man put her off her stride.

'Okay. I get that most social media is not strategically significant. Or significant in any way at all, in fact.' This was said with patient confidence. She was one of the few women in a room full of men drinking, and almost certainly the youngest. 'But if you look at how it's weaponised by certain regimes, especially Russia and China, they're able to use it to achieve things that would have previously required huge power.'

'Like what?' Simon wondered if he sounded aggressive.

'Like election outcomes. A year ago, Americans were being bombarded with stuff on Facebook which was cooked up in St Petersburg and designed to spread disinformation, chaos in their election. You could say that it worked rather well.'

'But how much impact does this stuff have? Nobody should believe things they see on Facebook.' Simon still didn't have a

Facebook account and admitted to being slightly mystified by its purpose.

The young woman seemed to be trying not to laugh. 'Facebook has become the main source of news for most Americans.'

Simon grimaced. This seemed very unlikely. 'What did you say your name was?' He was wondering whether he might get another drink. Should he offer her one? But he didn't want to seem sleazy.

'Evie. Evie Howard.'

'And who do you work for, Evie?' The pub had been taken over by a network of what were euphemistically known as 'corporate intelligence professionals' – spooks for hire – for the sole purpose of exchanging the sort of gossip that would get them sued if they committed it to writing.

'I don't, at the moment. I'm a student at King's. My friend Sophy brought me along,' she said, gesturing into the crowd. Simon had no idea if Sophy was a real person, but in his world, initiative was more important than strict honesty, so he wasn't too bothered if she was or not.

'And you're into online research? Open source, that sort of thing?'

'Я увлечён разведкой,' – I'm passionate about intelligence – she had replied in perfect Russian.

The combination of the background noise and this being unexpected meant that Simon missed what she said, and looked at her blankly.

'I was told you speak excellent Russian…' she said archly.

'I do,' he replied, irritated.

'Вам хорошо меня слышно?" – Are you hearing me okay?

Again, the arch smile, but this time Simon heard her fine and noted that her Russian was perfect.

'Я хорошо вас слышу, спасибо,' – I hear fine, thanks – he replied, and as he did so, he realised what he'd heard her say earlier. 'You're into intelligence. What do you mean by that?"

'I mean that I speak Russian like a native, have a master's degree from King's in Intelligence and International Security, and that's what I'd like to do for work... Be good to keep in touch,' she added.

Simon was about to reply, but she had already stepped away.

Chapter 3

Kyiv

February 2022

They called it a silent pistol, but Chovka had always winced when it fired. It was quieter than any other gun in the world, designed for covert assassinations and undercover missions. But the PSS still made an audible click, like someone snapping their fingers.

Click! Click!

Chovka had shot Stolyarenko in the back of the head. Twice, to be on the safe side. In spite of being the real deal, an actual Chechen assassin, Chovka never enjoyed these wet jobs. But there had been a mess which needed clearing up. Several messes, in fact. After the job in the woods at Holosiivskyi, he had then been supposed to rendezvous with the FSB units and wait for Russia's invading forces to show up in Kyiv. They would be arriving at 14:55, Chovka had been told.

You could say it hadn't worked out that way: Stolyarenko wasn't the only person who had turned out to be a poor FSB investment. There was meant to be a whole network of Ukrainians, from the top of government all the way down the civil service and military, who were going to step up the moment Russia began its invasion. Everyone knew Ukraine's President wouldn't hang around. *A fucking comedian?* They had laughed about it. *Let's see if he finds this funny.* The network would implement a silent *coup d'état*. The comedian would have the last laugh by falling out of a window. He'd always been a master of slapstick. And then the new government would invite the Russian army to help *stabilise* the place.

That was the other point. It wasn't supposed to be a fucking invasion. Not a real one where you had to fight battles to take every fucking metre of ground. The Russian army was going to march unopposed into Ukraine and *rescue* all the Russian speakers.

Chovka, who'd grown up speaking Chechen and practising Islam, had once been aware of the irony of his own situation. But that was some time ago. Chovka was a survivor, not a hero. Survivors figure out which people have power and make themselves useful to those people. Over the years, Chovka would make himself very useful.

But there had proved a limit to his usefulness in those chaotic days in the spring of 2022. Instead of rolling into a wide open Ukraine, the Russian army had got stuck in an epic traffic jam on the E95 highway, their tanks being picked off by Ukrainians armed with Javelin missiles. Chovka had helped do some tidying up: people who might have been important in the version of Ukraine's future under Russian control were now liabilities to be removed from the balance sheet. When the Russians decided to retreat from Kyiv, most of the FSB guys had already long since fled back home. But Chovka's handler had other ideas for him.

'There's a few million people heading west from Ukraine. Become a Ukrainian refugee. Russian-speaker from the Donbas, obviously, I've heard you try to speak Ukrainian. Get to Moldova and keep your head down. We have something you need to do there.'

–

As usual, Chovka had made himself useful in Moldova. Some of it was boring work: a lot of waiting around. But he was good at that. There had been some necessary – if unpleasant – tasks. And even opportunities to get some extra benefits. Not the worst job he'd ever had.

One night he was driving his recently stolen car back to his seedy hotel on the edge of Chişinău when his encrypted phone started buzzing. It was Ilya, who called himself a 'co-ordinator' and seemed to specialise in telling people things they already knew. But on this occasion it was new information.

'Gotta get out. We're blown.'

'What?'

'We're blown. They've arrested Viktor. He'd just got off a flight and they were waiting for him.' Viktor was their GRU team leader. This was not good.

'Seriously?'

'Wouldn't be a very funny fucking joke, would it?'

'Shit.'

'Yeah. Shit. Now, scram. Get outta here. Find a way. You're on your own.'

You're on your own. Once again, Chovka was being told something he already knew. He still wasn't completely sure whether Ilya's instruction had the finality he'd suggested, so he kept his options open, stashing the car and his kit in a quiet bit of forest and slipping back into the comparative safety of Transnistria, where the Russians ruled the roost. Sometimes these things blow over.

After a few days of hearing nothing, he concluded it definitely was over. Going anywhere near a blown car didn't seem like a good plan, so he drifted back into the mass of displaced humanity that was moving through eastern Europe. After a few days he passed into Slovakia, where there were huge numbers of Ukrainian refugees and it was easy to disappear in the crowds. At the border, the system was almost overwhelmed: they were barely checking documents and possessions. In Bratislava, once he was settled in a refugee camp and had established a sort of routine, he spent a morning following a complex anti-surveillance route, at the end of which he sent a message from an internet cafe to his handler, awaiting further instructions.

None came. Chovka wondered about trying the Russian embassy in Bratislava, but it seemed too risky. It would likely have the local security services crawling all over it, and his cover as a displaced Ukrainian citizen from the Donbas would not stand up to much scrutiny. But a lifetime lived around the world of Russian intelligence gave him an instinct. Rather as a fishmonger can smell a lack of freshness before it is obvious to the customer, Chovka could smell even the faintest putrefaction of criminality, of dirty money and of latent violence.

He knew how the world of Russian influence worked in places like Slovakia and quickly figured out where the oligarchs spent their money: the bars, brothels and businesses that were part of the Russian organised crime networks. The unimaginatively named Disco Club casino was the venue from which Aleksandr Babakunov, a St Petersburg ally of the Russian President, ran his human trafficking network, where he entertained the Slovakian politicians who described themselves as 'NATO-critical' and whom everyone else called Russian stooges. It was where Babakunov could ensure that the Slovakian head of the government-owned arms manufacturer was fully entertained during his night out, the *kompromat* going straight back to colleagues in Moscow.

Chovka spent a couple of nights hanging around outside Disco Club, inhaling the whiff of corruption, the sleek Mercedes and BMW saloons purring up and disgorging their cargo: fat men in shiny suits, accompanied by rake-thin women in short dresses and platform heels. Once he felt he recognised the stench, he joined the regular punters queueing behind a roped-off gangway, waiting patiently for their turn to be ripped off at the gaming tables. Inside the club it was all as he'd expected: lit solely by coloured LEDs in the ceiling, glowing on the blue baize of the gaming tables. A raised 'VIP area' at the back was darker, populated with bald men sitting on red velvet sofas, trying to think of amusing things to say to the call girls sitting on their knees. Their grunts were uniformly greeted with delighted gasps at their wit and perspicacity.

Chovka didn't yet have a plan, so he leant against the main bar that afforded him a view of the gaming hall and nursed the smallest, cheapest drink he could buy whilst trying not to look like a Chechen assassin disguised as a Ukrainian refugee. His nose twitched as he tried to assess the potential arrayed in front of him. There were one or two brash Americans; superficially appealing, but you make a mess of an American and the FBI shows up two days later taking fingerprints.

He found what he was looking for at a blackjack table. The man was sweating profusely in spite of the air conditioning. He was piling in on stupid bets, twisting on seventeen and accusing the dealer of miscounting as he knocked back the vodka and cola that the waitresses, all hot pants and crop tops, were happy to provide. One in particular, with a bob of jet-black hair and a pixie smile painted red against her paper-white complexion, had caught his eye. He had a dangerous, hungry grin that Chovka recognised. As the waitress brought the latest drink, his sweaty hand looped around her bare waist and he nuzzled her neck. There was a single frame of disgust on her face and then the compulsory smile returned to her gleaming white teeth.

There was an upstairs at Disco Club. This was where the discoing happened, although there wasn't much of that, as the vibe was mostly gambling or fucking, the latter taking place in little playrooms down a corridor off to the side of the dance floor. After a particularly ruinous hand, Sweaty Man slammed his fat palms in frustration down on the blackjack table, before hauling his bulbous behind off the high stool and waddling towards the staircase. En route he grabbed the waitress, and the two of them began a slow, almost funereal progress up the wide steps. She was clearly reluctant, but didn't seem able to refuse. Chovka had clocked a couple of security guards. They took no interest.

He let the odd couple make their laborious way up the staircase and then took himself up via a lift he had spotted in one corner of the building. The dance floor was empty, save for an elderly man in a pale suit who appeared to be auditioning for a 'move like Mick Jagger' contest, contorting his limbs with surprising athleticism. Around the edge of the room, couples sat in little booths. From what Chovka could make out, this was where the negotiations were held prior to making use of the private rooms down the corridor. The whole operation was overseen by an almost entirely spherical madam, who sat on a green velvet throne at the entrance to the playrooms, dead-eyed. Sweaty Man had Pixie Waitress in a vice-like grip, his huge hammy hand capable of grabbing a significant chunk of her torso. As she was being hefted towards a vacant cubicle, she looked over her shoulder at the madam with an imploring glance. The response would have been invisible to most, but Chovka had a good eye for these things. The madam inclined her head, almost invisibly, and the waitress gulped as she was dragged down the corridor.

It happened more quickly than Chovka expected: the scream began at a low pitch and escalated up octaves and decibels to a piercing high note. Within a few seconds, he had bounded down the corridor and shoved open the flimsy door of the playroom. Inside, all was red velvet and a cloying odour of air freshener. The waitress was naked on a bed, her face bleeding from her mouth, her previously cute button nose now smashed flat. Chovka saw the man's naked back, presenting acres of plump, white flesh, standing in front of the bed. His trousers and faded underpants were round his ankles; his buttocks sagged almost to the backs of his knees. At the sound of Chovka's entrance he looked over his shoulder, alarmed. There was blood on one of his hands from where he had smashed her jaw. His other hand was on her neck, keeping her in place. Chovka grabbed the rounded, hairy shoulders, but they were surprisingly greasy with sweat. Even more surprisingly, the man turned his head and bit into Chovka's left hand.

The combination of pain and the purchase this gave him on the man's jaw shocked Chovka into intense action. He was what people called 'wiry': not tall or broad, but very muscular. He snatched his arm downwards, pulling against the man's jawbone, twisting the head down against his jowly neck. The shock and speed made him release the bite, and he seemed briefly unbalanced, both arms flailing. Chovka, still standing behind the man's back, grabbed the right forearm and then swerved his entire body weight against the elbow joint. There was a satisfying crack as it snapped the wrong way, the man giving a guttural howl before tripping over his trousers and thudding noisily to the floor, his arm flopping uselessly. Chovka took a free kick into his bollocks, just as two security men appeared in the room.

He felt a huge, muscular hand grab his arm. He had planned for this moment, and remained as still and as compliant as possible. *Figure out which people have power and make yourself useful to those people.* He felt detached, as if he was observing with interest to see what would happen. And it was much as expected: he was dragged out of the room, roughed up a little, but quickly let go as the security went to work on Sweaty Man, making a real mess of him.

Chovka had assessed that the loser who plays low stakes, shouts at the dealers and then smashes up one of the hostesses, doesn't endear himself to the management. On the other hand, the quiet man who spots that something is amiss and proves himself capable of taking remedial action, and doesn't even complain when he's given a kicking by security, might prove useful to someone. They brought him a drink and told him the boss wanted to meet him. He should wait to be summoned.

Being a professional assassin is a very boring job. Almost all of the time is spent waiting for the right opportunity, and half of that time, something goes wrong just when you need it to go right. Sitting around waiting was something Chovka was very good at, especially now he was no longer expected to pay for his drinks. He could put his entire consciousness into a kind of trance, where hours would drift by, barely noticed.

'Boss is ready for you,' said one of the no-necks who had roughed him up earlier. He had one of those especially shiny shaved heads. 'This way.' Chovka followed him into the lift and this time they went to the top floor, where a large open-plan office with plate glass windows looked out over an undistinguished suburb of Bratislava. In keeping with the rest of the establishment, it was ill lit. But the décor was classier: more boardroom than brothel. A middle-aged man in a well-cut suit was sitting at the head of a long shiny table that reflected the ceiling lights like little glowing spots. He was flanked by two aides, whose faces were blue in the light of their computers. The security goon caught the boss's eye and he nodded, motioning to the two aides to wind up. They folded up their laptops and headed to a side office as Chovka approached the table.

'Evgeny,' he said, gesturing to himself, then indicating that Chovka should sit down. He had a knowing smile in his untroubled face that said, *It is no surprise at all to see you here.* Everyone was playing their role beautifully. 'What do we call you?' he asked, seemingly aware that names are temporary labels.

Chovka replied cautiously, using the identity the FSB had given him to escape from Ukraine. 'I'm Andrey Solyov, from Donetsk.'

'Sure you are,' Evgeny replied, the knowing smile still on his face. There was a pause. 'I hope the security guys didn't cause any lasting damage?'

Chovka shook his head. His shin was going to have a big bruise on it, and his shoulders were a little sore, but that was all.

'So you're a refugee from Nazi Ukraine? And you need work?' Evgeny was nodding even before Chovka had started his answer.

'Yes, I do need work,' said Chovka, trying to sound as straightforward as possible. He still wasn't sure what the game was; if it was merely that he should keep an eye on troublemakers at Disco Club, that was good enough.

'We have some special projects sometimes. Things that might suit a refugee, a real *Ukrainian* refugee,' Evgeny added, with special emphasis on the exotic possibilities that went with Chovka's status.

'What kind of projects?' he asked, pushing his luck.

Evgeny, his face showing a flicker of impatience for the first time, frowned briefly. 'I think we know the kind of work you do and the people you do it for. The details will come later.'

'Right.'

'Prague? You ever been to Prague? That a place where people know you?'

Chovka had not been to Prague.

Chapter 4

Kyiv

July 2022

There was much about the war in Ukraine that was user-friendly. For a start, getting a drink was far easier than it had been the last time Simon had been in a war zone, somewhere in the Middle East. And he had been able to find a small apartment in Kyiv on Airbnb, an attic room in a handsome Haussmann-nesque building not far from the green and gold domes of the St Sophia Cathedral. Although Simon's new identity didn't come with much of a profile as an Airbnb user, the average host in Kyiv was happy to have the custom. And Simon appreciated the tiny bedsit, with a shower cubicle next to a plug-in hob and a microwave along one wall, with his narrow single bed less than two metres away along the other. It was sufficiently bijou that he could turn down his boiling noodles by simply reaching out of the shower and twiddling the knob, although he did wonder whether this risked electrocution.

The ground floor of the building was grand: high ceilings, decorative stonework and a stately entrance hall. Similarly, the next few floors had wrought-iron balconies, full-height windows and elaborate cornicing. But with each floor climbed, the building became shabbier, grubbier and seemingly closer to its Soviet period of existence. By the time you were at the very top, things were firmly in the Cold War period drama phase of interior decoration. Here, global capitalism would be defeated by lining walls with brown chipboard. In keeping with the socialist dream, his loo was theoretically a shared affair, down the corridor from the bedsit. But he had yet to meet another occupant of the attic floor, which was no bad thing, particularly as, in the hot summer days, he had taken to leaving his door open in an attempt to create a through-draught with the rickety dormer window.

As 2022 unfolded, Kyiv had been several different cities: in January, under its customary blanket of winter snow, it was deserving of its reputation as one of the most elegant cities of eastern Europe, an undiscovered gem for a winter break. Come for the colourful monasteries, the hearty borscht, the famously beautiful women, the historic buildings and the dramatic geography, the wooded hills above the mighty Dnipro River. As January drifted into February it had been unseasonably warm, and the snow had melted away. And Russia appeared to be threatening invasion – *of course, they won't actually go through with it* – but nonetheless, Kyiv became a city of international intrigue, of frantic shuttle diplomacy, visited by world leaders, all of whom had been happily ignoring the place hitherto.

And then they did go through with it, and it was a city under siege, Russia's forces not far from the northern suburbs, the railway stations a mass of fleeing humanity, the roads gridlocked with fleeing traffic. And there were those who stayed: a defiant people who stood and fought, led by a President who said, 'I don't need a ride, I need ammo.' And the Russians' military planning had proved to be a load of crap and the Ukrainians fought like tigers to defend their homeland. Even the ones who had let the Russians think they were working for them turned out not to be ready to hand their country over to the enemy. So Kyiv did not fall.

Rapidly the new normal was established. Sandbags were piled up around government buildings; windows were boarded up to prevent flying glass from explosions. There were check-points,a curfew. Burnt-out Russian tanks were left on pavements and in a makeshift outdoor museum in front of St

Michael's Monastery, where children would go to have their picture taken alongside a civilian car that had been shot up by the invading forces, now a reminder of the war crimes happening daily. The air-raid siren – *Putin's lullaby*, they called it – was increasingly ignored unless you knew it was going to be a particularly dangerous raid. The city still had a strange emptiness. The young men had mostly enlisted and the war whores were trickling in: journalists, aid workers, mercenaries and 'consultants' doing all the other stuff. But above all, Kyiv functioned much as before. The cafes served coffee, the bars served beer when they could get it, and people realised that their war effort was to carry on as before, if they could.

But it was a watchful city, full of people with good reason to be suspicious, to question your story, to follow you. And Simon's story didn't add up. Even Mike the Marine Corps veteran, exhausted from the front line and hardly a critical interlocutor, had seemed to find the holes rather quickly This was why Simon avoided the busy places and would spend a lot of time in his garret, drinking coffee and attempting to figure out what was happening on the front lines by trawling through a series of military blogs, Telegram channels and Twitter threads.

One part of the war was being fought, as wars always had been, by armies equipped with deadly weapons. But there was another war underway on social media, in which anyone with a smartphone could be a participant. This war involved reams of disinformation and propaganda, as each side tried to claim it was winning. But only one side celebrated its own brutality. 'Check Telegram. They post everything,' Mike had said. And Simon had started to realise the awful truth of this: on Telegram channels popular with Kadyrovites, he found deranged men boasting of their killings of Ukrainian soldiers, 'for encroaching on Chechen honour and Chechen blood.' And something called the Akhmat Battalion always seemed to be involved, an abandoned sanatorium in Pryvillya the backdrop to their crimes.

Simon drained his coffee, pulled his notepad towards him and waited for a pre-arranged secure Signal call to come through. Rudi von Pannwitz's number flashed up on the dot of 11:00, as punctual as you would expect for a Germanic aristocrat living in Prague. Rudi was a sort of one-man intelligence agency with extraordinary reach into Russia and its institutions. Prior to Simon and Evie's arrival in Prague, Rudi had heard a rumour that a couple of Russian hoods, probably Chechens, were coming over the border from Slovakia. In Prague, Russians would come and go all the time, and Rudi had not attached much importance to the story. He had never suspected that the Chechens were there for Simon and Evie. He had managed to get to Simon just in time, saving his life, but he was too late for Evie. She had been killed by the man Simon now knew to be Chovka Buchayev.

Over a series of encrypted calls from Prague to Kyiv, Rudi and Simon had been trying to get a fix on the elusive Chechen. Rudi had messaged earlier, hinting at 'something important' he had to share. Simon was feeling a brief surge of anticipation as he answered the call.

'*Ei gude*,' said Simon, using an idiomatic German greeting that he imagined would make Rudi smile.

'*Wotcher, mate*,' said Rudi in an exaggerated mockney before reverting to his usual plummy German-accented English. 'Care to talk about Moldova?'

Moldova. Simon's spirits deflated. *What's that got to do with Chovka?*

'You remember Evie was working on it with me?' Rudi continued. 'GRU cell trying to start a coup. Fake political movement, false-flag assassinations. You know the form. Punish them for wanting to be in NATO. *Pour encourager les autres.*'

Simon recalled Evie's excitement as she and Rudi had uncovered and leaked the GRU's planning document for the coup, seeing the impact it was having, her quiet satisfaction when the would-be ringleader of the plot was arrested at the airport, the network exposed. 'Of course I remember,' he replied. 'GRU whacked someone and blamed it on the Moldovan government, deep state, CIA. Usual bollocks. Story spread everywhere, rent-a-mob in the streets—'

'Yes, yes,' interjected Rudi. 'But there's something new. Just reached me. The Moldovans have had a lucky break. Someone in a village outside Chişinău complained about an abandoned vehicle in the forest. So the police took a look and it was a car that had been reported as stolen about a month earlier. And in the boot they found a submachine gun, plenty of ammunition, plus a kilo of TNT, a mobile phone paired to detonators, and a pistol. Not any old pistol, but the PSS. The thing the Russians make for their professional assassins. Makes almost no noise at all. Just a click.'

'The weapon they used to kill the politician?'

'Exactly. Apparently they matched it to the two rounds they'd dug out of his skull... Doesn't tell us who fired it. But this might: concealed inside a door panel, they found a Russian passport. In the name of Tahir Akhmedov. I doubt it's his real name, but the alias suggests a Chechen. They didn't have any record of it being used to enter the country, but that doesn't tell you very much. Moldova, after all.'

'Tahir Akhmedov?' Simon repeated the name, wondering if it meant anything.

Rudi continued, delighted to have someone to share the information with. 'Now: the photo in the passport matched someone the Moldovan surveillance team had spotted a couple of times. Apparently, he had been casing the homes of possible targets, but he was good at anti-surveillance and they weren't sure they knew what he was up to. There were reports of a few other activities: he went to a bank a couple of times, was seen meeting a possible source – but whoever that was, they weren't able to identify them.'

'And they lost track of him?' asked Simon. 'Chap in the passport?'

'Yes, but I did some thinking, had a good idea.'

'Oh, yes?'

Rudi was particularly ingenious. If he thought it was a good idea, it would be.

'You know the thing about Russian alias passports used by GRU operators? Remember with the Skripal poisoners? Passport numbers were from the same batch as the guy doing the coup in Montenegro.'

Simon had heard about this. A whole series of suspected GRU operations in different places had been carried out by people with Russian passports whose numbers came from a narrow sequence. 'Sometimes, they're so used to us letting them get away with things, they cut corners. My theory is that they *want* us to know it's them. They know we won't do anything to stop them, so they make it easy for us to know what they've been up to.' Simon could see where this was going. 'Same with the passport in the car?'

'Just so,' replied Rudi. 'Same batch. Something like seven numbers away from the Salisbury ones. So the car, weapons, explosives, and so on were all part of a GRU op.'

'Agreed. So who *was* using the car?' Simon wanted it to be Chovka. But there could be any number of Chechens doing wet jobs for the GRU in Moldova. 'Any fingerprints? DNA? Something we can link to Prague?'

'Nothing at all,' said Rudi firmly, before signing off, explaining that he had to rush to a meeting, but not before sending a snapshot of the passport to Simon's smartphone via the Signal app. Eagerly, Simon opened the image, using his thumbs to zoom in on the face. It was clean-shaven, with dark eyes and a sharp mouth, dark hair cut in a straight line across a low forehead. Was this the face of an assassin? Was this the face of Evie's killer? A bewildering array of facts were swimming around Simon's brain: Moldova... Slovakia... a sanatorium in a place called Pryvillya... What did any of it mean? There were too many possibilities and not enough facts.

Chapter 5

Kyiv

July 2022

Since his call with Rudi, Simon had felt that he should be making progress, but didn't seem to be getting anywhere. He had been trying to link the Moldova story to the Chechens committing war crimes in the forests of the Donbas. But he wasn't getting anywhere, spending hours at the Kobzar, scrolling through inconclusive social media posts and unreliable reports. He began to suspect that they were completely unrelated, part of a random series of unconnected events in a chaotic world.

Perhaps in an effort to put this confusion to one side, he found himself increasingly focused on what was going on back in his real home country, the UK. Prior to his hasty departure, he had played a role in unearthing a political espionage scandal: a spy ring at the heart of the British Establishment, recruited at Oxford University in the 1990s by a mysterious Russian intelligence organisation called COSTELLO. Simon's attempt to expose that had been, at best, a partial success. As nervous civil servants muttered about it all being 'a bit of a hot potato', the members of the spy ring continued to stalk the corridors of power in Britain. One of them, Kamran Patel, had been appointed National Security Adviser, a job that put him at the top of Britain's security state, with access to the most sensitive intelligence. Another, Rory Gough, was now chairman of something called the National Security Strategy

Board, whatever that was. And Simon was in Ukraine, under a false identity, wanted by the British police.

The news from Britain was not encouraging: Patel was rumoured to be looking into the 'value for money' of aid to Ukraine. On the face of it, a sound piece of public resource management; the online rumours suggested that Patel was using this to argue for reductions in support, to limit the risks of 'escalation'. *We mustn't humiliate the Russians*, went the argument, as the Russians continued their war crimes, uninterrupted.

Simon left the cafe in a bad mood, taking a quiet side street that led to a winding walkway known as the Peizazhna Alley. This ran behind the main drag, tracking along the top of one of Kyiv's many parks, with views down through the trees and across the city. The path followed what had once been the ramparts of the old town. It was a sultry day, but there was a welcome breeze on this exposed ridge, which lightened his mood a little. The path had been made into a children's attraction, dotted with colourful statues of cartoonish animals and outdoor play objects. Simon made a point of stopping often, ostensibly to enjoy the views down over the wooded hillside. In reality, it was to try to see a certain shape. At a distance, all bodies have a distinctive outline. Long before you can make out a face or be able to describe someone's clothing, the shape of the body is distinctive.

He had noticed this particular shape a couple of days earlier: a stick man, like a child's drawing. It was always moving slowly. Long strides, but never hurried. Dark suit, heavy-rimmed glasses. At the first sighting, Simon had been in the Maidan and felt the familiar, unwelcome sensation of a marginal image, little more than a dark spot, that would reappear more times than was explicable. Training had taught him not to look directly at it, but to remember the sensation in his peripheral vision. This shape would reappear several times over the next few days: climbing into a taxi; appearing to turn away down no-exit side streets whenever Simon turned his head; and on one occasion, visible from his garret window, motionless on the pavement at some distance from the building, but visible nonetheless. The same shape.

Simon was an experienced intelligence officer; spotting a surveillant wasn't out of the ordinary. But he was finding this experience unsettling because he knew it wasn't real. He recognised the stick-man shape, but he knew it couldn't possibly be in Kyiv. But he had seen it again, earlier that morning on his way to the Kobzar, and he had decided it was time to settle this mystery. The curves of the path at Peizazhna Alley would give him lots of opportunities for looking at his tail, to force the issue.

Except this didn't seem to be working, contributing further to his sense of unease: the shape had gone. Instead, Simon sat down on a bench, brightly coloured with mosaic tiles depicting jolly animals. Perhaps the thing that could not have been true had, in fact, been in his imagination. *Too much stress and time spent alone, and you start seeing things.*

And hearing them. The sound of shoes crunching on gravel. He looked up, and then he saw it: a tall, very thin man in a smart Savile Row suit and bright eyes behind thick-rimmed glasses was walking along the pathway, slowly, but straight towards him. He was old, and had a slight stoop from years of leaning forwards to speak to people. But he had a sharpness about him that suggested age had not withered him. Without asking, or waiting to be asked, he plonked himself on the bench next to Simon, with one of those little sighs that older men make whenever they move in the vertical axis. The newcomer leant forwards, resting his elbows on trousers that had a perfect, sharp crease running down them.

'Don't worry.' The voice was patrician languid. 'You're not dreaming. I *am* here... You don't mind me sitting down?' asked the newcomer, solicitously. 'I mean, nobody else is sitting here, so I can't see why it would be a problem.'

Simon shook his head in bewilderment. 'I don't get it. What are you doing here? *Here –*' he pointed at the bench – 'and here in Ukraine? There's a war on.'

'Steady on, old boy, sounding a bit like Lady P, there.'

This did not help to answer the question of why Jonathan Vosper, known to friends and colleagues as Jonty and to the wider world as Lord Pelham, was sitting next to him.

'You're not being followed, far as I can see. You spotted anything?' Jonty asked this in such a routine manner that Simon just shook his head, without really thinking that it was bizarre to be having this discussion with someone he was certain would not be in Ukraine.

'Jonty, I thought I'd seen you, except it was impossible that you'd be here.' Simon was still grappling with the improbability of it all. 'I mean, seriously, how did you know where to find me?'

'Let's just say, a few of your friends and, possibly, some of your enemies have been keeping tabs on you.' He said this in his usual way: avuncular and generous. They say never meet your heroes, but Simon had always regarded meeting Jonty as one of the better things that had happened to him at the Pole. His first impression had been prejudicial: a lanky, languid aristocrat with a silly name, impeccable connections and a beautifully tailored suit. But then you found out about what he'd done: working under non-official cover in war-torn Beirut; in Moscow at the height of the Cold War, when every room was bugged, every step followed. In Peshawar he had run an Afghan *mujahideen* network that had proved particularly adept at shooting down Soviet gunships. After 1991 he'd popped up all over the former Soviet Union – Georgia, Kazakhstan, Moldova – forging relations with these newly independent countries. And Ukraine, where he seemed to have an extraordinary range and depth of contacts. By the time Simon had joined the Pole in the mid-90s, he was close to retirement, a legend of the service, but always discreet and humble about his extraordinary achievements.

Jonty had taken a shine to Simon because he saw in him someone who was smart and a good agent handler, not someone who played the office politics game. After his retirement they had kept in touch, Jonty treating Simon to an occasional Dover sole at his club and offering to help him find a job on the outside if he was interested. Simon was interested, but hadn't wanted Jonty to think he was the type of person to get a job stitched up for him by an aristocratic patron, so he'd missed that particular opportunity. But the lunches had continued, although at a lower frequency. Jonty was spending more time at his family estate, Simon imagined.

In fact, Simon couldn't recall when they'd last met. 'Christ, Jonty. It's been ages. And now you're here?'

'You know I've always loved Kiev. Sorry, Kyiv,' he corrected himself with an apologetic grin. He took a quick glance around to make sure none of the passers-by were taking any interest in the two men on a bench speaking English to each other. 'And where else would you expect to find me? I'll take a few days off in August, of course.' Simon wondered which of the compulsory events for posh people he was referring to: Henley Regatta? Glyndebourne? But otherwise, Simon could see the sense of it: Jonty had been involved with Ukraine since its emergence from the Soviet Union in 1991. And, in spite of his age – past eighty, Simon thought – he was the last person to be scared off by some Russian air raids. 'Anyway, glad we've caught up, so to speak. I bring greetings. From Sarah.'

Sarah.

And then Simon felt a rush of warmth, of giddiness and adrenaline, and even a slight lump in his throat. Because a spy alone is the loneliest person in the world, and now he was no longer alone.

Chapter 6

On the very same day, exactly 2,132 kilometres further west, the new National Security Adviser, Professor Kamran Patel, was trying to put his stamp on the biggest international question facing the British government. As he had hinted at in numerous interviews and opinion articles, he was going to take a neutral, dispassionate look at the question of whether Britain was getting 'value for money' from its military aid to Ukraine – whether it was, on balance, 'in the national interest'. For several weeks, people who took pleasure from being on the inside track of British politics had talked about Kamran Patel's 'Ukraine Neutral Policy Review'. If you wanted to show that you were well informed, you would call it 'the Patel Review', or just '*Patel*'. This latter usage would take the following form: 'It's not clear that this initiative would survive *Patel*,' a Foreign Office desk officer might say. 'Post-*Patel*' started to become a byword for a point in the near, but indeterminate, future where current Ukraine policy would no longer be in place.

But for real insiders, the word to use was *Ukneupore*, Patel's own clumsy portmanteau abbreviation for his policy paper. This sounded a little like an Indian city in an E M Forster novel, and given the professor's South Asian heritage, some people jumped to this conclusion, assuming, for reasons that didn't reflect very well on them, that it was a codeword chosen by Patel himself. Claiming to have an idea of what this document might say, or even to have seen a working draft of *Ukneupore*, was the mark of real access to the heart of British political thinking. A political podcast presented by two former Cabinet ministers included a discussion of the paper and the arguments it contained, but there being so many of these shows, it got little or no attention beyond the tiny number of subscribed listeners.

Throughout this period, Patel himself refused to confirm whether *Ukneupore* had any official status, or was just a bit of blue-sky thinking. And as the summer holidays took hold, interest started to die down as ministers and their media tormentors disappeared from Westminster. It was then, with the risk of serious scrutiny reduced, that Patel took action, releasing a small number of draft copies and background briefings to a select group of recipients across government. Theoretically, this included the Prime Minister, who was holed up at Chequers with his latest wife (who was also, unusually, his current lover). But Patel knew very well that the PM never got through his official documents even when he was supposedly at work. When he was on holiday, it was guaranteed that he would take no interest at all. With this in mind, Patel had scheduled the meeting.

–

Even people who have worked at the Foreign Office for years easily get lost in that labyrinthine building. There were competing theories on its bemusing layout. It had been built to house three separate ministries – the Colonial, India and Foreign Offices – and this meant that the passages, staircases and floor levels never quite matched up. You could be confidently heading down a long, straight corridor to your required destination, only to encounter a solid wall just as you thought you'd arrived, necessitating a long detour to find another way through. There were little maps of the floor plan dotted around the place, but the average user found these just as confusing as the overall layout.

The décor in the building was similarly bewildering. There were vast portraits of dead white men interspersed with modern posters, commissioned by the living white men who now ran the place, to try to emphasise that not everyone who worked there was a white man. As the visitor ascended higher, the posters – relics of long-forgotten public diplomacy campaigns – became ever more anachronistic. If people felt bemused by the relentless smugness of the *GREAT Britain* branding, a reminder of 2012 Britain's Olympian self-confidence, they were completely baffled by the time they got to the third floor, where the *Panel 2000* campaign celebrated something lost to history known as Cool Britannia.

Ordinarily, big meetings involving participants from across government would be held in one of the oddly named 'fine rooms' at the Foreign Office: there was the Map Room, with its huge cabinets containing charts of Britain's colonies; the India Office Council Chamber, from where the vast subcontinental empire had been administered; and greatest of them all, the huge Locarno Suite, with its soaring gilded ceilings decorated with zodiac patterns and Victorian bombast. The meeting Kamran Patel was holding was not ordinary. The fact that it was taking place in the Foreign Office at all was a small act of deception by its convenor, who had chosen not to bring people to the more obvious setting of the Cabinet Office, his normal place of work. Further camouflage was offered by the choice of an obscure room on an attic floor, accessed by a narrow staircase that was so hard to find that some people wondered if it was the inspiration for Hogwarts' Room of Requirement.

Like all meetings held in the Foreign Office, the start time was more aspirational than a fixed point. True to form, the Ministry of Defence attendees had arrived five minutes early, the all-male quartet marching across Whitehall in single file, wearing jackets and ties in spite of the summer heat and equipped with Moleskine notebooks and military-grade water bottles. At the head of the flotilla, Captain Codrington,

Director for International Security Policy, stalked into the room, talking loudly about his recent sailing exploits in the Solent. A few minutes after eleven (the hoped-for start time), a middle-aged South Asian man, slight to the point of intangibility, his grey suit flapping around his bony frame, entered, looking both harassed and resentful. He tsked at a pale-skinned underling who had followed him into the room, struggling under a stack of cardboard folders. This younger man looked about fourteen but, given the setting, probably had a postgraduate War Studies degree from King's College.

'…you should have got here earlier to find the way. This *always* happens in this bloody building…' As he caught sight of the defence crowd sitting, straight-backed, close to the middle of the long board table, the speaker's demeanour adjusted instantly. 'Ah! MOD. Military timing, very good, very good.' His accent was Asian-plummy.

Codrington stood up sharply and thrust a hand towards Patel. 'Peter Codrington, D-ISP. Hello, Mister Patel.'

'*Professor* Patel.'

'Yes, sir,' Codrington responded, with just a little too much emphasis on the 'sir' for comfort. As this awkward exchange was unfolding, several other people were dribbling into the room; most had quietly gone to an unoccupied space at the scuffed table. Others huddled in small groups, speaking in low tones, wondering if there was a seating plan. Patel's minion was walking round the table, putting a folder in front of each chair.

'Sam, is there tea?' Patel asked irritably of the minion. Sam Bonham looked up, clutching his diminishing stack of folders.

'Umm, Professor… it's an internal civil service meeting, so the drinks aren't provided. We have to get our own.' As if to back up his point, he gestured vaguely to the other attendees, many of whom were clutching paper cups from the coffee shop on the ground floor. 'I can go down and get you one,' he suggested.

This information did nothing to improve Patel's mood. The room, lacking any sort of air conditioning and located in a converted attic, was stiflingly hot. He dismissed the idea of tea, huffily taking a seat in the middle of the table. Codrington was sitting just to his right, Sam to his left with a few excess folders piled in front of him on the table.

'Where's Greg?' he asked. Greg Galton was a self-described 'futurologist' with a penchant for eugenics. His main output had been to compose policy papers on enforced contraception for teenagers, but Patel had used him to build a prediction model for the Ukraine war. Galton's conclusion that a nuclear exchange with Russia was the most likely outcome had proved highly influential on Patel's thinking.

'Tube strike,' replied Sam.

'I know there's a Tube strike, but all these people seem to have got here.'

'Yes, but Greg predicted that the union would call it off. He's probably waiting for a train somewhere.'

It was eight minutes past eleven and most of the seats around the table had now filled, with the exception of the three opposite Patel, which remained empty, as if pre-booked by some complex Whitehall reservation system. By a sort of aural osmosis, the room fell silent and Patel looked round, evidently frustrated. He then sighed and cleared his throat in headmasterly fashion for the benefit of the other people in the room.

'Foreign Office? It's their building and they don't appear to have turned up,' he said, indicating the empty seats opposite him.

With impeccable timing – albeit poor timekeeping – a Black woman in her twenties appeared at the doorway, where she stood, frozen by the multiple eyes turned in her direction.

'Ah… Here's Her Britannic Majesty's Diplomatic Service! Yes? Well, come on in, you'd better sit down,' said Patel, indicating the empty chairs across from him. 'And what about Mitchell? Olivia Mitchell,' he added unnecessarily, since everyone knew both names of the Foreign Office's Director General for Defence and Intelligence.

The newcomer sat down, putting both hands on the folder in front of her, perhaps to steady herself. 'Olivia works from home on Tuesdays,' she said apologetically. Codrington seemed to be muttering something to one of his MOD colleagues, who smirked.

'*She works from home on Tuesdays.*' Patel's repetition of this statement had not added to the overall level of understanding in the room. But he hadn't finished. 'The *Guardian*-reading, tofu-eating wokerati in action, ladies and gentlemen. As some of you know, I have been talking both to the Prime Minister and secretaries of state of the relevant departments about the... the *incompatibility* of working from home and maintaining Britain's national security. The eagle-eyed among you may have read my recent column in the *Telegraph* on this very subject.' He let this statement resonate for a few seconds, hoping that someone would admit to having read the relevant op-ed. Since nobody did, he addressed himself to the young woman sitting opposite, apparently the only representative of the Foreign Office at this important meeting. 'And who are you, young lady? Are you in a position to cover for Ms Mitchell? Or were *you* working from home when the briefing was sent round?'

The hands were now clasping the sides of the folder, hard. But when she spoke again there was a surprising firmness in her voice. 'I'm Kemi Williams, desk officer for Ukraine External. Olivia has secure VTC kit in her house. I just need to switch this thing on...' She reached for what looked like a large television zapper that was in the middle of the table, pointing it at the flat screen mounted on a wall at the end of the room. A murmur of conversation had begun to develop as Williams pressed a series of buttons on the remote. Hopeful prompts were appearing on the screen: *Initiate New Call*, followed by the promising-looking *Enter Participant Joining Code*, at which point she confidently typed a series of numbers that she had written down on a Post-it note. And then things took a turn for the worse: *Code Not Recognised*. A few more attempts generated the same result. In desperation, Kemi navigated to something called *Settings*. But everyone knew that wouldn't help.

'Would it be all right if I got my phone to check the code?'

Patel slammed his hand down on the table. For a slight man, he was able to make a surprisingly loud sound.

'About the only thing you seem to have taken on board about this meeting is that it's a strictly no phones session. If Olivia Mitchell can't be bothered to come to work, then the Foreign Office will have to be represented by... by a *desk officer*.' He said these last two words as if it were a particularly offensive slur. Williams blinked several times, but didn't say anything. Patel looked round the room. 'Well, if *everyone else* is content, shall we begin?' He shuffled the rickety wooden chair closer to the table and opened the folder in front of him. There was a swishing noise as most of the others at the table followed suit.

'You have all seen a draft of my submission, the Ukraine Neutrality Policy Review. *Ukneupore*. In front of you are numbered copies which will be returned to Sam at the end of the meeting. I will briefly introduce the paper and address comments or suggestions, if there are any.' Patel's tone suggested that there would probably not be. His pitch changed slightly, the diction a little slower. The academic in the lecture theatre, apparently reading from a prepared script.

'We are approaching the sixth month of the war in Ukraine. This necessitates a dispassionate and neutral review of our policies, including strategic questions of national security and value for money. The strength of Ukrainian resistance has surprised most people, including those in Moscow. Russia has retreated from the Kyiv area and the north of the country. It remains well established in the Donbas and secure in Crimea. Kharkiv and Kherson are in contention by both sides. Ukraine can match Russian forces on the ground, but is unable to make significant advances. It has neither navy nor air force. It is entirely reliant on Western support, and without it would collapse rapidly. Russia has strategic depth, huge stockpiles of ammunition and ordnance, and a willingness to enter into a battle of attrition. But it is unwilling – or unprepared – to commit the resources necessary to achieve a full military victory.' Patel paused, perhaps wanting to ensure that he still had his audience. Codrington nodded sagely, as if to encourage him.

'This presents a conundrum: do we continue responding to increasing demands for weapons and support from Ukraine, always risking escalation with Russia and – inevitably – reducing our own strategic reserves? Or do we accept a status quo de facto, in which neither side is able to dominate the other? Russia occupies a part of Ukraine but is tied down there, unlikely to have the resources for further military adventures elsewhere; for its part, Ukraine is locked into its defence against Russia. Its NATO ambitions are on hold and its EU membership is unlikely to progress.

'Some might hope that Ukraine could become a full member of Western institutions, such as the EU and NATO. But it's not clear how that's going to happen. For as long as Ukraine is at war with Russia, it can't join either organisation. All the while, the West risks being dragged into a nuclear conflagration with Russia. So, what we need to consider is a neutrality plan for Ukraine. If it poses no threat to Russia, there will be no need for war. And Russia, no longer feeling threatened, ceases to pose a threat of its own to wider Europe. Its experience in Ukraine has been painful enough that it won't try to encroach on any NATO territory as long as it no longer feels threatened by Ukraine. A new normal will be established and over time, the gradual reintegration of both countries' economies into the global trading system becomes possible, reducing acute inflationary pressures in the world economy. The risk of nuclear war is averted and we can focus on the real issues that confront our society, rather than being dragged into one side of a long-running civil war in the Donbas. Neutrality for Ukraine delivers security, stability and economic growth.

Have I summarised that adequately?' Patel looked round for approval from the people in the room he had decided were the grown-ups: Codrington, Michelle Maguire from the Home Office, who was sitting at one end of the long table, and the chap from the Joint Intelligence Directorate, who never gave his surname but answered to Alex, sitting at the other end. There were murmurs of comprehension, if not approval. Patel did not make eye contact with any of the others in the room and it was clear that their input was not encouraged. Least of all, Kemi Williams.

'Right,' concluded Patel in a brighter tone. 'So... policy conclusions: we *balance* our support for Ukraine against our wider national security needs. Ukraine cannot be allowed to trump other considerations, such as our own weapons stocks and our long-term energy security. And we must not reward failure. The Ukrainian army's solid defence should not be mistaken for an ability to drive the Russians out of the Donbas and Crimea. And since we know this, the best thing we can do for Ukraine is propel them towards a settlement from a position of comparative advantage. They won the battle for Kyiv, which could be the starting point of a negotiation—'

'Subtly done, Kamran. Well done.'

The voice, female and authoritative, appeared to come from the door, which was swinging open. A middle-aged woman, slim, with long dark brown hair and wearing an expensive-looking trouser suit, was walking purposefully towards the gap in the table opposite Patel. She was holding a large envelope with some kind of official seal on it, which she was in the process of untying. This was all sufficiently unexpected for the room to fall silent. The newcomer sat down next to Kemi, pulled a sheaf of papers out of the envelope, smiled at Patel and spoke again. 'Kamran, I'm terribly sorry for arriving so late. My invitation must have gone into the spam folder,' she said, a smile playing around the edge of her lips.

'Sarah.' Kamran's tone was flat and he spoke oddly quietly. Unlike when he had raised his voice at Kemi, it was clear that he was now really angry. 'Actually, you weren't invited to this meeting.'

Sarah du Cane, Professor of Contemporary Slavonic Studies at Oxford University and strategic adviser to the British government on Russian affairs, didn't seem particularly concerned, nodding in agreement. 'Well, I'm here now anyway, so shall we get on?' she asked, before turning to her neighbour and saying, in the sort of *sotto voce* that could be heard throughout the room, 'Hello, Kemi, always good to see you.'

'Sarah, you cannot just barge in here like that... This is a closed door meeting,' Kamran added.

'Yup, I closed it behind me. Shall we crack on?' She flashed her most brilliant smile. Codrington was sitting up straight, blinking excitedly at Sarah. The mononymous Alex from Joint Intelligence was motionless, as if terrified he might betray an opinion. Sarah was leafing through the paper she had extracted from the unsealed envelope. 'You make some interesting points here, if I may...' She paused, looking around the room at the dumbstruck attendees. 'But the conclusions are, perhaps, a little *ambitious*? I mean, if I was going to paraphrase, this says, "Ukraine can't win so we should let Russia keep the bits it's already taken." That's basically it, isn't it?'

'Sarah, that's ridiculous and simplistic. We have to consider Ukraine in the global context. People are treating it as if it's the only security challenge we have. It's diverting attention from far more important issues. China. Climate change. I hardly need to say these things. And while I'm at it,' added Patel irritably, 'I'd like to know how you had a copy of the submission? Sam, did you send Sarah one?' Sam shook his head quickly, as if horrified by the suggestion. 'That could be a security breach, Sarah,' said Patel, a smile forming around the edges of his mouth. 'Perhaps I need to organise an investigation?'

There were little gasps and snorts of shock at this escalation. Sarah stood up. Was she leaving? Probably not: she was walking purposefully towards the window. With a grunt, she pushed up the rickety sash. An immediate breeze of fresher air could be felt floating into the room.

'Let's not overheat, shall we...? As I'm sure you know,' she added, twirling the security pass she was wearing on a lanyard, 'I have an office in this building. Your submission was hand-delivered to me under secure seal...' Sarah had walked calmly to her chair and had gone back to smiling at Patel. The breeze was causing the net curtain to billow, but it did not appear to dissipate the tension. Most eyes were fixed on the table, excruciated with awkwardness.

A sullen silence settled, broken again by Patel, who was looking up and down the table, pointedly not at Sarah. 'Does anyone have, er, *substantive* comments? Or are we in broad agreement at the direction of travel?'

There was an apologetic clearing of throats. A few people at the table seemed to have found their voices. First was Maguire from the Home Office, flanked by her honour guard: a rotund man who looked like he'd been manning Border Force check-points for several decades, and a pasty youth who had been scribbling notes throughout, even when nobody said anything. 'The Home Secretary is pushing back against the idea that the Ukrainians get permanent status without some additional process,' continued Maguire. 'A stalemate in Ukraine means their return home is less likely, no? And the manifesto commitment remains in place—'

'The manifesto commitment to keep net migration to a level we have never kept it to in real life? *That* manifesto commitment?' This was from John McCaskill, a Treasury man wearing jeans and a polo shirt. 'Coming back to the main issue,' McCaskill continued, waving Patel's paper as if it were a promising assignment submitted by a sixth-former, 'we like it.'

'That's the Treasury "we", isn't it?' Sarah asked. A collective consciousness of bean counters who couldn't see beyond quarterly public sector borrowing figures.

'Not that *we* take a position on the international security matters, of course,' McCaskill added. 'Just the economy stuff. Seems like you're saying we should be spending less on Ukraine in order to balance other budgets. Normally you're asking us for more money, so it's a welcome change, actually. Ha ha ha.'

Patel, perhaps not expecting any help from this quarter, seemed mildly flustered by McCaskill's endorsement. 'Well, of *course* it's more complicated than that,' he added ingratiatingly, 'but I'm glad we're *somewhat* on the same page.' He paused. 'Now: any more for any more? Sarah? Since you're *here*, you might as well give us the *line*.'

'*We've* got a couple of things, Professor.' This was Codrington. 'From the perspective of MOD, it's about getting the right balance. Left of arc, the UK maintains satisfactory missile and artillery stocks, hangs on to its Challenger tanks, but the Ukrainian army collapses. Right of arc, Ukraine defeats Russia, but our military is just a paper force with no stocks or resilience. So, yes, we want to find the right balance.'

'Balance.' Patel was impatient. 'I'd have thought you chaps at MOD weren't very enthusiastic about nuclear war with Russia. Balance is a polite word for not doing anything. Sometimes you have to take an actual decision. *To govern is to choose.* That was also in my *Telegraph* article,' he added helpfully, given that the article was seemingly unread by the assembled company.

'Yes, but this is your private agenda, isn't it?' replied Sarah, as if she was asking something inconsequential, like where the National Security Adviser had been on holiday.

'I beg your pardon?'

'This isn't about government. This is you. You're doing this because the PM is distracted by some ridiculous money dispute.' The country was convulsed with a bewildering scandal over whether the Prime Minister had lied to the Cabinet Secretary about who'd lent him the cash to renovate his apartment and pay for his latest divorce. 'Number Ten's turning itself inside out about the PM's loan, and you've taken the opportunity to try to slip in a major realignment of our Ukraine policy.' The same tone, almost a hint of levity, and finished with a bright smile. But Sarah was pushing at the limits of what you could get away with saying in a civil service meeting, even if she suspected the person she was talking to of being a Russian agent.

'I won't respond to that *absurd* suggestion. Change is difficult, which is why people like you – the Establishment, I might even say the *deep state* – prefer that we keep things as they are. This paper is trying to answer real questions about Britain's strategic position. I'm sorry,' Kamran's tone was now loaded with sarcasm, 'that you find it difficult to engage with specific and actionable responses. Now, unless you have something *serious* you'd like to raise, Sarah, I think we can agree that your attendance at this meeting is no longer required. After all, from what I hear, you have some, er, *serious* questions to answer about a fugitive currently believed to be in Ukraine.'

For the first time, Sarah allowed her smile to slip, a frown spreading across her forehead. Her face coloured slightly. Not a blush, but a flush of annoyance. 'Okay, Kamran,' she said, tapping her forefinger on the table in time with her words. 'Okay, you want serious? Let's do serious. I think I just heard you say "if Ukraine poses no threat to Russia, there will be no need for war." I'm not making that up, am I?' She didn't wait for Patel to confirm. 'So, exactly what "threat", to use your word of choice, did Ukraine pose to Russia when it decided to invade in 2014? Or again this year? Or when it cut off Ukraine's gas supplies in 2006? Seems to me the threats are all coming from Moscow, not from Kyiv.'

Patel looked as though he was about to say something, but Sarah didn't give him the chance. 'Ukraine is everything. *Everything*. No point talking about "context" and "balance". If Russia can redraw the map of Europe and be allowed to get away with it, two things happen. First, Russia doesn't stop at Ukraine's borders. If Ukraine poses no threat, then Russia just moves on to its next target. Moldova? Estonia? More of

Georgia? Could be any of those. All of them, actually. And let's not pretend that Ukraine's neutrality is the only thing Russia wants. "Just give us this and we'll be fine about everything else." That is total crap. They've made it clear that they don't think Ukraine should exist at all.'

Patel tried again to interject, without success. 'Then,' continued Sarah, 'what's the lesson that other powers take from this? China? Turkey? Even bloody Venezuela will probably try to invade Guyana… To be fair, Kamran, you did well: you held the meeting in an obscure location. Number Ten's distracted, Parliament's in recess so ministers are all away in Tuscany or wherever…' She looked around the room. 'No disrespect to present company, of course, but these aren't the people in charge. You picked Olivia's work from home day, which you knew about when you scheduled the meeting. You made it hard for people to read the paper properly in advance, you pack the room with Home Office and Treasury who can't see the geopolitical wood from the trees. Like I said, you did well. But we both know there are things I can't say in this room. I know what you're actually trying to do here. And a lot of people will need to be made aware.' As she spoke, Alex from Joint Intelligence had nodded along in agreement, before catching himself and returning to sphinx-like stillness.

Codrington now felt bolder, straightening himself in his chair and saying, 'I think Sarah has made, umm, in her own way, some important points.'

At this point, Patel could see that he was going backwards. It had been an opening salvo and it hadn't worked. Now the only point in continuing was to save face.

'Sarah, you seem to have forgotten that I am the Prime Minister's *personal* appointee. I…' He corrected himself. '*We* are drawing together a policy process that has been agreed in principle at the highest levels.'

Sarah scoffed. 'You've got a lot to learn.' The smile had returned to her face. She turned to Kemi. 'Come on, I think we've done our work here.' She put the paper back into the envelope and retied the seal. Kemi left her copy on the scuffed table in front of her and the two of them left the room. Patel stared at the wall behind where Sarah had been sitting, trying to demonstrate that he was completely indifferent to whether she had been there or not.

'Now,' he said, looking round for approval, 'does anyone have any final points they want to make?'

There was another awkward silence.

—

Sarah and Kemi walked down a dingy corridor lined with photographs of wildlife endemic to Britain's remaining overseas territories. Britain's last imperial subject seemed to be the West Indian whistling duck, holding out in the wetlands of Turks and Caicos.

'Well, that was a good result, wasn't it?' asked Kemi, slightly diffident in Sarah's assured presence.

'Not bad. He has no idea how these things work. I think he really believed he could write a paper, send it round the houses and change our entire Ukraine policy.'

'We don't have to worry about *Ukneupore*. What a ridiculous name! But that's just his opening salvo. He's inexperienced, but he's a bloody fast learner. He'll come back stronger...'

They had descended a staircase and were now in a wide, airy walkway with a handsome curved ceiling. Along one side were windows giving onto the ornate grandeur of the Durbar Court, a spectacular glazed atrium in intricate carved stone. There were tiers of red granite pillars supporting arched colonnades. Stone busts of imperial notables stared down impassively at a gleaming marble floor, patterned with green mosaics. The click of their shoes reverberated on the stone floor, masking their voices.

'What do you think he'll do?'

Sarah paused. She didn't know the whole answer. 'It's what I'm trying to work out. Can you tell Olivia I'd like to have lunch with her soon? Needs to be off the premises.'

'Sure. And...' Kemi seemed to be weighing up something. *Will I ask it? I will.* 'The fugitive – that's our tailor of Kyiv?'

'You only have to pay attention to some of what Kamran says.'

Chapter 7

Kyiv

July 2022

'So, here you are, on your uppers in Ukraine. Bloody good job on the COSTELLO thing. I think you can be pleased with what you did there. By the way, I'm working on clearing up any awkwardnesses you might have with the Northumberland Constabulary. That should all go away pretty soon.'

Coming from Jonty Vosper, this meant a lot. Both the praise and the promise.

'So you know the whole story with COSTELLO?'

Spies don't tend to answer direct questions. 'I was involved in a small way. Very interesting series of discoveries you made there.' Simon had never understood exactly how Sarah had found the resources to fund the investigation that had uncovered COSTELLO. Had it been Jonty? And some of his wealthy friends?

'And you're here in Kyiv helping out?'

'Juggling a few balls, my dear boy. But the main thing is connecting the people who need things with the people who have things. People at home want to give, but don't know who to give to. I know my way around here, so I can plug a few people together.' This understated admission probably meant that Jonty was central to a significant proportion of the supply of war matériel going to Ukraine.

Simon had spent so many days in Kyiv expecting something to go wrong that there was still a part of him that wondered if this was an elaborate sting. Even with Jonty there, was there some kind of catch? Had he been sent to reel Simon in? *Who's the person you trusted the most at the Pole? That's the person they'd use.* He had about three seconds to get up and walk away. But even if he did that, and there was a plan to arrest him – or worse – walking away now wouldn't change very much. His will to continue against all odds and all comers, usually strong, had been dulled by always being on his own, talking to almost nobody since he had escaped Britain in a small boat a few weeks earlier. And here was someone whom he'd known and admired for years, who was working with Sarah, the person who had arranged his escape.

'You bring greetings from Sarah. Anything else?'

Jonty didn't seem to be listening. At least, he wasn't ready to talk. Instead, he was taking in the wide vista, the wooded hillside, the river below, the huge cityscape. There was a long pause, which ended with a loud sigh.

'You know this was once the ramparts of the old city? Up here? The original Viking princes of Kyivan Rus built their palace on this hill.'

'I didn't know that. D'you have some sort of a message from Sarah?' Simon was trying not to sound impatient.

'Shall we walk?' replied Jonty, as if he'd not heard Simon's question, pulling himself to his feet with a sigh. 'Doesn't get any easier,' he added, grinning ruefully. He puffed out his cheeks rodentially and began strolling at an unexpectedly brisk pace, forcing Simon into a quick skip to catch up with him. 'Right. Where to start? Sarah told me you're trying to find someone. Here. Let's trade. Where've you got to?'

Simon felt as if he was back at the Pole, in the old days, sitting in front of Jonty's desk, talking through his operational plan, hoping he'd be impressed by his efforts. And Simon was not empty-handed: the passport that Rudi had got his hands on might contain a photograph of Chovka. And there was something important about the reports of a torture centre at the Pryvillya sanatorium.

'Have you been in Moldova recently, Jonty?' With Jonty you never knew where he had travelled, what he'd been up to. But he shook his head, not wanting to break Simon's flow. 'Well, you've seen what's been happening there: Moscow trying to destabilise the place, divert attention away from Ukraine. I've been talking about it with Rudi, this guy who helped us out in Prague.'

'Ah, yes: Sarah told me about your splendid fellow in Prague. Rudi von Pannwitz. Let's just say I know of the family. Bit of a rum cove, if you ask me, but you're right: he definitely seems to know everything. And everyone.'

Simon wanted to talk about Moldova, but the shadow of Prague hung over them. Jonty filled the gap. 'I'm very sorry about Miss Evelina Howard. She did something of great value to the free world. Russia's victims are everywhere, and we must not forget any of them...' Jonty put an arm on Simon's shoulder. 'Bloody thing to have to deal with. Especially alone. Bloody awful.' This was about as close to the acceptable outer limits of emotion as an Englishman could get with one of his fellow countrymen. So they moved on.

'Back to Rudi,' said Simon, an attempt at brightness in his tone. He outlined the story of the GRU plot, the alias passport with a Chechen-sounding name discovered in the car, along with the weapons used for an assassination. Simon felt he had done pretty well, even if there were plenty of questions left unanswered. Jonty had stopped walking and seemed to be looking at him very intently. Simon gestured towards a railing, from where the ground dropped steeply down the grassy hillside. Maybe his age was finally catching up with him, as he didn't seem to have the lungs for combining walking with talking, and he leant gratefully on the banister, staring outwards.

After a brief pause, Jonty spoke. 'Interesting, of course, but what, if anything, does this have to do with Prague?'

'Well, at this stage I'm just working on a theory: that the man who killed her, Chovka, is also the Moldova assassin, alias Tahir Akhmedov. One and the same.'

'Interesting.'

Simon was wondering why Jonty had gone to the trouble of tracking him down. He hadn't actually told him anything; Simon had been doing all the talking. In the spy school at Cardross they'd been taught to be the listener, not the talker. On the hillside below them, a group of schoolchildren armed with clipboards were being cat-herded by their teacher. Whatever the task was, they weren't paying attention, giggling delightedly at the opportunity to be out of their classroom on a sunny day. The strange banality of a country fighting an existential war.

Simon found himself talking again. 'There was one more thing. This car had clearly been used by a pro. No prints on it anywhere. Same with all the weapons.'

Jonty nodded, taking it all in. 'That's not Russian mafia behaviour. That's an experienced Moscow Centre hood showing you what he can do.' He held up one of his long, pointy fingers, as if he were in a crowded room trying to call for silence. 'You've done very well, Simon. Very well indeed. My turn. Here's what Sarah wanted you to know: from CCTV, the Czech police found images of the two guys. One of them was seen at the wheel of a BMW 5 Series. The car that hit Evie.'

Simon's heart was pounding, and he knew that if he let go of the railing his hands would be shaking. Instead, he gripped harder, knuckles white. He could sense what was coming next. A passer-by seemed briefly interested in the two men speaking English.

Jonty was fumbling in his trouser pocket, pulling out a folded piece of paper. 'Sarah got hold of this.' He unfolded the paper, which had a large, fuzzy image from a security camera, and handed it to Simon.

Simon had stopped talking and pulled out his smartphone with the screenshot of Tahir Akhmedov's passport photo.

It wasn't a perfect match. The printed photo was grainy, showing a bearded Chovka, his head turned to one side. On the Akhmedov passport he was clean-shaven, staring at the camera.

It took Simon a few moments, staring intently at the line of the nose, the shape of the mouth, his eyes flitting from one image to the other.

And then he was sure. Simon was looking at two of the many faces of Chovka Buchayev.

Chapter 8

London

July 2022

Halfway down Great Smith Street, in the shadows of Westminster Abbey and government offices for departments that most people had never heard of, was a red-brick building of an institutional kind. To the uninitiated, drifting past on the upper deck of the number 88 bus, they probably thought they were looking at some obscure part of the Church of England's administrative structures. The eagle-eyed might have spotted a large galleried room with handsome shelving and concluded: public library. But it had stopped being a public anything a few years previously, when Westminster Council had decided that libraries cost too much and wasn't everything on the internet now anyway? So the shabby public library had become a swanky private club.

For Sarah du Cane, not a particularly clubbable person, it had the advantage of being very close to Whitehall, meaning that even the most self-importantly busy politician or civil servant could find time to get there for a discreet meeting. The other advantage was that, thanks to an overzealous membership policy, it was frequently empty. On this occasion the slightly creepy bartender was looking at the only customers, two women having lunch at a quiet corner table. They weren't a particularly interesting sight. Two middle-aged women, attractive and smartly dressed, both probably in demanding professional jobs, eating salads and talking animatedly. The crashing sounds from the restaurant's open kitchen meant that he couldn't hear what they were saying, which was probably a good thing.

'...on one level it was almost amusing. Or it would be if it wasn't so serious. The idea that you can end our support for Ukraine on the basis of a quick Whitehall meeting... But it's just his first salvo.' Sarah took a long swig of something sparkling, but it was only elderflower. The man at the bar had been disappointed that they'd turned down the special promotion on Prosecco.

'But we're solid on Ukraine,' said Olivia. Her fair hair was pulled back in a tight bun, emphasising her high forehead. 'Isn't this just low-level nuisance? I sometimes feel with this government that we're going through phases. A bit like my boys. You just have to be patient and we find our way to the right answer, having tried a few of the wrong ones.' Olivia Mitchell had combined her very successful Foreign Office career with being a mother to what seemed to Sarah like a huge number of small boys. Were there four of them?

'My concern,' said Sarah, 'is that it's going to be a long war and people aren't taking on board what that means. This isn't about whether we're giving them NLAWs now. It's about artillery. It's about tanks next year. About cruise missiles. Fighter jets. Are we going to be doing this in three, five years' time? Moscow is banking on the idea that we aren't. They aren't going anywhere and they think we'll get tired of it all.'

Olivia nodded. She hadn't come to debate Russia's long-term intentions with Sarah. They'd reached the point of their lunch where the small talk, the social catch-up and the Whitehall gossip was all finished, and it was now time for the main course.

'So you think there'll be more of this stuff?'

'Oh, I know there will,' replied Sarah. 'You know there was this flap with Powerstream a few weeks back? Big setback for Rory Gough. He's gone a bit quiet—'

81

'Yes, but that's what I'm talking about. That was another thing that was *never* going to get through. At this moment? It's crazy it got that far, really. I mean, it's not even clear to me that Rory knew exactly what the Powerstream project was about. He must have investments everywhere.'

'I'm not a hundred per cent about that.' Sarah wasn't doing a perfect job of hiding mild frustration at mandarin complacency. 'It *would* have got through, if it hadn't been exposed. They'd built the damn thing. Just needed plugging into the grid.' Olivia nodded, making a point of not asking whether Sarah had been involved in the exposure of the Russian links to the project that had become a national political scandal worthy of a -*gate* suffix.

'But Rory's wings have been clipped and we're doing the right things with Ukraine. We're good, aren't we?'

It was more complicated than that. Ahead of the lunch, Sarah had wondered how much she would tell Olivia. In an ordinary world, the recently appointed Director General for Defence and Intelligence at the Foreign Office was supposed to know most things about the secret state. But Sarah's knowledge of the Oxford spy ring had not come from inside government. And she had learned the hard way that even the good people could not always be told everything. Sometimes for their own benefit.

Sarah took a deep breath. 'I need to tell you some stuff about Rory and Kamran.' She paused again.

'Go on, then,' said Olivia with a hint of impatience.

'You know that Kemi – she's brilliant, by the way – did a secondment with Grosvenor Advisory? Before she joined your team?'

'Of course. But Grosvenor sort of imploded, didn't it? It was all very odd.'

'Odd' is one word you could use.

'One of Marcus's people was murdered,' said Sarah. 'My working assumption is: by the Russians. Probably not by Russian *hands*, but commissioned in Moscow, certainly.' She delivered this in the most neutral tone she could manage, but it had still left Oliva blinking, hard and fast. 'And then Marcus did something very stupid and drove his car on a tidal road in a storm.'

'What? So it was just an accident?' asked Olivia, deep scepticism in her voice.

'Yes, in fact,' Sarah replied, glancing out of the window as she did so, her mind swirling with images of the storm-lashed North Sea. She sighed and started again. 'Let's rewind a bit. I'm about to tell you something that's incredibly sensitive. I know you deal with these things all the time, but this is completely radioactive.' Olivia nodded, with a look of impatience. Spies loved to impress on other people how terribly secret their world was, as if nobody else had things that needed to be kept confidential. 'Rory Gough has had a relationship with elements of the Russian secret state since the 1990s. This was part of a network which originated at Oxford and included various people, here and some in Europe. Recruited as students. An Oxford spy ring, if you like. And one of the members of this network is Kamran Patel.'

Olivia opened her mouth to speak, but the words didn't seem to be coming out. Her eyes flickered, checking that nobody could be listening in, and then she leant closer to Sarah, speaking in a stage whisper. 'You mean they're *Russian agents*?'

Sarah nodded. 'But not in the way you might imagine. Forget Minox cameras and dead letter boxes. What they bring is political influence. Rory and Kamran have their agenda, their ideology, you know that. And the way they see it, it's an alignment of interests, not some sort of agent situation. But the important thing to know is that they co-ordinate with Moscow. And sometimes they take instructions. I doubt they'd accept that description, but it's what happens.'

Olivia was shaking her head. 'Sorry, Sarah… Ideology? That can't be right. I mean, Rory's only ideology is to be rich and influential. He doesn't *believe* in anything. None of us do,' she added with a chuckle. 'We're British, for God's sake. We don't *do* ideology.'

Sarah sighed, smiling ruefully. 'This is one of those rare occasions when I remember I'm not from here.' Olivia looked mortified, as if she'd said something inappropriate. 'My mother is an Italian Jew. We're always being kicked out of places over the centuries because of things we believe in. Even as recently as the 1940s. Ideology matters.'

Olivia was very flustered. 'Sarah... I hope you don't think I'm in *any way* antisemitic... Er, medieval Europe was *very* different—'

'Of course. I haven't expressed this very well. What I'm saying is, that with my background you probably see people doing things for ideological reasons rather more easily than if you're British. I think Rory, and Kamran and these others in the Oxford spy ring act *because* of their beliefs. It's hard for British people to understand because nobody here is remotely interested in grand ideologies.'

'What – and the Russians are? Don't they just believe in power?'

'It might not be that simple. Some people say we're in a post-ideological age, but I'm not sure. I think we just haven't found the right terminology to describe the things these people believe now. But Rory definitely has an ideology. He wants a world transformed, untrammelled business, the sovereignty of the individual and the nation state, a technical–intellectual elite running everything. He *believes* in that. As does Kamran. And they think working with Russia helps them achieve it. In that sense, they're not unlike Philby and Burgess. Perhaps it was easier when the ideology had a name. You could at least talk about communism.'

'You really think that's what's happening? Not just cynics jumping on a bandwagon?'

'Of course, there's always some useful idiots ready to help. Politicians who'll pick any side if it gets them power. Who probably don't even understand which side they should be on. But they're not the main event.'

'Who are the others?'

'The ones I know about – there's Ben Archbold, Tom Harkness and Heinrich von der Wittenberg.'

'The German politician?' Olivia was shaking her head again. 'And Tom Harkness? *Really?* I mean, at least with Ben you know he has been an apologist for Stalinism most of his life. But Tom? Oh, my goodness.'

'Oh, I forgot to mention: Zak Camondo. Swiss banker.'

'I can afford not to care very much if a Swiss banker turns out to be on the Russian payroll.' Olivia sounded almost relieved. 'But you're saying Rory and Kamran and these others are part of an ideological group that takes *instructions* from Moscow? Really? You're sure of that? That's not very sovereign-individual of them.'

Sarah didn't say anything, just raised her eyebrows, causing Olivia to think better of this question. 'Sorry, of course you are.'

Olivia was shaking her head, trying to take it in. Then she sat up sharply, as if jolted by an electric shock. 'We need to sort this out! Brief the Joint Intelligence Committee, the Pole, that sort of thing...'

'Of course, that's what *should* be happening. My original plan was to collect the info on Rory – you know, the *intelligence case* – and then put it in front of the right people, including you, of course. Write an elegant submission and it's job done, the wheels turn, the ship of state sails on... No scandal – that's not the British way – but Rory would quietly be removed from the picture. But that isn't how it worked out. I'd underestimated the scale of the problem. We got the intel, not just Rory, but the network with Kamran and some others, and then it became clear we couldn't actually finish it off, take the thing apart.'

'Why?'

'Because this goes right to the heart of political power in this country and those guys are in there, able to stop us. We thought we'd stopped Rory and then they get Kamran in as NSA. Our system doesn't seem to have the capacity to fix this stuff.'

'Oh, come on, Sarah.' Olivia had found her voice, and she was prepared to push back with some energy. 'I mean, look at Ukraine: we're leading the way with our support. Nobody could mistake us for pro-Russian. I honestly think you might have called this wrong. I don't like Rory and his crowd, but *Russian agents*? Seriously?'

'You can't publicly be pro-Russian any more, I agree,' said Sarah calmly, as if this wasn't the first time she was answering this particular question. 'But what really matters to Russia? We can send a few NLAWs, maybe we'll get as far as sending air defence and tanks. How many Challengers can we spare? Fifteen?'

'It's not nothing. It all adds up.'

'Okay. But where are the shipbrokers, the lawyers, the insurers who keep Russian oil moving around the world? All here in London. Is the government doing anything to stop them? No, it isn't. And where's this oil going? It's being laundered through refineries outside Russia, so it's not considered as sanctioned Russian diesel any more. And then commodity traders here in London sell it back to us. Whatever label we put on it, it pays for their war. And Rory Gough, who has fingers in all of this, continues to benefit. Whilst benefiting his friends in Moscow.'

'Well, it's difficult to get a handle on the oil piece. I mean, you know we've tried. Tightened things up. Price cap, that sort of thing.'

'Olivia, I'm not judging you. Or the MOD guys trying to supply the Ukrainian military. I'm talking about how, at a national level, at a certain point, we're not prepared to confront the realities. To unpick these structures. MI5 won't touch anything political. The NCA, Serious Fraud, all that lot have no resources. So the decision becomes: do nothing serious about the financial stuff but keep sending the weapons.'

'But we've done *unprecedented* sanctions. You can't say they don't make a difference.'

'Olivia, we lead the world in having people who specialise in advising you on how to get round sanctions. They aren't going to defeat Russia.'

'But we can't afford to upset the financial sector. Not post-Brexit. Half the City has already left for Dublin, or is threatening to.'

'Maybe. I'd still like to think they could have stronger guardrails. They always hide behind the line "We're not getting into politics." But what they're doing is playing a significant role on the wrong side of the most important geopolitical question of our era.'

Olivia was momentarily quiet, as her mouth was full of rocket leaves.

'Coming back to the beginning and Kamran: the point about all this is that he might be an annoying academic making a nuisance of himself. But he's also part of something bigger. He and Rory co-ordinate a lot with their fellow travellers. In places like Italy, Hungary, Germany. And in the US as well. Anyone who's against supporting Ukraine. They dress it up as caution against "provoking" Russia, or a kind of sovereignty thing: "We must look after our own interests first." Kamran can't be as obvious from inside government, but he's following the same agenda, just more subtly. So what I'm trying to get a feel for is: how? He has to work inside the tent, so to speak, hence the ridiculous *Ukneupore* paper. But that hasn't worked, so what else is he trying? We need to think about what his next angle will be.'

'He's very hot on the corruption. In Kyiv.'

'In what way?'

'Well, we all know it's an issue. And of course it's nothing like as bad as in Russia. But, if you're trying to undermine support for Ukraine, just keep saying that hard-earned taxpayer money is going into the pockets of Ukrainian oligarchs in the middle of a cost of living crisis.'

'And Kamran's saying that?' Sarah was frowning, twirling her long brown hair with one hand, a nervous tic.

'He's saying we need to be "taking a close look at the integrity issues around aid to Ukraine", which on one level is completely reasonable and sensible. The issue is *how* you do that.'

'Well, how *is* he doing that?'

Olivia seemed to be going off on another tangent. 'You know how these people are obsessed with loyalty? There's that insulting assumption that the civil service is plotting against them. The *blob*, for God's sake.' Sarah nodded, raising her eyebrows. 'We all know it doesn't work like that. That crowd have always had the Foreign Office down as especially ideologically unsound. We're part of the "surrender agenda". Did you hear that particular gem from the PM? And they all have this thing about bringing in "wider expertise" from outside government, by which they mean people who agree with them already. I mean, look at Mystic Greg,' she said, spluttering with laughter and holding her hand over her mouth.

'Who?' Sarah sounded baffled.

'You know, Greg Galton, the super-forecaster who's predicted that the Russians will win the war. They're calling him Mystic Greg...' Faced with further bafflement from the other-worldly Sarah, who didn't get the nickname, she ploughed on. 'Kamran's latest thing is he says he needs more "reliable"–' she made the quotation mark symbol with her fingers – 'reporting from the embassy in Kyiv.'

'Really? And how is he planning on getting that?'

'He says he wants "alternative perspectives" from the existing diplo team, which means someone who can be relied upon to tell him what he wants to hear. So he's brought in a guy from a Tufton Street think-tank who's going to be his "Special Correspondent", based in Kyiv. Working out of the embassy but reporting directly to Kamran. And of course, on things like the corruption stuff, you can expect him to be saying exactly want Kamran wants. The reports practically write themselves.'

'How brilliant,' said Sarah, shaking her head slowly. 'I mean, it's ridiculous, but from their perspective, it's brilliant.'

'I know. Foreign Office has been lobbying for months to get extra people in Kyiv and we've been told that security and numbers are all restricted, funding problems, so on. And then Kamran's guy shows up and he's all funded immediately, logistic challenges all fixed. No problem.'

'Funded how?'

'The think-tank. I think it's called the Sovereignty Foundation. Fancy offices in Mayfair, dark money financing, revolving door of advisers in ministers' offices. You can imagine.' Sarah could imagine it, as she had long believed that the institution in question was laundering funds for Moscow via a cut-out in the Gulf, all of it cleverly structured by Rory Gough.

'I see. Kamran will tout it as a new model for diplomatic assignments: public-private partnership, perspectives from outside government, that sort of thing. People will say how clever it is to be spreading the costs to the private sector.'

'That's *exactly* what he did. Ambassador's pretty pissed off, as you'd expect, but nobody in Number Ten cares about that.'

Sarah was nodding, taking it in. 'This new person got a name?'

'Hayden Edgworthy. Arrived in Kyiv a couple of weeks ago.'

Chapter 9

'Hit the ground. Running. That's my instruction from Kamran Patel.'

Hayden Edgworthy, who had the demeanour of a man who has been on personal impact training, looked in turn at the three other people sitting round the shiny meeting table, as he tried to gauge the impact of this particular statement. He had grown a beard to try to hide his youthful chubby cheeks, and his hair was swept backwards with lots of shiny product on it. It was possible that his mum thought it looked dashing. There was some eye-rolling in the room as he continued: 'A massive inflection point has been reached, and we're concerned that UK political, media and civil service elites aren't getting it.'

'And you're suggesting my team here in the embassy isn't getting it either?' The Ambassador, Andrew Mallory, sounded as if he was straining to keep it civil; deep frown lines striated across his forehead.

'Yes, what *exactly* is it you think we're missing here, Hayden?' asked Clare Tobin, head of the political section, feeling less need for civility.

Hayden took a deep breath, as if it was painful to have to explain such things to these *non-player characters*. 'What you're missing is the difference between setback and defeat. Russia has failed in its initial attempt to take Kyiv. It has not been defeated. I don't think *SW1*,' he found a way to say the Westminster postal district with particular disdain, 'has learned to live with that reality.'

'Thanks for the insight. And just remind me...' Tobin paused to scoff at the idea. 'How's your Ukrainian language training going? 'Cos I heard you've only got Russian. And people get a bit sensitive about that round here.'

If the sarcasm wasn't obvious, the Ambassador spelled it out. 'Clare makes a good point. There are a few bear traps you might want to avoid. Speaking Russian to Ukrainians is one of them.'

This diversion seemed only to add fuel to Hayden's fire. 'Groupthink,' he said, folding his arms in a gesture of triumph. This was greeted with frowns of confusion, leaving Hayden realising he might have to explain his argument. 'Perhaps it's time people from this embassy started talking to the huge number of Ukrainians who have *Russian* as their first language. Just because the Russians have been held up here in Kyiv, everyone's now decided that the Ukrainians are going to win the war. Groupthink on an epic scale. Do we actually think the Russians are about to be swept out of the Donbas? Crimea?' Mallory and Tobin looked at each other and exchanged a grimace.

'If the West provides them with enough matériel, then yes, they might well do that.' This from Colonel John Maxwell, the Defence Attaché.

'Right.' Hayden sounded unimpressed. 'And where are the hundreds of armoured vehicles they'll need? British Army's got more horses than tanks, last time I checked.'

'Tell me something I don't know,' responded Maxwell wearily.

'Okay,' interjected Mallory, gesturing in a conciliatory fashion, 'I think everyone's had a chance to set out some of their, er, *thinking*. Perhaps, Hayden, you can talk us through your priorities.'

'The thing I really want to dig deep into is the R3 Fund; you know, Relief, Recovery and Reform. Professor Patel is keen that I get into that.'

A confused-looking Mallory turned to Tobin. 'Clare, do you want to give me a refresh on that one? That's the international funding mechanism, isn't it? I don't think it's something we've looked at very closely before.'

Tobin looked only slightly less bemused, twitching her nose as she tried to recall the details. 'Ukraine Relief, Recovery and Reform Fund, known as R3. It's that big thing in Geneva. Everyone is supposed to pledge funds for fixing bombed-out bridges, that sort of thing.'

'Ah, yes, the one with the glitzy launch at Davos?'

'Yes, I think so: retired footballers, keynote from Prince Harry,' added Tobin, reaching the limits of her knowledge.

Hayden sniffed, underwhelmed at this ignorance, and proceeded to offer a condescending precis of R3's founding principles of 'partnership, transparency, inclusion and multi-stakeholder engagement'.

'It's not exactly the first item on the agenda,' said Clare dismissively. 'I'm sure it's important, but we have to prioritise. I can see if our LE economist is keeping an eye on it.'

'LE?' queried Hayden.

'Locally engaged.' Tobin seemed happy to have found a gap in Hayden's knowledge. 'We have very tough limits on the number of diplomats we can keep in the field at one time. Somehow you seem to have got round that. So we have a strong LE team. Daria is our local economist – very smart. Kyiv School of Economics. Much better informed than anyone sent out from London would be. What is it you want to know?'

Hayden gave a sort of snorting sound which was supposed to sound like spontaneous laughter.

'I'm pretty sure that whatever I want to know cannot be told me by a *Ukrainian*. This is about value for money – "VFM", as Professor Patel likes to call it. I want to get my head around the whole R3 funding mechanism. Including whether there are any corruption issues. *Far* too sensitive for a local hire. I'll need to analyse the material myself.'

Mallory was now looking a little more relaxed. 'Right, well, that's quite a task to be getting along with. Obviously, you can count on the support of my team…'

'Of course,' agreed Tobin, smiling disingenuously.

—

Hayden Edgworthy's first few weeks in Kyiv proved less problematic than everyone had been expecting. Mallory had been fully prepared to write 'in the strongest terms' to the Foreign Secretary about having Edgworthy foisted upon him without consultation, reporting to someone else entirely, 'a cuckoo in the nest'. But none of this had been necessary. Hayden seemed disinclined to do difficult things like request visits to the front, where he'd need a full security detail and take up valuable resources. In fact, as far as Tobin and Mallory could tell, he was spending a lot of his time in the especially poorly appointed office they'd selected for him, poring over spreadsheets. Mallory had almost felt embarrassed they'd consigned him to little more than a broom cupboard, without air conditioning and next to the loud hums in the server room.

In fact, Hayden had not been idle. He'd been producing a bewildering flurry of reports, memos and policy papers. He just hadn't bothered to honour a promise to share his output with the Ambassador and his team. Unlike Foreign Office telegrams, sent out in the Ambassador's name and working their stately way through the bureaucracy in King Charles Street, Hayden's missives went straight to Patel, where they became ammunition in a low-level war of words that had broken out in Whitehall.

But it was mostly small-bore stuff: Hayden's take on the campaign, his sense of the 'atmospherics' in Kyiv (as insightful as anyone else's emails home) and a few bits of scuttlebutt about rumoured corruption in Ukrainian political circles. None of this was of great interest or impact, even after Patel had started to refer to 'the CRITON material', as if giving Williams's output a codeword would endow it with superior qualities. Patel continued to summon Whitehall officials to discuss Ukraine strategy, but the people in the room with the National Security Adviser at his *Ukneupore* Working Group were increasingly junior, there on behalf of absent bosses.

Due to the ever-decreasing turnout, Patel had taken to holding the meetings in his own Whitehall quarters, a small space somewhere in the Cabinet Office which had been created years earlier with partitions from a grander suite, resulting in a room that was taller than it was wide, a strange column of space furnished with a desk and meeting table squished against one wall. Visitors had to edge their way into the seats one by one, like diners in a crowded restaurant. At one of these, the long-suffering Sam Bonham hovered anxiously as Kemi Williams slid her petite frame into the narrow gap between chair and wall, making it easier for the MOD representative to take his place in the corner, where there was more space for his expansive belly.

'Is this it?' asked Patel from behind his desk, where he appeared to be tapping away at an email before joining them.

In answer to the question, a mousey and bespectacled young lady from the Treasury entered and was ushered to a chair by Bonham.

'Treasury?' asked Patel, talking to Bonham, as if he couldn't talk directly to the new arrival.

'Yes, Treasury,' she replied, able to speak for herself.

'Nobody more senior available? Nonetheless, Treasury can't afford to miss this. I suspect there are others who'll come to wish they had been here,' he added enigmatically. The newcomer exchanged a glance with Williams, neither of them any the wiser. 'Let's make a start.' Patel had realised that waiting for potential attendees only drew attention to their absence.

He cleared his throat theatrically, surprising everyone by speaking from his desk; heads turned awkwardly in his direction. The professor spoke in an odd monotone and at a volume that would have suited a room with fifteen people in it, rather than five, reading from a sheaf of papers that had been sitting on his desk.

'There have been major developments in the CRITON material which deserve far wider attention than the attendance at this meeting would appear to reflect. Leaked emails and documents reviewed by CRITON, and now in our possession, have exposed the dimensions of a wide-ranging corrupt enterprise in the Ukraine Relief, Recovery and Reform Fund, otherwise known as R3. Put simply, it has become clear that the money that has been donated by Ukraine's allies is being stolen by its politicians. On an industrial scale.' He looked at his minuscule audience, awaiting a suitable response. Instead, he had a row of blank faces.

—

That suitable response came a few hours later.

'I see I've finally managed to attract the interest of the grown-ups,' said Patel to Olivia and Sarah as they sat in chairs arranged in front of his desk, headmaster's study-style.

'Good to see you, too, Kamran,' said Sarah, smiling.

'Let's not waste time on pleasantries. You've obviously heard about the CRITON material. We've now demonstrated that a group of Ukrainian operatives linked to the intelligence services, as well as to oligarchs and politicians, have been stealing from the R3 Fund. I don't think I can overstate the significance of these findings. You have Ukraine's President going round the world giving us his sob story about how they need our support, only for us to find they need our support so they can use it to line their pockets.'

'Shall we talk a little about what you're calling CRITON, Kamran?' asked Sarah, not taking the bait. 'Up until now, it's just been opinion stuff from your guy in Kyiv, hasn't it?'

'*Opinion stuff?*'

'I think, what Sarah's getting at here is that it's been more in the nature of atmospherics. A bit like diplomatic reporting,' said Olivia. 'Whereas what you're talking about is very different.'

'The CRITON material has been consistently improving in its reach and—'

'No doubt, Kamran,' Sarah interjected, 'but what I want to understand is where he's getting this stuff from. Kemi says you've got leaked emails and documents. How are you getting hold of these?'

'Ha!' scoffed Kamran. 'What's sauce for the goose turns out not to be sauce for the gander, if you'll excuse the pun.'

'I'm not sure that is a pun, actually,' said Sarah.

This did little to mollify Kamran. 'How many times have I been fobbed off by the intel people, the Pole, GCHQ, you name it? "We don't discuss sources and methods," they say. Even when the source is the most obvious thing in the world. And the *method*…? Well, what do you expect the method to be in a HUMINT agency? But I get it. You don't trust people outside your world, you have to protect assets. Well… so do I.'

'We just need to try to understand how much weight we can attach to this stuff,' observed Olivia mildly.

'How much weight? *How much weight?* Admittedly you have yet to read the material, but this is what you people like to call "documentary reporting": leaked documents and emails that have come into the possession of the CRITON operation, and as such can be taken as reliable. Not just some single source paid to say whatever you want. This isn't your Iraqi WMD, ha ha ha! So, it's impossible to reach any other conclusion than that the war is being used as a self-enrichment scheme by Ukraine's leadership. As you'll see when you read it.'

'Yes, about that. Reading the reporting, I mean. What's the arrangement?' Olivia asked.

'Well, in view of the *exceptional* sensitivity of the material, I will personally control its distribution. The experience with the original *Ukneupore* paper, which seemed to find its way into your hands, Sarah – I *wonder* how? – and you have no appointment, no formal government role, you aren't even a British citizen as far as I know. Well, we won't be letting that—'

'Actually, Kamran,' Sarah broke in, 'let me correct you there. I did the citizenship thing a couple of years ago. Proud owner of one of those dark blue passports which your lot were so keen on. The Italian one still gets me rather faster through most queues, but I'm sure you'll tell me there's a Brexit benefit somewhere in there.'

Kamran huffed. 'Passport, maybe. But you have no status here in government.'

Sarah sounded as if she might be enjoying herself. 'Wrong again. I have an advisory role here, fully vetted. And that means,' she smiled, 'I think I have higher clearances than Rory Gough, who managed to have a Number Ten email address for reasons that still remain unclear. No job or official role at all, as far as I know. Or has that stopped now?'

Kamran pursed his lips, then raised his index finger imperiously. 'Nevertheless, access to this particular stream of CRITON material will be as follows: there will be a secure reading room, in this building. Nothing leaves the room. I will personally supervise the provision of a read-only copy for specifically named individuals. Or Sam Bonham, in my absence. But the list is controlled by me.'

'I think we can all agree this needs not to go any further until we can validate the reporting,' added Olivia.

'So can we talk about that?' This was Sarah again. 'You want to protect sources and methods. But as far as I understand, your guy in Kyiv is working on his own. I don't think it's very safe for him to be handling ultra-sensitive internal communications, if that's what this is. I mean, if these are leaked emails from Ukrainian officials, politicians, so on. Documents. There's a reason people from the Pole and SIS have secure comms. Imagine what would happen if the SBU found out the UK had this stuff.'

'Your concern is duly noted,' he replied, placing his arms on the desk in front of him, touching his hands together at the fingertips. His mouth assumed a pensive pout.

After an awkward silence, Olivia broke in. 'Can we talk about the content? What's the specific allegation?'

'It's a commissions game, basically. On every transaction, every purchase, every contract. A slice goes to the people running the country. But you'll have to read the reports. They speak for themselves,' he added piously, before making some noises about not allowing Sarah to have access to the special reading room 'in view of her anomalous position' before backing down, grumpily.

Chapter 10

Kyiv

July 2022

'Simon, let me clear up *exactly* what I'm doing here.'

Jonty looked very comfortable leaning against the railing, enjoying the view down the grassy hillside at the expanse of Kyiv spread out below them. He was letting the sun catch his face and looking like a retired English gent on a continental holiday.

'Of course, always lovely to see you. Lady P sends her best. Forgot to say. But we could do all this over lunch at the Garrick when you're back. The important bit is this: you want to find Chovka. I can help. But I think we need to agree on the objective. And I need you to do something for me.'

For several weeks, Simon had felt a sort of numbness, as if nothing he did actually mattered. As if it was all a performance. Easy to claim that you're hunting for someone when you have literally no idea what he looks like or where he might be. Now he was feeling a sudden surge of determination. And fear. The prospect that he would ever get close to finding Chovka had felt distant and improbable. He had doubted that he was really going to track down a dangerous assassin and deliver righteous justice. He had felt responsible for Evie's death, and had a need to expiate his sins. The journey to Ukraine had been a penitential pilgrimage, barefooted and hair-shirted. Meaningful to its protagonist and perhaps to God, but without any real-world impact. And now he seemed to be making progress.

Much remained unclear. His initial lead on Chovka had come from Vasya Morozov. He'd known Vasya for years but, of course, he didn't trust him. Who trusts a former GRU officer? But Vasya had liked Evie, giving Simon at least some reason to believe him in this particular case.

'I don't understand. The objective is to find Chovka. What else?'

'COSTELLO. I said I'd been involved with Sarah in the background. You did a brilliant job on the UK side of it, finding the Oxford set. But Gough is still causing trouble, chairing that national security board.'

'Does that give him real power?' asked Simon.

'It's like all these things. Job title is half the story, identity of the incumbent is the other half. There are rumours he's been coming and going from Chequers, no doubt trying to put the PM off supporting Ukraine. Let's hope he fails.'

'I don't see what I can do about Rory from here.'

'I'll tell you exactly what you can do: the issue is, we know almost nothing about the COSTELLO organisation at the Russian end. An entirely separate intelligence organisation targeting Britain. Chovka is one of the very few leads we have. He could be a gold mine. We can't let that go.'

Simon found himself swallowing uncomfortably. He wanted to find Chovka and make him pay for what he had done to Evie. He had not been thinking of this as an intelligence-gathering opportunity. Simon spoke cautiously, almost dismissively. 'Well, first we have to find him. It's brilliant we've got the photo, of course. But that's just a small step. And even if we can find him, why would Chovka tell me – or you – anything? The guy's a fanatic. Cold-eyed killer. I can't imagine he's recruitable.'

Jonty smiled. There was almost a smugness in his face. 'Because he has a big problem with his people, and he is operating in an unforgiving environment.'

There was a pause as this new information sank in. Simon was starting to understand, his years of working with the complex, fissiparous peoples of the Caucasus region opening his eyes to the challenge. A region where people living in neighbouring valleys might have a completely different language, religion and set of traditions. Where the red thread of a blood feud could be traced down generations. 'Ahh. So he's under some kind of *chi'r*, the Chechen blood revenge feud. Has he offended his *teip*, his tribe?'

Momentarily, Jonty looked completely baffled. And then he chuckled, incongruously, Simon thought, given the gravity of the question. 'Thank you, *Florence of Arabia*. Don't get bogged down with the tribal crap. No – he is *not* in trouble with his own people because of an ancient Chechen blood feud. It's not the bloody eighteen-hundreds. You said he was seen going to various banks in Moldova? Yes?'

'Yes.'

'He's in trouble because he stole twenty thousand dollars of operational funds.'

'Ah. So you knew the Moldova stuff already.'

Jonty smiled enigmatically.

Simon had always admired Jonty. Believed in him. But that didn't mean he knew what he was up to.

'I checked the Prague name and picture with some chaps in DC. Big data wallahs. There was some banking intel – a suspicious activity report of a Chechen suspected hit man who wired funds from a Moldova bank.'

'Oh, right. Yeah, I can see that would be a problem if he nicked the money.'

'There's more. What he did with it is an even bigger problem. He was sending it to a bank in Istanbul. To an account in the name of Mansur al-Sharma. Yes, who is Mansur al-Sharma, you ask?'

Simon nodded, trying to order the story in his mind: *Chechen hit man in Moldova sending stolen funds to an Arab-sounding name at a Turkish bank. What does it mean?*

'I have no idea.' Jonty paused, evidently enjoying the effect. 'But I asked my American friends about the account. They think it's associated with Syrian rebels.'

'With what?' Simon was genuinely baffled.

'Yes, Syrian rebels. Jihadists. Maybe ISIS. Let's not forget that the Chechnya he grew up in was basically an Islamic state. Deep down, Chovka might be a fundamentalist. If you look at what he's done, that seems quite possible: he's stolen GRU money and sent it to Syrian radical Islamists.'

'Seriously?'

'It's very serious for him. I mean, it seems he is working with Syrian terrorists and he has been disloyal both to Russia and to the Chechen leadership. That gets him in even bigger trouble in Grozny than sending the money to Kyiv...'

'Bloody hell.' Simon did not bother to conceal his amazement. In the brutal world of Chechen politics, this was the sort of transgression that would be immediately fatal if discovered.

'I think we'd have significant leverage over Chovka,' said Jonty quietly, smiling at the awful prospect.

And now, Simon was starting to understand Jonty. 'I'm not really looking for leverage. Just revenge.'

'Yes, I know. But let's be brutally frank for a moment. I don't believe you're the cold-blooded killer type. I think you don't really know what you're doing here. Which is why, since you got to Kyiv, you've hardly spoken to anyone. Not exactly typical behaviour for an intelligence officer of your calibre.'

Coming from someone else, Simon might have been able to brush this off. But from the man he regarded as his mentor in the intelligence world, it stung. 'I've been keeping my cover intact,' he said indignantly. 'I've got a lot of stuff hanging over me back in the UK.'

'That's not what's stopping you. Know what I think's happened? You've realised you don't know why you're here. You're on a revenge mission but you haven't got the stomach for it. You're happy digging away online with Rudi, piecing together the backstory. But you aren't going to track down Chovka and shoot him in the back of the head. We both know that.'

Jonty had begun to walk, his hands thrust into his jacket pockets. He turned away from the parapet and headed to a flight of concrete steps that led down the grassy hillside. He took the steps slowly, with the caution appropriate to a man of his age. Simon followed, resentfully. At the bottom of the steps the ground flattened a little. Between handsome trees there was a scruffy pink object that had started life as an avant-garde bench and was now covered in graffiti tags. Jonty leant against it and spread his arms, perhaps a conciliatory gesture.

'Simon, this isn't about his rights or just desserts. Here's where I'm coming from: I'd like to find out some things, and I think we have a way to, er, *incentivise* him to talk. I'll help you find him if you're willing to try to get the intel.'

'Help me *find* him? Do you know where he is?'

'No. But we know he's here in Ukraine and that the Chechens, the Kadyrovites, are active in the Donbas. You know me: I connect people who have things with people who need things. I know some of the special units working down there. And those guys are very interested in Chechens like Chovka.'

'Which guys?'

'This is a coalition, Simon. You know what it's like in a war: people everywhere doing their bit, and you just hope it all adds up to our side winning. Sometimes it's a bit chaotic. But as long as the other side is more chaotic, we're probably going to be okay. The Ukrainians have a lot of intel on the Chechens around Bakhmut. It's now Russia's main objective, and Kadyrov's people are there in the fight. That's where you'll find Chovka. So we're all after the same guy, basically.'

'Pryvillya. Find a massacre and you'll find them,' Simon found himself saying, more to himself than to Jonty.

'What what?'

'I haven't been *completely* useless over the past few weeks. Got a tip-off about this place Pryvillya, where the Chechens have been torturing their prisoners. Victims, you might as well say. Nobody comes out of there alive. I was told they couldn't resist boasting about their crimes on Telegram. Thought it was an exaggeration, but it turns out to be true.'

'Well, I'd say that's bloody interesting. You *haven't* been completely useless. And this is on Telegram?'

'Once you know which channels to look at, you can find the stuff. The important point is that it's a hotbed of Chechen activity. Either Chovka is there, or people who know about him are there. Either way, it might prove useful.' Until Simon said it, he hadn't quite realised that he could have found something important. His time in Kyiv had not been the listless inactivity that Jonty was suggesting.

'Simon, this rather points to what it is you can do here. You need to do what you have always done. What you've been doing already, so it turns out. You're not an assassin. You're a HUMINT specialist. A brilliant case officer. You like the puzzle, the chase.'

I might be an assassin, thought Simon. *Perhaps that's what I'm here to find out.*

'So what exactly do you want me to do? What's the tasking?'

'We need to go on the offensive with COSTELLO. We can't keep waiting for them to make their moves. We need to go after them and learn as much as we can, so we can work out how to bring them down.'

'Okay?'

'Imagine the value of a source inside COSTELLO. We start to disrupt, not react. If the Ukrainians can lead you to Chovka, then maybe you can recruit him. Bring him in. And if you've found everything we're likely to find, you can then do whatever you want to him.'

Find out the truth. Expose Chovka, leave him a broken man. That will be my revenge, thought Simon. He didn't need to share this with Jonty.

'Is this a Pole operation, Jonty?' Simon wanted it to be. Back on the inside.

'No.' But Jonty had turned his head away, as if he didn't want to make eye contact.

It doesn't need to be a Pole operation, thought Simon. *It just needs to matter... It needs to make a difference...* For the first time in several weeks he felt purposeful. *The credit belongs to the man who is actually in the arena.*

There was a rustling in the trees. Was it a slight breeze taking the edge off the summer heat? Or did Simon shiver with the anticipation of recruiting a dangerous assassin on the front lines at Bakhmut?

Chapter 11

London
February 2018

Simon leant down to adjust the small fan heater under the desk. He had found that if he got the angle right it would counteract the draught from the rotting window frames. He had spoken to the landlord about replacing the windows, but not with any expectation of success. He did not pay much rent for his 'office', a single top floor room above a vape shop off the Edgware Road, and at those prices it was unreasonable to expect the windows to close properly. In addition to the lack of insulation, the glass in the windows rattled whenever a large truck passed by, and the floorboards had a sort of creaky bounce to them that suggested they might give way some day. But, in spite of these things, Simon liked the place. He found it easier to work when he wasn't in his own home and he liked having people around to work with.

Except, the latter was proving to be a bit of a problem. His sole employee, a combustible young Georgian called Irakli, had stormed out after an altercation with someone whom Simon had hoped would become a valued client, a Russian exile called Alexei who was wanted on trumped-up charges by the Kremlin. Alexei needed to prove to an English court that he was being framed by Moscow. If he failed to do so, he could reasonably expect extradition and death in a Russian penal colony. But they had not got as far as discussing the details of his case, as he and Irakli had managed to start shouting at each other within seconds. Alexei followed the Georgian out of the room a few moments later, shouting that he had been 'disrespected' by Simon's colleague. As Alexei stomped down the stairs, muttering to himself furiously, his temper, which his friends called 'effervescent' and his enemies 'psychotic', overwhelmed him and he shouted in guttural Russian at the empty hallway.

—

Evie Howard looked down at the map screen on her phone and then looked up at her supposed destination. But something was obviously wrong: in front of her was a dodgy-looking vape shop and a door that gave access to the upper floors. When she looked up, all she could see were grimy windows. She sighed with annoyance and checked the email.

'Huh?' It was the right address. She stepped forwards and tried the buzzer for the second floor, but it didn't seem to be wired to anything. It did not seem likely that any enticing job prospect could lie on the opposite side of that door, and she wondered about giving the whole thing a miss. Job hunting was proving a frustrating experience: interviews with over-attentive married men who would then call back and explain there wasn't actually a job available 'at the moment, but why don't I buy you dinner and we can see if there are things we can do together?'

I speak native Russian and have a postgrad degree in intelligence studies, and the only thing these people want to recruit is a new mistress. I'm not looking for a fucking sugar daddy.

Evie needed a job. Her parents were helping her out, but she was determined not to live off the Bank of Mum and Dad, particularly as her dear father, a retired army officer, had been better at serving his country than his bank balance. She was going to go to this interview, however unpromising the situation. The door was swinging on an ineffective latch and she pushed on in, steeling herself for whatever was coming.

This turned out to be a man on the staircase shouting in Russian. 'Fucking useless! He knows nothing! *NOTHING!*' he bellowed, slamming the wall with his fist. Evie assumed that the anger was masking the considerable pain the punch must have caused him.

The man did not appear to have noticed the young woman by the door, looking rather unsure of herself, and Evie coughed self-consciously. Alexei gave a semi-apologetic grunt as he massaged his bruised fist.

'I'd say he probably knows more about Russia than most Russians,' said Evie in her mother tongue, not very loudly, and Alexei wasn't sure if she was talking to him. He flicked his chin aggressively in Evie's direction.

'You say something?' he asked in deliberately idiomatic Muscovite.

Is this all some kind of weird test, thought Evie, *like one of those stupid Oxbridge interviews? Just going to have to roll with it...*

'Yes, I did say something,' she said steadily in her native Russian, doing a good job of masking her nerves. 'Simon Sharman knows more about Russia than most Russians, and that's why I'm going up to see him.'

'And who the hell are you?'

'Evelina,' she said, smiling and using the Russian pronunciation of her name.

'And you're part of this?'

'Yes... May I?' she asked and squeezed past Alexei.

–

There was a knock on Simon's office door.

'What now?'

'Oh.' A young woman, smartly dressed as you might be for an interview, was standing on the landing, looking unsure of herself. 'You said to come at four-fifteen.'

Simon took a deep breath. 'Sorry. Yes, I did... Remind me...'

'Evie Howard. We met at the Ship and Shovell…'

'Right. Yes, Evie. You're the one into social media.'

She smiled patiently. 'Well, yes, we spoke about that…' She had a determined look, but something about Simon's demeanour was off-putting. She began again, slightly deflated. 'Umm, I can see this might not be a good time. Do you want to reschedule?'

'Oh dear.' Simon was finally catching up with himself. 'Did you encounter an angry Russian on the staircase? Or an angry Georgian followed by an angry Russian?'

'Just the Russian, I think. I must have missed the Georgian.'

'Right… It's not always like this,' he said. 'Er, perhaps we should reschedule. There's rather a lot going on at the moment.' Simon didn't really feel like talking to anyone, least of all a pushy youngster hoping to get a job.

'Of course,' said Evie, trying not to look disappointed. 'Fine. *Completely* fine. Just let me know when's good for you.' She shook his hand and turned to leave. At this point the door swung open and the bulky frame of Alexei stomped back in, almost colliding with Evie, who gave a small yelp of surprise.

'Sorry, Evelina,' he said in Russian. 'Come, have a seat here.' He indicated one of the two armchairs in front of the desk.

Simon's head turned in bewilderment to the two people now sitting in his room. 'Umm, are you guys together?'

Evie looked nervously at Alexei.

'No, Mister Sharman,' said Alexei in accented English. 'I meet Evelina downstairs and she tell me you know Russia very well. So, prove it to us. How are you going to help me? My life depends on it.'

Chapter 12

Oxford

August 2022

As a rule, Sarah tried to avoid spending too much time in Oxford in August. The bewitching air of a city devoted to scholarship was largely absent, along with the majority of its students and faculty. Instead, the academy had been replaced by hordes of tourists, swarming around the colleges before sampling Oxford's 'retail offering'. Even in the safe space of Sarah's rooms, tucked away on an upper floor of Peckwater Quad near the back of Christ Church, you couldn't rule out the risk of a stray Harry Potter enthusiast finding their way up the staircase on the hunt for the Gryffindor common room. But Sarah needed to do some of her day job, and that required her to be in her office where she had access to the books and journals needed to be able to finish her paper for an upcoming academic conference.

For several days Sarah had buried herself in monographs, scholarly articles and recondite texts in Old Church Slavonic. This had always been her preferred way of working. Since winning a fellowship at All Souls College, Oxford's academic summit, just after her undergraduate final exams, she had taken an immersive approach to scholarship, preferring to disappear for days at a time, meals, sleep and the outside world all temporarily suspended. She would call this being 'in the tunnel', and was relaxed about ignoring almost all external stimuli during these periods. In Simon's first years as a junior intelligence officer he had thought that he might be able to have a relationship with Sarah, who was dividing her time between graduate work at All Souls and an analytical role in the Joint Intelligence Directorate. With their undergraduate years behind them, and some of the more intense social competition that went with that also dissipated, Simon hoped they would find time for each other. But Sarah's intense working pattern had rendered this dream an impossibility. Or, at least, that was what he had told his friends.

With Sarah in the tunnel, she had only skimmed her various Proton emails and Signal messages, deciding she could afford not to reply to them for a few days at least. As for the news, or other media from the world outside, she had ignored this altogether. As she neared the completion of the final version of her paper, she had a nagging sense that something not entirely welcome was happening, but she couldn't put her finger on the details. It was like waking from an intensely realistic dream of a bad event that leaves a memory of unease, the event itself forgotten.

–

A few days earlier, Sarah had submitted herself to Kamran's demanding security strictures and read through his CRITON dossier, under the watchful eye of Sam Bonham. The first thought that occurred as she leafed through the dossier was: *If these are fake, they did a decent job with the faking.* The originals, which were in an appendix to the dossier, were in earthy, colloquial Ukrainian, some of the words unfamiliar despite her considerable fluency in the language. And they had a convincing authorial feel to them – different voices appeared to come from different email accounts (most of which were in alias names or non-intuitive email addresses). And from her experience of reading private correspondence, leaked or otherwise purloined in the pursuit of national security, there was an authenticity in the way the messages were sometimes incoherent, misspelled, failing to answer the previous message. In short: true to life.

The story they told was damning: nearly fifty billion dollars had been paid by governments all over the world into the Ukraine Relief, Recovery and Reform Fund. A portion of this had been earmarked for a special 'public-private partnership framework' designed to bring in commercial investment alongside international aid funds, all to be used for the rebuilding of Ukraine's damaged infrastructure. It was all managed from Geneva by a bland-sounding institution called the International Credit Bank. But from Sarah's reading of the documents, this was little more than a front. Not a front in the classic sense, for it was a real bank carrying out plenty of the sort of business that at least other bankers regarded as legitimate. But it was a front in that it had lent its name and credibility as the 'lead partner' to a consortium that included a range of smaller entities that were willing to take a chance on the risky business of trying to rebuild Ukraine whilst Russia was trying to destroy it.

As Sarah read the documents she began to piece together a narrative. Financing had been for a series of reconstruction projects – repairs to water and electricity networks, rebuilding an office complex in Kyiv, a damaged port in Odesa, bridges over various rivers. And with all of these, members of the Ukrainian elite, government ministers, their business associates and family members all had companies ready to carry out these patriotic endeavours. From there it was straightforward: the international funders would seek a Ukrainian joint venture partner. Since the Ukrainian businesses were shell companies with no employees or ability to do any actual rebuilding, the money went straight to the politician or oligarch that owned the company, with a generous kickback to the bankers and advisers involved along the way. The same bankers would then make sure the Ukrainian beneficiaries were able to put their money offshore in cleverly arranged, tax-efficient 'structures'.

The story was depressingly familiar. Inflated contracts, kickbacks, money laundered through offshore accounts and shell companies in British offshore jurisdictions, places like the Cayman Islands and Bermuda, with meaningless names like Business Now Limited and Celestial Dawn Incorporated. But was any of it true? As Sarah combed through the documents, she employed the classic intelligence analyst's trick of being less interested in the content of the emails and more interested in the context. The email addresses, the recipients' names, the cast of characters. She was looking for a lead, for something that might offer an opportunity, a way in.

After two hours of study, with Sam Bonham's fidgeting and sighing becoming more frequent and impatient, she thought she might have found something. Buried in an email chain, between hundreds of documents that were, on the face of it, incriminating, but which offered no detail of operational value, was a mundane exchange relating to a series of financial transfers that a Swiss bank would make for one of its supposedly corrupt Ukrainian clients:

> On Mon, 13 Jun 2022 at 12:13,
> <dg347564@protonmail.com> wrote:

Can I get Patrice to make the arrangements for the wire transfer as before?

DG

> On Tue, 13 Jun 2022 at 12:21, Christophe Lyon
> <clyon@icbanque.ch> wrote:

Hi Danylo,

Patrice is no longer with ICB so please deal with Gabrielle Devaux who is cc'd on this email. gdevaux@icbanque.ch. I will have her reach out to you directly.

Cordialement,

Christophe L

Sarah set Kemi to work immediately with this slender lead. Over a coffee she explained her thinking: 'If these documents were real, someone called "Patrice" had worked for International Credit Bank in a period after the Russian invasion in February but had left by mid-June. So the dates could help narrow it down.' What Sarah had realised was that this Patrice, according to the email, had direct knowledge of payments from the framework fund. Payments that looked corrupt.

'And he no longer works there,' said Kemi, cottoning on.

'If we can figure out who he is, we might be able to find him. Speak to him.'

They had taken a corner in the tiny cafe in a side street between Westminster Abbey and St James's Park, its chief attraction a nostalgic shabbiness rarely seen this close to the centre of London. On the table in front of them were sheets of paper spread out with hand-drawn spider diagrams of the possible corruption network, lists of names, Sarah's memorised notes of the companies and transactions because she had not been allowed to take actual notes by the diligent Sam Bonham. It was the sort of collage that might be expected to attract attention from other customers. But this was a cafe where every customer thought their conversation was a secret of national importance: on the neighbouring table, two senior Treasury civil servants were planning which major infrastructure project they would axe in the next spending round; behind them, a special adviser from the Home Office was briefing the *Daily Mail*'s lobby correspondent on an innovative plan to use wave machines to deter small boats laden with refugees from crossing the English Channel. Nobody was remotely interested in Sarah and Kemi's investigation of corruption in a faraway country of which they knew little.

Kemi had got the point immediately. It didn't take her long to find Patrice Devouassoux, whose online profile suggested he had worked at various lower level roles in banks in Geneva, including International Credit. Was he someone who found it

hard to stick at a job, or someone who proved not very profi-
cient at the jobs he got? The effect was much the same: a résumé
with too many entries on it. But like many of his generation, he
did not conform to the lazy cliché of the millennial leaving his
entire life open to anyone with internet access. His Instagram
and Facebook accounts were private, and it took Kemi some
time to figure out a likely Twitter account, which was basically
inactive. What little they knew of him was from LinkedIn: that
he was #Opentowork, which was the most important thing.

'All we need now is access to the world's most dynamic
human intelligence network,' said Sarah, when she met up with
Kemi a couple of days later.

'You mean, get SIS involved?' asked Kemi, confused.

'No. Recruitment consultants.'

'What?'

'Best spies in the business. They have cover to ring up just
about anyone, ask them how they feel about their job, what
their background and motivations are, whether they want to
move. And if someone says, "How did you get my number?"
they just say, "It's confidential, but you were highly recommended."'

'Huh. And I imagine you have a tame consultant who works
with you,' Kemi said, rapidly getting to the point.

'Well, it's someone that I know worked well with...' She
paused, as if she didn't want to mention Simon's name, even
though Kemi had worked closely with him and Sarah before
his hurried departure. 'There's a guy called Hamish Sanderson,
typical head-hunter type, knows everyone, very charming and
connected. We'll get him to call Patrice and say there's a job
coming up in a private bank in Geneva. Something like that.
Hamish will figure it out. He does this stuff in real life. That's
why he's good at it.'

'But don't you need a cover office? A real business that will
vouch for Hamish and confirm it's a real job?' Kemi sounded
sceptical, as if Sarah had been making things up on the hoof.

'No, that's the beauty of it. The consultant can say "The client's in the banking sector in Geneva", but the actual business name is always confidential. And that's normal during the initial stages of a recruitment search. It really is a great way to get intel out of people.'

Kemi had not expected a response to a couple of messages she had sent Sarah. But one morning she rang her phone, having sent a quick *need to speak* text. No answer. But Kemi was not the sort of person to be put off easily, and rang again. Twice. And continued until Sarah finally picked up.

'Yes?' Sarah was standing in front of her desk, strewn with books held open at the relevant page with empty coffee mugs. The floor of her large study was paved with printed papers. Her hair was tied up in a messy bun and she looked like she had not slept properly for several days.

'Sorry. But it *is* important. I've sent an email. Check BBC News. I'll stay on the line.'

Sarah, frowning at the inconvenience, held her phone out as she navigated to the webpage. She squinted, frowned again, and then put her hand to her mouth. It wasn't quite a gasp, but it was surprise.

'Oh. Crap. This is the CRITON stuff?'

'Well, it certainly looks like it.'

Kamran Patel had insisted that his supposedly top secret intelligence of graft in the Ukraine reconstruction fund was handled in the most restrictive fashion possible. And now Sarah seemed to be reading about it on the BBC News website: 'Ukraine's President denies corruption at recovery fund' screamed the banner headline.

'How did it get out?' asked Sarah.

'Working on that. But it's going viral. BBC report is as bland as you'd expect. But there's all kinds of stuff popping up on social media. Memes, deepfake images of Zelenskyy on a superyacht, in a tux drinking champagne, that sort of thing. They're saying he's going to buy Highgrove.'

'Has Hamish got anywhere with Patrice?' asked Sarah.

'Yes. That was my other email to you. Couple of days ago. Patrice is up for a meeting. Wants to work for something less bureaucratic than the R3 Fund. That's what he said, anyway. He seemed very keen to talk about his reasons for leaving R3, but said it had to be in person. Said "you can't believe what you see in the media" but wouldn't elaborate. Like he has something to share. Hamish actually said he sounded a bit desperate...'

'We like desperate. And are you looking into where this story leaked from?'

'I am,' said Kemi, always a few steps ahead.

Chapter 13

What Kemi was trying to get to the bottom of was perhaps the most powerful and effective weapon that Russia had: disinformation. Sitting in Europe or North America, it seemed that Russia's incompetent attempt to seize Kyiv had gone from blitzkrieg to traffic jam in a few days, and Ukraine's heroic defiance had created remarkable global consensus. Who would have foreseen Germany upending decades of reliance on Russian gas, surging its defence budget and embracing the so-called *Zeitenwende*, the historical turning point forced on them by Russia's war? Or once-neutral Finland and Sweden applying to join NATO? But Kemi knew this consensus was an inside-the-bubble delusion that was easy to slip into when you've spent your life working in the British civil service. Her own range of influences were far broader than those of her bosses. She had cousins in Nigeria sending her TikTok videos that explained how Russia had been 'forced' into a 'defensive war' as a result of NATO's 'aggressive expansion'. She knew people who vehemently asserted that the 'military-industrial complex' needed a war to keep defence budgets inflated after a period of sustained peace.

Kemi didn't have to believe these stories to know of their purchase. She knew that Russia was a world leader in spreading lies online, but for all her instinctive Gen-Z tech savvy, she realised she didn't know exactly how this happened. Neverthe-less, Kemi knew who to call when things in the online world didn't make sense: the Welsh Wizard. She had never met this person, and had never been told his real name. He was just one of a cast of characters that Simon and Sarah seemed to be able to call upon to carry out tasks that called for obscure skills and extreme discretion.

The Welsh Wizard was Simon's affectionate nickname for Dylan Ifans, a former GCHQ hacking expert who had left the service in high dudgeon around the time of the Iraq war. From his home on a windswept Welsh mountainside, he had made himself a significant but invisible figure in the cyber-universe, offering help to investigative journalists, campaigners and activists. And, occasionally, Simon, whom he regarded as a serviceable back channel into government. A few weeks earlier, the Wizard had engineered a breakthrough in the investigation into the Oxford spy ring. It was his phishing attack that had enabled Simon and Sarah to figure out the identities of a series of Russian intelligence officers. These people had been travel-ling on alias passports bought from the government of St Kitts. Rory Gough's admission that he had met 'the St Kitts guys', as he had disingenuously referred to them, was decisive evidence of his interactions with Russian intelligence.

An obsessive guard of his own anonymity, Simon knew the Wizard's real identity because they had worked together in the years when they were both servants of the British secret state. But for Kemi, he was just a voice, a strange, distorted basso profundo emanating from a dark screen. Even getting to the voice was far from straightforward: to access the Wizard's bespoke messaging platform, Kemi had to use a dedicated computer that had never been sullied with any other activity, connect online via two layers of VPN encryption and memorise a bewildering number of passwords. For Simon and Sarah, these were mildly inconvenient hurdles. For Kemi, living in a cramped shared apartment in Croydon, it was rather more difficult. Her flatmate believed she did nothing more interesting than write civil service policy papers. The existence of a second laptop in Kemi's small bedroom, hidden under the mattress, was a hostage to fortune, but not one that she could avoid.

'Four–one,' said a disembodied, distorted voice coming from the laptop propped on Kemi's knees as she sat on her bed. She had chosen to work from home, waiting for the reassuring slam of the front door as her flatmate left in the morning. The Wizard insisted on the use of numeric identifiers, on the basis that an intercepted call would not feature any actual names, or even a recognisable voice. With Simon and Sarah, he would usually switch on his camera, on the basis that they already knew what he looked like. No such privilege for Kemi.

'Hello,' replied Kemi, trying to inject some brightness into her voice. She wondered whether it came out normal at the other end or whether she also was being distorted.

'Saw the message,' said the Wizard, not in the mood for small talk. 'Disinformation. Ukraine corruption story?'

'Er… yes,' replied Kemi, momentarily dislocated by his directness. 'Trying to work out how it blew up so quickly.'

'Yeah. It's CIB,' he said, as if it was rather boring to have to explain.

Kemi didn't enjoy it when someone made a technical reference she didn't understand, so she paused, hoping the Wizard might elucidate. He didn't.

'CIB?'

'*Co-ordinated inauthentic behaviour.* Proof of an online campaign rather than a story spreading organically.'

'Right?'

'You know what happened with the #IstandwithPutin hashtag? At the start of the war? It suddenly trended on Twitter. That was done by a Russian network set up to manipulate the algorithm. It worked, especially in the global South. You'd be amazed at how popular Putin is in Africa.'

Since Kemi's camera was also turned off, the Wizard could not see the roll of her eyes at the mansplaining.

'Thanks, that's helpful,' she said with some effort. 'What I'm trying to understand is how you *know* it's a Moscow network? Couldn't it just be a genuine social group? You know: things go viral. In parts of Africa, Russia is seen as standing up to the West.'

Kemi could hear the Wizard sigh. With exaggerated patience he began to explain. 'This stuff was being put out by bot accounts that had only been set up in the previous few days – and they were a tight network, all appearing online at the same time, all retweeting one another. Those are the seeders. We're past the days when these accounts are registered to Russian cities. But we still know it's them: it's the way they operate. And they deliberately targeted non-Western audiences.'

'Go on.' Kemi just needed to listen and make the occasional noise to reassure him she was still there. He explained that the seeders were doing the 'information laundering', moving the story from Russian-owned Telegram channels on to mainstream social media. 'And then it gets picked up by pro-Kremlin news sites, far-right bloggers, that sort of thing. This is *layering*: building up from the random bullshit accounts, via slightly batshit accounts, to the point that you have something that gets traction. At some point, these stories find their way into the mainstream.'

'Define mainstream.' Kemi had regained her stride a little.

'Tabloid news sites, cable TV. That's where a lot of Kremlin narratives first arrive in front of a mass audience. A lot of it is culture war stuff: "The Russian people still know which bathroom to use." That kind of thing. At a certain point, even the middle-of-the-road media decides it has to report it and it takes off.'

'How many of those media players are *wittingly* helping Russia, do you think?'

'Not my strong point, four-one. I don't try to understand people. I just look at the data.'

Who can blame him? thought Kemi.

'Okay, so where did it begin? If it started on Telegram, who put it on there?'

'Yeah, that's kind of your job, I think. But it first came up in a Telegram channel that seems close to Russian intelligence sources. It's not one of the big ones, but that makes it more interesting. If you were trying to do something a little bit subtle, you'd have a basically obscure channel come up with the original line, maybe one that sometimes criticises Russia in the war. Makes it look more authentic. And then that gets picked up by bigger channels. And so it goes. Looks organic.'

'And the date? The date it first appeared on Telegram? On the obscure channel?'

'Twenty-ninth of July.'

The exact date that Patel had announced his 'bombshell' CRITON material.

Chapter 14

London

August 2022

Sarah needed to speak to Kamran. She didn't want to give him the opportunity to know that she was coming to see him, and nor did she want to be inside a government building when they spoke. She wondered about staking out the entrance to the Cabinet Office, but there was far too much risk of running into someone she knew in that busiest part of Whitehall. Much better to find him at his home. She didn't know where he lived, but he had left a correspondence address on the filings of a limited company he appeared to be a director of. It had been fairly easy for Kemi to cross-reference this with a few other data points to be sure. Patel might be an intellectual revolutionary, but he was plotting to tear apart British foreign and security policy from a leafy cul-de-sac in a Hertfordshire commuter town.

She had set Kemi on the long-suffering Sam Bonham to gather pattern-of-life intelligence.

'I'll take him for lunch,' Kemi had said. 'Try to get something out of him.'

'Yes, but nothing fancy, don't want him to get suspicious.'

''Course not. Civil service date-style. Sandwiches in the park.'

–

A few days later, Kemi and Sam were eating their purchases companionably on a St James's Park bench, surrounded by all the other civil servants doing the same thing. Given the evident tensions between their respective bosses, it wasn't out of the question that Sam and Kemi might try to get to know each other, perhaps even find some common ground. With a bit of gentle flirtation and shared tales of the unreasonable demands that very senior people make on their hard-working desk officers, Kemi was quickly able to get Sam talking about what she needed to know.

'It must be a fascinating job, though, really at the heart of things.'

'Yes, I suppose it is,' agreed Sam, with a slight weariness.

'Fascinating and demanding. Is that fair?' asked Kemi, turning towards Sam and looking coolly into his eyes.

'Well, you know he's very, er, exacting. And I think he doesn't always feel he has many allies in Whitehall.'

Kemi laughed. 'That's an understatement. They *hate* him. It's almost enough to make you feel sorry for him.'

The casual confidence seemed to warm up Sam a little. 'Oh, I wouldn't go that far. He can be incredibly annoying.'

'Is he hard to work for? I mean, like, seven-day weeks, all that stuff? At least Olivia has a good work–life balance.'

'Yeah, well, he doesn't seem to know what a weekend is. I get calls on Sunday mornings. I'm on the point of claiming to be a fervent Christian. The thing with that crowd is that they have to pretend they admire Christianity 'cos it's a sort of old-school thing.'

'Long hours? I imagine you aren't allowed home until he's gone?'

'To be fair, lots of evenings he leaves at a fairly sensible time so he can get to some think-tank event or whatever. But if there's nothing on it's never before eight.'

'Sounds relentless,' she said sympathetically. She chose not to mention that she had assumed that everyone worked until eight.

'It is. Best is when he's travelling – then it cools off quite a lot. Or when India are playing a Test match. It's amazing how he'll make time for that. They're in the West Indies at the moment. 'Cos of the time difference it doesn't matter in the mornings, but come the afternoons he has this habit of disappearing on the dot of five.'

'What? Is he watching in the pub?' Kemi found this hard to fathom.

'No, I don't think pubs are a happy place for him. He'll head home. I know, because the calls still come to me thick and fast. Sometimes he's on a video call and I can see he's at home, and you can hear the sound of the match in the background.'

'Oh. So, you've become strangely attached to the schedule of the Indian cricket team?' Kemi said this as if it were a joke.

'I literally have. Next match starts in two days and I can't wait.'

–

Armed with this intelligence, Sarah planned a visit to Harpenden, a town about thirty miles from London that epitomised suburban respectability. Where golf courses and garden centres were the key drivers of the local economy, and the high street was one long stretch of coffee shops, Italian restaurants and hair salons. But to reduce the risk of a pointless journey, she decided to have Kemi follow Patel from the Cabinet Office. There were risks with this idea, as he undoubtedly knew what she looked like, but Sarah's judgement was that Kamran Patel was not the sort of person to take much of an interest in his surroundings.

A couple of days later, just before five, Kemi left her desk at the Foreign Office and made the very short walk past Downing Street to the Cabinet Office's entrance on Whitehall. There was usually a small crowd of people milling around outside the doors: the rigours of getting through the security inside were such that it was easier to arrange to meet people outside. But

Kemi avoided the area by the doorway, choosing to put herself at the far corner of the building near the grand entrance to the Scottish Office, under the welcome shade of a plane tree. Here, she could lean against a low stone wall and pretend to be waiting for a bus whilst keeping her eyes trained on the Cabinet Office entrance.

At six minutes past five, she saw Kamran emerge from the building. He was instantly recognisable: shambling in his creased suit and carrying a small leather satchel like a schoolchild's music case. He was staring at his phone, intently reading, only briefly looking up to pick his way down the steps onto the pavement before heading down Whitehall to Westminster Tube station. Although the end of day rush hour had yet to kick in, the pavement was busy, and Kemi had no fear that Patel would see her from fifty metres ahead, even if he did turn around.

Kemi had checked the likeliest route that Patel would take home: Google Maps said Tube on the Jubilee Line to West Hampstead and then the above-ground Thameslink to Harpenden. Her instructions from Sarah were clear: 'Make sure he's on the Thameslink. I'll take it from there.' The Tube was the riskiest part of the journey: Westminster station was huge, always busy, and he could be headed in almost any direction. It was only their guesswork and the attraction of the cricket that had him headed home. So Kemi made a point of walking quickly to reduce the distance as he approached the entrance, a flight of stone steps disappearing down from the pavement on the corner of Parliament Square. When she was about twenty metres behind Patel, Kemi could see he was wearing earbuds, the little white blobs standing out against his brown complexion. This felt like a good sign – perhaps he was already listening to the cricket commentary; he would certainly be less aware of what was going on around him.

Kemi felt a mild surge of anxiety as Kamran disappeared down the staircase. She had to force herself not to speed up, knowing the subway below led in only one direction. He couldn't escape. Sure enough, as she descended she regained her sight of him, still walking purposefully, his phone now in his hand by his side. The funnel effect of the walkway meant that it was much more crowded than on the pavement above, and Kemi had to zigzag past the slower movers to keep him in view. She knew she wasn't supposed to look purposeful or hurried, in spite of feeling both.

The passageway twisted a couple of times before opening out into the huge ticket hall, fed by entrances from all sides of Parliament Square. Here there were hundreds of people swarming through the ticket barriers: tourists on their way to see Big Ben; civil servants who'd made sure they'd left the office on the dot of five p.m.; politicos attracted by the magnetic lure of the parliament buildings. The space and the crowds gave Kemi a chance to get closer to Patel as he shuffled towards the gate, touching his phone on the yellow contactless reader to swipe the barrier open. A man seemed to be holding people up, not having the right card to get through. *Come on, Tall Man*, muttered Kemi, biting her lip in frustration. Finally, this neophyte figured out how the system worked and he paced quickly towards the escalator, a flood of frustrated regulars in his wake. Kemi was only a few steps behind him, spotting Patel further down the escalator to the Jubilee Line.

Good, thought Kemi. Patel was headed in the right direction and on the right line for West Hampstead, and she felt comfortable giving him more space on the platform. When the train arrived they were not in the same carriage, but she could keep an eye on him through the glass partition into the next car. He was sitting down, which fitted the profile of someone travelling through several stations, staring at his phone again.

That was when she saw it. Or, more accurately, saw him.

When Kemi had done her surveillance training, arranged for her by Sarah and delivered 'off-books' by a retired Royal Ulster Constabulary officer, she had taken to it readily. The intellectual game, the memory puzzles – 'Have you seen this face before?' – and the buzz of being in an obscure competition all played to her strengths. In spite of coming from a completely different background, generation and world view to Billy, her monosyllabic trainer, she was impressed by his professionalism and experience. The only thing that had jarred slightly was when he started talking about sixth sense.

'We all know when we're being watched. You just have to tune into that sixth sense,' Billy had said, as he debriefed her in a shabby cafe after a training route across Horsham.

'Seriously? That's not a real thing. What does that even mean?' she asked with a derisive chuckle.

Billy seemed unmoved by the possibility that he was being laughed at. 'So you're telling me you've never looked up at someone to find they're looking straight at you, and they look away immediately? You've never experienced that?'

'Yes, but...'

'Yes, but. That's your sixth sense. That's it working.'

'It's just coincidence. You happen to lock eyes, feel a bit awks and then you look away.'

'But when it happens you're not looking around the room at different people. Something is guiding you straight to the person who is staring at you.'

Kemi had conceded to Billy that this had in fact happened to her on many occasions, and that she had never before thought seriously about the phenomenon. But for all the sense that it was not entirely logical, the lesson had been learned. Stored away.

And now she was using it. She positioned herself in the train on the little perch by the door that connected to the next carriage. The door you weren't supposed to use unless there was an emergency (the only exception seeming to be people who would use it to go through the train asking for cash from embarrassed passengers). They had just left Bond Street, and she had flicked a momentary glance through the smudgy glass to confirm that Patel was still in his seat. She then resumed her own natural pose, back towards him, staring at her phone. She wasn't really looking at anything on there, but it was what you did on the Tube.

It was only in the immediate seconds afterwards that she realised what she had done: involuntarily, guided by that sixth sense that she had dismissed a few months earlier, she glanced up again through the glass partition. Not to look at Patel, but to lock eyes with another man, whose gaze dropped downwards immediately. Tall and angular, with a body like a pair of compasses, it was the man who had held people up as he struggled with the ticket barrier. His wrist was looped over the handrail as he stood by the doors that Patel would need to use to get off the train. His body was completely motionless, as if he had been ordered not to move on pain of being shot. No phone, no evening newspaper or diverting magazine. No headphones. No attempt at a cover story.

Is this just a guy on the Jubilee Line from Westminster?

Hundreds, maybe thousands of those, particularly in the late afternoon. But his trouble getting through the barrier showed that he was not a Londoner. Or had that been a deliberate ploy to put a bit of distance between him and Kamran? Kemi knew that her one job was to make sure Kamran was headed home. But she reckoned she had now found someone whose job was to follow Kamran.

Second sighting around the target – that's a hit.

And now he seemed to have spotted her and she needed to do something about that. As the train pulled into Baker Street, a large number of passengers were waiting patiently to get onto the train as a similar number poured out onto the platform. Kemi joined this exodus, heading briskly down the platform. She passed the carriage containing Patel and Tall Man, who appeared to have clocked her departure, but she was quickly enveloped in the crush on the platform. Once she was level with the end of the next carriage, she stepped back into the train just as its doors were closing, struggling for space and assuming the classic London commuter pose: her nose thrust into a stranger's shoulder, her arms unable to move. The carriage and platform were thick with people and she was confident that she had not been seen getting back on.

She now had four stops on the line – maybe ten minutes left – to figure out what to do. Tall Man, standing within a few metres of Patel, did not appear to be very interested in subtlety. Perhaps he had an even lower opinion of the professor's observation skills than Kemi had. When the wi-fi connected in the next station she fired off an encrypted Signal message to Sarah.

> *Patel has a tail. Not someone I recognise.*

She waited a few seconds for the ticks to show that the message had been read. A reply appeared almost immediately.

> *OK. Keep a close eye. Let's see what happens at WH.*

The train had emerged from the tunnels and was now in the open air under a summer evening sky, minutes from West Hampstead station. The crowd had thinned out a little and Kemi had been able to get a view through to the next carriage, confirming that both of her targets were still there. As she felt the train slowing, she noticed Patel getting out of his seat and moving to the door, where he stood, awkwardly close to Tall Man.

Kemi rang Sarah. No time for messaging.

'They're both getting off at West.' Even as she said this, the doors were bleeping and Tall Man shifted round to let himself off, followed by Patel. From her carriage, Kemi joined the flow of passengers onto the crowded platform, keeping her back half-turned, hoping this and the rush hour would obscure any view of her.

'You'll have to get rid of him, then. I need Kamran on his own.'

Even the usually composed Kemi was alarmed at this prospect, asking in an urgent whisper, 'Get rid of him? What, like *end him*?'

'That seems a bit drastic,' deadpanned Sarah. 'Just give him a reason not to be there. He won't use a gun in a busy station.' The phone went dead. Kemi said 'fuck' a few times under her breath and began weaving her way down the platform, her pulse now racing. The back of Tall Man's head was visible through the crowd, and Kemi manoeuvred so she was within a few metres of him. She could also see Patel's shabby suit a few steps further ahead.

Get rid of him. What the hell was she supposed to do in a station rammed with commuters, CCTV everywhere? She suddenly felt very hot. Was her pounding heartbeat and shallow breathing obvious? Nobody seemed remotely interested. The crowd was sweeping up the stairs like a single organism. There was a ticket barrier and a one-minute walk to the connecting overground train.

Tall Man was fumbling for his wallet as he approached the barrier. *You have to do something in the next few seconds.*

Kemi took a deep breath.

Thanks to her ethnicity and a twang of multicultural London in her speech, the middle-class white people whom Kemi encountered in her working life tended to assume that she had grown up in grinding poverty and in a rough neighbourhood. Sometimes, in more excruciating moments, she had been asked about her knowledge of 'street' culture by mildly titillated men who assumed she had a detailed understanding of London's drugs trade. In fact, her parents, who were both qualified accountants originally from Lagos, had run a small but profitable audit firm in Catford, looking after local businesses and people's tax returns. They had brought up their three daughters in a pleasant house not far from the South Circular and inculcated in them the values of hard work, education and spending plenty of time at church. Kemi, their eldest, was a particular source of pride: straight A's in all her exams, first-class Cambridge degree, followed by a prize for her master's thesis. A job in the civil service had followed soon after.

So, whatever her well-meaning bosses might have thought, Kemi had not had a tough childhood of petty criminality, drugs and unsuitable boyfriends. But she had grown up in south London. A boy in her year at her large secondary school – not someone she had been close to – had been a low-level dealer until he was stabbed, bleeding out in an unlovely dog-walkers' park near Loughborough Junction. Kemi had witnessed plenty of shoplifts, wallet snatches, phone grabs. This was the reality of an ordinary, teenage London life.

Kamran Patel calmly pointed his phone at the card reader and passed through the ticket barrier like the regular London commuter that he was. Tall Man was behind him, shuffling inefficiently through his wallet, trying to find the same card that he had used to enter the Tube at Westminster. Kemi positioned herself in front of the neighbouring barrier, to the left of Tall Man, hanging back. She flicked her phone at the card reader, ensuring the gate in front of her was open. Then, a pause as she stuffed her phone back into her coat pocket. *Count to three.* It seemed like an eternity.

'Come on, sweetheart!' called out a man's voice behind her, cockney geezer accent.

Tall Man had found the right card and was jabbing it at the contactless reader, his wallet in his left hand. The gates in front of him swung open. Kemi made a sudden swiping movement. She raced through the gap, sprinting out of the station onto the busy pavement outside. Tall Man's wallet was in her hand.

There was an angry shout. 'Hey! Stop!'

Sounds American. Didn't expect that.

West End Lane was busy with traffic, but she took a chance and shot through a gap between a white van and a double-decker bus, which honked angrily at her apparent indifference to being run over. Kemi had some advantages: youth, adrenaline

132

and having once been a reasonably promising school athlete. Her disadvantage was that she was wearing wedge loafers that kept flopping off her heels as she ran. She wondered about stopping to take them off.

There isn't time.

She chanced a look over her shoulder and could see Tall Man in pursuit on the other side of the road, his long legs scissoring down the pavement. Kemi could feel her sprint turning, inevitably, into a jog. As a committed south Londoner, she had always felt rather scornful about places like West Hampstead, but as she whizzed past sushi bars, gourmet burger outlets and a charming early twentieth-century fire station that had yet to be transformed into executive apartments, she had to admit it seemed quite nice. Her lungs now heaving, she could see potential salvation up ahead. The number 139, a proper red double-decker, destination Golders Green, was at a bus stop, preparing to pull back into the traffic. With one hand raised to persuade its driver to give her a chance, she raced towards the closing doors. With her other hand she lobbed the wallet in the direction of Tall Man, the square of brown leather spinning up into the air. Whether by luck or design, on its descent it caught the breeze so that its contents – a large quantity of receipts, an assortment of currencies and some dog-eared business cards – fluttered out into the road. Tall Man caught the wallet cleanly. But he allowed himself to be distracted by the contents that were now scudding in the wind along the pavement. Some well-meaning passers-by were helping retrieve the wayward items, huffing about crime in London as they did so.

On the bus, the driver gave Kemi a momentary stare as she swiped her fare and moved down into the interior. Had he just witnessed an attempted theft? *Best not to get involved*, he thought, and released the clutch.

Kemi flopped into a seat in huge relief. In a sweaty palm that shook slightly, she was holding a small plastic card that shone in the evening light, from which Tall Man's face stared out at her, peevishly. It was a US driver's licence, from Virginia, issued in the name of Leigh Delamere III.

CIA? thought Kemi.

Chapter 15

Harpenden

August 2022

Oblivious to the excitement that had been unfolding around him, Kamran Patel had joined the overground train for the short run to Harpenden station. He had the Test match commentary running in his ear buds and was settling into a Virat Kohli innings at the Kensington Oval that might prove to be a classic. As he climbed off the train and walked across the large car park, threading his way through the SUVs, he was barely aware of the small slice of Hertfordshire in front of him. His mind's eye was firmly located in Barbados, visualising Kohli as he played an inside-out, sending the ball for six.

Both Harpenden's critics and its advocates agreed that it was 'leafy'. Indeed, there wasn't a huge amount you could say about this small, wealthy commuter town, but that it was definitely leafy. This factor, combined with Kohli's heroics in Bridgetown, was helpful to Sarah. Part-concealed by an unkempt hedge and pretending to make a phone call, she had watched him cross the car park. As Kamran passed by, oblivious to his surroundings, she allowed a few other pedestrians to head in the same direction before starting her follow. Initially, she kept herself a little way behind, as the pavement was narrow and people were forced fairly close together. Sarah was reasonably sure Kemi had shaken off the only tail, but she needed to be certain.

As the road broadened and the walkers found their space, she watched as possible surveillants turned down side streets or headed in other directions. Once she was comfortable that Tall Man had no backup she took her opportunity. Patel was about fifty metres ahead of her now, so she quickened her pace, whilst trying not to look like she was jogging. She realised with a burst of frustration that she was wearing the wrong shoes; her stiff leather pumps with a bit of a heel on them were starting to click on the pavements as she sped up. *Simon wouldn't have got that wrong*, she thought, biting her lip.

The shoes added a layer of challenge to what Sarah was trying to do. She had reached a point where she was only a couple of paces behind Kamran's right shoulder, at which point she said in a steady voice, with a tone that tried to channel simple pleasure at running into an old friend: 'Hello, Kamran.'

The idea had been to sound not in any way threatening. In the event, she probably didn't sound at all. Kamran was continuing to walk, completely oblivious. He could only hear the mellifluous tones of the West Indies cricket commentary coming through his AirPods. Sarah wondered about raising her voice, but wasn't sure she could do so without drawing undue attention. Instead, she reached forwards and touched his arm lightly.

Kamran reacted as if hit by an electric shock, jerking his arm away and whipping round. On seeing Sarah, his eyebrows shot upwards and he let out a little shriek of alarm. A man walking past with a small child in tow looked up nervously and moved to cross to the other side of the road.

'Hello, Kamran,' tried Sarah again. His face remained a gaping hole of surprise.

'Sarah?' He said this at high volume because he was speaking over the sound in his ears. A passing jogger slowed and looked round, intrigued why this man was speaking so loudly. Sarah tapped at her ears in the hope that Kamran would realise what he was doing and then moved to be very close to him, hoping that her proximity might quieten him down.

'Lovely to see you! Sorry, didn't mean to shock you,' she said at a volume that might satisfy intrigued passers-by.

Kamran removed the little white blobs from his ears. He now spoke in an outraged hiss. 'What on earth are you doing here?'

'Harpenden is lovely, isn't it?' She grinned. 'It's so... *leafy*.' She put a hand lightly on his back to propel him forwards.

Kamran had resumed walking, his voice now quiet but shaking with anger. 'You're not here to talk about... about *leafiness*... I wonder, perhaps I should be calling the police? This is *harassment*.'

'It really isn't, Kamran. We happen to be walking down the same street on the same day, in this charmingly, er, leafy neighbourhood. Which is a lovely coincidence, because I wanted to discuss something with you.'

'Then you can come to my office,' he replied with exaggerated stiffness. 'Make an appointment with Sam, in the usual way.'

'Yes, I could do that, but given what I want to talk about, I'm pretty sure you wouldn't want me to do this in your office.'

Kamran frowned and shook his head. 'Well, if you think I am about to invite you into my home, you are very much mistaken.'

'Nope, not your home. Not much better than your office, I'd say. Let's just go for a nice evening walk.'

Kamran sighed. Perhaps he could get the Kohli innings on catch-up? 'Please get to the point. This is all most irregular, but if you insist then let's get it out of the way.'

They had passed through the main part of the town and the pavement was now quieter. Kamran had stopped walking again, perhaps unsure if they were going to continue. Behind him on a lamp post someone had put up a missing cat poster. It was dated months ago, the cat's sad face staring out hopefully.

'There's a park down here, I think,' said Sarah disingenuously. She had recced it thoroughly earlier in the afternoon.

'It's a *nature reserve*.'

Strictly speaking, Kamran was correct. The unkempt land at the end of Station Road came with a signboard explaining that hedgehogs and grasshoppers had been spotted in the vicinity. The two of them followed a path that wound between scrubby blackthorn trees. Sarah and Kamran saw neither grasshopper nor hedgehog, although there were a few of those little bags with dog poo in. Sarah could feel the dampness of the ground through her shoes.

'I think you know what I want to talk about. The Ukraine corruption story. All over the news.'

'The CRITON material has been fully corroborated. I can imagine that is very annoying for you.'

Sarah paused, searching for the right words. 'Here's the issue, Kamran: you came up with some potentially interesting material. You declined to share any background, sourcing, chain of custody, that sort of thing. Your prerogative, of course, but it doesn't help to validate it.'

'But now it *has* been validated,' he said, triumphantly, his wide mouth stretched into a grin, white teeth gleaming.

'So you say. But I just want to go back a little. You insisted on *very* tight handling procedures for CRITON. We all sat in the room with poor Sam Bonham looking over us. Utmost secrecy. Again, your call. Source protection, close-hold. I get it.'

'I did exactly what you would have done in the circumstances.'

'Well, that's the point, isn't it. "Exactly"? Did you do *exactly* what I would have done? Or did you do an *impression* of what I would have done? Because this super-secret corruption report now seems to be all over the global media. Feeding an argument that Ukraine is corrupt and doesn't deserve our support.'

They walked in silence. Sarah didn't fill it. Kamran gave in to the awkwardness.

'As our material showed, a range of people were involved. Something as significant as this was always going to get out, sooner or later. Of course, even *you* wouldn't go so far as to claim I leaked it.'

'Even I wouldn't go that far,' agreed Sarah. 'I know *you* didn't leak it because I've looked into where this story originated.'

'You have? And, er, what does looking into it tell you?'

'That it's a classic Russian disinfo campaign. Story originates on a Telegram channel used to surface pro-Kremlin stuff. Then it gets magnified by inauthentic social media networks controlled by your friends in Moscow.'

'My friends in Moscow? What's that supposed to mean?'

She ignored the question. 'The bots get the story to a certain level and then it gets breakout – picked up by a few hard-right voices here and there. And before you know it, it's on the bloody *Daily Mail* website… At which point the BBC feels it has to run the story. That's how they do it.'

'Just supposing I accept that this is what happened – which I don't, by the way – what makes you think it has anything to do with me?' Kamran's voice had a triumphant tone to it.

'Twenty-ninth of July. Does that date mean anything to you?'

'Not really.'

'It was on the twenty-ninth that you announced the arrival of the CRITON material. Olivia and I came to your office.'

'Yes, you came running when I had something that disturbed your preconceived view of events. We didn't sit on anything – it was the same day my man in Kyiv had received the dossier.'

'Thanks for confirming that. On exactly the same day, these allegations first appeared on a pro-Kremlin Telegram channel. So, it's an *interesting* coincidence, isn't it?'

Sarah had stopped walking and turned towards Kamran. The grin was still fixed to his face, but was there a hint of discomfort around its edges?

'It's a coincidence, yes, but I don't find it very interesting.'

'You don't find it interesting that *on the very day* the Kremlin launches a disinformation campaign to undermine international support for Ukraine, you, through means you haven't chosen to share with anyone, become the happy recipient of a so-called dossier that contains identical allegations? That isn't interesting? Remarkably incurious.'

They had emerged from a spinney onto a grassy area. A large, friendly Labrador bounded in their direction, following a ball that was bouncing erratically. Kamran flinched, clearly scared of dogs, even overweight Labradors. Sarah took a small step back and did something with her hand. Whether guided by Sarah, or just from a lucky break, the dog jumped up at Kamran, who threw his hands up in alarm. The dog responded to this exciting development by jumping up, trying to get sloppy jaws around Kamran's arms. For the second time in a few minutes, he let out another shriek.

'Get it off me!' he cried, staring at Sarah in horror.

'Oh, he seems *soppy*!' she said, smiling.

'*Please* help,' he gurgled, his arms flailing.

Calmly, Sarah reached out and caught hold of the dog's collar, pulling him to a sitting position and making a fuss of him as she did so. She picked up the ball and chucked it across the grass in the direction of the likely owner, sending the dog careering after it.

'Don't you like dogs?' she asked sweetly.

Kamran's hands were shaking, so he folded his arms, attempting to conceal it.

'We were talking about coincidences, Kamran,' Sarah continued, as if nothing had happened.

'*You* were talking about coincidences. Not me.' He had regained a little composure. 'If you have proof of something, you can no doubt talk to some of your many friends in the deep state. But if all you've got is this, you are really going nowhere.'

Sarah surprised herself by letting this statement annoy her. 'The real issue here is what the hell you think you're doing. Corruption in Ukraine? Sure, they have corruption. But what are you doing about corruption in Russia? Or the corrupt billions looted from Russia that have flooded through this country? If you have an anti-corruption agenda, what are you doing about that stuff?'

'If Russia steals money from its people, that isn't my imme-diate problem. If Russians steal money from their people and invest that money in this country, it might be to our benefit. Of course, I am in no way supporting kleptocracy,' he added with a tone of mocking piety. 'I'm just pointing out that it might not be a terrible thing for Britain. As house prices in Mayfair seem to demonstrate.'

'Seriously?'

'Whereas,' Kamran continued, ignoring Sarah's incredulity, 'when Ukraine steals money, that's *our* money. We gave it to them. Money that could have been spent on *our* defence, *our* military, *our* national security. Hospitals. Schools. You name it. Our money. How dare they steal it?'

Sarah took a breath, trying to fight her desire to whistle the dog back or just to kick Kamran in the bollocks. 'Right. But, just putting that stuff aside, what the hell are *you* trying to achieve. You? Professor Kamran Patel? I know what *I* think about your relationship with Russia. I know about the meetings in Europe. Aachen. With the St Kitts people. You and Rory and Tom Harkness. Others, too, no doubt. Okay, so Rory is a billionaire – who knows what he's making from all this? Maybe it's just about money for him. You, though? You're not in this for the money. What are you hoping for here? Not what you believed twenty years ago. What do you want *now*? In 2022? Russia's army is humiliated, its assault on Kyiv failed, its kit has turned out to be crap. Sweden and Finland are joining NATO. What's in this for you?'

'I don't know what you're talking about,' said Kamran lamely. The sun was low in the sky and there was a chill on the breeze. He seemed to shiver slightly.

'Look, I get it. You and your Oxford friends have managed to get away with it so far. You've managed to outmanoeuvre the British state, so you feel protected. But that doesn't force *you* to carry on. You can say, "Okay, we've crossed a line here. Russia is a gangster state and not even any good at being a gangster, I'm out." You could say that. I still don't understand why you, Kamran, someone as smart as you, is sticking with this nonsense.'

He shook his head and frowned as if nothing Sarah said made any sense to him.

She ploughed on. 'You're not going to shift British policy on Ukraine. Every bloody village in this country is flying their flag now. It's become the most mainstream thing in British politics. I just don't understand what you're trying to do.'

Kamran broke into a smile. He shoved his hands into his pockets and, for the first time that evening, looked relaxed.

'I'm pretty surprised at you, Sarah... You're much more cosmopolitan than I am, and yet you go on and on about Britain. Do you actually think Britain is the issue here? Is Britain on its own going to keep Ukraine afloat? Do you even think what we do matters?'

'Well, obviously the main show in town is the Americans,' said Sarah. And at that moment she felt furious that she hadn't seen the most obvious thing of all. 'Ohh... The Americans. The MAGA people. You're trying to convince *them* the Ukrainians are corrupt. And they all love Putin anyway... *Fuck!* How did I miss that?'

'You seem to be talking to yourself, Sarah. I'm not admitting anything.'

'But seriously, I know these people say crazy things. But America isn't actually going to let Russia win a major war in Europe.'

Kamran was squinting against a low sun, holding up a hand to shade his eyes. 'Sarah, I won't patronise you. You know a lot about Russia, so you will know their willingness to suffer. To play the long game. To learn from their mistakes. You know that bit of it. But I think you don't know America. It's changing a lot quicker than you think. They're looking for a reason to walk away from Europe. You've got all these countries in Europe that are the richest in the world, and they still think it's America's job to defend them. And America has enough on its hands with China, but the Europeans still won't step up to protect themselves. Even when there's a huge war in Europe, they just won't spend money on their own defence.'

'That's all changing.'

'Is it really? Really actually? Listen, the countries of Europe have economies many times the size of Russia's. They have more people, they already spend much more on defence, they have better tech. If Europe wants to confront and dominate Russia, it should do so with its own resources. Why should it be America's responsibility? The issue here is that Europe isn't prepared to take on Russia. You mention Germany's *Zeitenwende*, but it's all talk. Their military is hopeless. So why should it be America's job? Let Europe sort itself out. And that includes Russia being given the right to secure its own borders in Europe without being threatened.'

'So, you're talking about a complete realignment of America's alliances,' said Sarah, shaking her head.

'Not me. That's what *they* say. America First.'

'Well, that sounds like an admission that this Ukraine corruption story is a Russian disinfo op, targeting America. That's what you're saying, isn't it?'

'No, Sarah. I'm telling you Russia has strategic patience and America is running out of patience.' He let that thought hang in the air for a few seconds. 'And now, if you'll forgive me, I want to go home and watch the cricket. I would say we should do this more often… But we really shouldn't.' He turned away, his hands fumbling in his jacket pocket for his AirPods, which he placed back in his ears.

Sarah opened her mouth to say something. But she realised that she had nothing to say. But Kamran hadn't finished. He turned back and offered a parting shot.

'One more thing: the Russians aren't losing the war. They're just fighting it in their way. Their willingness to suffer is greater than any other country on earth. If you don't believe me, take a look at Bakhmut.'

Chapter 16

Kyiv

August 2022

'Bakhmut. It's all about Bakhmut. They've made this little town the absolute centre of their fight.' Simon was sitting in a windowless meeting room in a building that had been hard to find and harder to enter, listening to a Ukrainian military assessment of the situation in the Donbas.

Since his unexpected meeting with Jonty Vosper, Simon's depressed sense of aimlessness had lifted. He felt less paranoid about the possibility that the Ukrainian authorities might choose to arrest him at some point for being a fake journalist with an alias passport. He had even allowed himself to emerge from his garret with slightly lower feelings of paranoia, spending some amusing evenings at the Havana Café, getting drunk with the war correspondents and security types. Simon had also started to believe that he might one day be able to return to the UK. The only problem was that, between where he was now and that possible future, lay the small matter of recruiting a notorious assassin at the front line of a terrifying war zone. He had a rising feeling that he was being propelled towards an intimidating destination by forces he could not control. That it was no longer an idea inside his head, but something in the real world that other people expected him to act upon.

Jonty had given him a contact inside the HUR, Ukraine's military intelligence directorate. 'Contact' was putting it strongly. Simon only had a mobile number with which he'd exchanged Telegram messages. The person at the other end did not offer a name and employed a curt epistolary style. After the briefest of pleasantries, Simon was told to turn up at an anonymous building far from the centre of Kyiv at a given time. He had methodically figured out his destination, done his dry-cleaning, changing buses twice and walking several blocks to find an unnamed building behind high walls that could have been a small apartment block. The presence of an armed guard in military uniform confirmed to Simon that he was in the right place. But said guard had waved him away with a frown and a waggle of his AK-47 that had not been encouraging. Simon had retreated around the corner and then exchanged a few more messages with his mysterious contact. Enjoined to try again with the guard, this time he was – very grudgingly – waved into a screening area where the contents of his pockets and his Italian passport were subjected to rigorous examination.

He waited and a young woman in a khaki T-shirt and military trousers appeared at the doorway. Some sort of assistant? She was skinny and the combat pants hung on her small frame like baggy pantaloons. She introduced herself as 'Yelizaveta, call me Liz' and had a confident way of looking straight at him with her blue eyes. She led him down a warren of corridors, Simon assumed, to his meeting with the mysterious contact.

'So, you are a friend of Sarah? Friend of mine, then,' she said once they were inside a boxy little office, prising open her laptop. 'How can I help?'

So, Liz *was* the contact. And she knew Sarah, not Jonty. Simon did not do a very good job of hiding his surprise. Liz seemed to give a little smirk of triumph at his Gen-X prejudice.

'You know Sarah, too?' he asked.

She nodded, as if it was obvious. In a way it was: Sarah had worked in Ukraine over the years, especially since Russia's 2014 invasion. She was bound to have contacts all over its intelligence services.

'She was the supervisor for my master's. At Oxford,' said Liz. Simon noticed she spoke almost accentless English. His underestimation continued.

'Right. Great. Um… I… Well, Sarah and I and some others… We've got some intel to share about a Chechen assassin believed to be operating in Ukraine. I suspect in the Donbas.'

'We call it the JFO zone,' she replied curtly, using the Ukrainian military designation. 'You *suspect* he's in the JFO?' she deadpanned. 'What does that mean?'

'It means I had it from a good source that he's here in Ukraine, and the Donbas seems the most likely spot.'

'Right. It's a fairly big area.' Liz did not sound particularly impressed.

Simon ploughed on. 'The thing that might be of interest to you is this: I think it's *possible* – I won't put it any stronger than that – possible he might be induced to co-operate. He could be a useful asset for you guys: inside the Kadyrovite cells operating in the east. And we care because he knows some important things about Russian operations in the UK.'

'But you and Sarah and Lord Jonty Vosper aren't our official liaison channel with the Brits, are you?'

This had seemed to be going too well until this point.

'This, er… sits outside the usual structures,' said Simon, not sure if he was making any sense. 'I think the main point is that I will share now what I have with you about this guy and it might be useful. To you. He's not just part of the cannon fodder. He's someone the GRU uses for targeted assassinations.'

Liz nodded. It wasn't clear whether she believed anything Simon had said, but perhaps that wasn't important. 'How much do you know about the situation in the Donbas?'

Simon admitted he did not know much.

'Yeah, okay,' she said, tilting her laptop's touchscreen and scrolling through a document with her finger, pausing with a map of the Donbas, shaded with areas of Ukrainian control and Russian advances. 'Here's where we're at: when the Russians pulled out of Kyiv they put all their efforts down here in the Donbas. At first, I think they were hoping they could surround the Ukrainian forces, take thousands of our guys prisoner and the whole region with it. Didn't happen. Instead, their ambitions got smaller and smaller, and a few weeks ago they launched their attack here.' She was tapping a fingernail on the map at what looked like some road junctions. 'It really isn't an obvious strategic target.' There was something in the way she spoke that suggested an ability to see humour, even in the darkness of what Ukraine was going through. She was explaining how the Russians were throwing everything at Bakhmut.

'But it's pointless, right?' he asked. 'The Russians take Bakhmut and it doesn't get them anywhere in particular. I mean, what's Bakhmut even known for?'

'Sparkling wine,' she answered. Simon laughed at her quirky Ukrainian humour. 'No, I am serious,' she continued. 'They don't grow the grapes, but in the old mines there's a famous winery.'

'Even the Russians can't be trying to seize Bakhmut for that.'

'This is true.' She flashed him a glimmer of a deadpan smile. 'I think they see the town as the next place on the road to Kramatorsk. And the rest of the Donbas. In that sense, it's kinda important.'

'But they're not making much progress.'

'Not yet, but they've decided to throw a lot at it: regular army, special forces, Wagner mercenaries. And Chechens. Units that report direct to Ramzan Kadyrov.'

'Are the Chechens a major force?' asked Simon.

'Not in number. But they're brutal. Even by the standards of Russia at war. Basically it's a terror network: they'll do things the regular Russian army won't. That's their, how you say, USP.' She looked at Simon, checking her English, which was, of course, perfect. He nodded encouragingly. 'Kadyrov keeps claiming he's here in the fight, too, but that looks like bullshit. We're pretty sure he's tucked away safely back in Grozny.' Liz paused, pushing her hair back behind one ear, wanting to be sure Simon was following. She needn't have worried. Simon found there was something comforting about being in an intel briefing. This was a setting he was familiar with, even if he had no real idea exactly who he was dealing with.

'It's all about his social media profile,' said Simon, grimly aware of Ramzan Kadyrov, who ruled Chechnya with an iron fist on behalf of Russia's President. A preening princeling, constantly posting delusional machismo online; this included pictures of him supposedly in combat in Ukraine, bristling with weapons and tactical gear that looked brand new. The general consensus was that he had been nowhere near the war zone.

Liz continued: 'There's a Kadyrovite group operating around Bakhmut at the moment. They're doing things you'd expect: torture, beheadings, killing POWs, civilians.' Simon had a flash-back to an awful image of a severed head jammed onto a metal fence. 'They go out in small raiding parties, cross the front line and cause havoc. They don't usually hit anything strategic – you know, like sabotage or something. They just try for soft targets. Ukrainian civilians or soldiers. Kill a few on the spot, leave the bodies fucked up for everyone to see. And take a few back alive for exploitation. Interrogation. One or two survive and get sent back to spread the word.'

Simon decided to risk a punt. 'One of the things I've picked up is that they might be operating a torture centre in the sanatorium at Pryvillya.'

Liz leant forwards. 'What do you know about Pryvillya?'

Simon knew not very much. But he didn't want to admit that. 'Of course, it's hard to get firm details of that sort of thing,' he said, trying to sound as if he was across a lot more intelligence than was actually the case. 'But I'm thinking this is where Chovka might fit in.'

Liz had sat upright at the mention of the name. 'Chovka? That's your target?'

'Yes. Chovka Buchayev. He was in Moldova earlier in the year and then in Prague. In both cases carrying out assassinations for Moscow.' Simon reached into his pocket and pulled out a folded piece of paper. It had been scrutinised by the guard, but he had not been prevented from bringing it into the building. He unfolded it on the table in front of Liz, the photo staring out impassively. 'This is him. We have reporting from a Russian source that he's currently active in Ukraine.'

Liz had taken hold of the paper and was nodding. She placed the page back down on the table and gave Simon an appraising look. For the first time in the meeting she appeared to be impressed. And pleased, as if this information was helping to piece together a complex puzzle.

'This is the detail of an alias passport he was using,' said Simon, pointing to some written notes on the photograph. Liz placed her finger on the paper, leaning down to read the details. 'In Moldova he went by the alias Tahir Akhmedov. But we think Chovka is a real name, or at least the name he uses here.'

'I think this Chovka is someone we know about already,' said Liz.

'Really?'

Liz smiled winningly. 'With Sarah, things tend not to be coincidences, do they?'

Chapter 17

Geneva

August 2022

Kemi Williams sat on the terrace outside the Mandarin Oriental Hotel, nursing a cappuccino and scanning the pavement from behind dark glasses. On the other side of the road that flanked the hotel was the River Rhône, beginning its long journey from Lake Geneva to the Mediterranean. Even at this stage of its meanderings it was already wide and deep, its waters a deep green that looked strangely delicious.

Kemi had a photo of Patrice Devouassoux on her phone, which she had looked at several times as she waited for him to walk down the street. Experience had taught her that people's LinkedIn profile photos didn't always offer a very clear guide to how they would appear in real life, particularly when they were attending a job interview. She had already had several false alarms. Geneva had an ample supply of serious-looking young men who could have been Patrice.

He had been told to ask in the lobby for Kemi Adeoye from the family office of the von Rosens, a dynasty of reclusive Swedish industrialists. It was a quick cover identity that Kemi and Sarah had thrown together; it was good enough for a job interview but wouldn't have stood up to much hostile scrutiny. Kemi, not used to operating under alias, had picked her mother's surname in the hope that she would find it easier to remember. Nervously, she kept repeating her assumed identity under her breath so that she could introduce herself correctly to Patrice when he arrived. In the event that Patrice were to become curious about these eremitic Swedes, Sarah could play the role of the backstop. She did in fact have Swedish cousins called von Rosen, who ran a very private family business. Kemi had printed a business card with the real address in Stockholm of the Von-Rosen-AB head office and a Swedish phone number that redirected to Sarah's mobile. It was a world Sarah knew enough about from her cousins to be able to take a phone call and make a convincing response.

As Kemi waited she scrolled the international news. The story of corruption in the R3 Fund had become a global talking point. A former US President, whose sympathies with Russia were widely known, had been posting about it obsessively on a far-right social media platform. His most recent missive, whilst barely literate, had a strange eloquence:

> After my perfect handling of UKRAINE, who's crooked politicians have been stealing from our beautiful country for years, the fake news media tried to make a witch-hunt against me. Despite the constant negative press covfefe its clear the American people do not want there people to get involved in a civil war in east Europe!

What mattered was not the quality of the prose, but the hundreds of millions who read the post, the interviews on cable news, the acolytes and sycophants who were now demanding an inquiry into the R3 Fund. And a superficially more intelligent version of this argument had started to surface: that Ukraine and Russia had long-standing historic grievances that were not the business of the American people. Particularly not if the Ukrainians were going to steal the aid that a generous America sent them.

Kemi's plan was to watch Patrice's arrival from the terrace, check to see if he had any sort of tail and then intercept him in the hotel lobby. When a Swiss banker meets an investment manager working in Stockholm, one thing you can be sure of is that the meeting will start exactly on time. Down to the second. With the clock on her phone reading 10:55, she knew he would be appearing at any moment. Kemi felt the irritability of rising tension. Had she thought of everything? Perhaps he was already in the hotel and she had missed his arrival? She stood up and walked through the coffee shop into the lobby. No sign.

This being an expensive hotel, the staff were over-attentive. A man from the concierge desk asked if he could help 'in any way'. Kemi had no desire to bring any attention to herself or her upcoming meeting, so she retreated back towards her outside table, waving away the offers of assistance. As she re-entered the coffee shop she noticed a lone young woman sitting very still at a small table, staring at her phone, an overnight bag on the floor beside her feet. She was pretty with long blonde hair, but also looked very tired. Even gaunt. Kemi's immediate thought was that she must be Ukrainian. Then she put the thought out of her mind. *She could be from anywhere. Concentrate on your meeting.*

As she sat back down at her table on the terrace, Sarah resumed her scan of the approaches to the hotel. 10:57. *Surely he must be coming now?* And then she saw something, approaching along the wide pavement that bordered the river. At first it was more the clothing that identified him. Dark navy suit, pale blue shirt, elegant knitted silk tie. More formal than was usual for someone of his age. And the gait: walking quickly, as if, with just three minutes to spare, his reputation for Swiss banker punctuality was at risk. A young man on his way to an important meeting. He was now less than fifty metres down from the hotel entrance, close enough that Sarah could see the sun glistening on his carefully styled hair. He turned diagonally to cross the road, pausing as a large dark Mercedes swept past.

Kemi was now focused on the pedestrians on the pavement behind Patrice. It was not busy, but there were several possibles. A lot of people in Geneva had a surveillant look to them – sombre middle-aged men with a *mind-your-own-business* frown. But none of those seemed to be taking the remotest interest in this young man heading for the Mandarin Oriental. No heads turned as he moved to cross the road. Nobody pulled out a phone to make a call. The flow of people walking on the pavement continued unabated.

He's clean, thought Kemi, the tension in her chest dissipating slightly.

Patrice stepped into the road, and then paused again. The throaty growl of a speeding motorbike caught Kemi's attention. Patrice waited and the sound came closer. Kemi could see the bike, with a passenger clinging on behind the driver, moving very fast. Both of them had full-face helmets, black visors. Then it appeared to be braking sharply, perhaps to let Patrice cross. But he was standing, waiting for them to pass. As the bike passed between Kemi and Patrice, blocking her view of him, there was a popping sound. The exhaust backfiring from the deceleration? Kemi's attention was diverted by the noise, and her eyes followed the roar as the throttle opened up again and the bike sped onwards, weaving around traffic and out of view down the road. She blinked and turned her attention back to Patrice.

He had disappeared.

She shook her head involuntarily at this impossibility, raising herself higher in the chair to get a better look. He was lying in the road with a bloody hole in his forehead and another dark red stain spreading across his sky-blue shirt front.

Her hand flew to her mouth, a physical action to stop herself from screaming. For a second that felt like a full minute, she wondered if nobody else had seen what had happened. And then there was a sound which began as a low wail and turned into a high-pitched shriek. This came from an elegant *grande dame* sitting at a neighbouring table on the *terrasse*. She pointed frantically and a waiter rushed across the road, waving his arms at the oncoming traffic. A car skidded to a halt and the driver stepped out, furiously.

'*Merde, qu'est ce qu'il y a?*' he growled. But he had barely uttered these words when he saw the waiter, now crouching down, and Patrice's body. The waiter had his hand under the bloody mess of the skull. The screaming had turned into a torrent of panicky words. Another guest who had been sitting at the outside tables raced across the road where a small crowd was now forming, several of the passing pedestrians joining. There was more shouting now, and Kemi heard the words '*pompiers*' and '*médecin*'. A solicitous man in a suit with a little gold name badge that identified him as a hotel manager rushed out of the hotel's main entrance, wringing his hands nervously. The Mandarin Oriental Genève did not appreciate murders on its doorstep. Very untidy.

Kemi stood up from the table, feeling furious with herself. Someone must have been watching for Patrice's arrival, ready to tip off the motorbike crew, and she had failed to notice. All her preparations for being in Geneva – her laboriously constructed cover story, her research into Patrice, her mugging up on Swedish industry – all of that was to no end. And a young man had ended up with a hole in his head. What was she doing, playing at spy operations, when she had no real experience? She'd only worked in close proximity with one real spy, and not for the first time she found herself wishing that Simon had been there. He had years of experience. She was just an amateur.

Kemi was now standing at the edge of the crowd, craning to get a view of the body. She wondered whether she should step in to help. But she had no particular knowledge of first aid. Anyway, he looked like he was far beyond that. For a hopeless moment she wondered whether the body was someone else. She pulled out her phone and opened the LinkedIn profile picture. The top half of his head was a mess but the jawline and mouth, handsome and well formed, were right. Undeniably Patrice Devouassoux.

Her thoughts started to catch up with her. Whoever had known that he was coming for the meeting would probably know what she looked like. She turned and looked around, searching. The realisation hit her. *You need to get out of here.* She stormed back through the coffee shop, her eyes briefly locking with those of the young woman she had spotted earlier. It was almost as if she had been recognised. Was it someone she knew? A Ukrainian she'd met in her proper job, working for Olivia? The woman's face was florid with distress. Was this the face of an assassin's assistant? For a brief moment the young woman looked as if she was going to talk. But Kemi shook her head angrily and strode into the hotel lobby. There, a junior manager was handing out bottled water to distressed hotel clients. A free bottle of Evian washes away all trauma.

Kemi needed to think. To figure out her next steps. She had pulled her large sunglasses over her eyes in the manner of a mournful film star. She declined the generous offer of refreshment and said firmly that she would go for a little walk to 'get some fresh air'. Feeling desperate with frustration, she strode quickly out of the hotel and across the road. She walked along the broad pavement for a few metres to get some distance between her and the crowd around Patrice's body. And then she stopped, leaning her arms on the railing above the smooth green waters of the river.

She took a huge breath and then said, as loudly as she dared, '*Fuck!*'

Within a few seconds she was conscious of another person beside her. She turned and found herself looking at the rake-thin blonde woman from the coffee shop. Kemi looked around frantically. Surely they wouldn't try another hit now? What did this woman want?

'Is there a problem?' she asked in English. Angrily.

'No. No problem…' Then a gulp. 'Yes. There is a problem.' The accent was definitely Eastern European.

'Why have you followed me?'

The woman was flustered, red blotches on her face. She let out a small sigh, pulling her hair over one shoulder. She was shorter than Kemi and seemed younger, too. Her clothes were shabby, not in a chic way.

'Were you going to meet Patrice Devouassoux?' She mangled his surname but there was no mistaking who she was talking about.

Is there anyone in Geneva who didn't know about this fucking meeting? thought Kemi, ready to scream. She decided not to answer the question. But this didn't stop her interlocutor.

'You were waiting for him to arrive. I saw that. Then... Then someone killed him.' She stole an involuntary glance backwards and shuddered.

Kemi looked over the newcomer's shoulder. About thirty metres away, the crowd around Patrice's body had started to take a more structured shape. Someone was directing traffic around the body. A person in hotel uniform was walking out with what looked like a folded bed sheet. She thought she could hear the siren of an approaching ambulance. She looked back at this skinny blonde woman standing in front of her. Scared.

What do people agree to do when they're scared? Why assume she's Ukrainian?

Doing her best to sound calm, Kemi responded. 'You were the spotter, right? Where does that leave you now? Sacrificial lamb? Is that why you want to talk to me?'

The woman turned round and stared at the crowd around the body. The sheets had been laid over Patrice's body, covering his head. Red smudges had seeped through onto the white cotton. They could now see the flashing blue light of an approaching ambulance. She turned back to face Kemi. 'I don't know who did this,' she replied.

'Oh, really? And would you care to explain your excessive interest in what I am doing here?'

'Please listen to me. I had no idea this would happen.' Her lip was twitching as she said this and she was blinking away tears.

Kemi realised that she, too, was shaken. The blankness of Patrice's eyes as blood flowed out of the back of his head onto the tarmac was preying on her mind. 'I am walking in this direction,' she said, relenting very slightly. 'If you choose to walk with me I can't stop you.'

They followed the river towards the mouth of Lake Geneva, the water glistening in the hot sun. The pavement became busier again and Kemi felt the false reassurance of safety in numbers. The younger woman appeared not to want to say anything, instead making deep sighs every few paces.

'You were going to explain,' prompted Kemi, after they had walked in silence for a couple of minutes.

She took a deep breath, as if there was a lot she needed to get out. 'My name is Oksana Amelina. I work for Integrity Ukraine. We see anti-corruption as the second front in the war. I am here to speak to Patrice... I *was* here to speak to him,' she corrected herself.

Kemi was not ready to let her guard down. She was probably taking out some of her frustration on Oksana. 'How did you know Patrice?' she demanded.

'I've never met him. He wanted to share information with me. About the corruption issues.'

'And you're campaigning *against* this? The corruption?'

'Of course. I came here because Patrice had some sensitive information. He wouldn't speak to me over the phone so I came to meet him directly... Please can you tell me what your interest is?' Oksana was fishing inside her shoulder bag and pulled out a magazine-sized report, printed in English. *Anti-Corruption Activism in Ukraine: Lessons for International Assistance*; she appeared to be the author. There was something pathetic about this thin woman in shabby clothes, looking like she needed a long sleep, brandishing an earnest report. They, whoever they were, had motorcycling assassins. She had a report on corruption that few people would read. This could be an elaborate cover story, but it would be very easy for Kemi to check whether 'Integrity Ukraine' was a real organisation and whether Oksana worked for it. She began to wonder whether this might be that rare thing: a person who was what they claimed to be.

They had reached the Jardin anglais, a pretty park by the side of the lake complete with bandstand and wrought-iron benches. Its pretensions to Englishness were undermined by an absence of public drunkenness or litter. The lakeside was thronged with tourists taking pictures of the *Jet d'eau*, a huge fountain whose spurt of water dwarfed the masts of the boats in the marina and the handsome buildings on the waterfront. They sat on a shady bench and Kemi stretched her legs out in an attempt to squeeze the tension out of her body.

'Please. Can you tell me what is your connection with Patrice?' It was the third time Oksana had asked. The tone was becoming insistent.

'I suppose you have just as much reason to be suspicious of me as I do of you,' reasoned Kemi aloud. The two women looked at each other briefly, a moment of commonality exchanged between them. Kemi wondered whether she should put an arm on Oksana's shoulder. 'I realise you have probably seen many good people killed in this war. But perhaps you didn't expect it to happen in Switzerland.'

Oksana was shaking her head. 'I'm so exhausted by the war they have waged on us that I cannot feel anything. I am numb. Death is everywhere.' She rubbed her eyes. Kemi noticed that her nails were bitten to the quick. Oksana continued, finding strength from somewhere. 'Patrice told me he had a job interview at the Mandarin Oriental and he would meet me straight afterwards. That interview was going to be with you, wasn't it?'

'Yes.' They sat in silence. A street vendor who might have been West African was carrying a bewildering array of goods on his arms and shoulders. Balanced on top of his head was a huge pile of sun hats. He lingered, hopeful that these two women were in sudden need of a new pair of sunglasses or a fridge magnet of the Swiss flag. Kemi shook her head apologetically.

'So who are you? What was the job?'

There had never been any job. And Patrice had never known Kemi's real name. What did Oksana know? You keep your cover unless there's a reason you can't keep it any longer. 'I'm Kemi Adeoye. I work for a foundation in Stockholm. In a way it's related to what you are doing. We take an interest in things like corruption. We understood Patrice was unhappy at the R3 Fund.'

Oksana sniffed. A frown had appeared on her forehead. 'It seems like it's a strange coincidence that you are also interested in corruption in Ukraine. I don't often come across people with that hobby.'

'The coincidence is that we were both here to meet Patrice. So it's not surprising we're both interested in the same things.' Oksana nodded, partially satisfied by this explanation. 'And specifically, it seems like we found the same things about Patrice and the R3 Fund.'

'Basically, yes. He hated what he was seeing. Theft. That's why he contacted us.'

'And now corruption in Ukraine has become a big news story around the world. I'm sure you've seen the reports.'

'Yes.' Something in her tone and body language suggested Oksana wanted to tell more. That she was desperate to have someone to share with. Kemi willed herself not to fill the silence. 'There's something wrong with those reports,' Oksana continued. 'I spoke to Patrice three days ago. He said, "It was like someone had taken the truth and then written a novel based on it."'

'A novel written in Moscow. Which gives people good reasons to argue against supporting Ukraine.'

Oksana turned to look at Kemi. Her face wore an expression of gratitude. She had found someone who understood her perspective.

'Exactly. So corruption, which we are tackling ourselves, with our own institutions and civil society, is turned into an international reason *not* to support us. Patrice said he had to show me something. He wouldn't say exactly what it was on the phone. He said it wasn't safe. Well, that turned out to be true.'

They sat in grim agreement. 'Did he give you any idea, any sense of what it was?'

'He was very cautious. But I know the big picture. The media had the story wrong. He said that they'd flipped it round. He kept saying that he could show me the details when we met.'

'What do you think he meant?'

Oksana paused as if searching for the right framing. 'Well, it's no secret there is corruption in Ukraine. And the people doing the most to tackle that corruption are Ukrainians themselves. I'm part of a coalition of anti-corruption defenders. But some of this corruption has been driven by long-term Russian business interests. Even now, they have powerful networks. They have people inside ministries, they have oligarchs that own whole industries. They have hollowed out our institutions. But in this news story, it's one hundred per cent focused on Ukraine only. On the idea that our politicians are using the war to make money. He said "they flipped it round", and I think he meant they flipped a story about Russian networks and made it into a story about Ukrainian ones. With the result that now people are pushing to stop supporting us.'

'Was Patrice agitated when he spoke to you? Stressed?'

'Yes! That's exactly what he was. Like, saying it was so important for me to speak to him. That everything with the news reports was going in the wrong direction. That it was urgent. But that it had to be in person. That I had to travel immediately. But it's slow for us, coming out of Ukraine. With the train and everything. This was the quickest I could get here. I haven't slept for… for I don't know how long…' She leant forwards, her elbows on her knees, head in hands. 'They get everyone. And now they have got Patrice.'

Oksana was slipping back to a sort of hopelessness. Kemi's tone was firm, trying to keep her motivated. It was the tone of someone who had realised how important this conversation could prove to be. 'Something made you trust him? Made you decide the journey would be worth it?'

'What Patrice was saying didn't come out of nowhere. We have a lot of research, a lot of materials. All of which points to certain facts.'

'You knew about this already?'

Oksana leant back on the bench and pushed a stray lock of hair out of her eyes. 'How much do you know about gas transit? About Russian gas and how it crosses our country?'

The truth was that Kemi knew a lot about this subject. She had written briefing papers for ministers on the subject. She had contributed to analytical estimates of the Russian leadership's strategic intentions regarding gas supplies to Europe. But in the circumstances, playing the role of an executive with a Swedish foundation, she replied cautiously: 'I'm sure there is a lot I have to learn.'

Oksana looked into the middle distance, which in this instance was the white railing on the waterfront, and the blue lake water behind it, dotted with swans bobbing in the sun. 'Russia has used the pipelines that cross our territory as a kind of economic colonialism. Long before the war, before 2014, they knew that they could control Ukraine this way. By controlling the gas that came into our territory and the gas that continued to the rest of Europe. It was a crucial source of revenue for Ukraine.'

Kemi had not expected the history lesson to begin here. 'These R3 stories weren't about the gas, were they?' she asked.

'No, but I see the pipelines crossing our territory as part of Russia's system of control. Like ropes tying us to Moscow. They never thought of Ukraine as a separate country. You know that the name means "borderland"? For them, it's just a space between Europe – your Europe, this Europe –' she added, waving her arms at the definitively European sight of Geneva on a summer's day – 'and Russia. And when they put the gas pipes there it tied us into the dependency relationship. We needed their gas for our own industry and we needed the revenues they paid to transport their gas across our territory. So we just continued to be a borderland.'

'But this isn't about gas. Not now.'

'In a way it still is about gas. Europe became addicted to Russian gas, so they ignored what Russia was doing to our country. And a lot of Europe was depending on gas that came through Ukraine. So the most powerful Ukrainian oligarchs were the ones responsible for the gas transit.'

'Yes, but most of Europe is switching off that supply now, isn't it? Even Germany. The Russians have blown it. Not a great time to be a pro-Moscow Ukrainian gas oligarch, I'd imagine.'

'True, but it's what it did to our economy. A small number of people became ultra-wealthy, and the ultimate source of their wealth was Russia, not Ukraine. Some of them are now even claiming to be helping the Ukrainian war effort. But if their way of helping is to steal money from the R3 Fund through inflated contracts, then whose side are they actually on?'

Kemi was leaning forwards now, fully engaged. 'Is this a theory or an actual case study?'

'Both. We've been investigating Denis Dudnik,' she said, naming a Ukrainian oligarch known equally for being the middleman for Russia's gas exports and the middleman for the Russian mob. 'He's sitting here in Switzerland, but he made billions from the pipelines into Europe. Even now, with the war raging, the gas is going through Ukraine to Russia's friends in the EU: Austria, Hungary, Slovakia. And Dudnik makes money from all of that.'

'But hasn't he claimed to be on Ukraine's side now?'

'Exactly. He makes the money from the gas transit, claims to be supporting Ukraine's war effort, and then – this is the important bit – he's deeply involved with the corruption networks with the R3 Fund. We have gone deep into this,' she added earnestly, as if Kemi doubted her evident seriousness, 'and there's all the usual stuff: shell companies, nominees who've worked for Dudnik all their lives but aren't formally linked to him, politicians he has on his payroll, even politicians who are supposed to be for Ukrainian independence. It's all a fantastic muddle. But the bottom line is clear: the oligarch who got rich from Russian gas flowing through our country is now getting richer by stealing Western aid to Ukraine.'

'And you think that Patrice had evidence of that?'

'I think he had proof. Corroboration of all of our work. Which probably explains why he is now lying dead on the fucking street up there.' There was a quiet fury in her voice, and the two of them fell into a dispirited silence.

'What will you do now?' asked Kemi.

'Go back, I guess. I have a few people I can see on the way. In Germany and Poland. Some of our supporters. Funders. That kind of thing.'

'Maybe my foundation can fund you.'

'I'm not sure you've explained what your foundation is,' Oleksa replied sceptically.

Kemi found herself giving a version of the cover story she had planned for Patrice. 'I represent a long-established Swedish business family. They have investments all over Eastern Europe. Long-term. That's their style. They do things over decades, not months. It's the Nordic way. And they are involved in industries that are heavily affected by political events. Agribusiness, commodities, defence. Things like the territorial integrity of Ukraine and Poland affect their interests.'

'And you were expecting Patrice to help with that?'

'Well, we saw that he had been in the R3 Fund and that he was unhappy there and, yes, we thought he might have useful insights about what is happening in Ukraine. About the long-term economic trajectory of the country.'

'This sounds a lot like espionage,' said Oksana.

Kemi threw back her head and laughed. Perhaps too loudly. 'Gosh, no. No, no, not at all. We have *commercial* interests. But

163

things like the corruption picture, they're very important to us. As you said, it's the second front in the war. If Ukraine can't get on top of corruption, if Western countries decide not to support Ukraine because of corruption… Well, if that happens, then Russia will win the war. That's true, isn't it?'

'That's our point, yes. If we don't win this battle, then Russia wins the war.'

'And you can imagine how my employers would be affected by that. With investments across the region. Including in Ukraine. Knowing about the corruption situation is an important part of business.'

'So it's about *business*? We're fighting a war of survival and for you it's just business?'

'No – we all care a lot about the survival part. Of course we do – Sweden is about to join NATO because of this. But if I said our primary motivation was to defeat corruption in Ukraine, you would be right to be sceptical. You don't deserve to be bullshitted.'

Oksana nodded. 'So if your "foundation" started to support us, what is it you expect in return? You said it's a business. What are you buying?'

'We just want to understand the corruption situation. The real details, not the superficial media reporting. Like with this R3 story – what's really going on behind the scenes.'

'And what would you do with our information?'

'It would help guide my client's understanding. They'd treat it completely confidentially.'

'And you don't interfere with our work? Try to make us reach certain conclusions, that sort of thing?'

'Definitely not.' Kemi sighed understandingly. 'Look, we've just met. In, er, difficult circumstances. We could both wish they were different. But we seem to be on the same side. Perhaps we can share knowledge. Dudnik, for example. I knew his backstory, the gas stuff. But I thought he was just hunkered down here in Switzerland. Not nearly as active as he used to be.' This was, in fact, very far from Kemi's understanding of the sprawling web of influence that Dudnik had created for himself across Western Europe, including in Britain.

'Yes, he's done a good job there. Spent a lot of money in the West, going around lobbying for him, saying that he loves Ukraine. In Britain he seems to have particularly high-up friends. But the point about Dudnik has always been this: he came from nowhere. The Kremlin just picked him to be their man taking the cut on the gas. They didn't even need to do that. So why did they pick him? Who is he fronting for?'

'I've heard the rumours about the Russian mob,' said Kemi, keeping to her cover as someone who was interested, not someone whose job was to know these things.

'These aren't rumours. Russia is always playing a balancing act: they need different people for different jobs. They have smooth guys like Dudnik, and then they have rough mobsters who can arrange to have a young banker killed here in Switzerland. You have to fund the mobsters as much as you have to fund everyone else.'

'So that's the story? Dudnik is taking the aid money and using it to finance the Russian mob?'

'The mob. The war effort. War crimes. It's all wrapped up together.' Oksana's voice tailed away. She seemed to be succumbing to the sense of hopelessness again. Kemi should have let it go, but there was still something she wanted. A stone unturned.

'You mentioned he has all these connections in Britain. Know any more about that?' She tried to make it sound unimportant, but it felt clumsy.

'Not a huge amount. We started looking at it but didn't get very far. Usual oligarch stuff – big house in the middle of London, throwing a bit of money around at a charity connected with the royal family. And there's some finance guy he seems to be connected with.'

'A British finance guy?'

'I don't know. But I think he's involved with politics there. People seemed to know about him. I'm sure I can send the info when I get back. There were some other things we never got to the bottom of, but I don't think they're important.'

'What sort of things?'

'Well, according to some leaked documents he spends a lot of money on something in England every year which has a code-word. We can't work out what it refers to. But the codeword is "Glorious Twelfth".' She said the words in English.

Kemi let out a brief chuckle; not her world, but she'd met enough of them. 'If that's what I think it is, it's the name posh British people give to the day they go out and fire guns at wild birds.'

Oksana gave one of those looks that come from people who are a little tired of being underestimated. 'Yes, we know. We do have access to Wikipedia,' she added drily. 'But that doesn't explain the *actual* meaning. I mean, you couldn't spend a hundred thousand pounds in one day on shooting at birds, could you? It's just some peasant thing if you can't afford meat. And anyway, why would Dudnik spend money on that?'

Kemi smiled. 'Well, in the British system, killing birds is an activity for aristocrats. Or people who wish they were aristocrats. I think it's incredibly expensive. If you're an ambitious billionaire finding your way in British society, it's probably a good way to make connections.'

'What – you think he might *actually* have spent hundreds of thousands of pounds on firing a gun at some birds? How is that even possible?'

'Britain can be a very strange country,' said Kemi.

Kemi wasn't sure if Oksana believed her about the Von Rosen Foundation. But perhaps that wasn't important. Oksana was dedicated to her anti-corruption work and saw a potential ally. Kemi might be able to get her much-needed funding. That was enough.

They walked again, along the lakeside promenade. The sun was lower in the sky, throwing long shadows from the plane trees and the grand buildings. Holidaying families were out in force, the children mesmerised by the *tableaux vivants*. On the lake, pleasure boats promised 'sunset cruises' with complimentary drinks. The tall, angular man from the hotel, legs like a pair of compasses, was walking along the promenade, tracking their progress while keeping his distance.

Kemi and Oksana embraced and parted, with Kemi promising to connect Oksana to some 'useful colleagues'. Oksana walked in the direction of Cornavin station. Kemi sat down on a bench, staring across the lake, her mind turning over what she had just encountered.

Outside the Mandarin Oriental, the manager nodded approvingly as a workman used a power hose to clean the unsightly marks off the road surface.

Chapter 18

For years, the CIA had operated a network of safe houses across London and the rest of the UK. These anonymous properties, their ownership disguised by opaque shell companies, allowed case officers to meet their sources away from prying eyes. It also allowed some of the more louche case officers to enjoy their extramarital affairs in an environment of complete discretion, even if that wasn't the primary purpose. With thousands of its more desirable homes empty most of the time, central London was, in some respects, one of the easiest places in the world to run a safe house. Nobody thought anything of hearing that the owner of an empty multimillion-pound property 'lives in Dubai', and certainly no neighbour expected to recognise them or their guests. Nevertheless, they were still an administrative headache for the CIA's London station, requiring an entire team to service, clean, maintain and manage them.

Then someone invented Airbnb, and the CIA realised that they could access tens of thousands of properties in London, have them rented through a network of fake user accounts and never have to use the same place twice. No longer did they have to worry about who owned it, whether a hostile intelligence agency had figured it was a CIA property or just whether there was bog roll in the loos. All taken care of and no trace of the US government anywhere.

The main challenge remaining was the proliferation of security cameras all over London. Britain led the world in its enthusiasm for putting members of the public under constant video surveillance. So the CIA's London station expended considerable effort in finding places to rent in those rare corners of the city that remained off-camera.

On this occasion, that meant a quiet cobbled mews near Paddington station, which Sarah approved of because it was convenient for the train from Oxford. She knew she was supposed to do a lengthy dry-cleaning route around London before heading to the property, but she worked on the principle that her American hosts had much better resources than she did and they would make the effort to ensure that nobody was following her. If someone was, the meeting would be called off. Deliberately, she had left her phone in her rooms at Christ Church. If she'd brought it, the Americans would insist on her putting it in one of their special Faraday boxes which she assumed was actually downloading everything on the device. Better not to have it at all.

Sarah had been sent an image of the property and the safe signal the day before on a Signal message that disappeared within a minute of her opening it. The upper sash of the left-hand window was slightly open: this was the safe signal. Meeting going ahead. She pressed the brass doorbell on the tidy little mews house and the front door swung open immediately. She walked into the narrow hallway and waited for the click of the door closing behind her before opening her mouth.

Standing in front of her was a tall, angular man, his long legs like a pair of compasses, stooping slightly under a low ceiling.

'Hello, Leigh,' said Sarah. 'Nice little place you've found here.'

'Hello, Sarah,' replied Leigh Delamere III in his New England drawl. 'Something to drink?'

–

'I'm sorry about your wallet, Leigh, but Kemi was improvising.'

They were in an open-plan living room, sitting in armchairs and grazing at the food spread out on the glass-topped coffee table. The repast was classic safe house: indoor picnic food that Leigh had picked up on the way and a screw-top bottle of wine. He was taking notes, but Sarah knew there would be a recording device somewhere.

'She gave it back, minus my driver's licence. Coulda been worse.'

'Bit of a giveaway, that. Going on an operational mission with your regular wallet on you.' She said this with a disarming smile. Leigh rolled his eyes, shaking his head.

'Let's just say it's not in the training manual, but we had a bit of a scramble: someone we didn't recognise following Kamran. Turns out I shoulda just called you up... Anyway, we heard about Geneva. Your Kemi made a new friend, I understand.'

Sarah looked up sharply, doing a bad job of hiding her surprise that there had been a CIA surveillance team on the ground in Geneva.

'Who is she?' asked Leigh. Sarah assumed he already knew the answer.

'Ukrainian. Oksana Amelina. Anti-corruption campaigner. Was there to speak to Patrice.'

'Weren't we all?' he said, sighing heavily. 'And you buy that? About her? She coulda been the spotter for the wet team.'

'That was my first thought, except Oksana was sitting inside when it all happened, according to Kemi. She wouldn't have been much use to them. More importantly, I think her anti-corruption network is real.'

'Doesn't stop her from working for the Russians.'

'I agree. I'm just saying I don't think she was. Check her out. But shouldn't we be talking about Patrice?' There was a hint of exasperation in her voice.

'What's to say? He was trying to prevent a Moscow disin-formation op. Guess he underestimated the risks that go with that.'

'That's it?' Sarah wasn't doing a very good job of hiding her surprise at Leigh's insouciance.

'No. There's plenty we could say. But we both know he was killed in order to stop him talking about what was *really* going on with the aid money. So what more is there worth saying?'

Sarah was impressed at the world-weary cynicism. Leigh Delamere had seen a lot of things in his long career at the CIA. He refused to let anything surprise him.

'What *might* be worth saying is that Oksana had an interesting theory about the real R3 corruption. Not what was in the Russian story. She thinks it revolves around Denis Dudnik. And she thinks that's what Patrice was trying to tell us.'

'Really?'

'Yes. And there's a UK angle.'

'There always is, Sarah,' he said, smiling at the inevitability of it all.

'Some kind of financial link to Dudnik. A guy who sounded to me a lot like Rory Gough.'

'Funny how all paths seem to lead there.'

Sarah turned towards Leigh, her hand tightly clutching the stem of the wine glass in her hand. 'Yes.' She paused, discomfited, and addressed her next remark to the wine. 'Jonty spoke to Simon. And he went to the HUR building. So that's all done.' She said this as if it were mildly distasteful.

'Do you think HUR will play along?'

'Don't know. I think I might need to be there. In Kyiv. Make sure they take Simon to the front.' She looked imploringly at Leigh, her brown eyes fixed on him.

'We'll make sure he's okay, Sarah.'

'You'd better do that. I am fucking serious about this.'

'Yeah, I know. I get it,' said Leigh, leaning his head back to take the stiffness out of his neck. 'We get Chovka and it's a done deal. Simon will be fine. When have I ever let you down?'

'Yeah, let's not go there. Fuck! I hate this war,' said Sarah, shaking her head at the awfulness of it all.

Chapter 19

Pryvillya, Luhansk Oblast, Ukraine
August 2022

Chovka Buchayev drove at breakneck speed down the country road. The car was a crappy old Peugeot that they had liberated from a Ukrainian family before setting fire to their house. They had sprayed several big black 'Z' letters on the white bodywork, which seemed to be working as a signal to friendly forces. His wide-brimmed hat, which he liked to wear to keep the sun off, flapped in the rush of air through the open window. There was a manic energy in the car, the other members of Unit Jackdaw laughing and hollering with the adrenaline that comes from a fresh kill. In the boot, their only prisoner, hog-tied, howled in pain whenever they sped over a pothole.

Chovka hated it. He hated the other men in the unit. Their wanton violence, their crude sadism, their essential cowardice. He hated the stupidity of their missions – the absence of strategic or military value. Pure terrorism. He hated the fact that they seemed to be filming just about everything they did. Had these fuckers never heard of The Hague? Or Bellingcat? He hated the fact that he could be blown up at any time by a stray artillery round or a well-flown drone. And he hated the victims. The soldiers who wept with fear as they tortured them. The children, fearful, their eyes growing ever larger as they saw the evil that men do unfolding in front of them. The elderly, who seemed braver than anyone, calmly awaiting their fate. Wordlessly.

For a man who had seen a lot of violence in his life, Chovka had been surprised at how much he hated this war. He had tried to work out what it was that troubled him. It wasn't the violence in itself, the loss of human life. Chovka had seen so much of it that over the years it had lost its capacity to shock him. It was the stupidity that got to him. He realised that he had become a craftsman. Yes, it was the craft of killing people, but the actual taking of another life had never been pleasurable. It was the challenge that had given him satisfaction. The target... What did they do? Who did they know? What was the pattern of their life? When were they vulnerable? Chovka had been good at this. At doing jobs cleanly.

Other people had realised that he was very good. In Kyiv he had been given a lot of responsibility. Denis Dudnik had made Chovka the point man between him and the people who would take control of Ukraine when Moscow gave the green light. It was a complex job, including the complexity of removing various people who were seen as having failed to deliver on their promise. Chovka had carried out these demanding assignments with aplomb and Dudnik had taken a shine to him, even taking him to his chalet in Crans-Montana at one point. This was ostensibly for Chovka to do a stint as Dudnik's security officer, but really as a reward for work well delivered.

And then in February the Kyiv plan had fallen apart and Chovka had to get out in a hurry. But he was good at making himself useful, first in Moldova and then in Prague. He'd liked the Prague project: another demanding test of his skills, working with a new group of people. His partner had thought using a car was a bad idea, but it had worked perfectly on the first target. They had very nearly made it with the second. And then things had got messy. Only Chovka had made it back to Slovakia, his partner bleeding out in a Prague cellar.

He had hoped to sit out the war in Bratislava, but his life didn't really work like that. With a sense of inevitability, he received the summons back to the Donbas. 'Mother Russia needs you. The nazis could win this. We throw everything at Bakhmut.' And so he found himself in the Akhmat Battalion with a bunch of savages causing mayhem. A craftsman, sent on demolition jobs.

Chovka had been ten years old when his home town of Grozny had been demolished by the Russian army. He might have been a proud Chechen nationalist in the first ten years of his life, but at a certain point – whether you have a distinctive, centuries-old culture and language, or not – it stops being as important as whether your grandmother has just been dragged out of a cellar and gang-raped by Russian soldiers. Chovka, who'd hidden undiscovered in the same cellar, had crept up the stairs, following her screams in horrified fascination, watching from behind the door frame with eyes wider than saucers.

The soldiers had mostly been blind drunk. They'd looked like grown-ups to Chovka, but the oldest was barely in his twenties, with a bumfluff moustache on his upper lip. After they'd finished, they decided they'd better kill her, which they did mercifully quickly, spraying her body with their AK-47s, bullets ricocheting around what little remained of the tenement building. And then they had tried to take her gold teeth. But that proved harder than you'd imagine and they got angry, shoving at one another and shouting as each tried fishing around inside her gaping mouth.

It was at this moment that one of the soldiers had spotted a petrified Chovka, not able to move, not even able to make a sound with his mouth. He knew they'd kill him. That was what they did to anyone who saw what they did. A rake-thin trooper swayed towards Chovka, rearranging his private parts with one hand, his other jittering around the trigger of the AK-47 slung over his shoulder.

'Get a knife. Kitchen knife. Big one,' the soldier said, as if he'd known Chovka had been there all along and didn't care that he'd seen.

The boy stared at him, trying to say something.

'Go on! Fucking hurry up. Haven't got all day.' Chovka nodded desperately, and ran into the ruins of what had once been the kitchen in the family apartment. There was that big knife that *Deda* would use to slaughter the lamb at Eid. The staircase in the corner of the building was still standing, and their apartment had only been on the second floor. Chovka's lungs were heaving from fear and the run up the stairs. There was something bracing about a kitchen that was now open-plan to the outside world, the wall having been helpfully removed by Russian bombers a few days earlier, affording a view of the devastated city, plumes of smoke puncturing the winter sky. There was still that faded photograph on the kitchen wall of Chovka's family, smiling at their uncomplicated lives, no horror or fear.

Chovka tore his eyes away and grabbed at one of the kitchen drawers, the utensils jangling as he did so. He reached for the knife, long, with a slight curve, a glisten of oil on the blade. *Deda* always oiled it, kept it razor-sharp. Chovka's fingers closed around the horn of the handle. Its continued presence in the bombed-out kitchen was a reminder of their panicky retreat into the cellar only a few days earlier. There had been no time to grab anything except bare essentials. Chovka still had a family then. But now he had the knife.

He knew what to do with it.

He returned down the stairs quietly, steadying himself with one hand on the remaining wall, the knife in his other, outstretched hand, like a character in one of those fairy tales *Deda* would tell him. As he came out of the shell of the building he could see the four soldiers, taking a well-earned rest from their exertions. Two of them were smoking; another was knocking back what looked like vodka. The fourth had slumped against a pile of rubble, possibly dozing. None of them took any notice of what was left of *Baba*. Chovka could take them by surprise. Perhaps he'd not get all of them, but he would die a martyr's death. He'd be a hero, like Zelimkhan. They would be proud of him.

Who? Who would be proud?

His last family member was lying in a bloody heap, surrounded by drunken Russian soldiers.

'I'll take that.' The soldier had seen Chovka and was walking towards him, purposefully, his hand out, open palm, as if he was going to shake hands. Chovka tensed his grip. These people had destroyed Chechnya. They'd destroyed his family. This was the moment.

'Here,' the soldier said in Chechen, looking him in the eye. Brown eyes, like Chovka's. 'Don't do anything stupid, now. Be a survivor, not a hero.' His accent was from Grozny.

Chovka held his hand out, turning his wrist so that the soldier could reach the handle, his hand shaking. He was surprised that the soldier's seemed soft. Even with the knife, they'd practically taken *Baba*'s head off before they could get those gold teeth out.

Chovka had learned an important lesson on that day. When one of your formative memories has been the gang-rape and dismemberment of your last surviving close relative, it might be reasonably supposed that this would set you up for a lifetime of implacable opposition to the perpetrators. But the lesson was about survival: you could be a hero or you could be alive. You could not be both of these things.

–

The car passed through a small settlement and they reached an abandoned sanatorium, a blocky concrete building hidden behind thick trees. No doubt its designers had thought they were creating something beautifully functional for the worthy *nomenklatura* types who visited for their enema treatments. Now it was slowly disappearing back into the surrounding forest, its eerie emptiness giving it a horror-movie aesthetic.

As with the enema days, it remained a place where shitty things happened. Unit Jackdaw had found it was a good place to bring their captives. It was a few miles back from the front line, largely out of range of the Ukrainians' artillery and drones. It was far enough from other settlements that nobody would hear the screams. And there was lots of space for stashing bodies, or even keeping people alive for a few days, if that was really necessary.

On this occasion, it was not necessary. The car jerked to a halt in front of the building, skidding slightly on the gravelly earth. Movsar, a manic psychopath who drove Chovka to violent fantasies of his own, leapt out of the car and ran round to the back, pulling open the boot. He bundled the prisoner over the lip and threw him to the ground, where he grunted as he landed.

'Okay, nazi fucker. This is where we end it.' Movsar spoke in a high-pitched shrieking sort of voice that sounded as if someone had kicked him in the balls when he was a teenager. To be fair, Chovka wanted to kick Movsar in the balls most of the time. Kerim, a slow and stupid type who spent most of his time grinning because he couldn't understand what was going on in front of him, had climbed out of the front passenger seat and was pulling out his phone to film the excitements. Dzokhar, a powerfully built ex-wrestler, was dragging the prisoner along the ground as Movsar pulled on blue surgical gloves and fondled a large, curved knife that reminded Chovka of one in his grandparents' kitchen, many years earlier.

Dzokhar dropped the prisoner a few metres from the car and aimed a hefty kick into his ribs for no particular reason. Movsar was waving the knife and shrieking. Chovka kept his distance, leaning against the car door.

'Fucker! Now you see what happens to nazis!'

The prisoner rolled forwards on to his knees with some difficulty and looked squarely at Movsar. He was slim, with an exhausted grey complexion and dried blood streaked down his forearms. But a flame seemed to burn in his eyes.

'*Slava Ukraini!*' Artem Shevchenko spoke in a firm voice. They often started out defiant, thought Chovka. A little moment of heroism. But it never ended that way.

'Kerim, make sure you're getting this,' said Movsar. He then nodded at Dzokhar, who took up a position standing behind the prisoner, one arm gripping the prisoner's bound limbs, the other reaching around his front.

Movsar stood in front of the prisoner, brandishing the knife and addressing Kerim's cameraphone. 'Now we see what happens to traitors. Yes! Traitors!' He pointed at the captive. 'You are a Russian. This is Russia. But you serve a fascist army that is devoted to the destruction of our country. That makes you a traitor, for which there can be only one punishment.' He grinned as he held the blade of the knife against Shevchenko's neck.

'I defend Ukraine. *Slava Ukraini!*' A thin red line appeared across his neck and he gasped. But the gasp turned into a roar of angry pain. '*Slava Ukraini!*' This time his voice echoed off the concrete wall of the building. Chovka stepped forwards, uneasily.

'Fascist *khokhol*,' screamed Movsar, pulling the knife up and plunging it into Shevchenko's neck, which began to spurt blood.

Another roar which turned into '*Slava Ukraini!*' Movsar was exhibiting poor technique, Chovka felt, going in too near the spinal cord. It's harder to make an entry there, and the voice box still functions so they make so much fucking noise. Better to start at the front of the neck.

Shevchenko did not stop shouting. Movsar tried to hold his mouth shut with one hand as he worked the knife with the other, blood splashing onto his grimacing face. Movsar cried out in pain: Shevchenko had bitten his hand, a final act of defiance. The sound of agonised growls and Movsar's shrieking fused into a discordant mess of voices. Dzokhar was shouting, too – 'Pull the knife forwards!' – but nobody seemed to hear him.

'*Slava Ukraini!*'

A shot rang out. Brain matter splashed across Movsar's face and spread across Dzokhar's chest where he had stood behind

Shevchenko, whose body slumped to the ground, the back of his skull torn off by the bullet. Chovka holstered his pistol.

'You couldn't even take his head off without making a fucking mess of everything. And put that camera away,' he added, turning to Kerim. 'That video needs not to get out.'

Movsar growled angrily, yanking the knife out of what remained of Shevchenko's neck. His hands, wet with blood, slipped on the handle.

'Get rid of the body somewhere and then go and clean yourselves up,' said Chovka curtly, turning back to the car. Nobody spoke. In the summer afternoon, the cicadas buzzed rhythmically and a light breeze disturbed the treetops.

–

That day, Chovka decided it was time to do something different with his life. *Survivors figure out which people have power and make themselves useful to those people.* Chovka was a survivor, and he wasn't confident that Unit Jackdaw was very interested in survival. He needed to get out of the war. But first of all he needed to get away from this group of murderous idiots.

He had made up his mind. That was the hardest part. The next step was obvious.

Chapter 20

Kyiv

August 2022

It began with Hayden Edgworthy, grandstanding as usual at the Ambassador's morning meeting. He was hearing reports, he said. This was met with some eye-rolling and a little sigh from the Ambassador, Andrew Mallory. But Hayden didn't let that stop him. 'Credible reports,' he reiterated, that Ukraine was going to launch a dirty bomb, using nuclear waste seized from the Zaporizhzhia nuclear power plant.

Clare Tobin made a grimace. 'What do you understand to be Ukraine's motivation?' she asked politely, but with heavy scepticism in her voice.

'Their motivation,' replied Hayden, assuming the tone of a storied military expert in a seminar, 'is perfectly straightforward. Ukraine wants to win the war and it has limited access to advanced weapons systems. It has no nuclear arsenal. Using an RDD gives them a bit of an edge.'

'RDD?' asked Mallory wearily. He was very used to having to get Hayden to spell out some technical term or other.

But on this occasion it was Clare who obliged with a definition. 'Radiological dispersal device…'

'We have advance warning,' continued Edgworthy, 'giving us the opportunity to consider our response. That's the point.'

'I think the point,' responded Clare, 'is that you have been pushing this sort of stuff ever since you got here and it has proved mostly to be idle speculation. So until you show some compelling fucking evidence to back up your "credible" reports, it will be easy for the rest of us to treat this in the same manner.'

'Don't worry, Clare. You can be absolutely sure I will do that.' Hayden seemed to be delighting in his self-righteousness.

'Good,' said Mallory, relieved to be able to put this awkward discussion behind them. 'Now, let's focus on the main agenda.' An unusual level of energy had entered his tone of voice. 'Annual HR survey. How are we looking? This is one of my top priorities. I want this embassy to be on the leader board for highest response rates.'

—

Edgworthy was, perhaps unexpectedly, as good as his word. Although, the format in which he chose to share his 'compelling fucking evidence' was rather unusual. Later that day he emailed his colleagues a link to a document on the UN website. This turned out to be a letter addressed to the UN Security Council from the Russian Permanent Representative, Vassily Nebenzia. It was written in the bloodless language of international diplomacy but the content was explosive.

I would like to draw the Security Council's attention, wrote Nebenzia, *to the alarming information received by our Ministry of Defence about the plans of the Kiev regime to commit a provocation by exploding a so-called dirty bomb in order to accuse Russia of using a tactical nuclear weapon.*

From a technical perspective, a dirty bomb is a container with radioactive isotopes and explosive load. Once the load explodes, the container is destroyed and the radioactive substance is dispersed by a blast wave that produces radioactive contamination and can cause a radiation morbidity.

The Kiev regime has technological as well as industrial capacities to develop a dirty bomb. According to our Ministry of Defence, the Ukrainian Institute for Nuclear Research have received direct orders from Zelenskiy's regime to develop such a dirty bomb. The work is at its concluding stage.

Under a heinous scenario plotted by the Kiev regime in partnership with the Western countries, a Ukrainian special services sabotage team has targeted the Zaporizhie nuclear power plant located in the liberated territories adjacent to the sovereign Donetsk People's Republic. As the evidence we present to the Security Council clearly demonstrates, Ukrainian commandos were able to gain entry thanks to the assistance of a corrupt Ukrainian employee at the power plant. These commandos were able to leave the compound in possession of a sufficient quantity of radioactive substances for a dirty bomb.

This incident provides irrefutable evidence of the Kiev regime's nuclear terrorism as well as the necessity to exclude Ukrainian citizens from working in sensitive facilities inside liberated zones under the control of the Russian Federation.

The Kiev regime plans to camouflage the explosion of such a dirty bomb as an explosion of a Russian low-yield nuclear warhead that contains highly enriched uranium. In this scenario, the presence of radioactive isotopes in the atmosphere will be recorded by the sensors of the International Monitoring System installed in Europe and presented as due to the use of a tactical nuclear weapon. By this provocation the Kiev regime seeks to intimidate the population, increase the flow of refugees and accuse the Russian Federation of 'nuclear terrorism'.

These reckless Ukrainian provocations would lead to large-scale radiological contamination and may cost thousands of innocent lives.

The authorities in Kiev and their Western backers will bear full responsibility for all the consequences of such irresponsible actions.

Clare Tobin had barely reached the end of the document when she stormed into the Ambassador's office.

'You've read it, right?' demanded Tobin.

The modern Foreign Office encouraged informality. Open-door policy. First-name terms. Mallory got that an ambassador did not need to be referred to as 'Your Excellency' by members of his own staff. But he had to admit to being discombobulated by Tobin's willingness to breeze into his office without even so much as a brief greeting. On his first posting back in the 1980s, this would have been out of the question.

But he *had* read the document, with a mixture of alarm and dismay.

Clare spoke again, her voice quivering with anger. 'Isn't this proof that he's – somehow – in bed with the Russians? I mean, I can hardly believe I'm saying this, but how else did he know this was coming up?'

'Well, I don't think we should jump to *hasty* conclusions. There could be many ways for Hayden to come across this information. Lots of people in the Russian hierarchy could have known about this,' said Mallory hopefully.

'But we're talking about the *Russian* hierarchy. Why is one of our diplomats getting stuff from inside the Russian system? I mean, what exactly is Hayden doing here? What's his job? Who does he talk to? How is he getting this sort of info?'

These were difficult questions that Mallory knew he was unable to answer. But he had spent a lifetime avoiding difficult questions and it seemed to have worked so far. 'On the other hand, we could see it as rather useful, having someone who can give us the inside track on what the Russians are up to.'

'Don't we have the intelligence agencies for that?'

'This is a cross-government approach,' mused Mallory. 'I think we should at least allow Hayden to tell us himself... Let's hear his side of the story,' he added. For Mallory, a lifetime in service of bureaucracy had taught him there were always at least two sides to every story.

–

Russia's bombastic missive to the Security Council had all the classic features of the Kremlin at its most tendentious. Many supporters of Ukraine ignored the story altogether – just another absurd Russian lie from a country that was renowned for them. Experts pointed out that dirty bombs weren't really a thing: they existed on the pages of second-rate spy novels and in the fevered imaginations of alarmist journalists, but not in the real world.

But that didn't stop a certain sort of media commentator, claiming expertise they were unlikely to possess, to speculate in return for an appearance fee. Without nuclear weapons, these useful idiots reasoned, Ukraine might resort to other tactics, including a dirty bomb. They postulated that the story, whilst startling, was not completely implausible. These voices provided just enough credibility for those who liked to take Moscow's side of any particular story. Kamran Patel produced a memo urging that the British embassy 'get to the bottom of this heinous scenario' which 'appeared to be one of a series of reckless provocations by Ukraine'.

Clare was instructed by Mallory to 'look into' the dirty bomb story. The instruction was delivered with a weariness that suggested he had no expectation that she would find anything of significance. Exasperated, Tobin had stomped into her office and tapped out an email to Olivia Mitchell. The message was clear: *Send help!*

—

Two days later, Sarah du Cane stepped off the overnight train from Poland into the bustle of Kyiv's central station. She had been travelling for many hours, was underslept and desperate for good coffee. But she forced herself to focus as best she could. Clare was there to meet her, and the two of them climbed into an embassy vehicle that began to weave its way through the morning traffic. They passed the mirror-glass 101 Tower, looming over the railway station, and continued uphill towards the city centre.

Clare had chosen to drive the car herself, in order to give the two of them the chance to speak without a driver listening in. Instinctively she turned the radio up in case of planted microphones, and the two of them leant their heads towards each other, giving their discussion a strange intimacy.

'Hayden's definitely being used as a disinformation conduit,' said Clare, 'but I've no idea where he's getting it all from. I just don't have the resources to do a proper job on him,' she added, exasperated.

'Of course,' replied Sarah. 'You must be off your feet... I think my first job is to get Mallory to take this more seriously.'

'Good luck with that.'

'We go back a long way. He's a good man, but not very robust. Typical Foreign Office, really: very bright, heart in the right place, but *terribly* weak.'

'You doing anything else while you're here?' asked Clare, tentatively. She had heard of Sarah, but never met her, and was sure that she couldn't be in Kyiv just to deal with the infuriating Hayden Edgworthy.

'Oh, you know,' said Sarah. 'I'll try and get a feel for what's going on here. Talk to my friends in the ministries. That sort of thing. But it's just a quick visit, in and out. So don't worry, I won't be in your way,' she added. Clare felt slightly deflated: she very much wanted to be in Sarah's way, a wallflower in the rooms where it happened.

They reached the embassy, an elegant low-rise building on Desyatynna Street, painted a muted green with plaster mouldings around the white window frames. It was surprisingly quiet inside the office, with several rooms unoccupied. In spite of Britain being an important member of the coalition supporting Ukraine, the Foreign Office health and safety regulations did not permit many diplomats to be based in Kyiv, and its well-equipped embassy lay half-empty. Clare led Sarah up a wide staircase to the Ambassador's office and strode in purposefully, Sarah in close pursuit. Mallory was sitting at his desk, peering at the screen of his laptop, and his face had a brief flash of irritation which broke into a fixed smile on catching sight of Sarah. He bounded to his feet and greeted her with a grin and a shuffle.

'Sarah! It's been too long.' The grin had slipped and a wariness was knotting his brows.

'It really has, Andrew,' replied Sarah.

He shuffled to the door and closed it carefully. Like every action he took, he did this in a manner calculated to avoid offence. The furniture in the office was *Ambassador Level Three* from the Foreign Office catalogue; Sarah had seen identical items in British embassies all over the world. Level Three got you a glass-fronted cabinet for those glossy picture books that ambassadors were always being presented with, a director's desk in teak veneer, and a set of comfy chairs around a glass coffee table. If he'd been Level Two they'd have thrown in one of those brass table lamps with a green glass shade. But that would have needed the Estates Committee of the Foreign Office to upgrade the embassy.

On the wall were framed photographs of Mallory shaking hands with various people in military uniforms and a large colour print of the Queen looking young and beautiful at her coronation. There were also some baffling modern pieces picked out from the government art collection, and an indoor flag stand with the Union and Ukrainian flags displayed to ensure a suitable backdrop for official photographs.

They sat in the comfy chairs and Mallory cleared his throat nervously. To Sarah's chagrin he didn't offer coffee, but then he probably hadn't had time to book it through the e-procurement system. Anyway, this was a meeting he didn't want showing up on any digital register.

'Quick visit? I know you're here now and then, Sarah.' Was that an admonishment for not calling on him every time she passed through?

'Trying to squeeze a few things in.' She let it land and waited for Mallory to speak.

The pause was just becoming awkward when he folded. 'So... I suppose we're here to discuss Hayden.' Clare sighed a little too loudly at this, and he flashed her a single-frame glare of irritation before resuming his management-trained composure. He cleared his throat. 'You have to understand, Sarah, that the

186

modern embassy is a *platform*. We are a platform to enable cross-departmental working in international settings. As Ambassador, my responsibility above all is to ensure the integrity and functionality of the platform.' He smiled, pleased with the clarity of his words.

Sarah and Clare looked at each other in bafflement.

'Um… Not really worried about platforms, Andrew. Can we talk about Hayden?' asked Sarah.

It was Mallory's turn to look baffled. 'I *am* talking about Hayden. Our job is to provide the platform for people from across HMG. That includes Hayden.'

'Right. But I think we can agree that there are some serious concerns with Hayden. He's a conduit for Russian disinformation. Aren't you troubled by that?'

'I won't pretend I'm happy about it, Sarah,' he said, wearily. 'But I have no control over him being here. Way above my pay grade. This has been cooked up somewhere between Kamran Patel, Rory Gough and the Sovereignty Foundation. What do you expect me to do about it?'

'I expect you not to give up.'

'But it's not necessarily the worst thing that could've happened. Him being here. Better inside the tent and all that. We get an insight into Moscow's disinformation.'

'You really see it as your job to read Russian disinfo?'

'We can't ignore it.'

'Well, I think you should be suppressing it. But at the very least you shouldn't give it any oxygen. So, in fact, why *can't* you ignore it?' asked Sarah, her voice rising in frustration.

'Because it's *there*,' said Mallory.

'Well, I'll tell you what is *not* there: a dirty bomb about to be launched by the Ukrainians using nuclear materials stolen from Zaporizhzhia. That's a heap of crap. And it's the sort of disinfo the Russians pull all the time.' Sarah rubbed her eyes with thumb and forefinger, sighing. 'Where is Hayden, anyway? At the moment?'

'He's on a short trip to Poland. Back in a couple of days.'

'Well, perhaps you should ensure he doesn't come back.'

Mallory looked disturbed. 'I would need to go through the short-tour process. There's a panel. And a right of appeal. We can't just tell him not to come back to his post. It doesn't work like that.'

Sarah and Clare looked at each other, shaking their heads. Sarah stood up. 'Andrew, we can't afford to be defeatist about this stuff. I'm not going to waste any more of your time, but please don't imagine this is the end of the matter.' She and Clare swept out of the room. Mallory looked after them, making fish-like shapes with his mouth.

'Why can't a woman be more like a man?' he asked the empty room.

Chapter 21

Kyiv
August 2022

With his swept-back hair, sharp suits and dismissive manner, Hayden Edgworthy had done a good job of projecting self-confidence in his interactions with his embassy colleagues. He was iconoclastic. He was willing to tell hard truths. He had stepped outside the delusional blob consensus that dominated political discourse in the West. He was not downloading his groupthink patches from the NATO mediasphere. He was immune to memetics and in-group tribalism. There was a nobility – even a savagery – to his brutal honesty.

At least, that was what he wanted you to think. The reality of his situation was rather different: since his arrival in Kyiv he had felt vulnerable and very alone. He had taken the job on a bit of a whim: a way of getting out of the stultifying boredom of life at the Sovereignty Foundation think-tank in central London, where his main job was editing poorly written policy papers dashed off by ambitious politicians. Yes, he wasn't one hundred per cent sure of Kamran Patel's take on the war. But it was one of those opportunities you didn't turn down: to be there, on the ground in Ukraine, working on the great geopolitical challenge of the age.

At the beginning, he had enjoyed himself. He got to own the embassy libs whilst questioning their lazy orthodoxy, like a sort of one-man red team. The actual work was pretty undemanding: he could write think-pieces and send them to

Kamran, who treated them as if they were dispatches from the front line, rather than from a well-protected office in the British embassy. But then things had got more complicated. In one of his regular video calls with Kamran, Hayden had been surprised to find a second person floating in from a screen that suggested a corporate office somewhere. The setting might have been grand, but the person was anything but: a skinny, pinched face and scruffy white hair above a tatty T-shirt. There were dark circles under his eyes, and he mentioned something to Kamran about staying up too late 'with AI people'. Whilst Hayden had never before been spoken to by this man, Rory Gough needed no introduction as 'Founder and Chairman' of the Sovereignty Foundation. In his virtual presence, Kamran had lost a little of his usual bluster, deferring immediately to Rory, who didn't bother with small talk.

'Guy you need to meet. In Kyiv. Next few days. Fixed it up,' said Rory, twitching his fingers as he did so, as if even this curt instruction was taking too long.

'Right. Thank you, Mister Gough—'

'Why are you thanking me?' he asked sharply, the Cumbrian accent showing through.

Hayden had not expected this line of enquiry, and muttered something about it being a great opportunity for him.

'How is it a great opportunity when you don't even know who it is or why we're introducing you?' Hayden attempted to explain himself but was quickly cut off. 'Whatever. Just go to the Hilton tomorrow at 1600 Kyiv time. You'll be meeting Valentin Melnik. Who will you be meeting?'

'Valentin Melnik.'

'Correct. He is well connected: works with Denis Dudnik, who, as you know, is on the advisory board of Sovereignty. Melnik will provide you with important data on the activities of the Ukrainian mafia state. Our government's policy is making us look like a bunch of total fucking jokers. Melnik might be able to help with some of the damage limitation.'

A day later, Hayden found himself having a coffee in a Kyiv hotel lobby with Valentin Melnik, a Ukrainian who spoke fluent English with an American accent and boasted of owning an ocean-front property in Florida.

Melnik seemed to know everything and everyone, name-dropping politicians, judges and oligarchs. He claimed that his big priority was 'combating corruption in this great country' and offered to 'share some important intel'. A few days later they met for a second time and Melnik had handed over a USB drive full of what seemed to be highly significant documents, which Hayden had sent as top priority back to Kamran in London.

Hayden had felt euphoric as he saw his dossier begin to make waves in Whitehall. Not long after, at another meeting with Melnik, he was told that the Ukrainians were planning a false flag dirty bomb attack which they would blame on the Russians. Melnik's sources appeared to be as good as ever: within days, the Russian mission at the United Nations was making the same claim, and Kamran tasked Hayden with getting to the bottom of the story.

—

This was when things started going wrong for Hayden. They'd had another meeting, this time in Poland. Melnik had said he was in Kraków on business, and had selected an expensive restaurant near the majestic main town square, where fine wines and wagyu steak were on the menu, and it seemed as if it would be in poor taste to note that there was a war on just over the border. Melnik was stocky, with a well-structured belly and a boxer's nose, his thinning grey hair in an untidy comb-over.

Hayden wanted to get to the bottom of the dirty bomb story – asking a range of questions about what the radioactive material to be used in the bomb was, how the Ukrainians planned to paint this as a Russian plot, the people involved, and so on. But Melnik seemed strangely unwilling to share any details.

'The details are not important, Hayden. What matters is that such a plot exists.'

'Well... I suppose the details are part of what proves the existence of the plot?'

'Some of the details will not be disclosable. To someone such as you.' Melnik looked decidedly unimpressed to be having to explain himself to such a lowly figure. Hayden tried again, tentatively reminding him that they were working for the same side.

And then the explosion happened: not of the dirty bomb, but the intemperate gangster. Melnik had consumed most of a bottle of Château Cheval Blanc and there was a slurring around the edge of his words. He slammed a powerful hand down on the glass table, making the cutlery jangle.

'Enough with the fucking questions! Jesus. Round here, people who ask too many questions do not last very long.' The two men finished their steak in a sullen silence and parted monosyllabically.

–

Hayden didn't like to admit it, but he was a bit of a sensitive soul. He hadn't liked Melnik shouting at him and left their dinner in a foul mood, vowing revenge of an indeterminate sort. Being a Gen Z-er, he began by doing the thing he should have done after their first meeting. Valentin Melnik had been convicted of fraud in a Florida courtroom, and had been tied up with a complicated conspiracy to try to swing the 2020 US Presidential election. In this, he had been working hand in glove with Denis Dudnik. As Hayden went down the internet rabbit hole he began to wonder if he was on the wrong side of history. He couldn't stop thinking of the meme of two SS officers asking, 'Are we the baddies?'

He tried to shake off this unwelcome thought. The alternative – falling behind the intellectually lazy consensus, *that bloody woman Clare Tobin and her lot* – was surely far worse? Anyway, Melnik's difficulties with Florida law enforcement didn't have to mean that his insights on Ukraine weren't worth having. Probably not hard to be found guilty by a Florida court, especially when you're a foreigner.

Hayden decided to focus on the substance of the dirty bomb story. He could see the incentive for Ukraine, if they were able to push the blame onto Russia. But was it real? He found himself reading a post from somebody based in Maryland called John Kalnins, who appeared to be a bit of an expert. Hayden wondered if this guy was a crank, but he seemed to be serious, having worked in the US military and the Secret Service. Whether it was by good luck, or from the fact that Hayden said he was 'working in Kyiv', Kalnins responded readily and they ended up speaking over an encrypted line. He had a gravelly American voice and a way of making complex physics rather easy to understand.

'Dirty bombs are largely a nothing burger. Nobody can actually point to a case of one being made and successfully used in real life.'

'But does that make them impossible?'

'Not impossible, but the claims made in this Russian statement *are* impossible: they're saying the dirty bomb detonation is going to be mistaken for a Russian tactical nuclear warhead. But that can't happen. The physics are totally different. There's no way modern sensors would mistake one for the other.'

'So you're saying it's not theoretically impossible that Ukraine could make a dirty bomb, but these specific claims don't stack up?'

'Exactly. This is an obvious Russian scam.'

After all the speculation, tendentiousness and full-scale bullshit that had been a feature of Hayden's interactions with Melnik, there was something refreshing about the certainty with which Kalnins spoke. For Hayden, it was a moment of clarity. Groupthink was just as much a risk from Kamran and his people as it was from Clare and hers.

Chapter 22

Kyiv

August 2022

In spite of the war, plenty of things still worked well in Kyiv. Ride-hailing apps were one of them. Sarah sat in the back of a taxi, headed for a building in the suburbs of Kyiv that looked like a small apartment block, except that it was surrounded by high walls. On arrival, she chatted to the security guard in Ukrainian as he leafed through her passport. He seemed quickly satisfied and went to the effort of leading her through to the waiting room, holding the doors open gallantly.

Liz appeared a few moments later and the two women embraced warmly. They chattered animatedly in Ukrainian, as old friends do, sharing news of marriages, of babies born and, this being a country at war, of colleagues lost. Liz led Sarah down a maze of corridors to a quiet office. After closing the door carefully she sat down, an expectant look on her face.

'Chovka's ready,' said Sarah. 'To come across.'

'Simon said that might be a possibility. I didn't know if that was the whole story.'

'It isn't. Simon didn't know the details. He was just relaying a message.'

Liz took this in, nodding slowly. 'But you *do* know the details? You know he's going to do it?'

'Yes. It's confirmed. Direct from Chovka.' Sarah looked away as she said this. 'He knows what he's doing and what it means.

And he wants to do it. He's just waiting for a green light from this end.'

'So we have to create the circumstances for it to happen?' Liz was looking straight at Sarah, her eyes level. Unblinking.

'Exactly. Your Mayfly network gives you a reason for knowing his likely movements. He can make sure he's in the right place for a contact. Kinetic. Make it all as natural as possible.'

'And access? Once we have him, who has access?'

'Needs to be Simon at first. And then the Americans.'

Liz looked up sharply. 'So where do we fit in?'

'Well, Simon will be in your hands. He can carry your brief. And it's for you guys to manage the handover to the Friends. You might take a little while over it. Give you more time. Just a thought.'

Liz nodded. 'And what are the Americans going to do with him?'

A blink of uneasiness might have passed across Sarah's face. 'I can't really speak for them. But you all have the same objectives here, don't you? I can't see it being a major problem. Ongoing access, that sort of thing. But you know I can't make promises on their behalf.'

'Nobody in this world should make promises, Sarah.'

The two women smiled, knowingly, at one another.

–

Sarah felt a rising irritation born of stress. There were too many things to do, too many contingencies holding them together. She could look at the next few days unfolding, like a complex child's toy with lots of small parts that had to be clicked together in the right order. Only one part had to be unclicked for the whole thing to fall apart. But she wasn't even sure that she would have time to assemble the thing in the first place.

She got a cab to take her back towards the centre of town and the Hotel Continental, twelve floors of five-star marble and plate glass, overlooking the Pechersk monastery, its golden domes and white walls glistening in the afternoon sun. In front of the monastery some of the trophies from the Battle of Kyiv had been laid out across the square: burnt-out Russian tanks and armoured personnel carriers, as well as civilian cars that had been shot up by Russians, killing the fleeing occupants. The Princess Olga monument, commemorating an ancient ruler of Kyiv who had embraced Christianity and stood up against foreign domination, had disappeared under an immense super-structure of protective sandbags, giving it a strange rounded appearance like monstrous beehives. Around the sides, crude banners had been strung up, with simple, urgent messages: *WORLD – HELP US*, written in blood-red lettering.

At the hotel, there were more sandbags piled against some of the lower windows, but it had the appearance of a tokenistic measure, more to reassure than to protect. Sarah had heard rumours that some of the signature buildings of the city were known to be safe from Russian air strikes, thanks to the complex loyalties of their owners. She wondered if this applied to the Continental.

In her room, she pulled her clothes off and stepped into the shower. She leant her face against the cool of the glass door as the rest of her body ran with hot water. She was motionless for a long time, her hands pressing against the sides of the shower. Then she let out a moan. Someone listening might have mistaken it for ecstasy. It was the agony of an unwelcome task in prospect that even a hot shower could not wash away.

She stepped out of the shower and wrapped herself in a towel. Leaving the water running and the bathroom door open, she stepped into the bedroom, where she turned on the television and put Fox News on high volume. Once she was comfortable that there was sufficient background noise, she pulled out a Polish SIM card, newly acquired en route to Ukraine, and fiddled it into her phone. She rifled through her notebook to find the number she needed, which was disguised as an

ISBN for an academic monograph that she was unlikely ever to read. Slowly and deliberately she typed the number. Her thumb hovered over the green dial symbol. She noticed it was shaking slightly, and she had to will herself to make the call.

'Yes?' Simon's voice was wary. And weary.

'It's me.'

Simon didn't say anything.

'Aren't you going to say something?' she asked.

'Sorry. I was just thinking how amazing it would be to see you.'

Sarah felt a wave of anxiety wash over her. 'That's the thing,' she said, as quietly as she dared over the Fox News bloviation. 'I'm here. I need to see you.'

'Oh.' Simon sounded, above all, confused. 'Oh, right... Amazing.'

'Tonight? I'm only here on a very quick visit.'

'Where, then?'

'I don't think you should come to my hotel. It's one of the big ones. Middle of everything.'

'Yeah. Makes sense.' Simon would have quite liked to spend the evening at a swanky hotel where someone else was buying the drinks. He was running out of money and didn't feel able to ask anyone to help him. 'Come here, then. I've got a garret. You'll feel like you're a bohemian novelist or something. I'll send you the address.' He was trying to inject some lightness into his voice and Sarah appreciated that. As she ended the call, she realised that she had a lump in her throat.

–

Simon knew what this meant. The moment that he had hoped for was also the moment he had dreaded. And it was now almost upon him. For the past few weeks he had spent many hours alone, lying on the mattress in his garret, staring at the attic ceiling, following the cracks in the paintwork like lines on a map, thinking. About Evie. About the choices he had made in his life that had brought him to this point. About whether any of it mattered. In England, as he had raced to try to expose the members of the Oxford spy ring, he had felt, for the first time in many years, as if he was doing something important. Something of value. An individual making a difference. But there was something about the war – a war in which thousands of people died daily – that left him feeling powerless. Evie was dead, and he couldn't bring her back. Nothing he did would make a difference.

He tried to shake himself out of this funk by showering and making his bedsit at least relatively presentable. The sun was dipping in the horizon and he enjoyed the view across rooftops to the green and gold domes of St Sophia's Cathedral. He had some vodka and a few snacks that were almost in date. He realised he was not just nervous about the next step in his mission; he was nervous about seeing Sarah. The last time they had been together, Simon was escaping Britain on a small boat in the teeth of a North Sea storm. They had only had a few moments, and too much to discuss. He had dreamed of when they might spend unhurried time together, relaxing, enjoying one another's company. But it seemed that their meetings were always to be rushed and freighted with significance. And tension.

There was a buzzing sound from his phone. Sarah was downstairs. Good tradecraft told him that he should wait for her to come up, to reduce the risk of a passer-by seeing the two of them together. *Good tradecraft can fuck off*, thought Simon. The building always seemed deserted, anyway. He walked to the landing and the little attic staircase that led to his floor, bounding down that to the grander steps that looped up the main floors of the building, spiralling around an airy drop to the entrance floor. Simon leant against the banister and wondered idly about jumping. He wasn't suicidal, but it was an interesting thought experiment.

He could hear Sarah's footsteps on the stone stairs, at least two floors below. Shoes were important in Simon's world. Over years of experience he had become good at listening to the foot-steps and guessing the shoe type. This was important to match sound to wearer. Sarah often wore smart shoes, leather soles that clicked satisfyingly. But these steps were soft. *Trip to Ukraine, you probably pack something comfortable. Trainers? Espadrilles?*

And then she was there, rounding the curve of the floor below. Trainers, but some smart type that you could get away with wearing to meetings. A summery dress and hair that glistened from a recent shower, tied back simply. She had a small rucksack on one shoulder and sunglasses pushed up on her forehead. Simon knew he should have announced his presence, but she hadn't spotted him and somehow it was good just to be able to look at her.

The curve of the wall put her in full view and she raised her eyes directly at Simon, whereupon she gave out an involuntary gasp.

'Christ, Simon! How long have you been there? Shock of my life.'

Simon didn't know what to say, so he just smiled, shrugging. Then he took Sarah in his arms and held her in the tightest of hugs. He wasn't sure how long it lasted, but he felt their breathing slow down and then synchronise. He put his hand in hers and said, 'Come on up.' He was leading her up a narrow staircase to his room and he had a brief, magical memory of decades earlier, when she had led him by the hand up to an attic room in Oxford and they had made love.

'Right, we've got lots to get through,' said Sarah, business-like, as if she regretted their embrace on the staircase. She paced around the space with an appraising air. 'This where you've been since you got here?' she asked, looking out of the dormer window into the Kyiv evening.

'Yes. It's not that long, actually,' said Simon defensively. 'Anyway, it's out of the way, very few people know I'm here. Does the job.'

'Good,' she said, not sounding very interested. It was as if she was trying to be professional, or just cold. Sarah sat down on the small sofa, plopping her rucksack on the space next to her. Simon knew to sit in the other chair, straight-backed and not very comfortable.

'Shall we get started? Chovka. You saw Jonty. And Liz. Well, it's now all good to go. Liz's people will intercept him around Bakhmut. You'll be there with them. Direct access. Debrief and recruit.' Sarah's words had come out quickly, staccato. Simon looked at her blankly, shaking his head slowly.

'That's it? After everything, you've just turned up here to give me my orders?'

'Well, er...' Sarah fumbled for the right words. 'Well, there's a lot happening—'

'What about the bit where you tell me what I've missed? In the country I had to escape from? Like what's happened with Rory? And Kamran, and all of that?' His voice had started to rise. Sarah had never had the experience of being a fieldman, out on your own, living off snatches of information from home, never feeling like you're fully in the picture. And now she had swept in and started talking about Chovka when the thing Simon wanted above all was to know what he had missed.

She tapped her fingers nervously on her thigh and then a lot of words tumbled out. 'Simon, I just wanted to be sure you had everything. About the Chovka operation. There's a lot that could go wrong... *Sorry*...' She seemed to gasp slightly. Was it a sob? She steadied herself and then seemed to recover. 'Got anything to drink?'

'Only vodka. I'd meant to get something good.'

'Well, you'd better get me some vodka, then,' she said, a smile playing around her eyes.

He had put the vodka in the freezer and found a bit of lemon. They had their shots out of coffee mugs, but Simon had an OCD side to him, so they were at least clean.

'Start again?' asked Sarah after she had downed her drink.

'I just want to know what's been going on,' said Simon. 'You have to understand what it's like being here. It's like the old undercover trips and you'd be desperate to get back home, let your guard down, but they only used to last a few days, max. I've been here for weeks. And seeing you…' His voice tailed off but his eyes kept looking at hers.

Sarah blinked heavily and looked away. 'God! Where to start? Rory is hovering, but he's keeping out of the limelight…'

'He can cause plenty of difficulty from behind the scenes.'

'Yes, but he's being very cautious. I'm sure he's making money from this war, helping the Russians sell their oil, get round the sanctions. But he's not visibly interfering in the government like he was before. We're on him there.'

'So that's good, then?'

'It would be if it was the whole story. Instead, he's playing the PM behind the scenes. Spending all this time with him at Chequers with nobody else there to correct him.'

'Yes, Jonty mentioned that. But it doesn't seem to be working.'

'Rory's far too clever to do anything obvious. He won't be telling the PM to pull the plug on Ukraine. He'll be doing the subtle stuff: which oligarchs should escape sanctions, making sure the City is still financing Russia's oil fleet. That sort of thing.'

'And what about Kamran?'

'That's the current issue. He's basically Rory's eyes and ears. Arms and legs, too, come to think of it. The system is generally on the right side, but Kamran is working away, finding ways to undermine us. Keeping a check on him has become one of my main jobs. Some of it's stupid. He thought he could change our policy while everyone was on holiday. We stopped that. But he's sent a guy here who's at the embassy, acting as a channel for Moscow's disinformation. That's actually a big problem.'

'Here in Kyiv?'

'Yes. Name's Hayden Edgworthy.'

'Fuck. How did that happen?'

'They've badged it as some sort of partnership with the Sovereignty Foundation. Public-private, joined-up working. You can imagine.'

Simon scoffed. 'Sovereignty Foundation? So it's back to Rory and COSTELLO again. You make billions from the kleptocrats in the former Soviet Union and then you launder it through a think-tank and nobody, ever, seems to get what's really going on there.'

'Did you see all that reporting about the R3 Fund? Ukrainian politicians trousering the reconstruction money?'

Simon nodded. In his many hours alone he had ample time to read the news. It was about all he did.

'Well, that story was a Moscow hit job.'

'Next thing you'll be telling me bears shit in the woods.'

She smiled, properly, for the first time. 'Fair enough. But Kamran, and Hayden, his guy here, were some of the key seeders of the story. It was getting pushed around Whitehall. Online, as well.'

'You know who else was pushing the story? Heinrich.'

'Really?' Heinrich von der Wittenberg, an aristocratic German, had been at Oxford with Sarah and Simon decades earlier. He had since become a prominent politician in his home country and, they suspected, was part of the same COSTELLO network as Kamran and Rory Gough.

'Yes.' Simon was happy to be the one with something useful to share. 'The moment this story surfaced I looked on his Twitter. I just had a feeling he'd be up to something. Sure enough, he was giving speeches about it. Even did one in the Reichstag.'

Sarah was now seriously interested. 'What did he say?'

'That the German people, more than anyone, should know the value of peace and should be wary of escalating tensions with Moscow. That the importance of Germany being able to trade freely with Russia should not be overlooked. And, of course, that Ukraine is full of "actual nazis" and they, as Germans, should know what that means.'

'Huh. Kind of proves the point about it being a network, I guess…'

'Exactly. This wasn't a random set of occurrences. And it has real impact in Germany. Perhaps more than anywhere.'

'Yes. Well, not quite *anywhere*… You know one of the mistakes we made with COSTELLO?' she asked.

Simon shook his head, unsure where she was going.

'The Germany thing reminded me. The mistake is that we've been overly focused on the UK.'

'It's an Oxford spy ring. Clue's in the name.'

Sarah disagreed amiably. 'A spy ring *recruited* in Oxford, yes. But its members reach far wider: Heinrich was always going to go back to Germany. Zak was never going to stay in Britain, either. And Kamran worked in America for a while. That's the other thing about COSTELLO. In fact, Kamran told me himself.'

'He told *you*?'

'I tried to put him on the spot. Thought I could scare him off. Well, I got that wrong – he was happy to tell me to bugger off. But not before telling me something rather important…'

'Which is?' Simon was starting to sound impatient.

'Which is… that the main event is the US. Germany's important, yes, if Moscow can scare them away from giving Ukraine what it needs. But America's the big one. Kamran's exact words were, "Russia has strategic patience and America is running out of patience." Do you see what he's getting at?'

'What? America will pull the plug on Ukraine? That's not going to happen.'

'That was my first thought. But then you see the way this corruption story has been weaponised. How some – not all – but *some* Americans say it's not their job to keep Europe safe. And then imagine if the America First people are back in power. Could easily happen.'

'Shit. How do you turn around the MAGA movement?'

'I don't think you do. So the best thing we can do is stop this at the source. Close down this Hayden guy. And make sure Ukraine can win.'

'Which brings us to Chovka.'

'Which brings us to Chovka. Yes. The HUR unit reckon there's a way to intercept him. Make it look like an ambush. So you need to head down to Kramatorsk. Join the team down there. They'll bring him over and then you pitch him.'

'As simple as that,' said Simon sarcastically.

'Well, if he doesn't want to be recruited, then you can take him off the battlefield anyway.'

'And what makes you think he does want to be recruited?' Simon was looking straight at Sarah, intensely. He wondered if she was blinking too much.

'I thought Jonty explained: he's a Chechen who's had his hand in the till and seems to be supporting jihadists. If that got back to the Russians, he'd be finished. He basically doesn't have a choice.'

'And the idea is that I pitch him but the HUR run him? Why don't they just recruit him themselves?'

'Because he's a lot more likely to respond to a pitch from you. He's probably not into Ukrainians. Anyway, you're good at this. And you want to do it.'

'And I want to do it...' Simon said this reflectively, as if he was talking about a third person. 'I came here because I wanted to kill him.' He lapsed into a pensive silence. Sarah held out her mug. 'Got any more?' They both took a larger measure this time.

Sarah pushed her bag off the sofa onto the floor, slapping the empty space for Simon to join her. He sat down next to her and felt a slight twinge of desire, something he had thought his body had stopped feeling. 'Did you *really* come here on a revenge mission?' she asked. 'You had to leave England in a hurry, Vasya told you Chovka was in Ukraine. So you came here because it gave you a reason to be somewhere.'

'Well, I couldn't go back, could I?'

'You might be able to now. I've been working on it. We needed time for the dust to settle and you had to get out. There's been enough time to see whether Rory is trying to pin something on you. And the answer is, he isn't. I reckon he is trying not to bring any extra attention on to the story, especially after the Powerstream stuff. And you aren't in the frame for what happened to Marcus. I made that one go away. It was an accident and the police have accepted it.'

'So I could go back?'

'Do you want to go back? Isn't that the question?'

'I'm not sure, to be perfectly honest. Back to a country I don't understand any more. At least here in Ukraine, things are simpler: it has to defeat Russia, or cease to exist. I can get my head around that.'

'I'd like you to come back.' Simon was unsure how to respond when the mournful howl of the air-raid siren broke out. *Putin's lullaby*. He was happy to have a reason to jump to his feet and walk over to the dormer window.

'Do we have to go somewhere?' asked Sarah, a note of anxiety in her voice.

Simon checked a security app on his phone and looked out. All he could see was Kyiv looking beautiful, the evening light catching the golden domes of the cathedral. 'Basically, no. At the beginning everyone would scram to the shelter. Now we hardly ever bother. These sirens usually don't mean very much. It's not Mariupol.'

'That's good, I suppose.' Sarah's voice surprised him; she seemed to be talking straight into his ear. He turned round and she was standing in the eaves, peering over his shoulder out into Kyiv. They were very close to each other, and his eyes held hers for a split second longer than was normal.

As the siren wailed in the background, he leant forwards and kissed her.

Chapter 23

It was all a bit awkward. The sex. It had been so long that Simon wasn't sure if he had it in him. And what the modern etiquette was. He kept asking if he could do certain things. *Consent is very important.* He knew that.

The kissing was good. They both seemed to like it and Simon, once he had established that he had permission, went exploring behind Sarah's dress and up the well of her back, his fingertips running along the smooth skin. He felt her arching against his hand, and then he reached her bra strap and thought he'd do a one-handed quick release. But that didn't seem to work. After some fumbling he brought a second hand in, but somehow it still wasn't going anywhere, so he beat an ignominious retreat to her waist. He liked that she was still slim, with a pronounced inward curve above her hips. Self-consciously he held his belly in, wondering if it was obvious. Sarah was more dextrous and seemed to know what she wanted. He felt her touch like a live current. It was too late to worry about his underwear; it was definitely clean, but he was not wearing his best pants.

The advantage of being in a bedsit was that they only had to stagger a few metres across the floor to the low bed. They slouched on the saggy mattress, struggling with buttons and buckles. Sarah still had her dress on, now unbuttoned at the front, the skirt pushed up above her waist, and then Simon thought he'd better ask again.

'Can I…?'

'For God's sake, Simon, just fucking get on with it.'

So he did. First with his mouth and then with everything. Sarah was ready for him, pulling him closer and deeper, making sounds that allowed him to believe it hadn't been a terrible experience for her. He didn't last very long, but he lasted longer than the air-raid siren, so it was a creditable performance. Afterwards, they lay entwined, listening to the sound of each other's breathing. Simon waited for his sweat to cool him a little before getting up. With socks still on and his trousers round his ankles, he stumbled as he went to open the window. He undressed fully and grabbed a large glass of water, flopping back on the bed. Sarah pulled her dress over her head and now, both naked, they resumed their close embrace, Simon's face buried in Sarah's neck, her hair tickling around his nostrils.

They held each other for a long time, as the room darkened with the setting sun. The sounds of the city outside – occasional motorbikes, the whir of cars, the groan of buses – were the only chorus. In some way Simon didn't really believe it was happening. But if he lay there holding Sarah's naked body, his arm nestled under the fold of her breasts, then the moment didn't have to end.

They talked quietly about how Simon would get to Kramatorsk and what he needed to do once there, and then they drifted back to sleep. At some point in the night, Sarah got up. Simon had been sleeping, but stirred as he felt her warm body leave the bed. But he turned over dopily, so he didn't see her looking for her phone and tapping something on the screen. After a few seconds she tucked the phone back into the pocket of her bag that lay on the floor. She padded back to the bed and curled her body up against his.

–

208

They woke with the daylight and made love again. But this time they both avoided eye contact. Simon was distracted by the thought of his mission in the Donbas. Sarah seemed upset, glad when it was finished. Wordlessly, she climbed into the shower cubicle. The white noise of the gushing water failed to clear the air. Simon had a towel round his waist in kilt mode, and made coffee on the little gas burner perched perilously close to the shower. When Sarah came out of the cubicle she covered her breasts with her arm and seemed happy to have a towel to hide herself in. She had taken a long slug of her coffee before she said anything.

'You're sure you want to do this?' Simon thought she was talking about them. About a relationship. About – *dare I imagine?* – a future together.

'Of course I'm sure,' said Simon, reaching to touch her bare shoulder. But she turned away, disconnecting.

She was now talking with her back to him. 'Only, it's very risky... Bakhmut is like the Somme with drones thrown in.'

She's talking about the mission. Simon felt the hot wave of embarrassment sweep over him. And the honest truth was that he didn't really want to go through with it. To travel to a dangerous war zone in the hope of persuading a murderous fanatic, or perhaps threatening him sufficiently, to flip sides. No, he was not particularly enthused at this prospect. But he found himself unable to suggest any alternative, as if everything had been preordained. He tried to rationalise and the best he could come up with was that, as an Englishman, he felt it would be impolite to back out. It would be inconvenient. So that left him committed.

'I'm going to do it. This is what I'm here for.' It wasn't exactly Churchillian, but it was the best he could come up with.

–

Sarah took her coffee and dressed quickly. She seemed to be in a hurry. Simon recalled that after you had slept with someone you were supposed to have 'the talk', where you reassessed your relationship with that person in the light of recent exertions. There was no sign that Sarah was interested in this. She pulled on her underwear and her light dress over her head, easing her long hair out of the way. She turned to look at him, perhaps the first time she had made eye contact that morning, and Simon noticed her eyes seemed to be welling up.

'I've got to go now. I'm around, but I'll be tied up with various things. Can't spend too much time in your company. Not here... Anyway, take care,' she said, her arms around him, squeezing tight. '*Please* take a lot of care.'

Simon was about to try to assure her that he would do exactly that, but she had already left the bedsit.

Chapter 24

Kyiv

August 2022

Sarah stood on the street outside the bedsit. She had none of the walking-on-air feeling that should follow a night spent with a new lover. Instead she was trying not to think about Simon, trying to distance herself from the reality of what he was going to do.

Keep calm and carry on.

Sarah messaged Oksana that she would meet her at City-Zen, a swish cafe where glass, steel and granite worktops were the house style and the waiting staff were young and hip. It meant good coffee and a constant clatter that drowned out any chance of being overheard.

This was their first meeting in person since Sarah had taken up the introduction to Oksana from Kemi. But they had held several Zoom calls in the intervening days, Sarah focusing on building a rapport designed to allay any doubts about their odd Swedish foundation. Oksana arrived late at the cafe, clutching a cardboard wallet file and looking harassed, her naturally pale complexion flushed. She managed a weak smile on seeing Sarah and asked for a double espresso, which she knocked back like a vodka shot. Then she ordered an actual vodka shot, which she knocked back like a double espresso. Oksana's hands were shaking, Sarah noticed, and her hair was greasy.

'Is everything okay?' It looked rather unlikely that everything was okay.

'I haven't slept for two days. There is so much to do.' Oksana had that strange mania that can take over in someone who is beyond tired. 'We wanted to get to the bottom of the Dudnik question. I knew you would ask me about it. And I think I have the full story now.'

Sarah nodded. There was an abruptness about Oksana, the way she had gone straight to talking about Dudnik. Sarah liked it.

'So you know that Dudnik has all the money from Russian gas here in Ukraine. But he's probably holding a lot of that cash on behalf of other people. Moscow people.' She was talking quickly, as if she wanted to get it done and then, perhaps, go to bed.

'Yep.' Sarah did not want to break the flow.

'You know that some of the cash goes to the Russian mob. And lots is being laundered offshore for the Kremlin – high-end properties, yachts, and so on. But there's still plenty left. And Dudnik spent it on building his profile. Particularly in the UK. Political donations, obviously. But also a charitable foundation, funding museums, and so on. And he was clever about it, making himself look like a patriot. A Ukrainian patriot. He even funded a Ukrainian cultural centre in London.'

Sarah was about to interject. As the occupant of the Chair in Slavonic Studies at Oxford, she was painfully aware of the story. Oxford had lobbied to host the centre. Even Sarah, with all her knowledge of the grubbiness of Dudnik's money, had briefly hoped that it might come their way. But to Oksana, Sarah was claiming to be an adviser to a Swedish industrial dynasty, not a Slavonic Studies professor, so she bit her lip.

'And the grouse shooting? Is that all part of the same scheme?'

'Yes,' said Oksana. 'Your colleague Kemi told me in Geneva that in England people can spend a lot of money hunting birds.'

'Shooting,' said Sarah instinctively.

'Yes. They hunt them and then they shoot them,' said Oksana, unsure why this distinction was important. 'The point is the money. We also got some of Dudnik's bank transfers. Well, transfers from one of his shell companies. We all thought "Glorious Twelfth" must be a codeword, because the sums were so enormous. He has paid more than a hundred thousand pounds every year for the past decade for a Glorious Twelfth shooting party. I thought that must be a front. A way of transferring money to someone. But from what you are saying, that might be a real thing.'

'As mad as it sounds, yes. A hundred grand is a lot, but it's not unbelievable for a big shoot. Where was it, out of interest?'

'Well, the payments go to something called the "East Dentdale Estate". We looked it up: it's in Yorkshire. Here...' Oksana was rustling the papers, and pulled out a printed photograph: Denis Dudnik wearing loudly checked tweeds that were so new the breeches had a crease on them. He was grinning at the camera and clutching a beautiful, and doubtless very expensive, shotgun that gleamed in the sunlight. Sarah could imagine all the old-money types on the shoot being ingratiating to Dudnik's face in the vague hope that he might favour them in some way, and then scoffing behind his back at his arriviste vulgarity. She squinted again at the photo, hoping to be able to make out some of the others, but only Dudnik's face was turned towards the camera.

'And who owns it? The estate?'

'It's a Cayman Islands shell company. I can't find anything about what sits behind it.'

'It isn't very likely to matter. Oligarch wants to do the British gentleman thing. He finds a fancy grouse moor that's happy to take his money and plenty of British gentlemen happy to get a few days' shooting when someone else is paying.'

'I still find it hard to believe that people spend that money to do this activity,' said Oksana, shaking her head.

'Do we know who joined Dudnik on those shoots?'

'You know, bunch of dinosaurs. Plenty of bankers, society magazine fodder. Nobody who matters in the real world.' Sarah nodded. She had too many things to deal with, and this over-priced social engineering by Dudnik did not seem to matter very much.

'Have you thought of the possibility that Dudnik is actually on your side? He funds Ukrainian culture, he says he's against the war...'

Oksana smiled and opened her folder, pulling out a wodge of printed sheets. 'That's where this stuff comes in,' she said, spreading the pages out on the marble tabletop. 'Dudnik is playing all sides – as you'd expect.' She pulled some printed sheets out from the pile of papers. 'He's there in Zurich saying he's against the war, but he makes millions every day from the Russian gas passing through this country. And that money is then laundered for Moscow.'

'But he was always making money from gas, right? He might still be against the war. The invasion.'

'Except, look at this,' said Oksana, holding up a sheet of paper that looked like a scan of an older document. Perhaps a contract. 'What we found was that many of the R3 disburse-ments were going to companies controlled by him. This sheet is a series of contracts to rebuild schools in Kherson, funded by the Norwegian government. Just an example; lots of donors have been taken for a ride. In this one, the Norwegian govern-ment grants money for "restoration of civic infrastructure in Kherson". Schools, clinics, and so on. It goes through the R3 structure in Geneva. And at the end of it, a construction company owned by a Dudnik associate has the contract to do the work. It overbids massively and there's a kickback for some of the people running the fund. Nothing gets built, of course. And then most of that money goes, in one way or another, to Moscow. To the mob, to the offshore accounts, but it's still part of the Kremlin's *obshchak*,' she said, using the Russian word for a shared criminal fund.

'So Norway's aid to Ukraine is paying for Russia's war?'

'Yes.' Oksana clasped her hands together nervously. 'Not just Norway's. Russia is stealing the West's aid and then using it to power its war machine.'

They both sat in momentary silence as they considered the absurdity of their world. And then Sarah revived.

'I suppose you might be happy to make money from it without being in favour of the actual war, though.'

'Maybe,' said Oksana, leafing through the papers and tsking as she knocked over her espresso cup with shaky hands. It was mostly empty, but the end of the drink dribbled onto one of the pages. She shook her head and blinked a few times. 'What matters more – the money being stolen, or the perception that it's been stolen?'

Sarah wanted facts, not discussion, but she needed to keep the flow going, so she responded earnestly. 'Depends on where these things lead. If the Americans decide they don't trust the Ukrainians any more, that will gift victory to Russia, eventually.'

Oksana nodded. 'The whole reason we wanted to speak to Patrice in Geneva was that he had the real story. Where the money was *really* going. The story I've just told you. Rather than the disinfo version about the President getting rich. But that version made the headlines.'

'Yes, exactly.' Sarah knew this already.

'The point is: Dudnik isn't just part of the system that steals the money, he's also part of the system that spreads the fake news. For Moscow.'

Sarah leant forwards. 'How so?' she asked, perhaps too quickly, more in the manner of an intelligence expert than an executive on a Swedish charitable foundation.

'Dudnik is under sanctions in America. He wants to make those go away, so he has made himself useful to the anti-Ukraine people in America. The ones who blame us, who say that we mistreated the Russian-speakers. Former US President, his supporters. It's win-win: they say Ukraine is totally corrupt and they claim the current guy in the White House had business here. Or his family, whatever. It doesn't have to be true; just believable. Moscow likes it, MAGA likes it. Everyone is happy.'

Sarah found herself thinking of Kamran, striding away angrily from an uninspiring nature reserve. *America is running out of patience*, he had said. 'This is the online stuff?' she asked. 'The disinfo campaigns?'

'Online and real world. Dudnik has a Ukrainian–American called Melnik. He talks to a lot of people. One of them is a guy at the British embassy.'

'Really? Have you spoken to the Brits about it?' Sarah was an executive at a Swedish foundation, not a British intelligence official. She didn't have a reason to ask for a name and her cover was wearing paper-thin.

Oksana scoffed at the idea. 'I don't think I have contacts like that,' she said, holding Sarah's gaze longer than necessary. 'No, *we* believe in transparency. That's why I am giving you these papers. We don't need to have secret discussions with foreign diplomats. Our next report will provide all the evidence. It comes out in a few days. One week, maximum. Then people can explain themselves however they like.'

'Okay.' Sarah needed to get this back onto ground that was vaguely plausible for her to be interested in. 'Back to the R3 scam. You said a "Dudnik associate" was running the construction company. Is there a link to Dudnik himself?'

Oksana nodded, unfazed by the question. 'Well, the way to that is here…' She was shuffling through a pile of papers, searching for something. Then she pulled it out. 'Dmytro Martynov. He's been involved with Dudnik all of his professional life. Co-director of businesses, shareholder, and so on. And Martynov is here,' she said, pointing her finger at a figure in a group photo that had been printed on an A4 sheet. The quality of the image was not brilliant, but Sarah could make out the face of Dudnik, familiar to her from numerous articles, profiles and even from secret intelligence files. He was posing in a slightly goofy group shot: a bunch of guys, just ordinary post-Soviet oligarchs, in a room that looked lavishly decked out. It was one of those places with a home bar – the sort of thing that real men have to entertain their buddies: spirit bottles upside down with dispensing taps, rows of matching beers and expensive mixers. And in front of this tempting array, a dozen men, paunchy, self-satisfied, over-tanned, some with brilliantly cosmetic teeth. Whatever the collective noun was for oligarchs. A guzzle? A rottenness?

'How did you get hold of this?'

'I'm surprised you think I can tell you. But let's just say that when oligarchs leave in a hurry, they sometimes fail to secure their possessions.' Oksana smiled. Sarah found herself remembering images of protesters looting the abandoned palace of a billionaire former President of Ukraine who had fled to Russia. 'Gold taps and a private zoo,' was how one person described what they'd found. In the chaotic circumstances of Russia's war, finding some old photographs didn't seem too surprising.

Sarah was now holding the photograph, looking closely at the faces. She recognised some of them: a Russian mobster here, an FSB officer there. 'Do you know where this was taken?'

'Yes, in Switzerland.'

'Dudnik lives in Zurich, doesn't he?'

'That's his main residence these days. But this was taken in a place called Crans-Montana.'

Sarah did something with her hand; perhaps she was brushing something off her face. Then she looked brightly at Oksana. 'Crans-Montana? Yes... I *think* I've heard of it. Posh ski resort.' She held the paper up again, looking very closely at the faces. There were two that she had not expected to be with Dudnik. One was Vasya Morozov, a former GRU officer who had also been an agent of British intelligence.

The other was Chovka Buchayev.

Chapter 25

London

February 2022

Simon and Evie were going through a rocky patch. Their inter-actions had always been professional, but they had also become good friends in the early days. Evie's charm and fluency in Russian had made her a very valuable colleague, and as their working relationship blossomed, so had the business.

But Simon had a self-destructive streak. If things were going well, he reasoned, it was only because they hadn't yet started to go badly. He disliked most of his clients and wasn't very good at hiding that. Most of his clients found it preferable to be working with more ingratiating advisers. And Evie had started to get a bit fed up with finding promising leads only to have them shot down by Simon, who was always able to find a reason the particular client would not work out.

Events in the wider world were not helping. Evie's Russian mother was no fan of Putinism, and had lived outside the country with her English husband for nearly three decades. But Evie still had Russian cousins and liberal Russian friends. She wanted to believe that a version of the future existed in which Russia was a functioning democracy, no longer a threat to its neighbours. Simon's attitude was hardening: increas-ingly he saw Russia as an implacable threat that needed to be contained, maybe even broken up. And as the prospect of an invasion of Ukraine loomed ever larger, this difference of emphasis simmered, like one of those rows between long-married couples that doesn't need to be spoken out loud.

'I can't believe they'll do it,' said Evie in one of their many conversations on the subject. Her scepticism was not because of any moderation on Russia's part, but because of her analysis of the situation. 'The forces amassed on the border aren't remotely sufficient to invade a country of that size. And Ukraine now has a large army. We're not in 2014 any more.'

'I'm not sure we should be judging them as rational actors, Evie.'

This was what really got to Evie: the idea that Russians were somehow incapable of reasoned thought. 'Yeah, that's right, because Russians can't make decisions based on logic. That's why they're so shit at chess.'

'I'm not saying Russians as a people are incapable of using logic,' replied Simon, exasperated. 'I'm saying the current leadership may not be.'

'The problem is not to understand how logic can be applied by bad actors. Russia, North Korea, Iran. All capable of acting rationally according to their own circumstances,' said Evie impatiently.

They had versions of this argument regularly, until the war began, at which point the awfulness of Russia's actions made the intellectual point-scoring seem distasteful. But like many arguments between people who've been in a relationship a long time, it was a proxy. For the dawning realisation that what had brought them together was no longer a reason for keeping them together. Simon was losing interest in his work, and increasingly behaving in ways that made that obvious. Evie was still in the early stages of her career, and was ambitious. She had built up a bit of a network and was happy to be bought lunch by Marcus Peebles, whose firm Grosvenor Advisory appeared to be big and successful. The lunch proved a bit of a disappointment: Peebles's main objective seemed to be flirting with Evie. His secondary objective was finding out what Simon was up to. Evie had been told that people who had worked as intelligence officers were supposed to be good at eliciting information. In her experience, this was not always the case.

In the absence of much satisfaction from her day job, Evie decided to devote more of her time to her passion for open source intelligence. She was one of a loose collective of net-savvy volunteers dotted around the globe who had become expert at winkling intelligence revelations out of obscure corners of the internet. They had proved that it was a Russian rocket that shot down the Malaysian airliner; they'd identified the GRU assassins sent to poison a defector living in the south of England; and now they were working on unmasking a series of Russian active measures unfolding across Europe.

Evie's main contact in this work was Rudi von Pannwitz, a mysterious Germanic aristocrat living in Prague whom she idolised for his ability to winkle the deepest secrets out of the Russian system. They had got to know each other well, in spite of never having met IRL, as Evie would call it. Rudi was impressed by Evie's quick wit and brilliant Russian language skills. For her part, Evie started to get a sense that Rudi might have access to important datasets that had been leaked from inside Russia. Things such as the travel records of Russian citizens.

Not long after, Evie contacted Rudi, excitedly asking whether she could come with her boss Simon to see him.

'You're always welcome, Evie, but you don't have to travel – I'm sure we can operate securely on this channel.'

But Evie insisted: 'This is something really unusual. I think it's best if we meet in person.'

'You know you're always welcome here,' he replied graciously.

Evie's reply began with a little red heart emoji. 'Amazing. Never been before, and Prague is one of those places you're supposed to see before you die, right?'

Chapter 26

Somehow, thought Simon, you could tell the size of the country from its landscape. Ukraine could only be a large country: vast flat prairies, single cornfields the size of entire farms in England, the geographical features spread miles apart, almost mesmeric in their sameness. The roads were straight and mostly empty. Simon twisted awkwardly on the bench seat, his bare arms sticking to the plastic covers, his head trying and failing to find a comfortable lolling position against the side of the bus. The vehicle had probably spent years ferrying schoolchildren around Kyiv's suburbs and bore the scars of those years of service. On the panel by Simon's head, someone had scratched a pair of breasts in exquisite detail. A caption underneath attributed these to 'Lyudmyla'; Simon suspected as subject rather than artist.

The air conditioning was limited to a single sliding window on each side of the bus. As Simon was sitting in front of these, the heat was oppressive, as was the noise of the straining engine. Many of the other members of this 'counter-disinformation practitioner orientation mission' had pulled on large noise-cancelling headphones and checked out, their orientation momentarily on hold. Simon, ill-equipped, looked on enviously at their apparently sound sleep and found himself having to listen to Kristoffer, an earnest and talkative Dane. The noise levels were enough that he had to lean in close to be able to hear, and even then he struggled to follow, in spite of being spoken to in perfect English.

This was because he didn't have the vocabulary. Nobody feels impostor syndrome more acutely than an undercover agent pretending to be something he isn't. With his cover as a journalist, Simon was in a field that he felt capable of emulating. *Appear curious, ask questions, take notes, look like you're always writing something... How hard can it be?* But now he was a journalist working on a strategic communications counter-disinformation project for a central European think-tank that he had never heard of until Sarah had come up with the idea a couple of days earlier.

'I can get you on a stratcomms visit to the Donbas, gives you cover for the trip down to Kramatorsk,' Sarah had said as they lay on the bed together. 'It's something the Ukrainians do, you know, help people understand the real situation on the ground. The others will be various contractors from around Ukraine's allies. Pretty harmless bunch, I expect. Consultants, you know the type.'

'And my cover for being there?'

'This war is a huge bandwagon. Every consulting company and think-tank from here to Alaska is getting contracts to do strategic communications, countering Russian disinformation, projecting Ukrainian narratives, all that stuff. I know the guys at NovStrat, it's a think-tank in Bucharest. I've done some work with them over the years. They'll vouch for you as an associate, remote worker, nobody has actually met you. You just need to learn the language.'

'What – Romanian?' asked Simon, momentarily perturbed.

'Not Romanian. Although that's actually quite easy if you know any Italian or Spanish. I'm talking about the language of international strategic communications professionals, which might be harder. Anyway, not your first cover operation, is it?'

Simon had spent the next couple of days reading up on a world of arcane terminologies, bewilderingly named programmes and grand-sounding technologies. He could understand the basic point: Russia was good at telling lies about its war and these lies were believed in much of the world, so Ukraine's allies were trying to push back. That was the easy bit. The confusion set in when he tried to understand what they were doing about it. How were they pushing back? As far as Simon could tell, by creating structures of such confounding technical complexity that it would take years before the intended recipients of this counter-disinformation heard any of it. Meanwhile, Russia continued to flood the zone with shit.

The delegation's meeting point for the long journey east had been the lobby of the Natsionalny Hotel in the centre of Kyiv, a cavernous place with dark walls and shiny marble floors in the late Soviet style. There was that awkwardness of adults all pitched into an unfamiliar environment, feeling like schoolchildren as they were briefed by Volodymyr, their liaison from the public affairs office of the Ukrainian ministry of defence, a straight-backed young officer probably chosen for his charming good looks and fluent English. There were about a dozen of them, mostly from NATO countries – a sprinkling of Poles, Slovaks and Germans – mostly young and smart in the way you'd expect from people with jobs in 'comms'. Simon found himself talking to the earnest Dane and Ava, an Australian of Ukrainian heritage who had been working in an ad agency in Sydney until the invasion, and was now fighting an information war for a country she was visiting for the first time. She combined long blonde hair and wide almond-shaped eyes with a Bondi Beach tan, and was polite enough to smile at Simon's attempts at witticism. But Volodymyr was being particularly attentive to this particular delegate, and Simon reminded himself that his priority was to keep his head down and get to the front without being memorable or interesting. He found this came naturally.

As the journey progressed, Simon was worried that his limited knowledge of the world he was claiming to be part of might become painfully obvious. But one of the things he'd learned in the years of trying not to attract too much attention was that people were always very happy to talk about themselves, especially when they appeared to have a willing listener. For the first couple of hours of the journey, there was a preening atmosphere in the bus as a group of mostly male young professionals tried to demonstrate to one another their superior credentials and knowledge of the task at hand. For Simon it was an educational opportunity – or, as his new companions would say, 'There are useful learnings here.' He muttered a few things about having worked in 'FCAS environments in Africa' (that was one bit of jargon he had picked up: *fragile and conflict-affected states*) 'before coming on board as an associate with NovStrat on their counter-disinfo programme'. Few took much interest, and Simon could listen and learn.

Gradually, most of the passengers lost the energy to talk in the bus over the heat and the engine noise, but Kristoffer seemed unperturbed by either, regaling Simon with his work, 'countering mal-, dis- and misinformation by using an AI-enabled deep and dark web scraping tool that generates curated metanarratives offering a full-spectrum response capability...'

Simon had largely tuned out, but there was a silence that he was probably supposed to fill. 'Yeah...' he offered. 'I mean, it's really tricky, isn't it?' he added, hoping that this could be an adequate catch-all response. Kristoffer's confused frown suggested it was not, but Simon was saved from further scrutiny by a roaring sound, like a huge waterfall.

Simon's first thought was *missile attack*. Frantically, he looked around for the source of the noise. And then they came: over a slight rise in the landscape, no higher than a normal house, two grey shapes loomed over the horizon. They appeared to be following the road, coming straight for the bus. The driver was braking, hard. Uselessly. Simon could see and hear them, but his brain couldn't work out what he was seeing. And then the two shapes had separated and banked up and away either side of the road. Instinctively, Simon's head followed the shape closest to him, like a spectator at a tennis match, and he realised he was looking at a fighter jet. He could see the helmeted figure of the pilot inside the cockpit outlined against the blue sky. Simon leant down to get a better view over the other side of the bus and caught sight of the second plane disappearing out of sight. As he did this, the bus jerked to a halt and he was thrown forwards from his seat. The roar of the jet engines was dropping away and there was a momentary silence in the bus.

'Bloody *hell*!' said Ava, her Australian vowels twanging. And then there was a peal of nervous laughter. At the front of the bus, Volodymyr pulled himself to his feet, his hands steadying himself on the seat back.

'We are close to Kramatorsk now. Those are our planes, by the way. Nothing to worry about. This sort of thing is quite normal in this zone.'

As they got closer to the front, they passed through villages that had an eerie emptiness. There were blown-out buildings, their rooves open to the sky, rafters black from fire, abandoned shops and road junctions without traffic. When they needed to buy food, they went to a market hall where elderly women bought and sold produce from one another in mournful silence. The contrast between the vastness of the country, and the sense that its people had disappeared, was unsettling.

The landscape had also changed, as if blue skies and fields of sunflowers were too jolly for a deadly war zone. It was darker, as they had entered a coal mining district. Pitheads were silhouetted against the wide continental skies, their winding gear frozen in time. Where the ground had been flat, stretching in all directions, it now rolled with wide, curving hills like an Atlantic swell. On the horizon there appeared to be dramatic mountains of great height, until they got closer to them and Simon realised they were huge slag heaps.

They were on the outskirts of Kramatorsk and the roads were busy with the traffic of war. Huge lorries and pickup trucks were swarming on wide roads, carving muddy ditches out of the soft verges. The asphalt had been churned up by tracked vehicles and the bus lurched over ruts and potholes, pitching its passengers violently from side to side.

Simon felt a knot of anxiety building in his stomach. In his previous visits to the war zones of the 9/11 era, there had been obvious dangers, but the conflict had been limited to insurgent or guerrilla attacks. You could be unlucky, be in the wrong place when a bomb exploded. Simon had experienced a couple of close calls in those years. But underlying all of that had been the knowledge that his lot – Western militaries – could always bring greater firepower to bear than the insurgents they fought. This time, it was very different. Simon was entering the one-thousand-kilometre front line of a war between two heavily armed, industrialised countries. He had never before faced an enemy with armoured vehicles and artillery, let alone a well-equipped air force and guided missiles. And in addition to all of these things were the new angels of death: tiny drones hovering unseen in the night sky, that could drop grenades with pinpoint accuracy. In this conflict where the dead were measured by the thousands, a spy, alone, was a mere pinprick, easily obliterated at any moment.

In spite of the heat in the bus, Simon felt a shiver pass through his body.

Chapter 27

Kramatorsk

August 2022

Kramatorsk was a spacious, dull city of flat straight streets laid out in a grid, its centre a monument to the Soviet love of crumbling concrete and smokestacks. But it was also a green city, its outskirts containing row upon row of low houses set in pleasant little gardens, many of them now overgrown thanks to the depopulation of the war. Intermittently you could hear a distant booming sound of artillery at the front, still more than thirty miles away.

The group had checked into a small hotel that hid its limited charms behind a high wall. The two-storey building was a monument to brown and beige, to Formica, linoleum, nylon and the advantages of wipe-clean surfaces. The sole member of staff, a lugubrious *babushka*, sighed heavily as she handed out keys. The door to Simon's room was so insubstantial that he wondered why she had bothered. Inside, it had a damp smell and was chilly with an excess of air conditioning. He lay on the crinkly bedspread, staring at the ceiling, thinking about what Sarah expected of him, what Jonty thought he would do, about Chovka. Years of HUMINT operations had taught Simon that recruiting intelligence agents was a pretty random business. When it went well, people would say the case officer had done a brilliant job. When it didn't, people would mutter that 'some people just don't have that necessary spark'. Simon had concluded that dumb luck was the crucial factor. Who really knew what was going through the mind of someone about to commit treason, risking their life, their reputation, all of their relationships and friendships for an uncertain and dangerous future? Would Chovka want to make that fateful choice? Even Chovka himself, wherever he was, probably did not yet know the answer to that question.

Simon knew there was a good chance it wouldn't work. In that case, he would need plenty of luck to get out in one piece. What would people say about that? The spies getting together to drink and gossip. *Heard what happened to Sharman? Yes, poor chap, he was completely out of his depth... Middle-aged bloke who thought he was James Bond, just ended up causing a lot of trouble for everyone.*

He knew he couldn't dwell on the enormity of his improbable task. The only solution was to do the next right thing. So he got up and wandered out to get a cold beer.

Simon sat outside the hotel on a white plastic chair under the covered terrace, nursing a bottle of Yantar. The sun was setting behind the building, throwing a fiery orange light onto the breeze block wall. Mosquitoes seemed to be operating with surprising ferocity, but that was fine because it meant fewer people wanted to be outside. He was pretending to be busy writing in his notebook so that people wouldn't try to talk to him. Patiently, he waited until the night-time chill had descended and he was the only person still outside, the sound of the cicadas and the traffic his only accompaniment. And then, once he was sure nobody was looking at him, he walked out of the hotel compound and crossed Hoholivska Street, using that action to take a good look up and down the road. It was ill lit, and he strained to see in the dusky shadows. He began ambling along the pavement, looking up and down for a taxi, his day sack slung over one shoulder. Under a street light he stopped, and waited, making sure he could still see the entrance to the hotel. He scanned the streetscape, apparently hoping for a ride. In reality, he was trying to imprint into his memory as many of the parked cars as he could. In particular, the one with two figures sitting in it, shadows in the dusk. There was no question what they were doing, just across from a hotel frequented by foreign visitors, aid workers, journalists and other persons of interest. The only question was whether Simon would be 'of sufficient interest' to merit following, or just a footnote to a dull surveillance shift.

He had not been waiting for long when he heard a friendly honk and a battered Toyota pulled over.

Simon used his best Ukrainian, although he was sure both of them were happier in Russian. '*Vidvezy mene do likarni.*' – Take me to the hospital.

The driver grunted and started to make conversation. Simon responded with 'English?' and a shrug, and they continued in silence. Squinting into the offside wing mirror at the line of parked cars stretching behind him down the road, Simon could see one car pulling out, perhaps a hundred metres behind them. Was it that same SUV, two-up, parked across from the hotel? It didn't indicate. Normal people use indicators; surveillance teams don't unless they have to: why signal to everyone else which direction you're going in? He tried to keep an eye on the car. It had two rather small, round headlights, but he lost track of it when the traffic became denser. Without turning in his seat and looking round in a way that would be obvious to his taxi driver, he couldn't distinguish it from other vehicles on the road.

Once the hospital sign was visible up ahead he tapped the driver's arm and said '*Tut!*' – Here! – pointing at the pavement. The driver said something that might have been a sweary complaint, but Simon was already waving a 200-hryvnia banknote at him. The taxi swerved to a halt beside a high pavement and Simon climbed out, walking immediately without looking round in the direction of the medical compound. As he did so, he tried to see if any other cars were slowing. The line of traffic seemed to be moving as before, but as one car sped past he thought he saw a face turned towards him. Was that an expression of surprise? Or annoyance?

He strode towards the hospital, trying to take in the scene in front of him. The first thing was the sound: a cacophony of sirens and horns. He knew that Kramatorsk was the first major emergency facility back from the front line, less than a half-hour ambulance ride away. As he'd expected, it was frenetic with activity – field wagons emblazoned with red crosses, pickup trucks and regular cars screaming in from the front at Bakhmut. Blue lights were flashing, harassed medical staff were marshalling arrivals as other vehicles were loading up to transport patients to the larger hospitals in Dnipro and beyond. A melee of onlookers, journalists, well-wishers and local residents thronged the scene. But it was dark and people were scurrying around, dealing with crises and challenges, uninterested in Simon.

There was always the risk of bumping into someone you knew: war zones have a habit of collecting the same crowd. *Simon? Is that you? The hell you doing here?* He ran that risk. But being spotted going to the hospital by a Russian informant was actually something he was pretty relaxed about. He had plenty of good reasons for being there.

In the occasional lull between sirens and horns, the ominous low murmur of distant artillery was audible once again. In the throng of people around the entrance ramp the air was not of desperation or panic, but calm defiance. Paramedics issuing instructions, grey-faced soldiers being unloaded on stretchers, their exhausted comrades holding up fluid pouches or applying pressure to blood-soaked field dressings, a worried mother following her injured child on a gurney. Simon lost himself in the small throng and then pulled a packet of cigarettes out of his pocket. He had never been a smoker, but they were always useful things to have on you. He stepped away from the entranceway as he fiddled with the wrapper on the carton. Other than where ambulances could drive straight to the admissions area, the site was barely lit. Within a few paces he was standing in the dark between the tall trees that surrounded the building. At another time, it would have been a pleasant convalescent place, close to leafy parks and avenues. He replaced the cigarettes in his pocket and leant against the wide trunk of a huge cedar, the pine sap tingling in his nostrils. He was certain that nobody could see him. His heart was pounding and he needed to collect himself. He wondered about smoking one of the cigarettes, but he didn't want its glow visible and, anyway, he'd probably just start coughing. Instead, he closed his eyes and a familiar scene played in his mind – just a few seconds, like a clip shared on social media.

A screech of tyres, a car appearing from the left side of his field of vision, about fifty metres ahead of him, slamming into a young woman. Evie. Perhaps because of the speed, perhaps because the car is low to the ground, her body is tossed upwards, cartwheeling in the air over the vehicle. And then the vehicle reverses, smashing her prone body with a sickening crunch, before swinging forwards, the headlights now pointing at Simon.

Simon opened his eyes, the reality in front of him preferable to the traumatic memory.

He walked, now purposefully and briskly in a straight line away from the building, crossing a narrow lane away from the hospital compound. He followed a small path that led between two high walls concealing empty lots. It was dark, but he knew what he was looking for. After a few metres he saw a white-painted metal door set into the breeze block wall. The white seemed to glow in the darkness and he thought about banging on it, worrying momentarily about the clanging noise this would generate. Now distant from the melee of the hospital, he could only hear his own breathing. He was sure that he was being watched on a CCTV camera and wondered whether the door would swing open, pulled by an invisible hand. He stood and waited. Nothing happened. Then he spotted a cheap plastic doorbell stuck on the side lintel. He pressed the rubbery grey button but heard no sound, wondering if, in fact, he was in the wrong place at the wrong time. Perhaps he should just walk back to the hotel? Forget about it all.

There was the sound of approaching shoes crunching on gravel. And then a voice.

'*Tak?*' – Yes?

'I'm here about the birdcage,' he said, feeling faintly ridiculous, as he always did when he had to use a recognition codeword. There was a brief pause. Perhaps the person on the other side had no idea what he was on about and was wondering why a random Englishman had come by to discuss aviaries. And then the door swung open on silent hinges. A tall man stood on the other side, grinning broadly from behind a luxuriant beard, wearing a grubby white T-shirt, shorts and flip-flops.

'Welcome to the madhouse,' he said in a Ukrainian accent, extending a powerful forearm and combining a bone-crushing handshake with a pulling motion that propelled Simon through the doorway.

He was inside. No turning back.

Chapter 28

'We weren't sure if you were coming in tonight. I'm Yuri. What shall I call you? This way,' he said, not waiting for an answer and guiding Simon towards a two-storey building that had the look of a school or local administrative centre.

They were inside a dark, high-walled compound. Plywood boarding had been used to black out the windows on the building, but there was a little light that emerged as the door swung open. Simon followed Yuri inside. The interior had been lined with more plywood, giving things a claustrophobic, low-ceilinged feel. Everything was lit by temporary strip lights that were held up by cable ties. Simon recognised these as the type used by special forces to tie up prisoners. There was a hum of activity. People were moving around busily, saying little and taking no interest in the newcomer. Yuri led him past a room where a man in jeans, T-shirt and hiking boots was checking over a compact, Kalashnikov-type sub-machine gun and filling up several magazines with ammunition as he watched Netflix on his laptop. He and Yuri exchanged some words in a very idiomatic Ukrainian which Simon couldn't follow. The other man nodded a greeting, but Yuri had already continued down the corridor and Simon was worried that he might get left behind.

A little further and Yuri tapped a code into a keypad which opened a heavy door into a larger office that appeared to be in the heart of the building. This room was also lined with plywood boards and lit by utility strip lighting. On the facing wall was a huge printed satellite photograph of a city, offering great detail of individual streets and buildings. It was the full height of the room, at least two metres wide and covered in annotations, arrows and labels. Next to it were three clocks showing 'Local Time', 'NATO HQ' and 'DC'. On the wall to the left was a flat screen of the sort you'd expect to find in a pub showing football games, except it was flickering with a series of images that looked like feeds from surveillance drones, the eerie green light of night-vision imagery lighting up the room. Against the right wall was a bank of computers of varying configurations. Most of these were idle, except for one, which had a woman – the only occupant of the room – sitting in front of it, typing quickly with her back to Simon. She didn't look round at their entrance.

Yuri wheeled an office-type chair from the table in the middle of the room and pushed it in Simon's direction.

'Tea?' he asked, walking towards a samovar.

'Sure,' said Simon, sitting down, trying to appear relaxed.

'Come and join us. Let's help Simon figure out what's going on.' The woman had swivelled round in her chair and was scooting it towards the table. Simon recognised a familiar face. Liz held out a hand for Simon to shake, smiling with her eyes. Yuri had sat down, handing Simon a glass of tea.

'Good to see you here, Simon.'

'Right.' Yuri slapped his hands on his bare thighs for emphasis. 'I don't know how much Liz told you already,' he began, 'but this is one of those units that doesn't exist. We do things that never happened. Below the radar. Recon, running sources, some more kinetic stuff. You get the picture.' Liz nodded, as if to dispel any doubts.

'I imagine you have help from Langley?'

Yuri waggled his head, as if to say, *interesting suggestion*, but kept his mouth shut. Instead, he turned to Liz and signalled that it was time for her to speak.

'When I saw you in Kyiv I said there were various Chechen groups marauding around here. Well, we've identified Chovka's group,' she said with a smile that suggested she was rightly pleased with the progress they'd made.

'Oh.' Simon wished he'd responded with more enthusiasm.

'We also have a source who has access to their planning. Based in Horlivka, Russian-occupied village just south of Bakhmut.'

'Access how?'

'It's *complicated*,' interjected Yuri. 'New source on trial. But we've been able to check out some of what they say. Over the last week or so it's proved pretty accurate.'

'A *week*?' Simon was used to a world where intelligence sources were tested and validated over months, sometimes years.

'Battlefield intel, Simon. Agent life cycle can be pretty short. The network codeword is *Podenka* – "Mayfly". Anyway, Podenka 4 is proving quite reliable.'

'And what are you learning?' Simon had addressed the question to Yuri, who nodded at Liz. She picked up the thread again.

'They do these raids, small groups of five or six. There's several different groups, each named for the leader's call sign. They're all animals.'

'I can imagine,' said Simon, an image of Evie's body in the air flashing through his mind.

'No.' She smiled, blinking with mild embarrassment. 'No and yes. I mean they use animal names for their units. Wolf, Tiger, Hyena. And Jackdaw. *Chovka*, when they use Chechen.'

Simon felt that he should say something. But all he could muster was a nervous gulp. He had the sensation of being swept along by fast-flowing water. Once you were in it, there was no choosing when and how to get out.

Liz continued: 'The last time Unit Jackdaw was out they hit a couple of villages south of Bakhmut – Kodema and Semyhirya. Killed some civilians, tied at the wrists and shot in the back of the head. And they took a few prisoners: there's about five soldiers missing. We don't know much about what's happened to them; Pod4 believes they're taking them to the sanatorium at Pryvillya. Seems your intel there was good.' Liz paused. There was the mournful wail of an air-raid siren. Kramatorsk was in a bulge of Ukrainian-held territory, with Russian forces to the south and north. The regular crump of distant artillery could be ignored. Ballistic missiles were another matter: Simon had a grim memory of the strike on Kramatorsk's railway station a few weeks earlier. That had targeted the crowds waiting to get on trains to take them to safety. More than fifty had been killed, most of them women and children. Grim pictures of twisted body parts had appeared on the news. With unusual honesty, the Russians had spray-painted 'For the children' on the side of one of the rockets.

'Should we head to the bunker?' asked Simon.

'That would be a great idea,' agreed Yuri, 'except we don't have one. Plywood should do the job,' he added, pointing to the panelling screwed onto the walls and ceiling. They waited a few more seconds for the sound of an explosion, but none came.

Liz stood up and walked to the huge map drawn from satellite imagery plastered on the wall facing her. 'According to Pod4, Unit Jackdaw will hit Zaitseve tomorrow night. That's another village around Bakhmut,' she added, bending down to point to a spot on the map. 'I said it's not very strategic or targeted, but there's a sort of logic to it – they're clearing the ground for the Russian advance. It's a shaping operation.'

Simon stared at the map, trying to wonder what it would look like from the ground. It was an area of huge fields, with a few curving lanes and small houses dotted spaciously – possibly farm dwellings. Liz had stopped talking and Simon was wondering if he was supposed to say something.

'The idea is an ambush, basically,' said Yuri, breaking the quiet. 'We'll be waiting for them. Liquidate the unit, except for your *Galka*,' he said, using the Russian word for 'jackdaw'.

'Chovka.'

'Either way. You'll come with us, put him on the spot. Use some of that famous British charm. We see if that works. If it doesn't, we take him out. If it does, we bring him back here so that you can get what you need. Then, we run him. Or if he won't help, the prosecutor's office can have him. Or you sort him out,' he said, shrugging as if it didn't matter very much. 'Remember, we don't exist,' he added.

Things were moving very rapidly from a strange revenge fantasy to what might now be a reality. A reality that would unfold in the next twenty-four hours. This sounded like a dangerous mission, but standing in a room with people who were doing this stuff every day, Simon couldn't think of a reason to object. Not for the first time in his life, his main reason for doing something that might be thought of as heroic was that it would have been a bit socially awkward not to. Anyway, having a plan, even one that involved travelling behind enemy lines, was preferable to blundering aimlessly. And he liked Yuri, a bearlike man of quiet competence. It was the boastful ones you had to watch out for, and he didn't seem to be that.

Simon knew that the key with black ops was to move quickly, get what you needed and get out again. It was doable, and what else was he going to do? The people he used to work with in British intelligence would probably describe him as having 'gone rogue', almost the worst judgement that could befall a former member of the deep state. Here in Ukraine he was just another invisible soldier on a huge battlefield. He would try to do what he felt was his duty by Evie.

Chapter 29

Kyiv

August 2022

Back in Kyiv from his short trip to Poland, Hayden Edgworthy had made his mind up: the next time he saw him, he would confront Melnik with the implausibility of the dirty bomb plot. This was perhaps an easy decision to make, because they had no immediate plans for a meeting. Melnik was back in Florida and Hayden had skulked back to work.

The following day, an important-looking woman swept into Hayden's poky office at the embassy.

'Who're you?' asked Hayden.

'I'm Sarah du Cane,' she said. 'I think we need to have a chat.'

'Right, pull up a chair,' said Hayden, smiling cheesily and feeling self-confident, even charming. 'What do we need to chat about?'

'Not here,' she said. 'In the tank.'

They padded through a shabby warren of rooms in the attics of the embassy to the safe speech room. It was a box within a box, its walls and ceiling separated from the building, its floor elevated on a series of short posts. The door had a heavy lever to open it and it sealed tight, like a walk-in freezer. Sarah pressed a red button on the wall, which activated the additional anti-intercept protections and bathed them both in a pallid fluorescent light. An unseen fan whirred to deliver air, but it was stiflingly hot. It wasn't quite airless, but it definitely wasn't the sort of place you could fart surreptitiously.

They had walked to the tank in a stony silence and Hayden assumed a petulant air once inside. 'Care to explain what we're doing here?'

'We're figuring out how to keep you safe,' said Sarah.

Hayden thought this was amusing. 'I think I'm perfectly able to do that myself.' He grinned.

Sarah ignored this and spoke with an exaggerated slowness, to make sure that her message could not be misunderstood. 'In the next two days, a report will come out from Integrity Ukraine. It's an anti-corruption NGO. It will detail, among other things, the role of the oligarch Denis Dudnik in stealing Western funds meant for reconstruction.'

'Good,' he said defiantly, perhaps with a slight quiver around the edges of his voice. 'This corruption issue needs as much ventilation as possible.'

Sarah was now speaking rather faster, and her tone was aggressive. 'You understand that this account of corruption is in direct contradiction to the version of events that you provided to Kamran Patel, in a series of documents he decided to call CRITON?'

'Well, since I've not seen the report I don't think I could be expected to understand that, could I?'

Sarah ploughed onwards: 'This report will also detail some of the ways that Dudnik has been feeding disinformation into the system. You are a part of that story.' She waited, hoping that Hayden would find the backbone to say something at this point. The silence lingered. Eventually, Sarah filled it: 'Anything you want to say?'

'Nope.' This time the petulance had disappeared, and he was harder to hear over the whirring of the fan.

'What does the name Valentin Melnik mean to you?'

Silence. Only the white noise of the tank's underpowered ventilation system. Sarah carried on. 'In the end it doesn't matter very much what you say, because this report will state that you have been a conduit for spreading Kremlin disinformation via the Dudnik network. This disinformation coming to you from your direct meetings with Melnik.'

Sarah was speaking with a sort of harshness to her voice that showed absolute command of her facts. But she was, in fact, winging it. She knew enough to know that the Ukrainian-American conman who worked for Dudnik was Valentin Melnik. She was gambling on his contact being Hayden. It wasn't at all likely to be anyone else. But the truth was she had no idea of the details of what would be in Oksana's published report. She stopped talking and listened to the whirring fan again. There was a squeak. Probably the tank had fallen out of use and everything had started to seize up.

Hayden was staring at the table, taking deeper breaths that tended towards hyperventilation. He put his head in one hand, his nose almost touching the table. Without looking up, he spoke.

'Oh, God. Oh, Jesus fucking Christ. Fucknuts… Fuckenstein.'

What are fucknuts? wondered Sarah. But she kept her mouth shut. He needed to drop a little deeper into his despair. There was another silence.

Then he spoke again. This time he looked up, pleadingly, at Sarah. 'Is there anything we can do? That you can do?'

'About what?' she asked cruelly.

His face had reddened and his eyes might have been watering. 'About the fucking report!' he stammered, desperately.

'Don't think so,' she replied in her most reasonable voice. 'I mean, I wouldn't want to interfere with very important work they're doing at Integrity Ukraine. And anyway, something that your boss Kamran is very keen on also applies here.'

'What's that?' asked Hayden huskily.

'Source protection. Our reason for knowing this is… well, inexplicable.'

'So what are we going to do?' Hayden's voice had risen by at least an octave. Sarah noticed that his hands were shaking. *He is a young man and this is quite possibly the worst moment of his short life*, she thought coldly.

'*We* aren't going to do anything, Hayden. There's a bit of an issue with your situation. I was talking to the Ambassador about it, actually. I understand you're here as part of some new-style public-private partnership with the Sovereignty Foundation?' Hayden nodded, miserably. 'Well, it sounds very innovative – creative, even. But the problem is, it seems you don't have diplomatic status. I suppose it's one of those old-fashioned things that don't seem very important when you're trying to break down the administrative state, or whatever it is you do. So there isn't much we can do to help you, I'm afraid. If Ukrainian law enforcement want to interview you, we'd just have to hand you over. Martial law, and so on.'

Hayden had started weeping, snivelling onto the sleeve of his navy-blue suit jacket. 'I don't know what to do,' he sobbed.

If you can make them cry, it moves things along. Sarah remembered Simon saying that about interrogations. She'd never done one properly before, but she felt that she was doing rather well.

'If you want my advice, and if you have any sense, get the fuck out of Kyiv, never talk to Melnik again, and don't talk to Kamran if you can avoid it. Maybe we can hold the Ukrainians at bay for a few days before the report comes out.'

'Oh, please. Please do that. God, yes.'

'We'll get someone to take you to the station immediately. You won't have time to get your things. Someone can send them onwards, I imagine. You're going to need to go off-grid for a few weeks. Disappear. No messages, no Insta posts, no bloody Snapchat. Nothing to anyone.'

Hayden snivelled in pathetic gratitude. Sarah had heard of the 'smell of fear' before, but had always assumed it to be a metaphor. But the air had become very hot and stale in the tank, with a sweaty odour, and Sarah was desperate to open the door. She felt that she had made her point. She stood up to yank on the heavy handle, and then remembered something.

'Oh, how did you meet Melnik, by the way? Who introduced you?'

'Rory Gough. He said he had someone he wanted me to meet.'

Sarah's hand tensed on the door lever but she kept her face level.

'Rory Gough? The finance guy?'

'Yes. He's the chair of the Sovereignty Foundation.'

'And how did Gough know Melnik?'

'I don't know the details... Please, I think I need to go now.'

Sarah opened the heavy, airtight door and a flood of sweet, clear air rushed in as Hayden rushed out, heading for the bathroom.

Chapter 30

After they had finished the briefing in front of the map, Liz led Simon to a well-equipped storeroom and introduced Simon to Aleks. This was a world where people didn't ask questions unless they had a need to know, so it wasn't entirely clear what Aleks did, but he seemed to be a sort of quartermaster. Simon had quickly been allocated a bunk, asked if he was hungry (he wasn't; the butterflies in his stomach left no room for food) and told to get some rest. The only thing that remained was for him to send two messages: one to Sarah, to say that he had found the right people, and one to Volodymyr, claiming that he had checked into the hospital suffering from appendicitis and was being transferred by ambulance to Dnipro.

He woke from a disturbed night, sure that he hadn't slept at all, but equally aware of strange dreams in which Evie kept trying to tell him something but Simon never seemed to give her the chance to say it. He was in a smallish room in a lower bunk. During the night someone had come in and climbed into the bed above, and was now in a deep sleep. As Simon rolled out of the low bunk, he saw that the newcomer had left his camouflaged body armour and webbing at the foot of the bed. The kit was muddy, suggesting that its user had been lying prone only hours earlier. He found his way to a shower room, hoping that a blast of warm water might dislodge the weight of anxiety on his shoulders.

It didn't, but he felt a little refreshed. His nose told him that there was coffee somewhere in the building. Maybe even bacon.

'Good morning!' said Yuri brightly, as Simon poked his head round the door of a kitchen. Half a dozen people were sitting around a large table, tucking into coffee and bacon rolls. Some of them were on their phones or listening to headphones. Yuri was chatting to Aleks and another man. He beckoned Simon to join them, pouring him a mug of coffee. 'Erik here will be my 2IC in the team tonight. Briefing at 0830 in the ops room. There's a lot to do.' He spoke a few sentences in their slangy Ukrainian and then there was a peal of laughter.

'Sorry. Yuri here is trying to convince us that his team is going to win tonight. We know how likely that is,' said Erik, smiling at the improbability of the notion.

'Confidence is more important than track record,' said Yuri, shaking his head and laughing as he did so.

Simon raised his eyebrows in alarm. He hadn't expected these men to be so casual about their prospects. 'Well, er, I guess your team's track record must be reasonably good, as you're still here?'

There was a baffled silence as Aleks, Erik and Yuri exchanged confused glances, and then Yuri burst into laughter again. 'Ah, I think we may have caused some confusion. These gentlemen are laughing about the prospects of my beloved Manchester United. Not this strike team. *Our* record is more like Manchester City.'

Simon flushed. 'You're talking to a West Brom fan,' he explained. The exchange had reminded him that the greater the jeopardy, the more the quotidian pleasures worked as distractions. Years earlier, he had spent much of his limited downtime in a Forward Operating Base in Afghanistan playing online Scrabble. Saved you from having to think about whether you might be blown up the following day.

They walked as a small group into the ops room. There were already half a dozen people there, including Liz tapping away at a tablet, standing in front of the wall-mounted screen. The others were men, sitting at the table in Under-Armour T-shirts and combat pants. Some had laptops open, others held notepads and pens. There was a low hum of conversation.

'Morning,' said Yuri, putting a hand on Simon's shoulder and standing in front of the group. 'We have an English-speaking visitor with us, so we'll try to make it easy for him today. Simon here will accompany us for battlefield exploitation of target Chovka. Not in the strike team. Liz?'

Heads had turned in Simon's direction. But this was a world where people focused on their own jobs and didn't go looking for unwelcome complications, so the heads turned back to Liz. She tucked a stray lock of hair behind her ear and tapped on her tablet. An image appeared on the screen: the same expanded passport photograph that Jonty Vosper had shown Simon.

'Chovka Buchayev. Chechen Kadyrovite, implicated in numerous assassinations and war crimes. We have intelligence from the Podenka network that his unit will hit Zaitseve tonight, around 0300 hours.' Liz had clicked forwards to a Google Earth image showing a small settlement surrounded by farmland, due south of Bakhmut. 'According to the intel, the village is being targeted because there have been reports of low-level resistance activity here since the Russian occupation began.

'Chovka's team will come south from Bakhmut, using this access road. We understand they usually travel in two or three pickups. Eight to ten operators.' She tapped again at her tablet and arrows appeared on the map, indicating a narrow lane that led to the village. 'Before they reach the houses in the village they have to pass through this area. You'll see the road is shaded by trees on both sides.' There was an arrow marking where the road passed through the wooded area. There was nodding in the room; the ambush point was obvious.

'Recce team were there two days ago. You can cross the line using dirt roads, by Kurdyumivka. Conceal the jeeps close to

245

the Bakhmut–Horlivka highway. Then it's about four clicks on foot to the ambush site. Any questions so far?'

There weren't any. Even Simon, with his limited experience of military operations, could see that this was a fairly straight-forward job: close to the front line; short distance between the target and the vehicle extraction point. Maybe it wasn't going to be as dangerous as he'd thought.

'The objective: liquidate the team, bring Chovka alive to the vehicles. We come back over the line and deal with him at that point. Well, that's Simon's job really,' she said, offering a smile for him. She then started talking in colloquial Ukrainian, although Simon could make out the word 'recce', and one of the men at the table – a slight man with dark hair and a cheeky smile – stood up. He was showing detailed photos of the route which had obviously been taken in the last couple of days. Aleks put his hand on Simon's arm and explained in a low voice that they should step out, 'so you can get your kit sorted. You've got the info you need for your part.'

Now that Simon knew the plan, he felt able to rationalise it. This wasn't far different from things he had done in the past: a strike team hits a target and brings out the prisoners for 'exploitation'. That sounded like a euphemism, but the key was to take advantage of the shock of capture: the bewildering displacement in the first few minutes that someone realises their operation has been rumbled, their comrades might be dead, their options rapidly closing down. Treat the prisoner firmly but humanely, and often you quickly got what you needed. He'd done this before in other war zones. The difficult and dangerous bit was the ambush. But that wasn't his job. They just needed to get back over the line with Chovka and they'd be okay. The only rule was: don't get caught. Ever. But that was no different from the old days. Getting picked up by Islamic State or the Taliban meant months of torture followed by your beheading being streamed on the internet. Maybe the Russians wouldn't stream his beheading, but you couldn't rule it out.

In the armoury, Aleks issued him with a PYa pistol, explaining it was 'the one all the Russians use, so you'll blend in'. Simon turned the unfamiliar object over in his hands. Most pistols were pretty similar; the thing Simon cared most about was whether it had a safety catch and how to make sure it was on.

'And a rifle?' asked Simon, looking at rows of modern-looking variants of the AK-47 racked on the wall behind Aleks.

'You won't need a rifle. If you do, things have gone very wrong,' he said, smiling.

They continued. Body armour, holster and belt, a handful of magazines. 'Three is plenty, don't you think?'

'More than.'

There was a helmet. 'It's going to be clear tonight, half-moon. Most of the guys on the ambush will use night-vision gear, but we don't have many spares. I can't see you'll need it.' Simon was happy to agree. One less thing to worry about.

Aleks showed him the radio and channel they used. 'But we go black during the op, so you won't need to carry a radio. You don't need to worry about anything, really. Basically, you just have to wait at a safe distance and we bring him to you.'

'Maybe I don't need to go across the line? If you succeed in capturing him you'll have him over this side in a few minutes. Fewer people on the op, lower risk.' Simon knew he was being cowardly, but there was a cool logic to his thought. Why risk going into enemy territory?

'You guys call it shock of capture, don't you? You have to get to them just at their moment of maximum weakness. Just after they've been caught. And also, many things can happen – plans evolve, the ambush occurs in a slightly different location. It's better to have you close by. If you're happy to do it, of course?' Aleks asked this in a non-committal way, as if there were nothing of particular difficulty at stake.

Why was he doing this? The tiny number of people who knew where he was might imagine that it was for Evie. And he cared that her death did not go unanswered. But he had to be honest – he wasn't trying to prove something to Evie, or Sarah, or Jonty, or any of these brave people he was about to join on their very dangerous mission. He was trying to prove something to himself.

'I agree, Aleks. Definitely better to have me there on the ground.'

Chapter 31

Kyiv

August 2022

When Sarah and Jonty met for a catch-up in the coffee shop at the Hotel Continental, they had not seen each other for a couple of days. Sarah had been busy at the embassy, clearing up the Hayden mess; Jonty had been glad-handing a group of donors who had come on a war-tourism trip that had been organised at the last Davos summit.

'Of course, they're a bloody nuisance, but they're a bloody valuable bloody nuisance,' observed Jonty, who looked as though he had thoroughly enjoyed shepherding a bunch of billionaires around Lviv and Kyiv. 'Far from the actual front lines or any real danger, but close enough to give them something to talk about once they're safely back home.' He took a gulp of his cappuccino and turned his attention to Sarah. 'How's our intrepid tailor getting on?'

She sighed, clearly stressed and perhaps a bit tired of Jonty's relentless bonhomie. 'He's there, with Liz and Yuri. They're going over tonight. I think everything's in place, as far as these things can be, anyway.'

'Good. We move to the next phase.'

There was a brief silence, broken by Sarah, who seemed keen to change the subject. She picked up a cardboard file from the coffee table, which she handed to Jonty. 'This is some of the work Oksana did. Fascinating stuff.'

'Oh yes?' said Jonty, leafing through the pages but not really reading them.

'Yes. Two really interesting things: Dudnik is everywhere. *Everywhere.*'

'Dudnik, you say?' Jonty sounded interested now. 'Everywhere how?'

'Well, you should read it. But the big point is that he was the ultimate source of the corruption disinfo.' Jonty had now pulled on some professorial reading glasses and was peering at the documents. 'But there's more,' added Sarah.

Jonty looked up, frowning. 'More?'

'Chovka worked for Dudnik.'

Jonty blinked a couple of times. 'You sure about that?'

Sarah reached forwards and pulled out the oligarch group photograph from the sheaf, spreading it out on the coffee table between them. 'There. Look: Chovka, Vasya and Dudnik. One big happy family together.'

'Well, that *is* very interesting,' said Jonty. 'Very interesting,' he repeated, sounding distracted. Then he seemed to find some new energy, drummed his concert pianist fingers on the coffee table and stood up. 'Sorry. Little boys' room. Occupational hazard at my great age. Back in a mo,' he said as he stalked off, his long legs propelling him swiftly across the lobby and out of Sarah's line of vision.

Chapter 32

Kramatorsk
August 2022

Over five hundred kilometres east of Kyiv, in Kramatorsk, Simon was having a busy day, happy to have something to keep his mind occupied. Getting kit ready, studying the maps and aerial photographs, familiarising himself with the comms routines, looking at the maps again, memorising codewords. But by late afternoon he had run out of things to do and he began to get stress aches in his neck. In the early evening the team sat down for a meal, although Simon didn't have much of an appetite.

'Take, eat,' said Yuri, holding a basket of bread rolls in front of Simon. Liz had joined the meal, and they were thirteen in all. He had learned most of the work names of the team members, but it had been made clear to him that he needed to be focused on Erik, Yuri's second in command, and Pyotr, who would be driving the vehicle that Simon would travel in. They both had the quiet monosyllabism he associated with the best special operations types, their inner world kept walled off from the horrors their jobs forced them to witness. Liz was more of an enigma: a young, attractive woman in a building full of warriors. Rather than being the target of flirtation and innuendo, she seemed to command greater respect even than Yuri.

The meal had finished – not that Simon had really eaten anything – and most of the team took the chance to have some downtime. Some took long showers, or watched Netflix. Most took the chance to get some sleep. They had four hours before they would need to start to get ready. Simon headed to his little bunk room, but felt far too wired to drift off. He was relieved to find it empty and lay in his bed, twisting and turning as he tried to settle. He found his mind wandering endlessly to that night in Prague: Evie's body cartwheeling through the air.

At some point, Simon accepted the inevitable: he wasn't going to get any sleep. He wished he could have a stiff drink, but he couldn't see a way to make that happen. Instead, he decided to make a cup of coffee and headed back to the kitchen. As he walked down the corridor there was a stillness to the building; the earlier sounds of banging doors and clanking bits of equipment had disappeared. He passed a closed door and heard Yuri's now familiar voice. And another, quieter – a man's voice with an American accent. He looked furtively up and down the corridor to confirm that nobody else was around and then leant his head against the door, straining to hear. He couldn't make out all of the words, but phrases came together that made sense.

'…a priority for us… access at an early stage…'

Then Yuri, who spoke louder and was easier to follow in spite of his accent.

'A lot of people want to get their hands on him. You know that I'm trying to help these Brits…'

'…primacy. We can share…'

Simon heard footsteps and whipped round guiltily. The corridor was still empty, and he tried to look as though he was walking normally towards the kitchen. Liz appeared around the corner and he said, perhaps too loudly and with a forced bonhomie, 'Do you fancy a coffee? I'm just about to make one.'

But she didn't seem to have noticed anything and they headed to the kitchen together, Liz saying something about trying to reduce her caffeine intake. Simon was straining to hear if there was any movement back in the corridor. There was an embarrassing silence when Liz had finished talking, but Simon hadn't been paying any attention. He apologised quickly, saying he'd been distracted.

'Yeah, I get that sometimes before missions,' said Liz.

Simon could hear a door opening and the voices were louder now, the American and Yuri. But they were just exchanging pleasantries, promises to catch up again soon. He wondered if he could feign a sudden need to go to the loo, to bump into the mysterious visitor. But it seemed too obvious. The voices drifted out of earshot, and he focused on making his coffee and a herbal tea for Liz. And then the door swung open and Yuri walked in, a preoccupied look on his face. On seeing Simon, he raised his eyebrows suddenly.

'Everything okay?' asked Simon. 'I'm just making coffee if you want some.' But Yuri was talking quietly to Liz in Ukrainian, which Simon struggled to follow. He repeated himself and Yuri nodded with a slight air of harassment.

'Busy day?' said Simon, in the hope that this would open up an explanation of the American visitor.

'Yeah, I guess,' said Yuri, taking his coffee and closing down the discussion. 'Excuse us,' he added, and he and Liz left the room, again speaking in low voices.

Simon sat down at the kitchen table, trying to order his thoughts. He had assumed all along that this unit had CIA support. There had been rumours of the agency keeping the fig leaf of no American involvement in the war in place by funding and equipping units that took the fight to Russia on its behalf. The Ukrainians had the native Russian speakers and the need to defend their country, but they would need support, kit, intel feeds, all manner of CIA inputs. It was reasonable to assume the Americans would know about all of the operations Yuri's team were carrying out. What he hadn't anticipated was that the CIA might have a direct interest in Chovka himself. He had heard talk of CIA 'primacy' many times before and knew what it meant: if Chovka was in their hands, neither he nor Sarah nor anyone else would ever hear of him again. If that was likely to happen, perhaps it would be simpler to finish him at the ambush?

With these questions bouncing unanswered in his brain, one thing was becoming clearer.

You're in over your head, Sharman. You don't actually know what's going on.

While he was grappling with this thought, the door opened and several team members came in. They had a jovial energy about them, making one another drinks and helping themselves to snacks as they did so. Simon felt guilty that he had spent so much time worrying about his limited, comparatively low-risk involvement with one mission, when these men were carrying them out day after day, apparently enjoying themselves as they did so.

He went back to his room to get ready, the previous feeling of deep fear now having given way to adrenaline. He just wanted to get on with it. Quickly, the pre-departure rituals that he remembered from his days of black ops in other places flooded back. He stripped naked and then went through every item of his clothing, slicing off any labels that he found. He checked and re-checked every pocket for scraps of paper, receipts, a stray ten-pence coin. He would carry no phone, not even a radio. He had a pen and an ad hoc notebook he'd created from some folded printer paper. He'd made sure the paper was from a new packet, so that there was no chance of impressions on the page from a previous writer.

He then pulled on his belt and holster. The sights on the PYa pistol seemed to catch as he practised drawing the weapon, so he made a minor incision to the holster to give him a smooth draw. Then his body armour, webbing, checking the magazines, adjusting his helmet several times. It was comforting to be reminded of distant muscle memories, of doing these actions many times before. And on all those previous occasions, he had come back alive. He had put a couple of field dressings into his daysack and he shoved these into the cargo pocket on his trousers. He then tidied up the small number of remaining objects that existed as his personal possessions. He had no idea what would happen to them if he failed to come back from the mission. He wondered if he should scribble a note to Sarah, but it felt a bit melodramatic. And anyway, he'd left it too late to come up with anything memorable. Instead, he stepped out into the corridor for the final pre-departure briefing in the ops room.

The atmosphere in the room was alert, but not tense. But Simon felt overstimulated and found it hard to concentrate. In any case, most of the detail wasn't for him: all he needed to do was wait for them to bring Chovka to him and present him with the grim reality of his position. Shock of capture.

They filed out of the ops room and made their final gear checks. There was a melee of people, bits of kit being handed around, most of the team tooling up with weapons and strapping on a bewildering array of additional pouches that looked very heavy and left Simon feeling under-equipped. Outside in the dark courtyard, there were three unmarked twin-cab Hilux trucks, the engines already running, doors open. Yuri told Simon to sit in the back of the second one. Around him were people looking busy with plenty to do, so he was happy to obey, getting out of the way. After a few moments Erik climbed into the front passenger seat, craning round to chat to Simon. Pyotr climbed into the driver's side, putting his pistol in a special holster attached to the inside of the central console of the vehicle. He and Erik were checking the radio and various other gadgets that were bolted to the dashboard. Simon stared out of the side window, resting his head against the glass.

There was a rustling sound as someone was climbing into the back seat.

'Hi,' said Liz as she stashed a stubby Kalashnikov rifle in the gap between them.

'Oh,' said Simon stupidly.

Liz smiled. 'What? Did you think I should be back in there making hot drinks?'

Simon stammered. To be fair, he didn't think she should be making hot drinks, but he was sure that she would be manning the ops room.

'We rotate,' she explained. 'My turn to go out this time.'

'Cool,' said Simon, immediately wishing he'd come up with something better to say.

'Don't worry,' said Liz, patting the rifle, 'I'm normally pretty good with this.'

'Definitely not worried about *that*,' said Simon, trying to sound nonchalant. There was a slight jerk as Pyotr eased the vehicle into gear, and the clanking sound of a metal gate being thrown open.

Chapter 33

Kramatorsk and Bakhmut
August 2022

It was blackout dark on the streets as the little convoy set off into the night. At first they were on roads with a few other vehicles, mostly military trucks and a few that looked like tanks. Simon could see that they had left the city and the convoy slowed. Up ahead were bobbing lights.

'Checkpoint,' Liz said. 'It's fine in this direction, but we have to be super cautious on the way back in. People get shot all the time. You can imagine, late at night, manning a checkpoint. Scary job. People get trigger-happy.'

After the checkpoint they extinguished the headlights and Pyotr and Erik pulled on their night-vision goggles, which illuminated their eyes with a ghostly green light. Simon realised that he was starting to see better, a clear sky and a half-moon opening up the landscape to him. They seemed to be descending a very shallow hill that stretched towards some kind of settlement. The darkness was occasionally illuminated by artillery shells, billowing globes of orange, still distant but clearly audible. Under the shells he could make out buildings, or at least the remnants of them. As they got closer to Bakhmut itself, the sounds became louder, more distinct.

Liz leant close to Simon, holding her finger up. 'Listen to that one,' she said as there was a faint whistle and a crumpling, crackling sound of explosion. 'That's incoming.' Another sound, this time a deeper boom. 'That's outgoing. Outgoing is a cleaner sound… It's okay,' she added. 'The incoming is still several miles ahead.'

Erik and Pyotr were talking to each other, and then Pyotr had a short exchange over the radio. The voices from the other vehicles sounded electronically altered, Simon assumed due to some encryption.

Erik had swivelled round so he could speak to the back seat. 'Simon, we're going to leave this road and head south for a couple of kilometres. Mostly dirt roads. Then we cross. All comms in Russian from that point. Time to make ready, also.' There was a clicking sound as he cocked his pistol and then did the same with the small machine gun he had in the footwell. Liz was checking her weapons, but Simon felt a strange self-consciousness as he pulled out his pistol, worried that he would look as if he had no idea what to do with it.

He stared at the black object, heavy in his hand, and wondered if he would have to use it. Would he make Chovka beg for his life? Would he tell him about Evie, about how special she was, about how much she had achieved in her short life? Ask him how he felt when he crushed her with that car? And then end him? Simon still didn't feel like answering those questions.

'*Pyat minut*,' said Erik in Russian – Five minutes.

The trucks were pitching violently on unmade roads. They were zigzagging around field boundaries, bumping over small ditches and tracking alongside stands of trees. Simon had put on his helmet, but that just meant that his head banged more often on the ceiling. There was some talk on the radio and the trucks were slowing. They seemed to have stopped at the edge of a field boundary, but it was clear there had not been a harvest for several years, as the wide, flat expanse was giving way to scrub. There was no sign of any human presence, but they opened the truck doors gingerly, trying to make the minimum noise possible. Simon was glad to be in the cool night air and he tried to take in his surroundings. Up ahead he could make out the line of a main road bisecting the landscape.

Erik stayed with the vehicles. The rest of them moved off quickly on foot, crossing the deserted highway and passing an abandoned farmyard, a sad collection of collapsing concrete buildings. They were walking quickly and in silence. The distant crump of explosions over Bakhmut and their footsteps on soft ground were the only sounds. They followed a well-worn tractor path across a ploughed field and then hit another smaller road – little more than a country lane – which they followed over a small bridge across a tiny river. Liz leant close to Simon at this point, saying, 'Welcome to Russian-occupied Ukraine.' Simon had expected something visible: barbed wire, a minefield or a trench. Not just a smelly watercourse. They dropped off the road into a muddy field and cut across until they had reached a line of trees that stood out against the moonlit sky.

They regrouped under the tall trees and Yuri spoke in a low voice, going over the plan again in Russian. Liz and Simon were to wait at the edge of the field as the remainder continued another hundred metres, through the trees, to the edge of the road to the ambush site. He watched them spread across the landscape, their bodies becoming dark shapes, indistinguishable from the trees. He could make out the road, the flatness of its surface giving a different hue in the low light. All they had to do now was to wait.

Simon sat in silence, his back against the trunk of a tree, thinking about Chovka. Liz was standing up, her rifle slung across her shoulder, facing out to the open ground. There was a strange intimacy between them as they shared the darkness. Simon had a lot of questions he wanted to ask, but didn't know if he was allowed to speak. Instead, Liz broke the silence.

'What are you going to do with him?'

'You mean if he *doesn't* talk?'

'No. I mean if he talks. If he doesn't talk, that's easy. I want to know what you are going to do if he co-operates.'

'Find out how they operated, I guess. He was working for a Russian intel organisation. One that nobody knew about, which targeted the UK. I want to know how that worked. Who was his handler. The rest of the network. That sort of thing.'

Liz didn't respond immediately. Was she turning something over in her mind?

'Because I guess there could be higher priorities here. If you're just wanting to do some historical debrief, perhaps that can wait.'

'Wait for what?' Something was shifting. First, the CIA officer in the team house, now Liz.

'We need Mayflies, Simon. Someone working on the inside with the Kadyrovites would be really useful. In this war that we are fighting right here.'

Simon felt like raising his voice, but he had to remind himself that he was behind enemy lines. Not a good place for a shouting match. He took a deep breath and spoke quietly. 'Okay. So I'm just trying to figure out why I am here. And why you chose to bring this up now?'

She smiled disarmingly. 'We're having the conversation now because if we'd had it earlier, you wouldn't have had any reason to come on the operation.'

'But why bring me at all? You're already running sources. You want to recruit him, you can do it yourselves. What do I bring?'

'I don't actually know. But he asked for you.'

'Who? You mean Yuri asked for me?'

'No. We're talking about Chovka. Mayfly 4 spoke to him. And he asked for you. For Simon Sharman, formerly of the British Joint Intelligence Directorate, known to all as the Pole. He asked for you, Simon.'

Chapter 34

Bakhmut
August 2022

Although it was dark and Liz was no longer looking at him, Simon was shaking his head. His mind was a turmoil of incomprehension.

Chovka asked for me? There must be some mistake.

He opened his mouth to speak to Liz, but she was holding her finger to her earpiece, listening to a radio message.

'They're approaching,' she said in a commanding whisper. 'Two minutes. If you have something to discuss, we'll do that later.' As she said this, she pulled out her pistol, double-checking it was made ready before doing the same with the rifle. Then she paced a few metres down the track to a point where the view of the road was clearer, motioning Simon to do the same.

Liz, standing by a tall tree, tapped at her ear. Simon could hear it, too. The sound of an engine straining. Perhaps two of them. He scanned the horizon, wondering if he would see lights. Would Chovka's men have night-vision goggles? The sound grew louder and Simon could see faint lights moving in the distance. Then the vehicles came into view. There were two cars, driving at breakneck speed, but they had to slow down for a corner. They only had their sidelights on, throwing out a dim yellow glow. With this illumination Simon could see the shapes of the ambush team arrayed among the trees, some kneeling, others standing behind tree trunks, weapons at the ready. Suddenly the forest erupted in a deafening barrage of machine-gun fire. There were flashes jumping out from the gun barrels and tracer rounds streaking like laser beams. The lead vehicle skidded off the road and turned over. The second one ground to a halt, its engine and tyres shot out. There was a momentary halt in the firing, and the dark bodies were swarming out of the trees towards the two vehicles.

Then there was the crack of an incoming bullet. Instinctively, Simon dropped to his stomach. He was fumbling for his pistol, pointlessly, as he couldn't see anything and had no idea where the round had come from. Liz was calmly taking cover behind the tree trunk, craning her head outwards, looking down the sights of her rifle. Two more rounds flew past in quick succession, and then Simon saw more flashes close to the vehicles and heard a cry of pain. Someone shouted some words that might have been 'not here!' in Russian. He could make out Yuri and at least three of the others peering into the vehicle, followed by the distinctive sound of the double-tap, repeated several times and coming from several different angles.

Silence.

And then he heard it. A high-pitched whirring sound, unmistakably electronic. *Drone*. There was a very brief shout, maybe a bellow of surprise, or a warning. And then a huge boom, and the rushing wind of the blast struck Simon in the face, his eyes filling with dust. He was trying to shout something to Liz, but his mouth didn't seem to be making any noise. Or had he been deafened? And then, as he turned his head towards Liz there was another boom, coming from the farther vehicle. But he felt that one more than he heard it. Liz had dropped to her knees behind the tree trunk and the two of them craned to look back at the ambush site. Both vehicles were now in flames and they could see movement. With a gasp of horror, Simon realised there was a body on fire, writhing and screaming. There were cries from other voices, but he couldn't tell where they were coming from. Without thinking, he stood up and sprinted forwards. He could feel the heat of the fire on his face. Liz was by his side and they were reaching the edge of the trees, the first car no more than twenty metres away. Simon hesitated, leaning on a tree trunk; he was trying to take in the scene in front of him: the burning vehicle, bodies on the ground, cries of agony. Liz was running towards the other vehicle, also in flames, shouting Yuri's name.

A pair of headlights appeared on the road, illuminating the scene. Almost instantaneously there was a roaring, thudding sound, like a colossal drum roll. Simon froze as the scene on the road in front of him was torn up by huge .50 cal rounds coming from the direction of the headlights. Bits of vehicle, body parts and road surface were all being churned up by the massive bullets. He realised he needed to turn round, to run back into the forest. He knew he had to do it, but he was mesmerised by the sheer power of the heavy machine gun. With an immense physical effort, he pushed himself behind the tree trunk, breaking into a run back where he had come from. He could see splashes of light on the trees up ahead of him. He realised people were behind him now, shining powerful torches. He drew his pistol and swung his arm over his shoulder, firing randomly. Immediately he heard the crack of a high-velocity shot fly over his helmet. He crouched down in a small ditch, trying to take cover.

He swung his shoulders round, pistol in hand, but he couldn't see anything except torch beams, dazzling his eyes. Some urge for self-preservation told him not to fire. His mind was whirring with contradictory instructions. *Play dead. They'll want you alive. You're valuable to them… Don't allow yourself to be captured… Torture is worse than death… Shoot yourself.*

But anyway, his hand had slipped and he had dropped his gun in the darkness. Too late to do anything. They were on him now.

A heavy boot crashed into his chest, but the body armour did its job and he felt bruised, not beaten. A torch was shining directly into his eyes, photo-bleaching his vision. He squinted and tried to look away. Another heavy kick made contact, this time on his kneecap, sending an electric jolt of pain through his leg, and he cried out involuntarily. There was shouting in Russian, but for some reason he was struggling to make sense of it. He felt a powerful hand grab the shoulder strap of his body armour and yank him to his feet. He tried to stand, but his knee gave way and he staggered. The torch was lowered and he was able to make out the shapes of several faces. They were all wearing helmets and military uniform. One was poking an AK-47 in Simon's face, shouting in Russian.

'*Kto ty?*' – Who are you?

Simon didn't answer, as he was calculating frantically. What was his story? Who was he supposed to be? Italian journalists didn't carry pistols. British spies didn't live long in Russian captivity. Perhaps a foreign volunteer fighter would be a high-value prisoner? Someone who'd be tradeable for one of theirs?

With a crunch, a well-aimed boot slammed into the same knee. It felt as if boiling water was spreading out from the joint. He screamed with the pain, but the hand holding his shoulder strap didn't budge.

'*Kto ty?*' This time it was shouted in his face. Little flecks of spit landed on his nose and mouth.

'International Legion!' he blurted, giving way to another gasp as the second wave of pain coursed through his body. The large, muscular hand that had grabbed his shoulder was now enveloping his arm, dragging him violently through the trees. He looked round, wondering if he could wriggle free and make a run for it, but he knew he was having the thought more for form's sake than anything else. The man was monstrously large, and his other hand held a pistol that he periodically jabbed at the back of Simon's neck. A single shot would mean instant death. He'd been through the SERE training like everyone else: Survival, Evasion, Resistance, Escape. He was at the Resistance phase, not Escape. The one thing he couldn't see was any sign of Liz: no body on the ground, nor evidence of her capture. The thought of her sprinting back to the trucks to raise the alarm gave him a surge of hope. He knew from the training that you had to have hope.

'You! *No hope.*' One of his captors, a balding man wearing a khaki brown T-shirt, was showing off his command of English. 'No hope,' he repeated for clarity – unnecessarily, Simon thought – his eyes wild and staring. He drew his finger across his throat to remove any room for doubt. They were now level with the technical, a pickup truck with a .50 cal machine gun welded onto the flatbed. Behind that was a boxy armoured jeep that looked a bit like a Humvee. The soldiers standing by the vehicle were smoking, and Simon's arrival did not appear to attract much attention. No-Hope and the Monster pulled Simon's arms tightly behind his back and he felt a cable tie being placed around his hands. They pulled it tight and Simon winced as it dug into his skin. Then they squeezed it again, and Simon briefly wondered if they had taken a sharp knife to his wrists. His helmet was pulled off and a hood thrown over his head. They went through his pockets and pouches. He got a small boost from the thought that they'd find nothing of use. He was then manhandled into the back of the vehicle; his shins crunched against a metal step, no doubt deliberately.

He heard the door clang shut and the sound of a bolt being drawn. He was in a heap on the floor of the jeep, waiting for something to happen. It was a surprisingly long wait, but he suspected the soldiers were busy going through the bodies of the team, looking for intelligence.

He tried to stitch together what had happened. He'd heard the words 'not here', probably from Yuri. That was just before the drones dropped the grenades. *Not here.* He assumed that had meant no Chovka. He had known they were coming. And he had asked for Simon.

None of it makes sense.

There was the sound of talking outside. They didn't seem to be in any hurry to depart, and he wondered what the wait was for. Eventually, after what felt like a full hour but he had no idea really, some people had climbed into the front of the truck, slamming the doors. The vehicle moved away and he felt them swerve around the kill zone, the wheels rumbling over the churned-up ground. After that they seemed to speed up, and he tried to figure out which direction they were heading in. In the movies, spies who had been hooded and cuffed seemed to be able to know wherever they had been driven. Simon didn't feel he had any idea.

Instead, he tried to figure out who these people were. Their arrival, just after the drones had dropped their payload, had not been random chance. As far as Simon knew, the Russians were playing catch-up with the Ukrainians' mastery of drone technology. So this had to have been a specialist unit with access to high-end equipment. Not some random bunch of conscripts, but a team acting on specific forewarning of the planned ambush.

There was plenty he couldn't figure out, but some things were coming into focus: Chovka must have been indirectly in contact with Liz, presumably via Mayfly 4. He had said he wanted to come in from the cold. To cross the line. And this was something the CIA had taken an interest in. Yuri's team had decided to stage an ambush so that Chovka's disappearance would look like a capture, not a defection. But he hadn't been in the convoy. *Not here*, Yuri had shouted. So the whole Chovka operation had been a set-up. A *dangle*, as they used to call it in the Pole. And part of that dangle had been to ensure Simon's presence. Why him? Who cared about him?

Simon let out a sigh which turned into a groan. He felt a sudden wash of cold, as if he'd stepped into a freezing shower. Chovka had been the bait. Simon was the prey. But who had led him to this trap?

Yuri? No. Yuri's dead. Liz? But she had sounded distraught when the drone hit. That wasn't acting... What about that American talking to Yuri? Whose side is he on?

But what benefit can the Americans possibly gain from handing me to the Russians? Not them.

That leaves Sarah.

Can't be right.

He started to unwind the thought process that had brought him to this point, searching desperately for another explanation. The first time he had been to see Liz, she had already known about Chovka. And Sarah had been the link to Liz and Yuri. Sarah, who had showed up at his garret a few days before, distracted, moody and sexually available, something she had never been to him in the past quarter century. He had let his guard down, allowed his groin to do his thinking, not his brain.

No. Doesn't make sense. She was the whole reason I started the COSTELLO investigation. Can't be her.

And then he went round the same thought process again and again, desperate to reach another conclusion. And every time, he landed back in the same place: Sarah.

It was obvious from the start. Idiot.

Simon recalled his first meeting with Liz. What was it she had said? 'With Sarah, things tend not to be coincidences, do they?'

How right she had been. Sarah had guided Simon to the trap. A trap set by COSTELLO.

Chapter 35

Bakhmut

August 2022

Simon felt the truck slowing. He had kept his eyes closed for much of the journey, even though the hood had shut out what little there was to see. That way it was easier to try to imagine he was somewhere else altogether. For tiny snatches of time, it worked.

But reality intervened as the truck came to a halt and the doors were thrown open with a brutal clang. Simon felt himself being dragged out, his feet hitting the ground awkwardly, strong hands on his upper arms, the cable ties digging into his wrists. He was marched over flat ground, rubble underfoot, and then down a small flight of irregular stairs. His knee was still throbbing with pain and he stumbled several times before reaching the flat ground. There was a musty smell and the air had a dusty chill to it. He suspected he was in some kind of cellar. He shivered; these were places where bad things happened. Then he felt he was being moved along a corridor and once again heard the clanging of a steel door. He was being pushed down onto a seat and he felt his arms being forced behind the back of the chair. A new cable tie was being placed over both arms and looped behind the chair. His legs were still free, and he thought idly that he could still run, but he would have a chair strapped to his back if he did so. Absurdly, he worried that he would look ridiculous.

The hood was whipped off, pulling some tufts of hair with it. But the stinging pain on his scalp was good because it diverted him from the awful throbbing in his knee. Simon was momentarily blinded by a bright light shining directly into his eyes. He couldn't really see the room, but he could see two faces staring at him. No-Hope from the forest was there, his wide mouth grinning at him ravenously. He slapped Simon hard. The stinging pain reminded him of being a child. There was another man who looked like the brains of the operation, although perhaps that was putting it strongly, standing very still, arms folded. Something about his face was familiar, but he couldn't place it clearly. In the background he could hear the sound of artillery. It was fairly close, and he guessed he must still be somewhere near the Bakhmut battlefront.

In his SERE training, Simon had been taught a dissociation technique to try to manage the pain of torture. Pull your mind away from your body. Become an observer of the situation, rather than the person at the centre of it. This recollection of his training was briefly helpful. Another memory was the need to have a plan: figure out what information you can afford to let go and do not give anything up too early. Because everyone talks in the end.

Simon wondered whether it would be better just to do the talking now. The quiet man spoke in reasonable English, clear Russian accent. He sounded tired, even bored. 'You are foreign mercenary? Carrying out terror activities here in the sovereign Donetsk People's Republic?'

It took Simon a couple of efforts and much throat clearing to get one word out. 'Journalist.' He swallowed, but his mouth was so dry. 'My name is Simone Sartori. I am a journalist.'

The interrogator nodded and held out his hand, leaning closer to Simon. 'Press pass, please,' he asked, as if he were manning a checkpoint.

Simon wriggled his shoulders, his arms tightly bound behind the chair. Even if he'd had a pass in his pocket there was no way he'd have been able to pull it out. The interrogator knew that and made a shrugging gesture, as if he was mildly put out that Simon had chosen not to help him.

'We already went through your pockets and you are not carrying any accreditation. You are wearing military uniform. You are mercenary. We have death penalty for terrorism in the Donetsk People's Republic.' Where had Simon seen that face before? It was like watching a movie where the actor was familiar but you couldn't remember what you'd seen them in.

'My name is Simone Sartori. I am a journalist.'

'You were captured with weapon. There is holster on your belt. Journalists do not carry guns. Who are you?'

Who are you? Who is this man, this familiar face?

And then it hit him: a few weeks earlier, on a rainy day in the north-east of England, Simon had been lying on his stomach, unobserved, watching a small group of men having a business meeting inside a Portakabin. He had been there. Sarah had told him the name a few hours later: Sergey Sazanovich, a known Russian intelligence officer. Identified as an asset of COSTELLO, the Russian intelligence unit that nobody knew existed until Simon had discovered it.

For some reason, the realisation that he recognised this man gave Simon a little burst of defiance. He knew he was in the hands of COSTELLO, but they might not know he knew.

'My name is Simone Sartori. I am a journalist—'

No-Hope launched a powerful kick at Simon's kneecap. Simon started screaming before the boot had even hit. The pain sent fireworks across his brain and he seemed to have been blinded. His arms strained involuntarily against the cable ties, as he was desperate to clutch at his knee. Instead, the waves of pain ran up into his groin and he had to fight not to piss himself.

Gradually, his scream dropped through the octaves to a growl of angry pain and his vision returned. The pain was no longer excruciating. Just terrible waves of intensity. He waggled his leg desperately, vainly trying to shake away the feeling.

Dissociation didn't seem to be working. Everyone talks in the end. Simon was ready, and they'd been going for only five minutes. It was not physical courage or mental strength that stopped him. It was that he wasn't even sure himself who he was. He could hardly confess to being a British spy when he had not been one in nearly ten years. He was not on a British intelligence mission. He was on his own, betrayed by the person he thought was his closest ally.

'I am a reporter embedded with the unit. In these conditions journalists wear uniform. I did not carry a gun. You did not find me with a gun,' said Simon, recalling the moment his pistol had tumbled out of his hand just before his arrest.

'We found your weapon on the floor. You are a mercenary and a terrorist... Another one?' Sergey said these final two words in Russian to No-Hope, who began to limber up for another kick.

'No!' Simon shouted out instinctively. Sergey raised his hand to stop the next assault.

'*Vy ponimayete po-russki?*' he said to Simon – You understand Russian? Sergey smiled at this new revelation. '*Ne nayemnik. Shpion.*' – Not mercenary. Spy. He switched back to English. 'Now, we are making progress. You were with a special services unit working with NATO intelligence. No journalist would be with such a unit. You are not *spetsnaz*, that is clear. You appear to have minimal weapons training. So you must be a spy. Which agency are you working for?'

The pain in Simon's knee was now pulsating, excruciating him in surges. Sergey had briefly disappeared to a dark corner of the room. Now he was looming back into view, holding a small metal object that looked like a nail file. As he came closer, Simon realised it was a surgical scalpel. Sergey leant down, so close to Simon that he could see the individual hair follicles and the tiny grey sprouts of two-day stubble. He was breathing heavily, deep sighs of rancid air. He fixed Simon with a lifeless stare as he pressed the blade against Simon's little finger. The edge sliced cleanly into Simon's flesh and he gasped. It felt like a clean pain. Perhaps he could endure it? He felt the scalpel edge slicing into the joint, the blood warmly wet against his ring finger.

Don't scream. You can do this.

Simon screamed. Sergey pulled the blade out and then it really hit. Searing, slicing pain that ran from the end of his finger up his arm and down to the end of his leg. He screamed again and looked at his finger. The end was still attached, barely visible among the blood.

Everybody talks in the end. He wanted to start talking, but he was sure the truth would make no sense to Sergey. 'I have contacts in the British government,' he blurted out desperately. 'I am a former official and I will share information with appropriate officials. But I am not a spy. I swear this is the truth.' His voice was quavering, and he hated himself for it. 'You can cut my whole hand off but it won't change anything. I have not been sent here by my government.'

'We have a saying. Once a Chekist, always a Chekist. Nobody is a *former* anything, *Simone.*' He said the name sarcastically. 'Should I just call you Simon? It is your name, after all. Simon Sharman, why don't you have a little think about the reality of this situation? And then we can start talking.'

With a sense of bitter despair, Simon realised they knew everything. They knew because Sarah would have told them. They knew who he was. They would know his reason for being in Ukraine. And they must have known about his work to uncover the existence of COSTELLO.

Once a Chekist, always a Chekist.

Chapter 36

Bakhmut

August 2022

Liz was washed through the woods on a flood of adrenaline. She barely felt her feet on the ground as she wove towards the open fields. Bullets were ricocheting off the trees around her. Some rounds passed so close that she felt the air displaced by their passing. One hit a tree trunk by her face, sending splinters cutting into her cheeks. But the intensity of the fire was reducing, and as she neared the edge of the copse she could only hear rounds from a single weapon. She landed herself in the shallow ditch that marked the edge of the field, where she waited. Another bullet flew overhead and she could tell that its shooter was close by. Lying on her side in the ditch, she pulled her rifle across her chest, slowly and silently. She placed her finger on the trigger and waited, straining to control her breath. She could hear the distant commotion from the kill zone, the sound of truck engines, shouting in Russian.

Then she heard it: no more than the scratch of a boot sole on uneven ground. Coolly, Liz shifted the selector on her rifle to rapid fire and waited. Another scratching sound, closer. It was enough. She had started firing almost before she needed to, executing a rapid sit-up and spraying a line of bullets into the torso of the Russian soldier, sending him flying backwards. He was so close to the ditch that his blood splashed onto Liz's face.

She wanted to run straight away, across the open field and back towards the trucks. But she couldn't be sure whether there were more of them. She would be in open ground, easily picked off. So she crawled along the ditch as far as she could without breaking cover. She could hear the sounds of soldiers talking, the clanging of truck doors. There was a heart-stopping moment when two voices came close. They were looking for their fallen comrade. She heard them come across the body, a mere twenty metres away. Straining a little, she could make out their conversation.

'Poor fucker,' said one. 'Better take him back.'

'Shouldn't we be going after the nazi who did this?'

'Long gone, I imagine. We've got what we came for.'

Liz stayed in the ditch as she heard the sounds of the two men dragging the body back to their trucks. They seemed to be taking ages and she became desperately uncomfortable. It was an act of physical will not to get up and run. Finally, there was a clang of doors and the sound of engines picking up speed as the convoy drove off into the night. She waited until she could no longer hear the engines and then gave it another ten minutes, just to be sure. The silence of the night resumed, broken only by occasional and distant booms from the battlefront. It was time to go. Staggering to her feet, she bounded out across the field, back towards the trucks.

She was surprised that Erik wasn't already heading in her direction. She knew they had to remain dark – no radio trans-missions – all the time they were across the line. But he would have heard the commotion unfolding, wouldn't he? Or did it just sound like the ambush taking place as planned? Where the trucks had been parked under an overgrown hedge was quiet. She stood still and pulled her rifle to her eyeline. There was just the faint sound of the wind in the trees and the distant growl of engines at the ambush site. The trucks appeared to be empty. But where was Erik? She crept forwards, trying to give herself a good angle so that the engine block of the first truck would shield her. Her senses were screaming that something was wrong but she couldn't see anything, not in the twin-cabs, not under the trucks. She continued to edge round the vehicles, her back to the open ground to reduce the risk of being surprised.

She crept round the front of the truck and Erik was in front of her, sitting against the wheel, looking as if he was taking a breather, his head leant back. She ran up to him. He had a surprised look, his face turned upwards and illuminated by the moonlight. There was a single neat bullet hole in the middle of his forehead.

Liz slammed her fist on the truck with a mixture of fury and devastation. But she quickly collected herself. Whoever had killed Erik might still be nearby. She grabbed his body and opened the rear door, groaning as she hauled him into the vehicle, laying him out along the bench seat. Then she ran to the driver's door and pulled herself up on the steering wheel, her hands searching for the ignition key. The engine grunted into life and she swung the truck back onto the dirt track, her foot slamming the accelerator. She had to get to safer territory before she could risk any comms.

'Come on. *Come on!*' She urged the truck round the sharp corners of the route they had followed earlier in the night. Liz, who prided herself on careful planning and preparation, was now disorientated. Somehow, she had taken a wrong turn and missed the little bridge that marked an ill-defended salient of the front line. 'Fuck!' she screamed, furious with herself and starting to dread the debriefs, explanations, reports, justifications and second-guesses that would inevitably follow this failed mission. She swung the truck round in a J-turn that made Erik's body fall off the bench seat into the footwell. She then gunned the truck back onto the track and found the right gap in the field boundary that led to the bridge. She crossed this so quickly that it felt as if all four wheels of the truck had left the ground.

The significance of this bridge in Russia's full-scale war on Ukraine was minimal. It marked a commonly accepted understanding of a border between Russian-held and Ukrainian territory. But it was an uncontested part of the line simply because neither side had tried to mass force at that point. The act of crossing the bridge did not reduce the chance that artillery shells, rockets or any other threat might strike her. But she felt safer, closer to home. She flicked on her radio and transmitted an anodyne message.

'Returning to base.' She gave their call sign, but not their location. No mention of the disaster that had unfolded. Someone had leaked their operational plan. There must be a mole somewhere inside the system, and she could not afford to trust anyone.

Almost anyone. With one hand on the wheel, she squirmed awkwardly to reach a pocket that was under her body armour, pulling out a small Nokia handset. She tapped out an SMS:

> *Svitlana can't make it. Sorry.*

The recognition word was Svitlana. But something caused her to add the apology. Was she apologising to her other comrades, who had just given their lives to Ukraine?

'*Heroiam slava!*' she screamed at nobody in particular, slamming her hands on the steering wheel, her eyes running with tears.

Glory to the heroes.

Chapter 37

Kyiv, Hotel Continental
August 2022

The sound of a message arriving was a welcome distraction. Holed up in her room, Sarah had been wanting to find the excuse to do some work, but Jonty had knocked on the door asking, 'What news on the Rialto?' and, there being none at that stage, had decided to hang around and talk incessantly. Had it been anyone else, Sarah would have said he was anxious. But as far as she knew, Jonty didn't do anxious, so she assumed it was enthusiasm. About the war, the Ukrainians' changing of the world order, pushing Russia backwards on the battlefield. She had rarely seen him so stimulated, in spite of his age. The war that he had spent his entire life preparing to fight had arrived – just a little later than expected – and he was doing everything to make sure he could make a difference, even in the autumn of his life.

'There's no way the Russians can win this now,' he had said, excitedly and not for the first time. Sarah nodded and fumbled for her phone, squinting at an SMS from an unusual number. She was about to delete it: random spam. Then she read it a second time.

'Shit.'

'What?' said Jonty, looking rather surprised to be cut off mid-flow with this discourtesy.

'Shit. Shit. Shit.' Sarah closed her eyes, perhaps hoping the room would disappear and all of this would prove a bad dream.

'Op's gone bad, hasn't it?' He hadn't needed telling. Jonty spoke with a quiet calm, born of years of experience.

'Svitlana. That was the word for… for a complete fuck-up, actually. Oh, *Christ*!' She leant her head back and stared at the ceiling, trying to steady herself. 'I had three girls with Liz. Three names. Ksenia – good. Chovka's over the line. Olga – no Chovka but they're all safe. Svitlana – everything's fucked up… Oh, Jesus! What has happened?' Sarah was breathing heavily, the hint of a sob around the edges of her voice.

'All right…' Jonty was trying to project steadiness. 'Let's gather the information. Sounds like "Svitlana" could mean a lot of different things. How do we speak to Liz?'

'She'll call as soon as she's safe to.' Sarah stood up, pacing the room in the way nervous people do.

Chapter 38

Sazanovich and No-Hope had left Simon alone with this despair. For him, it was a kind of release. He had thought he was trying to stay strong, to do the right thing for other people who cared about him. Maybe even loved him. But now he realised he had deluded himself. Knowing that he had neither allies or friends had the strange effect of removing the fear. There was now no advantage to surviving. He would still have to endure pain, but death itself would be the release. He looked at his left hand, sticky with drying blood, and had a momentary flash of defiance.

I will take Chovka down with me. It would be his final act. A decision that he could make for himself. Doing right by Evie. With this thought clear in his mind, he drifted into an uneasy stupor.

He did not know how many hours it had been when the door opened and a light was shone into his eyes again. He knew from experience that interrogators liked to leave their prisoners to wallow in hopelessness, but they would not have let him sleep.

Sergey approached the chair again, a new swagger to his gait. He knew that he had the upper hand, that Simon was as good as broken.

'Some tea?' he asked, with a vulpine grin. Simon appreciated that this was a textbook interrogation. Shock of capture, fear-up, inflict some pain, enough to scare but not enough to debilitate. Then, a reward. Some tea. 'Of course, Simon, we are both professionals. You know I can't bring you the tea before you give me something. You know how this works.'

'I was here to make a recruitment,' Simon said, plainly.

'So you admit that you are an intelligence officer? Simon Sharman of Britain's Joint Intelligence Directorate, sometimes known as the Pole? That is you, is it not?'

'I am Simon Sharman. I was here to make a recruitment of one of your operatives. He had offered his services.'

Sazanovich's smile disappeared and he slammed Simon's face with the back of his hand, more punch than slap.

'You do not get to denounce one of my people just to save your own skin.'

Simon's face was stinging and his eyes had filled with tears. 'Sazanovich.'

The one word had an immediate effect on his captor, and Simon felt a tiny flash of superiority. Sergey had not expected that.

'We infiltrated your COSTELLO network, Sergey Sazanovich. We know a lot about you. You were in England at the Powerstream site with Marcus Peebles. And I was here to make a recruitment. One of your operatives had volunteered his services. To me, specifically.'

Sazanovich had put the smile back on his face, but he swallowed uncomfortably. 'The name?' He tapped his finger on the bloodied mess of Simon's left hand, and he yelped at the stinging sensation. 'The name, Simon. We start with the name.'

Simon knew that the name was the ending. At that point he would be of little use to them. He accepted death, but some Darwinian urge in him forced him onwards, not yet ready to conclude the story.

'One of your most trusted operatives. Used in the most challenging and demanding jobs. He had been talking to our side, ready to come over—'

'The name. *The name!*' Sergey reached for his holster and pulled out a pistol, which he cocked angrily. He shoved it against the side of Simon's head and leant his head very close to Simon's ear. He could hear the heavy breathing of an over-weight middle-aged man who drank far too much vodka. He spoke very quietly and slowly now. 'We start with the name.'

Chapter 39

Kyiv

August 2022

Sarah's phone rang and she grabbed at it with clumsy hands.

'Yes? Liz?'

'They were ready for us. Chovka wasn't there. Simon is captured. Everyone else is dead.' Liz's voice held up, breaking only slightly on the last sentence.

Later on, Jonty commended Sarah's calmness, but she was sure he was just being kind. She had little memory of the rest of the conversation, as the awful reality of the situation had unfolded. But Jonty was in control, the years of experience obvious. Immediately he seemed to know what he needed to do, getting word to the right people, reassuring Sarah.

'Things look pretty awful now, but we mustn't give up hope.'

Sarah kept saying she didn't understand how this had happened, but Jonty had brushed that aside.

'We'll have lots of time for that later. Let's just get him back.'

Sarah appreciated what he was saying and why he was saying it, but she knew that the chances of Simon coming out alive were minimal. She knew this because she had sent him on this mission in the full knowledge of the risks involved. Jonty's busy determination almost seemed inappropriate.

'I'm going to call in a favour. Or two. We can still fix this, Sarah.'

Chapter 40

The door to the basement dungeon swung open and No-Hope entered. Never a good sign. Simon could briefly see another figure entering, silhouetted against the light outside, before the door clanged shut again. Sergey looked round irritably at the new arrivals and wandered over to speak to one of them. They huddled together, speaking in low tones. Simon could not make out what they were saying. There were just snatched words: *what?... Now? Yes, commanded ... artillery...* During the quiet of this whispered conversation, No-Hope had picked up the scalpel and was toying menacingly with it. There was a deafening crash of incoming artillery, this time very close to the building. If Simon had not been strapped to a chair, he would have flinched. There was a strange ringing in his ears and he wasn't sure if he could hear properly. The explosion had caused some loose mortar to flake off the roof of the dungeon and Simon felt the dust sprinkling onto his hair. No-Hope had moved towards the other two men, their voices now slightly raised. Some agreement had been reached.

'Okay, let's go,' said Sergey, and the hood was thrown over Simon's head again. He felt a thin piece of cold metal pressed against his arm where the cable tie held him to the chair. Then there was a ping as the cable tie was slit. For good measure, No-Hope slashed Simon's arm. But the cut wasn't deep, just an act of petulant frustration. The sting was almost welcome as it took Simon's mind off the agony in his knee. He was wrenched to his feet, No-Hope's thumbnail grinding into the open cut in his arm.

'Fucking sadist,' Simon growled. This earned him a slap in the face.

His knee briefly gave way, but he was able to tense his leg and stay upright. He felt himself being marched out of the cellar and up the stairs and was soon in the fresher air outside. He could hear a vehicle up ahead – a heavy chugging diesel engine – and they began to move him towards the sound.

Suddenly there was the banshee scream of an incoming mortar, the note dropping swiftly as it descended towards them, and he felt himself being pushed down. He let out a bellow of pain as he fell on his bad knee, just as the mortar landed. It was incredibly close and he felt a rush of hot air. He was momentarily deafened by the boom of the explosion.

Simon was wrenched to his feet again. There was a shout of 'Bystryy!' – Quickly! – and then he was half stumbling towards the engine sound. He could smell the diesel fumes and heard a heavy metal door opening. This time he did a better job on the step at the back and launched himself forwards into the interior, trying to put the pressure on his good leg. The clang of the door slamming behind him was almost instant, and he felt the motion of the truck moving. It was driving jerkily and at some speed, and Simon was thrown around in the darkness as he tried without success to wedge himself into a sitting position.

They had evidently emerged in the middle of a major military engagement. Artillery and mortar rounds, both incoming and outgoing were crashing around them. Some of these caused the truck to shake, and he felt them brake sharply and lurch into reverse. But then they seemed to have reached a better spot: the truck was driving fast along a straight road, the explosions seeming more distant. Simon wondered whether it would have been a good thing for the truck to have been hit directly by the artillery. At least he would have felt very little. Not a bad way to go.

There was another huge boom. It sounded as though it was right inside the vehicle. He felt himself being thrown forwards, his shoulder thudding painfully on the opposite wall of the box-like interior. He found it difficult to sit up and couldn't work out why. Then he realised: the entire vehicle had turned on its side; the wall had become the floor. With his hands still uselessly cable-tied behind his back, he rolled over and tried to stand up. There was a crack of gunshot and he heard a cry from the cab of the truck, little more than a metre from his head. Another few shots rang out, including one that seemed to have come through the skin of the rear box that he was in. And then there was the clanging sound of one of the rear doors being pulled down, now a horizontal slot at ground level.

A voice said 'Come on!' in English with a Russian accent, but it didn't sound like Sergey. He wriggled towards the opening and someone dragged him through the gap, pulling him to his feet. The hands were less firm on his arm, the intention to cause pain no longer obvious. But they were still moving very quickly and he stumbled, crying out in pain as he was quick-marched across uneven ground. Someone put their shoulder under his armpit to take the weight off his leg. He felt himself being manoeuvred onto another truck and was told to lie down. He could feel a hatch being closed and he guessed he was in the rear flatbed of a pickup, which immediately surged into action, bumping over the wrecked roads. He might have passed out, or just blocked the rest of that journey, the pain of his knee sending shock waves through his body with every pothole, the sense of claustrophobia in the coffin-like trunk he had been entombed in.

But these people seemed to want to help him.

The truck had stopped and there was the sound of several men talking, quietly. He could hear muffled Russian, but struggled to make out exactly what he was hearing. Then there was the crunch of boots on gravelly ground and he wondered if he had been left alone. Perhaps this was his coffin after all?

With a rush of air that felt sweet and cool, the hatch was levered up and a hand reached in, pulling Simon upright. Gently, it seemed. He was guided to the edge of the pickup and stepped down onto the ground, leaning his unsteady body against the rear of the vehicle. He felt a hand carefully pull the hood off and he blinked into a night sky, lit with the glow of an approaching dawn. A man was standing in front of him, looking windswept and tanned and grinning as if this was all great fun.

'Misha! You are really making a lot of work for me. What the fuck are you doing here?' asked Vasya Morozov.

Chapter 41

In the first moments that Vasya spoke to him, Simon did not realise who this person was, calling him Misha and asking him what the fuck he was doing there. Simon's legs were very unsteady, and after hours of being cable-tied behind his back, he had long since lost all feeling in his forearms.

After several blank seconds Simon had a burst of realisation. *Vasya. But that's impossible. Not here. Not in Bakhmut.*

He blinked several times and the person in front of him continued to be Vasya. Wearing Russian military fatigues, but unmistakably Vasya. Simon was sure he was supposed to say something, but no words came out when he moved his mouth. Vasya had stepped forwards and could have been clasping him in an embrace. In fact, he was reaching behind to cut Simon's arms loose. The cable ties had cut into his skin and his wrists had become crusted together with dried blood. It took an extra effort to prise them apart, the cuts stinging with new bleeding. His shoulders and back were burning with pain, and he put a hand on Vasya's arm to steady himself. That was when his legs gave way, his entire body weight falling forwards onto Vasya's shoulders. Vasya swayed slightly under the unexpected weight and then clasped Simon in a firm hug.

'I've got you, Misha. We're going to be okay.' Simon realised the stinging on the cuts in his face was from the tears.

'Water.' Vasya manoeuvred him to the passenger seat of the pickup and thrust a plastic bottle into his hand. Simon couldn't open it: his fingers didn't seem to grip properly, so Vasya had to help again. He took a huge slurp and the water was the sweetest thing he'd ever tasted. He let out a huge sigh, and there must have been some light in his eyes, because Vasya smiled.

'So I ask again, Misha, what the fuck are you doing here?'

When they'd first met, about twenty years earlier, Simon had used the alias Michael. Since then Vasya usually called him Misha, long after he'd learned Simon's real name.

'I reckon I should ask the same of you,' replied Simon. Vasya's wide mouth broke into a smile, which turned into a laugh. This was brought to an end by the distant crump of exploding artillery. Not close enough to matter, but close enough to make you stop laughing. Simon took in his surroundings for the first time. They were near some kind of abandoned coal mine. He could see the pithead gear against the light of the breaking dawn, and there were shabby buildings dotted around them. It was all dilapidated, with broken windows and rusting machinery. For a fleeting moment Simon wondered if they'd passed back across the front lines into Ukraine-held territory. But this seemed too much to hope for.

Vasya was laughing again, wiping his eyes and shaking his head. *Whatever it is, I'm not sure it's that funny*, thought Simon.

'Look at the pair of us,' said Vasya. 'Middle-aged guys dressed up as soldiers and stuck in a fucking war zone.'

'At least you *were* a soldier at some point.'

'Which brings me back to the explanations. What are you doing here, Misha?'

Simon was feeling seasick. He had expected to be tortured to death in a cellar. Maybe Vasya would shoot him, but he was sure he wouldn't torture him.

'You told me Chovka was in Ukraine in the first place. I reckon you know exactly what I'm doing here,' he said, boldly.

There was a silence as Vasya digested this point. He seemed to accept its validity, as he was nodding his head slowly.

'But you, on the other hand...' Simon continued. 'You should be living the high life in Switzerland.' There was another crunching boom of artillery. This one was closer than the last, drowning out Simon's words. The world was waking up, including the warring armies.

'Misha, we need to get to a safe place. Short drive. Some old coal tunnels. Then we talk. There's a lot to say.'

Briefly, Simon had a misplaced sense of shared adventure. The two of them, a pickup truck and all of their combined wits. Two spies against the world – was there anything they couldn't accomplish? Like the old days. Except, it was very different from the old days. For all of Vasya's throwaway laughter and bonhomie, Simon could tell he was anxious, chewing on his thumb and drumming his fingers on the steering wheel. For his part, Simon was ragged, his hands a mess, barely able to walk. And they must both be wanted men by at least one side in the bloody war raging on around them.

Vasya drove through a maze of tracks and ramps, part of a huge abandoned mining facility. They pulled up at a single-storey block that looked little different from many others they'd passed: smashed windows, a musty smell of decay. Vasya led the way, stopping to grab an AK-47 and a small satchel from behind the seat of the pickup. It was dark inside the unlit building and Vasya used a head torch to lead them to a ramp, which descended into the start of an access tunnel. Simon was moving painfully slowly, but eventually they reached what might once have been the changing room for the miners, rows of benches and lockers that reminded Simon of a school. Simon gratefully plonked himself down on a bench and took another slurp of water. Vasya seemed too agitated to sit and was pacing up and down, his torchlight bouncing in the dark.

'Come on, just sit down and tell me what's going on.'

He sighed and positioned himself next to Simon on the bench, rummaging in his bag for something as he did so. Simon felt a flat metal object being pushed into his hand and realised this was a hip flask.

'Have some,' said Vasya. 'You'll need it.'

Simon was reasonably sure he didn't need strong liquor, but he obeyed nonetheless. It was brandy, and tasted surprisingly good. That was something he liked about Vasya: even in a war zone he showed up with proper cognac. They sat in silence. Vasya was working out how best to explain something. Simon had had enough years as his handler to know what these pauses felt like, the strange intimacy of source and case officer.

'Okay, Misha,' he said, 'perhaps we begin at the easy bit. I am here in the Donbas doing what many former GRU guys are doing. Fighting for Mother Russia. I have a team, some ex-*Spetsnaz*, some grunts. Russia needs its people in this war. They pay for our work. So, I showed up.'

'What – like Wagner?'

Vasya spluttered derisively. 'Not like the Chef, because we follow orders and don't decide that we know better than the bloody minister of defence. But yes, this is a commercial operation. We're all mercenaries, aren't we?'

Simon had a memory of Vasya having used these exact words, only a few months earlier, when they had met on a Swiss mountainside. It had meant something very different then. 'It doesn't add up. I've known you too long. You were having a nice time getting rich in Switzerland last time I saw you. You didn't have to be in this hellhole. Something's happened.'

'I am a patriot and an entrepreneur. The Donbas is where these two things collide.'

'Bullshit. Yes, I'm sure you're a patriot, but something's happened.'

'Quite a way to thank me for rescuing you.'

'Fair enough. I am incredibly fucking grateful. Thank you. Now, what's the thing you are finding difficult to say?'

'The truth is rarely pure and never simple. That's your Oscar Wilde, isn't it? We do things for many reasons. I am here as an act of patriotism. It's making me money... And also, like any good business, it does not require me to be here all the time for it to function correctly.' He sniffed pompously, as if he were giving a talk on 'running modern private military operations' for an MBA course. 'But I said I would start with the easy bit. So now I go back one step. I can be a patriot from a safe distance. I can make money quite well in Switzerland. What brought me here?'

'I'm all ears,' said Simon sarcastically.

'Let me tell you a story. A young sports player makes a mistake. Maybe, since you're an Englishman, maybe he's playing soccer. It's a small mistake, but he's unlucky: his opponents don't let him get away with it, so he is presented with a choice. He can take his chances with his coach, who has a reputation for being unforgiving, or he can take the risk of working with the opposing team. He does this. But at a certain point he sees that his new team aren't playing the game any more. At least, they're not playing to win. He could stop playing, walk away from the game. But what if he gets an offer from another team? The number one team in the world? A team that is still playing to win. What should he do?'

'Yeah, but it doesn't work: in soccer you can't be on two teams at once. In our world you can.'

'That's why this is only a story. So, in the story, does the player take the call? From that number one team... say, Manchester City?'

In Simon's view, Manchester City was everything that was wrong with modern football. 'I wouldn't. But maybe that's why I haven't been very successful. For me, it's about values.'

'Values? In sport, value is winning. You have to play to win.'

'Shall we stop talking about football?'

'Sure. I'm a hockey guy.'

'Vasya, I just need to hear it from you straight.' Simon was starting to see where this was going, but he didn't want to follow it to its logical conclusion.

'In 2014, you, me and the Pole parted ways. Britain had given up. I wanted to get into business. You know this story. But you also know our saying: once a Chekist, always a Chekist. I wasn't ready to give up. So, I joined the other team. The one playing to win.'

Simon had the sensation of an optical illusion, where one picture was turning into another in front of his eyes, but the image was in fact unchanged.

'The Americans?'

'The number one team.'

Simon began with denial. 'No, sorry. This is crap. We both know what happened. My people didn't believe what you were telling them about Crimea in 2014. We were both angry and we went our separate ways. You, for your business, me for… Well, for mine. Except it didn't really take me very far.'

'The Crimea thing made it easier. It gave me a reason. I didn't have to make something up.'

Simon had moved quickly from denial to anger. 'Wait a fucking minute, Vasya. If you hadn't left, perhaps I'd still be at the Pole. Perhaps I'd be… I dunno, a senior guy now. Instead, I'm sitting in an abandoned coal mine in a fucking war zone with a busted leg, and I don't really know why I'm here. You've been playing me, all that time?'

Vasya laughed bitterly. 'You lost me at the bit where you didn't like being played. We're spies, Misha. What you mean is you didn't like being *out*played.'

There was a pause as Simon tried to take in what he was being told.

'But this doesn't make sense. The Americans. I mean, maybe they pay you better, but you never complained to me about money. You're loaded now, anyway.'

'Has it occurred to you that it was my relationship with the new team that made it possible for me to make some real money?'

This had not occurred to Simon.

'Misha… No, let me do you the respect of calling you Simon. There's a lot about Uncle Sam that drives me mad. If

I never have to see another fucking polygraph machine, I'll be very happy. But they do this stuff in a different way. For them, it's about making things happen. You Brits just wanted little reports. "This guy is now the Assistant Director for Administration in the Third Directorate of the Second Division of the Ministry of Railways." Who gives a shit? And what is your so-called Global Britain going to do with these reports anyway? Even the Crimea stuff? If your people had believed me, would Britain have done anything? Of course you wouldn't. You would have just sat on your hands, waiting to see what Uncle Sam was going to do. And if he wasn't going to do anything, you would just make a *jolly old cup of tea*.'

'Okay, so we align with the Americans. But we're nimble. We punch above our weight.' Vasya laughed again. This time the hilarity sounded genuine. Simon ploughed on. 'We work with the Americans for a reason. It's a kind of leverage. You could have told me that you wanted to do something bigger. Perhaps we could have done a joint operation with the agency.'

Simon was at the bargaining stage.

'A joint operation with the agency? You think the guys in Langley want to do the serious stuff with you guys? The stuff that really matters to them? Ever heard of NOFORN?'

Simon had indeed heard of NOFORN, the restrictive marking for 'No Foreign Nationals' that was stamped on top of much of the intelligence gathered by US agencies. Vasya would not have been material for a joint operation.

He had not finished. 'The thing about you Brits is you assume you should be treated as a world power. And at the same time, you run yourself like a village council. We all know you barely have an army any more. Or a navy. Why do you even imagine that someone would choose to work with you on something that *really* matters? This is the real world, not some fucking British Empire theme park.' Simon was stung into silence.

Depression, then acceptance.

Chapter 42

Bakhmut

August 2022

If Vasya's decision to ditch the Pole and work with the Americans had a brutal logic to it, Simon was still struggling to make sense of Vasya's behaviour when they had last met, in Crans-Montana, a Swiss mountain resort known to be popular with Russian oligarchs. He had railed violently against Britain's policy towards Russia, at one point holding Simon over the edge of a cliff. The recollection of that moment set his body coursing with adrenaline: the sheer drop stretching down hundreds of metres; the soles of his hiking boots gripping tenuously on to the cliff edge.

'When I came to see you in Crans you... you nearly pushed me down a bloody mountain. Because you said we'd fucked Russia and we were playing with you. And all that time you were actually working with the Americans? You expect me to believe that?'

Vasya had sat down on the bench again. Now that he had told Simon what was really going on, he was happy to be next to him, making eye contact. 'Simon, this begins with a mistake I made in Vienna. Sometimes I wonder what would have happened to me if you had not taken advantage. But you gave me no choice. If I hadn't become your source, you would have destroyed my career anyway. Once you had made me a traitor, I was stuck on a certain path. And then you guys let me down in 2014. There's that. I think the West has much responsibility for what has happened to Russia.' He stopped and looked at Simon, who was about to say something. But then he cut him off. 'These things make me angry sometimes.'

'You nearly fucking killed me.'

'Maybe. But I didn't kill you. And I helped you with something pretty big… The truth is rarely pure and never simple.'

'And did you report back to the Americans? About our meeting? About what we spoke about? About COSTELLO?'

'Naturally. But it was them that told me to expect you. And asked me to be helpful. I should think they were happy that someone in the UK was finally doing something about it.'

Simon slammed his hands down on the bench in frustration. The feeling was coming back, and it hurt more than he'd expected. Had the whole COSTELLO investigation been set up like a massive role-playing exercise? Had he been an unwitting American puppet? Someone had tipped them off.

Sarah. She would have known that I'd go to see Vasya. But Sarah has just betrayed me to the Russians.

Simon leant forwards, his head in his hands, massaging his brain in the hope that it would make things clearer. His head hurt, his knee hurt. Everything hurt. 'There's a lot that isn't making sense right now, Vasya.' But even as he said this, he felt he was beginning to understand something. 'Oh, hang on… The whole Oxford thing was a Langley op, wasn't it?'

'Simon, *Simon*. Really, the Americans? They don't spy on their allies, do they? Hah!' Vasya said this with the bitter sarcasm that often arises when two spies talk to each other.

'I suppose I can see how it could happen,' said Simon, thinking out loud. 'Washington was getting pretty stressed about the Brits selling our souls to Mother Russia. About the possible existence of a Russian spy ring at the heart of the British Establishment. So they decided to get to the bottom of that… When you told me about Kleshnyov, you knew the whole COSTELLO story anyway?'

'No. Remember: this was led by Langley, not me. I told you what little I knew, and you took it and did the work. Seems like you did a great job. Uncovered the whole story. I never doubted you were bloody good at this.'

Everything led back to Sarah. Sarah had commissioned Simon to investigate the Oxford spy ring. He had been told it was for a small subcommittee of the British government. Off the books, keeping it away from prying eyes around Rory Gough and the Prime Minister. But now he knew the Americans had been the puppet masters. And Sarah — adviser to NATO governments on Russia strategy, feature of the think-tank circuit in Washington DC — was the person they had turned to, to structure an operation that had no American fingerprints on it.

'Makes sense,' said Simon, 'to do it that way.' But then it didn't make sense that Sarah had betrayed the Chovka operation. Everything hurt again. 'How did you know I was in a dungeon with Sazanovich trying to cut my finger off?'

'Simon, like I said, I have a team. We carry out tasks that are given us by Langley... When your mission went south, I was told to get you out. What was impressive was how quickly the news came to me. Let's just say you seem to have better friends than I had realised. Jonty was on to me the moment you were picked up. Took us a little while to get organised, of course, get the full instructions from Langley. But the initial heads-up was Jonty, right on cue. That guy has your back. Seems I'm not the only one with a soft spot for you. We had to pick our moment, some artillery backup, and I showed up.' He smiled, as if it had been the easiest thing in the world.

There were so many other questions that Simon wanted to ask. 'What about Sarah?'

'Meaning what, exactly?'

Is Vasya being evasive?

'What was her involvement in getting you here?'

'Nothing. Like I said, first Jonty, then the people in Langley.'

'And Chovka? What about him? I was told he asked for me. So how come he wasn't there?'

'Yes. That's the bit I don't understand either. Chovka told me, personally, that he was ready to come over. He wouldn't talk to an American. So you were useful. I told him that you were the top British spy in Ukraine. Words to that effect. I mean, we both know that's bullshit, right?'

'*You* spoke to Chovka?'

'Yes. First met him in Crans-Montana, actually. He was working for a Ukrainian called Dudnik. One of those gas people.'

'I know who Dudnik is. What I'm trying to get my head around is that you already knew Chovka when he killed Evie.'

'I didn't know he was going to kill Evie, did I? Or try to kill you, come to think of it.'

'How would I know? I've got no reason to believe anything any more.'

'Look: I met Chovka at Dudnik's house. We chatted briefly. Kept in touch: you never know when it might be useful to know a Chechen tough guy. But we weren't in regular contact. Until I had a reason to be. And then I was just a messenger. I told Chovka that he had a problem on his hands. The timing was lucky. He wanted out. I told him that you were the guy. And then the Ukies linked him up with their Mayfly network.'

'And I'm the last to know. Sarah gets me to do things, you get me to do things, some fucker in Langley gets me to do things. And I'm just the idiot on the end of it all, not realising. Just a fucking puppet! But you got screwed, too, didn't you? Chovka wasn't there.'

'Someone must have leaked the plan.'

'Who? Who leaked it, Vasya?' Simon was sure he knew: Sarah. But he needed to hear it from him.

Vasya shrugged, infuriatingly. 'Misha, this is a war. Everyone is trying to be on every side at once.'

'That might be your way to fight a war. I still don't understand why you're here. Why you're doing this? If Ukraine wins this war, Russia is fucked. Wouldn't it be better to stay in Switzerland?'

'No, Misha. If Ukraine wins this war, the current leadership in Moscow is fucked. Not Russia. Remember: Russia tied down here, unable to fight anywhere else, that is great for America.' Simon had a moment of clarity. Vasya, whilst well connected in the Russian system, had never been able to reach all the way to the top. His Moscow background meant that the innermost circles, dominated by the President's friends from St Petersburg, would always be closed to him. The demise of the current ruling elite would present him with potential opportunities. Opportunities that might even make it worthwhile spending time in a deadly war zone.

Play to win.

'So, what do we do now? What about Chovka?'

'He's not the priority. Right now, my mission is getting you back. You're a long way from safety.'

Simon shivered. He had almost allowed himself to forget that he was inside Russian territory. And he wondered, if he made it back, whether he could avoid Sarah. She had delivered him to COSTELLO. His return from the dead would be a deadly threat to her. Simon's life was about to get even more complicated.

'You have one thing in your favour,' continued Vasya. 'This war is chaos. I guess they all are, but this one *really* is. There isn't one Russian army: there's the fucking Donetsk People's Republic morons with their weapons from the military museum. There's the regular military, the naval infantry, the *Spetsnaz*, the Chechens. And then there's the private military companies. Wagner everyone has heard of, but there are plenty of smaller ones. Nobody really knows what anyone else is doing. That's how I stay alive,' he added, smiling winningly. 'So, for the moment, you are okay. But you are like a piece of radiological waste, Misha. We've probably got a few hours, maybe a day. Any longer, and exposure to you kills me.'

'Do you, er, have something in mind?' Simon wasn't sure if it was reasonable to expect Vasya to have a fully formed plan. He knew he didn't have one.

'Obviously I can't just let you escape; they'd know what'd happened immediately. You're not exactly James Bond, are you? But if the Ukrainians were making some kind of advance and the fleeing Russian unit left you behind in the panic, that might work.'

'Right, so all we need is basically to stand in the path of the advancing Ukrainian army. That sounds great to me.'

'You've got it, Misha. Quick learner,' he added sarcastically.

Chapter 43

Kyiv

August 2022

'He's with Vasya,' said Jonty, plonking two coffee cups down on the table in the hotel room which had become an ad hoc operations centre. Sarah had seemed paralysed by the news of Simon's capture, unsure where to turn, who to speak to. But Jonty had kept up a dialogue with friends and allies in Washington, in London and in Kyiv. A lot of this he chose to do privately; even with Sarah he was old-school about preserving his contacts, popping out into the corridor to make calls. When he was in the room, he devoted his energy to reassuring Sarah, who seemed devastated, almost unable to help. As if she felt personally responsible for what had happened.

Chapter 44

Bakhmut

August 2022

They drove in Vasya's truck, with Simon playing prisoner, plas-ticuffed to the door handle in the back, a hood over his face. When Simon had asked if that was necessary, Vasya had insisted it was: 'Not to stop *you* from seeing anything. But the fewer people that see your face, the better.'

Before departing they had cleaned up his hand and dressed the wounds. Simon had also tried binding up his knee, which made walking stiffer, but slightly less painful. He was pretty sure he'd need to run at some point, and the prospect added to a long list of anxieties in his head.

As they were climbing back into the truck, Vasya had pulled out a Ziploc bag full of tablets in little sachets. Some were a light blue, others white or yellow in colour.

'Want some?' he asked.

'Morphine? Great.'

'What you think this is? Private fucking clinic in Geneva? I've got fentanyl for the pain and Captagon to get you through. Good shit, though. Hardly any brick dust.'

Simon swallowed uncomfortably. 'Nothing else?'

'There's paracetamol, I suppose,' he said, pulling out a sachet of white tablets, with which Simon dosed himself sensibly.

There was the warriors' cliché of marching towards the sound of gunfire. They were driving, but it was the same idea. For Simon under his hood, it was a mixture of confusion and fear. He could hear the sounds of the battlefield growing louder. But more immediate was the sound of Vasya, delivering a masterclass in how to deal with Russian checkpoints. At some, he was peremptory, barely slowing the vehicle. 'You don't get to ask who the prisoner is. Haven't you seen one of these before?' Simon assumed he was waving some sort of pass or special services identity badge. At others, it was clearly necessary for Vasya to show some respect. All of his charm, humour and bonhomie were on show. 'Special prisoner, yes. Sure, you can take a look at him if you want, but we fucked him a bit so it's not pretty! Ha ha.' This got a few laughs and they could drive on. And then there were the simple cases of bribery. Simon could hear someone say that it was 'irregular', to which Vasya would respond with an offer to 'regularise' the situation.

After some time, in which Simon had begun to wish he'd gone for the fentanyl, he felt the truck slowing, bouncing on an unmade road. The sound of artillery was much closer, and he could hear the rattle of small arms fire. But he couldn't hear the other vehicles that had dominated earlier. They must be near the front. Vasya pulled off the hood and Simon blinked in the light of another sunny day. He looked around himself to a scene of devastation. They were parked up against the wall of a destroyed building, the blown-out windows like gaping wounds in the summer sky. Beyond it he could see the skeletons of buildings, piles of rubble where houses had once stood and burnt-out vehicles quickly turning to rust. Vasya had released Simon's cuffs, and as they climbed out of the vehicle the sounds of the battlefield were now loud enough that he flinched with every artillery shell and mortar, even as he tried not to. Vasya had put on a helmet and passed one to Simon. He had to raise his voice to be heard, waving his hand at the devastation and announcing: 'See? We liberated them.' As much as he was horrified by what he saw, Simon appreciated that Vasya could still keep up his cynical humour.

Vasya turned to Simon and handed him his pistol. 'You'll probably need this. I've got my rifle anyway.' He shoved the weapon in his waistband.

They walked away from the truck and wound their way through a series of what had once been narrow streets where, even with ruined buildings, there was lots of cover. There were houses and apartment buildings without their external walls, allowing you to look inside the rooms like into a doll's house. At times, Vasya would run to cover across a small patch of open ground and then signal for Simon to follow suit. Every step was a struggle, but Simon forced himself onwards.

'Snipers?' asked Simon, looking anxiously around the ruined buildings looming over them.

'Not here. Not from their side,' replied Vasya, pointing a finger to the sky. 'Drones.'

The noise of explosions, gunfire and occasional shouting was now very close, but their sources were still invisible. Vasya beckoned Simon up to a large wall that had been punctured by rounds from a heavy machine gun. Gingerly, they peered out to the scene beyond.

It was as if they had chanced upon the Western Front in the First World War. Up ahead was a large area of open ground falling away in front of them, undulating with high mounds of coal-black earth and stumps of trees and bushes. In spite of the summer, it was a monochrome vista. Smoke drifted across the terrain, and with it the traditional battlefield smells of diesel, cordite and burning flesh. There were trench lines and passageways dug into the earth. These were not straight and neatly executed with planking, like the ones Simon recalled visiting on a childhood trip to northern France. Instead, they looked as if they had been dug in a hurried panic by ill-trained conscripts.

In a large hollow, perhaps created by an earlier shell, a group of soldiers were huddled together. They appeared leaderless and panicky, without any tactics.

'Look,' said Vasya, shouting over the sounds of explosions; none of them appeared to bother him in any way. 'These are our meat storms. Conscripts. We send them to run at the Ukrainian .50 cal.'

'Why? What's the point?' Simon felt hollow at the thought of the senseless human cost.

'They run and it shows us where the enemy have their machine guns. Then we can direct ours.'

'What if they don't do it? If they don't charge?'

Vasya pointed to a spot closer to them, at the edge of the buildings. 'We have our machine gun there to encourage them.' Simon shuddered.

They waited a few minutes, crouched in the corner of the building, and then the heavy-calibre machine gun close to them erupted in a roaring barrage of sound. Vasya stood up and peered out of the gap in the wall, beckoning to Simon. Dust clouds and smoke made it hard for them to see across the mounds of earth, but after squinting and searching, Simon could make out the shapes of men scurrying between trenches and dugouts. There were probably about ten of them, or there had been at the start. Already, some had been picked off by a sniper. Simon watched a fallen conscript crawl towards a patch of dead ground, where he waited to die alone. Moments later he saw a small group of men scramble up over a rise and run manically towards the Ukrainian positions. They were immediately cut to pieces. A wave of nausea washed through Simon and he crouched down, away from the window opening. He was breathing heavily to try to stabilise his stomach.

There was a lull in the gunfire as the doomed assault petered out. Vasya crouched down next to Simon. 'Ready for your turn?' he asked with a grim smile. Momentarily, Simon wondered if Vasya was about to tell him to run towards the Ukrainian machine guns. But he seemed just to be enjoying the chaos of war. 'At some point today we expect the Ukrainians to launch a counterattack here. You just need to survive it. We have to find you a place you can avoid things landing on your head. And then you wait for your rescue.'

Chapter 45

Bakhmut

August 2022

Vasya led Simon on a winding path around the ruins at the edge of the city. He was searching for something with an intensity of concentration that dissuaded Simon from asking any questions. They clambered between piles of rubble and through brick archways formed by blown-out doorways. The crackle of gunfire continued in the background, but the artillery was more of a whump than a boom. They reached a building that had once been some sort of shop. There were posters of home appliances and fancy televisions on the wall, but the shelves were strewn across the floor and the contents had long since been looted. Only a few toasters were left, forlorn and unwanted.

They picked their way through to a stairway that descended to a dark basement. At the top of the stairs, Vasya held up his hand and then called down. It was Russian, but Simon struggled to keep up. Too tired. Something about birds, but that didn't seem to make sense.

He saw a light shining up from the basement and he heard someone moving in the cellar below. The light flashed on and off three times and Vasya nodded, padding carefully down the stairs and beckoning Simon to follow. They stepped into a storage room that had also been thoroughly looted, although a few washing machines remained. Perhaps they had been too heavy to shift. A small, wiry man with dark facial hair was sitting on one of them, his feet resting comfortably on a lower box.

He was wearing combat fatigues and had a rifle slung behind his shoulder. His dark brown eyes were staring intensely at Simon.

'Let me introduce you,' said Vasya. Unusually, he was sounding a little unsure of himself. 'This is Chovka Buchayev.'

With extraordinary speed, Simon whipped his pistol out, training the sight picture on Chovka's face, his finger playing on the trigger. Afterwards, he tried to tell himself it had all been planned. But he was barely conscious of his action as he drew the weapon, almost an out-of-body experience. And then he had a crunching return to reality and he found himself in the arena: pointing a gun at Evie's killer, the muscle memory of the two-handed grip with the satisfying weight of the pistol in his hands. Simon could only hear the sound of his own breathing, heavy, but still in control.

Chovka's face was impassive, his stare fixed on Simon, his hands remaining by his sides on the edges of the washing machine. He had not tried to reach his rifle, tucked uselessly out of the way behind his back. Vasya had put one hand on his weapon, but he wouldn't be able to do anything from there. His eyes flicked inquisitively from Simon to Chovka and back again.

They said I wouldn't do it.

His mind was a swirl of connected thoughts. Evie on a summer evening in Prague, walking down a narrow street, moments before the end. Simon's call to Evie's father from a smelly telephone box in Pimlico. Henry Howard had been so brave. Jonty saying, 'You aren't going to track down Chovka and shoot him in the back of the head.'

Not the back of the head. In the face.

Simon began to squeeze the trigger, but his grip wasn't as steady as before. He looked across at Vasya, an unspoken question on his face.

'Plan B,' he replied laconically. 'I didn't want to promise because I didn't know if he'd be here.' Simon looked back at Chovka. He knew that the slightest additional pressure on the trigger would fire the gun. Chovka didn't seem to know how to blink.

'Honestly, you just have to do it if you want,' said Vasya, sounding a little bored.

Simon pulled the trigger.

Chapter 46

Nobody should ever have to bury their own and only child. But if such a terrible thing happens, let it be on a sunny day in May, in a small English country churchyard. The hawthorn was in flower and the sky had the milky blue of early summer. But there was a coolness in the breeze, and the mourners huddled close to one another.

With help from some mysterious bits of the British state, Henry Howard had managed to repatriate Evie's body, his soldierly practicality carrying him along, in spite of the waves of grief that threatened to drown him. But there was something about organising the funeral – the finality of it – that he found insurmountable. Evie's mother, who had been born a Soviet Russian citizen, had become almost mute since the news of Evie's death, unable to do anything more than the basic act of living from one day to the next.

The couple had met in Azerbaijan and lived and worked in various far-flung places, so Evie had been at a boarding school. She carried a close-knit circle of friends from there through her university years and afterwards; it was this group that stepped into the breach. They set about collecting memories, photographs and a playlist of songs that had meant something to her. In spite of her short life, she had touched enough people that the tiny church was full, with mourners having to squeeze together to allow the coffin through. She arrived to 'Ave Maria'

309

and left to 'Another Love'. In the churchyard, she was lowered into the plot that her father had bought for himself and his wife. It was a tiny solace to them to think that at some point in the future, all three of them would lie together once again.

At the graveside, one of her friends read some lines from Gray's 'Elegy':

Full many a gem of purest ray serene,
The dark unfathom'd caves of ocean bear:
Full many a flower is born to blush unseen,
And waste its sweetness on the desert air.

After the ceremony had finished, the mourners left Evie's parents alone with their daughter. After a few minutes, the stricken pair were approached by a short, barrel-chested man who stood apart and didn't appear to know any of the others in the congregation. He took Evie's father's hand in both of his and shook it, clearly struggling for words. Eventually, he managed to say something.

'Alexei is my name,' he stammered in Russian-accented English. 'I owe my life to your daughter.'

Chapter 47

Bakhmut

August 2022

Chovka's body jerked sideways. Vasya had pulled his rifle up to a half-ready position, peering over the top of the barrel. Simon was now holding the pistol in one hand, pointing it at the floor. He was shaking, but he hoped nobody else would notice.

'Was that the plan?'

'Fuck off, Vasya.'

Simon had made his point, hardly in cold blood: he had pulled the trigger on Chovka, who had wrenched his body to one side in an attempt to evade the bullet. But the gun had not been cocked, clicking bathetically. Harmless. Realising this, Chovka had straightened himself, taking his eyes off Simon and glancing briefly at Vasya.

'This is the guy?' he asked Vasya in Russian, unimpressed.

Vasya nodded. Chovka looked at Simon, expectantly. The fury in Simon's chest was preventing him from thinking clearly. He had handled defectors plenty of times before in his professional life. But this one was different.

I showed that I would do it and I chose to let him live. It was in my power. Now it is in my power to make him work for me. The thought, even with its self-delusions, calmed him a little.

'Hello, Chovka. You want to talk to the British?' Simon asked in Russian.

Just keep it simple.

'Yes. Once we're across the line.'

Simon shook his head. 'It doesn't work like that. I have to be sure it's worth taking you across.'

Chovka put his palm down on the hand-guard of his rifle. Simon, an uncocked pistol at his side, felt under-equipped. Vasya pulled the rifle up to his eyeline. He followed this up with a growling sentence to Chovka that Simon didn't catch, but probably meant something like 'Don't be a fucking moron'.

Chovka moved his hands back to his sides. Simon put the pistol back in his waistband. 'What do you want to know?'

Simon tried to keep the emotion out of his voice. 'I want to know what you did in Prague six weeks ago.'

'You know what I did.' Chovka's eyes were so level, his voice so flat, Simon wondered if he had been intoxicated in some way.

'How did you end up there? Who sent you?'

'Babakunov. In Slovakia.'

Simon nodded. It was a name he didn't recognise, but one of the things he knew about a debrief was that you didn't break the flow. He could go back for details later. 'You were based in Slovakia?'

'No. I was in Kyiv. Until the start of the special military operation.' *It's a fucking war*, thought Simon. 'Then the military assault on Kyiv failed, and I escaped.'

'What was your role in Kyiv?'

'I worked with Dudnik.'

'Only that?'

'Only.'

Vasya erupted: 'Listen, cocksucker. Have you forgotten just how fucked you are?' He waved his rifle barrel at Chovka, who started speaking again.

'Dudnik was supporting a group that was going to take over the country. A coup backed by Moscow. My job was to get people out of the way. People who were causing difficulties or knew too much. There was an FSB team on the ground. Led by Sergey. I will give you all the details.'

Simon nodded. There would be much to come back to. 'And how do you know Vasya?'

Chovka looked across at Vasya, who nodded back at him. 'Dudnik has houses in Switzerland. He took me there once. Said I was being his bodyguard, but it was really a holiday. Nice place. I had ice cream every day. And I met him.'

'Why did you decide to defect?' He needed to hear Chovka spelling out his own reasons for treason. Chovka sighed... And his eyes flickered uneasily. Perhaps in spite of himself, he was allowing a semblance of humanity to be displayed.

'I lost interest in the work here... It was good timing.'

Vasya broke in, impatient: 'Good timing? You stole from the op funds in Moldova and now you have no choice. Come on, Chovka, stop fucking around. Simon knows this world as much as you and I do.'

Chovka shrugged, unperturbed by Vasya's aggression. 'I do jobs for different people. That's how I survive. But I know that this is a one-way journey now.'

Simon cut in: 'You didn't show for the first RV. What happened?' His mind shot back to the doomed ambush: men screaming; the sound of the drone just before it dropped its payload.

'The command group found out about the plan, but they decided to let the ambush unfold. To catch me in the act. But I had a warning. One of the guys in the ops room told me. I had something on him and he owed me. So I let my unit go without me. Told them I had another mission.'

Vasya, a natural in the world of double- and triple-cross, stepped forwards, standing close to Chovka. 'Who warned the command group?'

'They had info that Simon was coming and that I was going to cross over. From Dudnik.'

'Dudnik?' asked Simon. 'How the hell would he know?'

Chovka shrugged, indifferent. To him, it was just another betrayal in a life full of them. 'He has friends all over. Maybe Vasya told him.'

'I don't think I'd be here now if I was the source,' said Vasya, smiling. Simon agreed that this made sense. But often the thing that didn't make sense turned out to be the thing that was true.

'Dudnik has friends in Britain,' added Chovka as a bit of an afterthought.

Of course he does, thought Simon. *Friends like Sarah.*

'I have done jobs for lots of people in different places,' said Chovka, perhaps in an effort to reassure. 'I know I have to do a job for you guys now...'

Simon knew that he didn't have time to get the full story. But he needed more than this. 'Let's go back to Prague. Who is this Babakunov?'

'Business guy in Slovakia. Has a casino. All the Russians know him.'

'What was the mission?'

'You saw the mission.' Chovka smiled in a way that made Simon wish he had cocked his pistol. But then he wondered, *Would Evie want me to shoot him in the head? I don't think she would.*

'What were your orders? Who was directing you?'

'We had your picture. And the girl. Knew the hotel you were at.'

'Who?' asked Simon insistently. 'Who gave you that?'

For the first time, Chovka looked uncomfortable, throwing a glance in Vasya's direction. 'They asked if anyone knew me in Prague. Then a few days later I go back and there's a new guy. Vlad. He gives me the orders.'

'Vlad who?'

Chovka pursed his lips. Of course, nobody had told him Vlad's full name.

'But you got the patronymic?'

'Vladimir Vladimirovich,' he shrugged.

Useless: most common names in Russia. Once again, Simon wondered about shooting Chovka.

'He asked me about what I'd done, who I'd worked with. He obviously knew some of the FSB guys from the Kiyv operation.'

'So he was FSB?'

'No. He made that very clear. Said, "This op is not run by FSB, or any other service you have heard of." Maybe he thought that mattered to me. I couldn't have cared less. But he wanted to make a point of it. Anyway, I found the passport he was using. Took a snap of it.'

'Oh?'

'Yeah. Strange, 'cos it wasn't Russian. It was from one of those English islands where they sell passports. St Nevis. Something like that.'

Vasya and Simon exchanged a knowing glance.

'Where's the image?' asked Simon.

'USB. I have a whole lot of useful ones. We can look when we're over.'

Chovka might be sitting on a gold mine. Simon was finding it harder to hate him. His blunt honesty, a man who did what he had to do, not usually knowing what the bigger game was, trying to stay alive. Betrayed, double-crossed, constantly braced for the next surprise, trying to protect himself by collecting information. It was strangely familiar.

And then he remembered Evie and hated himself a little more.

Chapter 48

Bakhmut

August 2022

As they had been speaking, even in the basement, the sounds of the battle happening above ground had become louder. And Vasya was becoming noticeably uneasy, constantly checking his watch and his cellphone. The lower rumble of noise turned into an insistent roar, and then they heard a shell flying directly overhead, the screech of the projectile followed by a deep thump and the sensation, even below ground, of the earth moving.

'I'm going to have to leave you guys to it,' shouted Vasya apologetically, sounding as if he was at a noisy nightclub and needed to head home early. The three of them climbed up to the ground level and Simon was suddenly struck by the noise. The battle was close now, artillery flying overhead in both directions. Simon realised that they were effectively in no-man's-land, although the dense buildings made it hard to get a sense of exactly where the action was moving.

Simon didn't know what to say, so he chose idle bravura. 'I guess the drinks are on me next time,' he called into Vasya's ear. They embraced, both men knowing they would quite possibly never see each other again.

Vasya turned to Chovka. 'Keep him alive. He'll make it worth your while.' Chovka nodded back, although it wasn't clear whether he'd actually heard, over the relentless crash of the explosions, now regular and close. And with that, Vasya turned around, picking his way over rubble, twisting his head around nervously as he tried to sense likely sniper positions. There was a brief lull in the artillery and Vasya sprinted, as best a man too old for urban warfare could be expected to, towards the far corner of a blown-out factory. Simon knew Vasya's truck was on the far side of that building. Nearly there.

Vasya was about a hundred metres away, only partially visible between the rubble. He turned back, raised an arm of farewell and then paused, waiting to time his run for the factory wall. Simon heard a loud crack, which echoed across the ruined buildings, and instinctively turned his head towards the source of the noise. He couldn't see anything, but he knew the sound of a sniper rifle. He turned back to where Vasya had been, but he was gone.

Good. Made it out.

And then he saw it. Vasya's legs on the ground by the corner of the building. Motionless. He couldn't see the rest of his body because of a collapsed wall in the way. It took him a few seconds to figure out what he was looking at. But then Simon realised.

'No!' he screamed, and started to hobble towards Vasya. A firm hand clutched his shoulder. Chovka spoke into his ear.

'You go there now and the same sniper will get you. We have to get out of here... Not get killed out there.'

Simon knew he was right. And what was he going to do, anyway? A limping idiot, on the wrong side of the front line, liable to be picked up and thrown into the nearest Russian dungeon. His only – slim – chance of survival was if they were picked up by Ukrainian forces. Very soon.

–

The artillery continued overhead, but from what Simon could tell, there was more coming from the Ukrainian side than the Russian. Did that mean that the Russians were retreating? The small arms fire seemed to be picking up, and he and Chovka spent a few minutes selecting a bit of wall to hide behind that he hoped would make them visible to the Ukrainians when they came over, without making them a target ahead of that time. Perhaps because of his leg, but probably because of the fear, Simon found it hard to stay still. He was racked with thoughts about Vasya. Had he died quickly? Had he felt a lot of pain? But perhaps the most important question: had he died feeling he was doing something worthwhile?

'Make sure this matters to someone,' he had once said to Simon. He could see now why Vasya had switched to work with the Americans. He wanted to be doing things that mattered. Not to be the sniping critic but 'the man who is actually in the arena'. Simon recalled their first ever meeting, in a wooden hut in the Vienna woods. 'I know the rules of this game. I hope you are a good player. That's all,' Vasya had said. These words might have been a throwaway remark, but they had stayed with Simon ever since. He wished he had told Vasya that.

Simon shifted uncomfortably, grappling with these thoughts. But Chovka seemed completely calm. He had learned how to wait, even in the middle of a major urban assault.

They could tell that the contested part of the city was off to one side of them: there was gun smoke and rapid fire coming from an area just a couple of hundred metres away. But they could also hear the rattle of small arms getting ever closer to their position. Simon wondered if they should show themselves, maybe find a way to wave a white flag. But Chovka cautioned patience.

'They'll get here. We're safe in this spot. Stand up now and there are snipers in every direction.'

Simon didn't need reminding of this. The echoing crack of the high-velocity rifle, very different from the rattling sound of the smaller arms, continued to ring out every few minutes. He glanced over to where Vasya had fallen, but he couldn't see him clearly. A fire had started where an artillery shell had landed on some kind of fuel store, and thick smoke made it hard to see across the open ground.

Simon had snatched a glance back over the wall and seen that the Ukrainians were advancing at an oblique angle to where he and Chovka were. These troops would not be running over the top of them, but coming up alongside them. The Ukrainians seemed to be making steady progress under a barrage of their artillery as well as endless drones – seemingly tiny, insect-like objects that flew overhead to drop grenades on the Russian firing positions. Two of the heavy Russian machine guns had been silenced, and the Ukrainians were so close that Simon could hear them shouting in the lulls between the gunfire. At a certain point he would need to make himself known. If he let them get too close, he would shock them and they'd probably shoot first before finding out who he was. But the last thing he wanted to do was stand up and present himself as a target. Instead, he waited for a lull in the shooting and then called out, at the top of his voice.

'*Hellooooo.*' He reasoned that it was likely that someone had been told to look out for a foreigner, maybe an Englishman. He scrabbled around and found a bit of broken plank, on to which he tied his pale undershirt in a makeshift flag. Making sure his head was well below the parapet of the wall, he waved this ragged banner hopefully. He could hear them now, no more than fifty metres away. There was more scrabbling, boots on rubble.

Chapter 49

Two soldiers came around the side of the building at a canter, their rifles held at the ready. The two men assumed a ready-to-fire stance, legs braced. Simon and Chovka knew to keep very still. Simon wondered about raising his arms, but decided even that might spook them. Instead he found himself staring at the barrel of one of the rifles. *Will I see the flash before it kills me?* he wondered idly. The two men had the sort of equipment that said 'special forces' rather than regular army: sleek, new-looking rifles with retractable stocks, lightweight helmets and uniforms devoid of any insignia. Simon thought he recognised one of them from the HUR unit in Kramatorsk, but he couldn't be sure.

'Simon?' called one of the men, pronouncing his name in the Russian way. He had to raise his voice to be heard above the sounds of gunfire, which continued unabated around them.

'Yes. That's me. This is Chovka,' Simon added, indicating with a flick of his head. He still wasn't ready to wave his arms around.

'Show us your hands,' said the other soldier, in Ukrainian. Simon and Chovka both obeyed, cautiously. The explosions had started again, so loud that Simon found it hard to think. The soldier used his hand to signal that they should get up. Simon had to struggle, but Chovka stood up easily. The soldier raised his rifle again and signalled Chovka to get rid of his gun.

He did this with immense caution, pulling the shoulder strap over his head and holding the weapon away from himself as if it were an object of disgust. Simon pointed at the pistol in his waistband and the soldier nodded, so he pinched the end of the grip and flung it a few metres away onto the ground.

With these rituals over, the soldiers relaxed, lowering their rifles. One of them smiled. 'Let's get out of here,' he shouted above the din in accented English. 'Dany,' he added, pointing at himself. The second soldier announced himself as Viktor.

Several other soldiers were now running across the open ground where Vasya had fallen. Simon found himself braced for the crack of the sniper rifle, but none came. The little group began their journey, Dany in front, Viktor bringing up the rear, picking their way around the edge of the ruined building and into what had been no-man's-land only minutes before. They moved quickly between stumps of wall and other bits of cover. The artillery was still screaming overhead, but their landing zone was now several hundred metres away.

Then he heard the crack of the sniper rifle again – several shots – and they threw themselves to the ground. Simon was behind Chovka and crawled painfully towards him, his bad knee dragging on the broken ground. Chovka turned his head towards Simon and smiled. He mouthed something, but Simon couldn't hear it. He wondered whether he had gone deaf. He leant in close so that Chovka's mouth was next to his ear.

'I've been hit,' Chovka said, in a strange bubbly voice. For an absurd moment Simon wondered if he was joking, but then he noticed a red stain spreading out onto the ground. A pallor was already beginning to appear on Chovka's face and his breathing was laboured. Simon called back, beckoning Viktor forwards desperately, who scrambled over at a low shuffle. He and Chovka exchanged a glance of recognition, or even resignation. Simon and Viktor dragged Chovka laboriously to the point of safety where Dany was waiting for them.

In the shelter of another ruined building they looked at him. He had a bullet in his chest. They dressed the wound but he was declining fast, sucking in air in little gasps. He beckoned Simon over to him, pulling him close so that Simon could hear his whispery voice.

'Do something for me?' He was fiddling under his shirt and his hands were covered in blood.

'You can do it yourself. We'll get you out fine,' Simon lied.

'I'm dying.' He gasped several times and then appeared to steady himself enough to be able to continue for a few seconds.

'Istanbul. My son.' Chovka was speaking Russian and Simon didn't have difficulty understanding the words. But they didn't seem to make much sense. Maybe he was delirious.

'Your son?'

'Yes… Mother Syrian… Aleppo.'

Simon paused. A shell screamed overhead and he couldn't hear properly.

'You were in Aleppo?'

Chovka gave a feeble nod. Simon had known that some of the Kadyrovites had been in Syria – Russia's alliance with the Assad regime. Chovka waggled a hand towards his chest and Simon realised he was pointing to a chain around his neck. *Do these people have dog tags?* Simon pulled the chain loose from the bloody mess around the chest and realised there was a USB drive strung along the chain.

'All on there,' Chovka said with considerable effort. His eyes had become very wide, pupils dilated. He then had a slight surge of energy, as if the life was leaving his body with a final flourish. His speech regained some fluency.

'I wanted to see my son Mansur… In Istanbul… Refugee… Won't happen now. Got Bitcoin. Key on there. He'll be okay…' Then Simon lost the thread. Chovka seemed to be talking about some numbers, but it wasn't clear what he meant. Simon leant in closer and asked him to repeat.

'1999… Apartment bombings.'

Simon blinked in amazement. In 1999, a series of explosions in Russian apartment bombings had killed hundreds of civilians.

Simon's view was that it was an inside job, a false flag carried out by Russian security agents and blamed on Chechens. The story remained shrouded in mystery.

'What do you know about it?' Why was Chovka bringing this up now?

'Istanbul. I know people who...' But Chovka was struggling to breathe again and the words stopped.

His eyes opened wider still and he gasped again. '*Spasibo*.'

His body became very still and Simon could no longer hear any breathing.

And Chovka Buchayev, assassin, torturer, mass murderer, orphan and loving father, died in Simon's arms.

Chapter 50

Bakhmut

August 2022

'Let's get the fuck out of here,' said Viktor grimly. Simon nodded, stuffing the USB drive into his pocket. He took a last look at Chovka, wondering what he should feel. Then a barrage of heavy machine-gun fire shook him out of his reverie and he followed Viktor down a narrow passageway between two walls, bent forwards to reduce his vulnerability.

They quickly made it into a trench system, the ground muddy underfoot, coal-black soil piled up on either side. Simon had the sensation of going against a tide of advancing infantrymen. At times they had to move to one side in the trench to allow men with fixed stares and bayonets to run in the opposite direction.

They crossed two more stretches of open ground at a gallop, but the firing was much less intense now. By the second stretch, Simon's knee was in such pain that he had taken to digging his fingernails into his forearm as he ran. He was sweating profusely and felt dizzy, but they had reached the point where the Ukrainian supply lines were better established. There was a truck waiting, Dany already in the driver's seat. Simon gratefully pulled himself into the rear and they sped off into the rubble-strewn outskirts of Bakhmut. It was now early evening and Simon wondered what day it was.

Viktor turned round in his seat and offered a hand for a high-five. 'You've made it out,' he said, grinning. Simon managed to slap his hand, but didn't manage to say anything. Instead he leant back, his head lolling against the rear glass. He wanted to feel elation, but felt very little at all, except intense tiredness.

—

They reached Kramatorsk quicker than Simon had expected. Perhaps he had slept on the way. He could see the hospital buildings and realised they were nearly at the HUR compound. And then he remembered that the story wasn't over. Somehow, in the elation of escape, he had managed not to think about all the questions that would now need answering. Viktor had told him that Liz was okay and had been sent back to Kyiv for a full debrief. But what about Sarah? And what would she be doing, now that he was coming back alive? Simon might be off the battlefield, but he was sure he was not out of danger.

The steel gates clanged open and the truck pulled into the compound. Simon saw a small welcoming committee: two guys he half recognised from his first visit to the HUR building. And Sarah.

Chapter 51

Kramatorsk

August 2022

Simon stared blankly at Sarah, standing in the yard waiting for him to get out of the truck.

Fuck. What's she doing here?

He climbed out stiffly and she bounded forwards, throwing her arms around him, holding him tight.

'Simon. Thank God.' Her voice cracked slightly. Simon felt his body stiffen, his mind racing.

She's playing it completely straight.

Sarah playing the role of relieved colleague, thankful that he had come home alive. Maybe relieved lover? Simon had a flashback to their last moment together and felt repulsed that he had allowed himself to be taken in. Sarah's behaviour could only mean one of two things: either she hadn't realised he had seen through her, or she was trying to brazen it out. He started to realise that he couldn't simply tell people what had happened. Who would believe him, the traumatised survivor of a disastrous mission?

Sarah had her hands on Simon's shoulders and was looking into his eyes. He was impressed to see that she had tears pricking around the edges of hers. 'What do you need?' she asked, convincingly solicitous.

He needed to get away, to order his thoughts. To make a plan. He was also dishevelled and filthy. 'I need a shower. And painkillers.'

'And then we have to talk.' This from one of the Ukrainians, a severe-looking bearded man called Stan. 'There is lots for us to understand.'

–

After a long shower and being reunited with his civvy clothes, Simon got Dany, obviously an accomplished combat medic, to put a proper bandage on his knee. With the dressing came powerful painkillers that Simon assumed were some kind of opiate, given the near-immediate hit they gave. Then coffee, which tasted amazing. But he couldn't prevaricate any longer and the debrief began in the same ops room. Last time he'd been there it was with Yuri and his comrades, who now lay dead at the ambush site. Stan and his colleague Maksym sat with Sarah on one side the table, all of them furiously scribbling notes as Simon spoke. He assumed he was also being recorded, although they didn't specify this.

Reliving the events of the past few days was not as hard as he'd imagined. It prevented him from having to grapple with what might happen next. They focused a lot of attention on Chovka and Vasya. Simon realised he hadn't done a very good job of finding out exactly what discussions had occurred between the two of them. Who had been Chovka's source who warned him off the ambush? What promises had Vasya made to Chovka? How had Vasya and Chovka agreed to meet in the ruins at the edge of Bakhmut? He sat there, with few answers to these questions, his hands thrust into his pockets. As the debrief unfolded, he was nervously fiddling with the flash drive with his right hand. He opted not to share what he had in his pocket.

He managed to learn things. Principally, that it had been Jonty who had got him out. Jonty had stepped up, spoken to the right people in Langley, got Vasya mobilised. After a few hours, during which Simon had emptied two water bottles and still felt a raging thirst, Stan and Maksym absented themselves, explaining they needed to make an interim report to Kyiv.

'Shall we sit outside for a bit?' Sarah asked awkwardly.

Simon nodded and they wandered out into the sun, where they found a couple of white plastic chairs at the edge of the yard. The urge to confront her was boiling in his chest, and he found her ability to play her role – gentle supportive colleague – chillingly impressive. They sat in a tense silence.

'How are you doing?' Sarah asked eventually.

'Seriously? Really want to know?'

'Of course.'

'How I'm doing is wondering where I go from here. You had a plan for me. It failed. So what next? Have I got a few hours or a few weeks? I don't expect an answer... But that's what I'm wondering about.'

Sarah had a look of blank incomprehension. She opened her mouth to say something, but appeared to think better of it. Instead, she shook her head. Her mouth seemed to be quivering with a mixture of rage and upset.

Simon ploughed on, remorselessly. 'It couldn't have been anyone else.'

She was still shaking her head, but had now found her voice. 'No... You're... You're saying *I* did this? *I* sabotaged this mission? You can't be that stupid.'

Simon felt angrier than ever. It wasn't that he expected her to admit to anything, but he didn't want her to have the satisfaction of thinking he didn't know. 'Chovka told me the leak had come from Dudnik. But who told Dudnik? I thought about whether it came from inside this unit. But Liz was the only survivor and I saw her reaction. It wasn't her. Then I thought about Vasya. But if he had let it leak, why would he have come to my rescue? Risking everything. *Losing everything.* And who else knew? You. Jonty, I guess. But he got me out, so that doesn't make sense. Who's left?'

Sarah was still playing dumb. 'You're really doing this? I get that this was a bad experience. God knows, horrific, even. But you're really doing this?' She spluttered at the madness of

Simon's accusation. And the edges of doubt started to form in his own mind. Before, when he had thought it through, it had made perfect sense. 'Why would I be here?' she asked, her voice rising with anger. 'I mean, if I'd arranged to have you killed off and then my cunning plan had failed to hatch, what the actual *fuck* would I be doing here now?'

'You're trying to find out what I know, so you can plan the next stage,' he said, feeling unsure of himself as he did so. Her eyes had narrowed to small points and she looked at him with pure, intense fury. Simon continued, but he felt as if he was blustering. 'One thing we both know, Sarah, is that in this world you never know everything. Like I didn't know Vasya was a CIA asset. Or that the whole COSTELLO investigation was something put together in Langley. Or that after I recruited Chovka he was going to be handed over to the Yanks. Those are things I didn't know because you chose not to tell me.'

'Right… And so your genius conclusion is that I'm a fucking Russian asset. Is that it? Is that your big investigative break-through?' she asked with evident sarcasm.

Simon did not feel ready to answer. So he went on the attack again. 'Okay, so if it wasn't you, who was it? What went wrong? Because this was a big plan you had stitched together with the Yanks and God knows who else, and it has gone completely to shit. Yuri, Erik, Aleks, all his people, Vasya, Chovka. All of them dead. Who are you holding responsible? Who's to blame?'

Sarah replied with icy self-control. 'I'm just going to put on one side the fact that you have accused me of trying to bring about your almost certain death at Russian hands… As for who is responsible, it may shock you to learn that I am one hundred per cent focused on getting to the bottom of that. And you might also be surprised to learn that Maksym, who is from Langley, not Kyiv, is doing something similar on the American side of things. And since you mention Dudnik, he has a lot of fingers in many spies, as the saying doesn't go.' She paused and looked at the floor, as if she couldn't bear to have eye contact with Simon any more.

Simon had been answering questions all day. Now he wanted to ask some. 'Okay, so how did you find out? About what had happened.'

'Liz. We had a codeword for if the whole thing had gone south. She only messaged once she was back over the line.'

Simon was feeling a lot less sure of himself, but he was sure there was something important here. 'And what did you do, when you got the message? You said it was Jonty who sorted everything.'

'Yes. I was with him, and the moment I'd got the message he knew what was up. Comes with all that experience. And he went out and started making calls. Jonty was brilliant, actually.'

'Where is he? Jonty, I mean.'

'He headed back once he knew you were going to be safe. You know what it's like with him... Always some project or other.'

'And why did you leave it to him? I mean, if I'm wrong, you'd be desperately trying to get me back, wouldn't you?'

Her reply was acidic: 'Because, Simon, I was so upset about what had happened that – maybe for the first time in my adult life – I froze. I didn't know what to do. Where to start.' Her eyes had welled up, and she looked away and hit the arm of her chair in frustration.

This didn't look like acting. With a sensation of falling through the air, Simon realised he had screwed everything up. Again. He reached his hand out to touch Sarah's. But she pulled hers away.

'Seriously. Just leave me alone, Simon. I am sure at some future point you will be able to explain the things you have just said. Not now.'

In the middle of the despair at his own stupidity, Simon felt something else. A voice telling him something. Or telling him not to forget something.

'About Liz. When she messaged you she was out, right? Over the line?'

'Simon. I really don't want to talk to you. I don't think it's good for either of us.'

'This is important. Please just hear me out.' Sarah huffed and turned her head in his direction, even if she was still avoiding eye contact. 'When Vasya found me, he said, "Jonty was on to me the moment you were picked up." He said he was really impressed how quickly that had happened. But you said Liz waited till she was over the line. Which is what you'd expect. Secure comms protocol.'

Sarah was playing with her hair, twisting her long ponytail around in her hand, something Simon knew she did when her brain was turning things over. She started talking, not really to Simon, but she clearly wanted to share the information out loud. 'Liz said it took some time before she could get in touch. She had to hide in a ditch, they took ages to leave. Then she had to get back to the truck, where she found they'd got Erik. And then back across the line. And she lost her way at one point.' Sarah shot Simon a direct look, her brown eyes intense. 'That's definitely not "the moment you were picked up". Is it?'

'I'd tell your American friends to ask Vasya. But it's too late for that.' As soon as Simon said this, he wished he'd not made it sound like he was blaming Sarah again. He owed her an apology, but felt too ashamed even to formulate one. To Simon's relief, Sarah ignored him.

'Vasya was sure about that? "The moment you were picked up"?'

'He made a point of it. How it showed I was well connected somehow. That Jonty wanted to help me by getting word to him as quickly as possible, and then people in Langley followed it up.'

'But the initial contact was straight from Jonty to Vasya? That's what he said?' Sarah's tone was insistent, now, with an urgency to it. 'Not Langley to Vasya?'

Simon could see something clearly now. But it was possibly even harder to believe than the thought that it had been Sarah who betrayed him.

Chapter 52

Kramatorsk

August 2022

'It was the same sniper.'

Sarah looked up, confused by Simon changing the subject. 'What?'

'Same sniper. Got Vasya and Chovka. Didn't get me. Or Viktor. Or Dany. Just those two. The people who knew the answers. Tidying up.'

'You're sure?'

'From the way Chovka fell. And Vasya – it was coming from the side. Not from the Ukrainian lines.'

Sarah nodded. She was looking pale and exhausted, and Simon wondered if he should give her a hug or something. Then he remembered that she was furious with him.

'And they found out from Dudnik…' Simon said. 'Jonty has questions to answer, hasn't he?' Sarah nodded again. It was as if she couldn't put it into words, but she had figured it out already. 'Oh, God, Sarah, I'm so sorry. I… I felt like I'd been betrayed. There was a lot you hadn't told me. I made a stupid mistake. I'm sorry. I fucked up. That's all I can say.' He tried again, putting his hand on her arm, but she twisted hers away.

She wasn't looking at him, but she did start to talk. 'Simon, one of the things about relationships… I mean, it's been a while, but one of the things I *remember* about relationships is that they rely on trust. I think you've shown that you don't trust me.'

He replied angrily: 'Did you trust me when you set up the investigation into the Oxford spy ring? I mean, you could have just rung me up. "Oh, Simon, some friends across the pond are a bit worried about the way Britain is being bought out by the Russians and I've been given a budget to look into it." But instead you hid that behind endless layers of... of lies.'

She huffed and made a face. 'Come on, Simon. The Americans spying on the UK? I mean, it's the great taboo. Of course I didn't tell you about it.' She sounded as if her point was completely reasonable. Maybe it was? 'I lied for a valid operational reason. That was work. Lies are part of what we do. The *core* part, actually. On the other hand, you created an insane story in which I was the villain. Can you see the difference?'

Simon spoke with an insistent anger. *How can this all be my fault?* He had been sent off on a deadly mission on a false premise. 'But you lied about Chovka, too. About the plan for him to be handed to the Americans.'

'But that's the same thing,' she said, exasperated. 'The Chovka plan is part of the whole bloody Oxford spy ring operation. Was, I should say.'

Simon felt in his pocket, twisting the flash drive nervously between his fingers.

I'll keep it to myself.

'I made very clear to the Americans that your safety was the top priority,' continued Sarah primly.

'Good of you,' said Simon sarcastically.

'Oh, shut up, Simon. You took yourself here on this crazy escapade to find Chovka. Nobody forced you to be in Ukraine. I offered you somewhere to hide out in Italy, but you had other ideas. And here we are.'

'Yeah. Here we are. I suppose this wasn't destined to work out.'

'No. It wasn't,' she said abruptly, turning away.

He looked angrily at Sarah, furious with her, with himself and the mess they had found themselves in.

Simon stalked back inside and started assembling his meagre possessions. He stepped back out into the courtyard and told Dany that he was planning to try to get a ride back to Kyiv. He and Sarah were studiously ignoring one another, but a certain point was reached when they couldn't keep up the charade any longer.

'Well. This is it, then,' he said, offering her a perfunctory hug.

'Yep.' She had something in her hand. A sort of paper file. 'Take this,' she said. 'It's a copy of a report. About Dudnik. Might be useful for when you speak to Jonty. He saw the report before you went over the line.' She patted his upper arm, as you might a child lingering at the school gate. *Off you go, then*.

'Take care, Simon.'

He didn't answer.

Chapter 53

Harpenden
September 2022

With its stretch of comfortable but unshowy houses shielded by neat privet hedges, Castletown Avenue in Harpenden was a monument to English respectability. It was the sort of place where driveways were free of weeds and windows were regularly cleaned. Potholes were reported immediately and leaves were swept the moment they fell from the trees. There were Neighbourhood Watch stickers on most houses; sticker or not, it was a very watchful neighbourhood.

Castletown Avenue was not the sort of place where you would expect to see media vans with large satellite dishes on the roof. Or where a group of reporters and photographers might congregate, cameras at the ready, outside number forty-three, a sturdy brick house with a neat cherry tree in the front garden. Even on a Saturday. This atypical assembly had already been noted by many of the avenue's residents. But Kamran Patel was not a Morning Person. On weekdays he could drag himself out of bed in time for his early train. But weekends were another matter. The chances of him being aware of the assembly outside his front door at seven in the morning were slim.

These factors came together in a way that was unfortunate for Patel's credibility in front of the world's media. He had opened the door in a bleary state, insufficiently prepared for what awaited him on the other side. He was greeted with a face-full of camera lenses and the shouted question: 'Professor

Patel, have you anything to say about the Integrity Ukraine report? Where's Hayden Edgworthy?'

His mouth made a small circle of surprise and he blinked repeatedly, before finding his voice. 'Ooh. Bloody hell,' he said, before slamming the door in their faces.

The image of Professor Kamran Patel, Britain's National Security Adviser, in T-shirt and boxer shorts, and with a severe case of bed-head, was beamed live on a few news channels that not many people watched. But a TikTok video of the moment, edited so that the professor's words were repeated, rap style, the door slamming in time with the hip-hop backing track, gained immediate traction.

Kamran Patel's career as a senior government adviser ended at that moment. It was not his appearance in Integrity Ukraine's report that did for him. It wasn't even the disappearance of Hayden Edgworthy, although that had brought the media to his door. Several of Hayden's closest friends were political journalists he knew from his think-tank days. They had been in regular contact with him in Kyiv, from where he liked to dole out 'off-record insights' he claimed to have picked up from the front lines. His sudden and unexplained departure had set these reporters on a trail that had led them to Kamran and to 43 Castletown Avenue. But what finished Patel was looking faintly ridiculous in a twenty-second video watched by millions. Of those millions, a tiny fraction – but still many thousands of people – took an interest in Oksana's work. The discovery that Russian-backed oligarchs were stealing Western support, whilst curating a disinformation network to undermine that support, hit hard at the sense of fair play that most people felt was Ukraine's due.

–

It was not long afterwards that the ever-vigilant residents of Castletown Avenue noticed removal vans at number forty-three. Kamran Patel had always been a very private resident. After his unwanted appearance for the world's cameras, he had gone from private to invisible. Nobody had seen a 'For Sale' sign, but he was definitely moving out.

Kamran wasn't really the type to hold a leaving party, but had he done so, he would have taken pleasure in explaining that America was 'changing a lot quicker than you think. They're looking for a reason to walk away from Europe and from NATO. You've got all these countries in Europe that are the richest in the world, and they still think it's America's job to defend them. Russia isn't America's problem any more. These days, when some European leader asks the USA if they would continue to protect them, the answer should be: "If you didn't pay for your defence, Russia can do whatever the hell it wants to you." That's the line I'll be recommending to the GOP, anyway.'

For the residents of Castletown Avenue, making polite conversation at a local drinks party, clutching their glasses of warm white wine, this might have been a slightly heavy message to imbibe. For Kamran, in his new role as a research fellow at the Washington DC office of the Sovereignty Foundation, this would be his mission statement.

–

It is often pointed out by management consultants and motivational speakers that the Chinese word for 'crisis' is composed of two characters, 危机, one representing 'danger' and the other 'opportunity'. This is, linguistically speaking, incorrect. Luckily, both for management consultants and motivational speakers, their work is rarely fact-checked.

Nevertheless, Kamran's departure lived up to this dubious factoid. The danger presented by his efforts to undermine America's commitment to NATO brought with it an opportunity: a vacancy in the office of UK National Security Adviser. This happened to coincide with the resignation of the Prime Minister after his addiction to lying about almost everything had finally caught up with him. In the brief vacuum of the interregnum period, some highly effective lobbying by Sarah got Olivia Mitchell appointed to the role. The longed-for goal – to make Britain's Prime Minister aware of Russian agents of influence hiding in plain sight – appeared closer to success than ever before.

Chapter 54

East Dentdale Estate, North Yorkshire
September 2022

It was an ordinary shooting weekend. There was a smattering of local toffs, banker-types up from London and a minor royal who kept complaining about Pizza Express. Nobody was very sure why, but as long as you kept him away from the younger waitresses he seemed harmless enough.

It wasn't very warm, but then it never was in East Dentdale, high in the Pennines, even in an Indian summer. The skies were clear and it was not too windy. Perfect conditions for an ordinary shooting weekend.

For Jonty – or Lord Pelham, as people tended to call him in these settings – it was a fine occasion. The year was hardly a vintage one for grouse, but the gamekeepers had done a bloody good job, burnt off plenty of heather and sorted out the hen harriers. After the disaster of the 2021 season, it was just wonderful to be outside, in a place he loved, doing something he was passionate about. Still, as with everything in life, there were compromises. He had to put up with a bunch of paying guns: loud people who worked in the City and wore even louder tweeds. Most of them had bought their own shotguns. One of them hadn't even shown up, rude bugger. Something about a 'super forecast'? The weather *was* super, so why had that stopped him? But they weren't uniformly ghastly. Some of the younger ones were jolly chaps with not many cares in the world. Nice contrast from all that misery in Ukraine.

They'd drawn lots for the stands, but Jonty had an arrangement with Shep, his head gamekeeper, which ensured that he got his favourite butt, a well-constructed stone bunker in a pleasant little fold of moorland that tended to offer an excellent line on the birds as they came over. There had to be some upsides from being the bloody owner of the moor, after all. A hunting horn sounded and the beaters came into view, bringing with them a reasonable, if not bounteous, quantity of grouse skimming through the air. The old guns did a thorough job, bringing most of the birds down. The City boys were mostly firing at fresh air, but they probably thought they'd made themselves useful. They seemed happy enough, and none of them did anything inexcusable like swinging through the line.

After a couple of drives they stopped for a warming bullshot. There was some appreciative banter about the quality of the shooting and the weather that Jonty had laid on. They climbed back into the Land Rovers and moved on to the next drive, Jonty in his usual spot at the end. There was a beautiful vista across the scarp of the moor and down into Dentdale. The remaining heather was in full bloom, a beautiful mosaic of soft colours against the grass and bracken. Phil, Jonty's loader, a naturally monosyllabic type, offered that it was 'a bloody fine day, sir,' and Jonty could but agree.

Lunch was a slightly windswept picnic in the lee of the parked jeeps. After his fair share of fruit cake and sloe gin, Jonty toddled off to a quiet patch of moorland to relieve himself. He was fumbling with the buttons on his breeches, his shotgun broken open over his elbow, when someone sidled up to him, dressed in camo gear and an odd sort of furry cap with the earmuffs pulled down. One of the beaters? Back in the days of his late father, the fourth Lord Pelham, a beater accosting his lordship during his rightful enjoyment of a quiet open-air pee would have been unimaginable. But Jonty prided himself on being able to talk to anyone. Even a beater at a shoot. Twenty-first century and all that. He turned to make conversation.

Simon pulled the cap off his head. 'Hello, Jonty.'

'Simon! Thought you were one of the beaters. The hell you doing here?'

'You know, Jonty. You know what I'm doing here.'

Jonty smiled, literally the master of all he surveyed. All 4,623 acres of it. 'Come to thank me for getting you out of that hellhole in Bakhmut, I shouldn't wonder. What are you up to tonight? Should've invited you to shoot, but I'd never had you down as much of a sportsman. Forgive me if I've got that wrong.' Simon shook his head. 'But you'll come to the shoot dinner, won't you? Lady P would *love* to see you.'

Simon had thrust his hands in his pockets. He looked relaxed, like a man enjoying a walk on the fells in the cool breeze of the late summer. 'You're right,' he said, 'I should thank you.'

Jonty gave a gracious smile. 'Come on, you didn't need to track me down here just for that, did you? Everything all right?'

'Everything's fine,' insisted Simon. 'And I really should thank you... For getting help so quickly.'

'I did what anyone would've done in the circs.'

'Still, it made all the difference, giving Vasya time to get organised.'

'Yes, yes,' said Jonty, a hint of impatience in his voice. 'The important thing is that I got you out, not who rang who.' He had finished fumbling with his breeches, and made to turn back to the rest of the shooting party. 'Come along,' he said. 'You don't need to shoot to enjoy the day... Sloe gin?' he added, holding out a silver hip flask with some sort of crest engraved on it.

Simon shook his head, even though he loved sloe gin. 'One thing, though. How did you know the op had gone wrong? Vasya told me you contacted him a good two hours before Liz had got out.'

Jonty shrugged and took a swig from the flask. 'Bit out of the blue, this, don't you think? Anyway, not sure you can back up your case, old boy,' he added, pulling off his tweed cap and wiping a bony hand over his swept-back hair before replacing his headgear. 'Impossible to know who called who at what time. Fog of war, so on.'

'Yes. That was the bit that didn't make sense. You knew the op had gone wrong even before Liz had told Sarah. But then you did everything possible to get me out. For which I should repeat that I am truly thankful. But it still leaves me trying to figure out what exactly you were trying to achieve.'

'Simon, are you… well… *all right*?' Jonty was looking round awkwardly, calculating whether he could fob Simon off on one of the loaders or beaters, but not sure whether he might say something incriminating. Better to deal with it himself before rejoining the group. 'You've been through some bloody awful things. More than ever's happened to me. You probably need a warm bath. And a bloody good blow job while you're at it,' he added, delighted at his risqué suggestion. 'Man's earned it, no doubt,' he said, as if there were a sympathetic crowd listening in, ready to titter at the idea. This little bit of moor was, in fact, completely empty. 'But I do have to get back. Plenty of chaps waiting for me who've paid real money to be here—'

'But that's the point, isn't it? East Dentdale,' said Simon, as if he was in a different conversation altogether. 'No doubt costs a bomb to maintain. Gamekeepers, loaders, beaters… all that stuff. So you get people willing to spend serious amounts to shoot here.'

'No sob stories, Simon. I think in the modern vernacular we call it a "first world problem".'

'I suppose so. But that's where Denis Dudnik features. He came shooting here a few times, didn't he? Paid silly money for the privilege, I understand.' Simon pulled a folded piece of paper out of his pocket, handing the photo of Dudnik in his tweeds to Jonty.

Jonty stared at the image, looking uncomfortable, but not fatally so. 'I helped Dudnik a little. Back in the early days. But anyway, he's not exactly an emissary of the Kremlin, is he? I mean, look at the work his foundation has done. The Ukrainian culture funding. He's hardly pro-war.'

'Depends who you ask, doesn't it? I know you're not in *Moscow's* pocket. But you *were* in Dudnik's pocket for a while, weren't you? Maybe you still are? I imagine the family pile in the Cotswolds is bloody expensive to keep going. And there's this place. But you're a Cold Warrior. I've seen you there in Kyiv: you're not part of the Kremlin crowd.'

'Oh, you're too kind, Simon,' said Jonty sarcastically.

Simon ignored him. 'To be honest, I couldn't make sense of it. But my mistake was looking for the big conspiracy. Trying to link you to Kamran Patel and Rory and all those other arseholes who think they're going to change the world. But that wasn't it, was it?'

Jonty seemed angrier now, a reddening in his face that wasn't just down to the sloe gin. His loader had started to approach, but Jonty waved him off with a promise to be with him 'in a minute'. He turned back to Simon. 'Dudnik paid silly money to come shooting here, and then he paid for a Ukrainian cultural centre, which I had a hand in arranging. I don't need to apologise for any of that.'

'I'm sure you justified it to yourself at the time. But you reckoned without the war, didn't you? What was just about okay five or ten years ago looks completely indefensible now. And that was before the link between Dudnik and Chovka became obvious.'

'Dudnik and Chovka?' said Jonty, searchingly. 'No. Didn't know anything about that.'

'Ah, but you *did* know,' said Simon, rubbing his hands together. He had caught Jonty telling a lie. 'Because you had seen the report Sarah got from Oksana. Photo of Chovka and Dudnik together in the house in Crans-Montana. I've figured out the sequence. I headed off to Bakhmut to meet Chovka. At that point, you were all for it. You bloody well proposed the damn thing. But then, *after* I'd left, you saw Oksana's report that Chovka had worked for Dudnik. That must have been while we were in Kramatorsk, just about to cross the lines. And if I'd succeeded in bringing Chovka over, he would start telling us about your relationship with Dudnik…' Jonty was looking at Simon with a fixed sort of grimace. A gust of wind caused the paper he was holding to flutter. Somewhere in the background, Simon could hear snatches of braying laughter. Lunch was proceeding successfully, in spite of Jonty's absence.

'This is all the most *ridiculous* speculation,' said Jonty, his voice rising.

'No, Jonty, it is what you taught me about intelligence many years ago: inference—'

'Oh, do shut *up*,' he interrupted, sounding furious.

But Simon also had a righteous fury propelling him. 'Once you had seen Oksana's report, you had a sudden realisation that we'd find out about your relationship with Dudnik,' he continued. 'As soon as that awful prospect reared its head, you knew you had to prevent it from happening. So you got word to Dudnik. And Dudnik told the Russians.'

A sole grouse that had somehow evaded the earlier slaughter was scudding along the escarpment. It gave its cry – *go-back, go-back* – followed by the long chuckle of a bird that was happy to escape.

'My theory,' Simon continued, 'was that you didn't plan for me to be captured. Far too risky. All you needed was for Chovka not to show up. Dry hole. Happens all the time. We'd all head back to Kramatorsk in one piece, none the wiser. But things got out of hand. I'm guessing Dudnik refused to play it the way you'd hoped.' Jonty was shaking his head, but some of his earlier vigour had gone. Simon continued: 'So I assume the Russians couldn't resist the opportunity to arrange a little massacre and capture a Western spy. Who can blame them? And then your only way out was to get Vasya to rescue me.' Simon paused. Jonty was staring at him, a mixture of incredulity and fear on his face. 'If it's any comfort, I never thought you wanted me dead.

And that's why you contacted Vasya so soon. Too soon, as it happens. You couldn't wait for Liz to get back over the line and contact Sarah. I'm genuinely grateful for that. The additional time probably saved my life.'

Jonty scoffed, as if the whole thing was an amusingly crazy idea. But he didn't seem to be able to find his voice. And Simon ploughed on: 'You tipped Vasya off, and then spoke to the Americans as soon as it was safe: once Liz had contacted Sarah. The only thing I'm not sure about is whether you arranged for Chovka and Vasya to be taken out. By the sniper. Or was that just their bad luck?'

Simon knew he was pushing it, but he was trying to goad Jonty into admitting to something. It wasn't working. Jonty spoke with a disdainful tone. 'It really is an impressive work of the imagination. You've been through a lot. My grandfather had shell shock. He would come up with these odd stories. Nobody knew what to make of them. PTSD they call it these days. You can get help. But don't go thinking I'll let you drag my name through the mud. Let's face it, I have many more friends than you do. Some of whom are waiting for me over there,' he added, turning towards the sound of lunch.

Simon felt he had a last chance. 'Jonty, I get it: you got into bed with Dudnik at a time when it was controversial, but not — in polite society, at least — indefensible. Problem now is that it's *become* indefensible. The whole Dudnik show: the Chovka link, the corruption, the mob money, his reach back to Moscow. It's not that I think you're a Moscow stooge. You did what a lot of people were doing at the time: you got fat on Russia's looted wealth. The difference is that you, of all people, should have known better. No wonder you're working so hard on Ukraine. You're covering your tracks, aren't you?'

It had worked: he was angry now. 'Simon, I think you've gone about as far as you dare. An oligarch having a few shooting days on an English grouse moor several years ago is proof of nothing at all. The rest is pure speculation. My professional record speaks for itself.'

'But it's *because* of your professional record that you did this. Your reputation is the most valuable thing you have. If this comes out, your life's work is finished. Your name, the supposed nobility of it, all discredited.'

Simon felt completely confident, perhaps because he knew nothing that could happen would be as bad as what he had already experienced. He pressed on remorselessly. 'Your reputation won't recover. There'll always be a record of those calls you made, somewhere. A time-stamped record. The Yanks will already have a transcript of that call to Vasya, given his relationship with Langley. You'll always think you've shut down all the avenues, expunged all the records, but there'll be something out there. This will *never* go away.'

Suddenly, Jonty looked very old. 'My reputation, Simon, my reputation... I have lost the immortal part of myself.' He said these words in a studied way that left Simon wondering if he was supposed to have recognised a famous quotation. 'What if I were to say that I acknowledge that mistakes were made. You and me, we go back a very long way,' he added pathetically, his voice starting to waver. 'In our line of work, not every operational call works out as originally intended—'

'Fuck off. Getting rich off looted Russian money, Ukrainian money... is not some kind of professional misjudgement. It's just shit. You're a money-grubber cosplaying some kind of Cold War hero...'

'Please,' he said imploringly, his rheumy eyes looking straight at Simon. 'I am asking for your forgiveness. This could just be between the two of us.'

Forgiveness. Be the bigger person. And then Simon thought of Yuri and his men, of Chovka, of Vasya. Of Evie. Who had asked *them* for forgiveness?

'My forgiveness is immaterial,' he said coldly. 'What you did will always be there.' Jonty's face had drained to a deathly pallor. Simon pressed on, a twist of the knife: 'Others will find out. You can *never* make this go away.'

'I can make this go away right now,' said Jonty. He slammed two cartridges into his gun and pushed the stock up. He kept the barrels pointing at the floor, but looked at Simon, his face a picture of devastation. Simon could see his hands were shaking.

Simon felt calm in a way that he would not have been able to before his capture in Bakhmut. Life had a different perspective now. 'Jonty, I'm reminded of something you said to me, not very long ago: "I don't believe you're the cold-blooded killer type." I think it applies to you as much as it does to me. I don't think you've got it in you.'

Jonty shook his head. With a desperate sigh he raised the gun.

The shot echoed across the moorland.

Author's Note and Acknowledgements

The battle for Bakhmut would rage on, consuming tens of thousands of Russian lives, as well as great numbers of its Ukrainian defenders. As Liz had remarked to Simon, it was a city known more for its sparkling wine than any particular strategic significance. When the city fell into Russian hands in May 2023, there was no Bakhmut left to seize, just the pulverised rubble of a place that had been under constant artillery barrage for more than a year. By then, the world's attention had moved on to the Ukrainian counter-offensive. Kyiv's NATO allies had high hopes that its inexperienced troops would be able to pull off a famous victory with limited training and minimal air power. It didn't work out that way: Ukraine made slight progress at the loss of many men and much matériel.

At the same time, Russia was advancing in other ways. The real-life versions of the propaganda networks that are represented in this story by Denis Dudnik, Kamran Patel and Valentin Melnik, flourished. In America, support for Ukraine became politicised. Russia's President was given a soft-soap interview by a top right-wing US news presenter. Even the pro-Ukraine side in Washington put endless restrictions around Kyiv's use of Western weapons. Some European governments began to lose interest in supporting Ukraine. In Moscow, there was quiet satisfaction that their people were returning to power in Western capitals, including in Washington. The threat that Ukraine's supplies of weapons could be cut off became very real. The war would not be won or lost in the battlefields of the Donbas, but in the battle for Western public opinion.

–

A kind reviewer described my previous novel, *A Spy Alone*, as a 'spy thriller with a social conscience'. My decision to write a sequel set in the Ukraine war puts the question of social conscience at the top of the list. It is reasonable to ask whether it is appropriate, in 2025, to be setting a work of entertainment in a devastating war that has exacted a terrible price in terms of casualties. My answer is that I hope that this book serves as a reminder to a war-weary world that the heroism of the Ukrainian people is undimmed, the importance of their fight for freedom never greater, their need for our support unchanged.

Where possible for the story, I have tried to use the real events of the first summer of the full-scale war as the backdrop to the unfolding plot. Several real-life incidents are described or referred to, but this is not a work of history or reportage, and where an incident in the text does not match what was really happening in the Donbas in July and August 2022, I hope my readers will allow the licence which all authors of fiction need to be able to do their jobs.

–

To be able to write this book I was privileged to be able to visit Ukraine more than once. Friends and acquaintances in Kyiv and elsewhere in the country were enormously helpful guiding me around. It isn't appropriate for me to name these kind people, but they know who they are and they have my heartfelt thanks. Any errors or exaggerations in my descriptions of Ukraine are my responsibility alone.

I have also relied on a lot of excellent reporting of the war. Doing proper journalism, particularly in a conflict zone, is an expensive and risky business and it deserves to be supported appropriately. Much of this is done by huge multinational news organisations, but there are also a raft of freelancers and small publications that rely on donations and subscriptions to continue their essential task. If you feel able to support some of these, or the Committee to Protect Journalists, a global charity that supports journalists in Ukraine and elsewhere, please consider doing so. You can find them at cpj.org.

Outside Ukraine, Dan Kaszeta, the world's leading expert on chemical, biological and radiological warfare, patiently guided me through the facts and mostly fiction around dirty bombs. My editor, Craig Lye at Canelo, and my agent, Michael Dean, have both been essential parts of the process of writing this and my previous novel. Without their professional experience and input, these books would be nothing. I owe them both a huge amount.

Finally, a couple of references are worth explaining. The character of Oksana Amelina, a young Ukrainian dedicated to the cause of anti-corruption, is *not* based on Victoria Amelina, a real-life Ukrainian novelist who became a war crimes investigator and was tragically killed by a Russian missile attack in Kramatorsk in July 2023. But my Oksana is unashamedly named to honour Victoria and the many other Ukrainians killed by Russia's deliberate strikes on civilian targets.

The other is Chovka Buchayev. The idea of a sympathetic Russian assassin may offend some readers. If this is the case, I apologise. Nonetheless, it seems to me that Russia's treatment of its own minorities (including its use of young men from the provinces as cannon fodder in the current war) has in many cases contributed to a multigenerational moral catastrophe involving deeply traumatised, damaged people. None of this is to excuse or justify the many war crimes committed by individual Russians and ignored by millions more. But it is an attempt, no doubt partial and inadequate, at an explanation. It is therefore not a coincidence that the name reminds us of

Chovka Gochiyayev, either a notorious assassin and terrorist, or a fugitive scapegoat for one of the greatest crimes in modern Russian history. It all depends on your perspective.

Slava Ukraini.

Charles Beaumont
December 2024